I0618553

PRAISE FOR
SO FELL THE SPARROW

"If you like ghost stories and are not afraid of a little mystery, *So Fell The Sparrow* is the book for you. The action happens in exactly the kind of small town that you would think a ghost tale would happen, and it has everything you need in order to enjoy it from cover to cover. Expect sudden turns of events, powerful characters, a unique love story, and a frightening storyline." **–Readers' Favorite**

"Oh, how I love a great gothic romance! There's something about the contrary emotions of falling in love and being freaked the hell out, that make for a fantastic story combo, but only if it's done well. Thankfully, *So Fell The Sparrow* strikes a great balance and had me hooked on all counts." **–Love Reading Romance**

SO FELL THE SPARROW

Copyright © 2013 Katie Jennings

All rights reserved. Except as permitted under the U.S. Copyright Act
of 1976, no part of this publication may be reproduced, distributed,
or transmitted in any form or by any means, or stored in a database or
retrieval system, without prior written permission of the publisher.

This book is a work of fiction. The characters, incidents, and dialogue are
drawn from the author's imagination and are not to be construed as real. Any
resemblance to actual events or persons, living or dead, is entirely coincidental.

Published by Sapphire Royale Publishing

ISBN-13: 978-0615908496
ISBN-10: 0615908497

Visit the author at:
http://www.katieajennings.com
http://www.facebook.com/authorkatiejennings
http://www.twitter.com/dryadquartet

ALSO BY KATIE JENNINGS

Up In The Pines
For Love & Bourbon
Things Lost in the Fire

The Vasser Legacy

When Empires Fall
Rise of the Notorious
Rulers of Deception

The Dryad Quartet

Breath of Air
Firefight in Darkness
A Life Earthbound
Of Water and Madness
The Dryad Quartet Special Edition

To Allison and Audra, my fellow fans of all things paranormal.
Thanks for making this book so much fun to write.

PREQUEL TO
SO FELL THE SPARROW

Gypsy of SPIRITS

"The beauty of this country is becoming part of me. I feel more detached from life and somehow gentler. I have some good friends here, but no one who really understands why I am here or what I do. I don't know of anyone, though, who would have more than a partial understanding; I have gone too far alone. I have always been unsatisfied with life as most people live it. Always I want to live more intensely and richly."

– Everett Ruess

GYPSY OF SPIRITS

On the day she was born, the world knew her as Mary Jacqueline Hart. When she ran away from home, she simply became Jackie.

She belonged to no one and everyone at the same time. Her favorite song was about a girl who talked to angels; her preferred vice a rich glass of elderberry wine. She craved the moonlight over the sun and carried a weathered copy of the Book of Psalms in her pocket.

Home was a place she had never truly found, though she gave up searching long ago. Instead, she made each new destination her temporary home. And as she traveled, the only constant that remained was her gift. Her sight. Her ability to talk to the dead.

The fire red Jeep she drove took her into the Ozarks, winding aimlessly through the endless rolling hills. With the top down, the cool night air swirled around her. It brushed her dusted-gold skin like a sweet caress and sent her long, ebony curls flying across her gypsy face. Her dark eyes filled with a peace that only the open road could give. She smelled the trees of the forest, the rusty cedar and the licorice aroma of sassafras. It blended with the cool, mineral scent of a nearby creek running fast with mountain water.

The clear sky rioted with stars; millions of them dotting the expanse of sapphire. There was no one for miles around. Not a single car, home, or any sign of life at all.

She didn't have a destination. None that she knew, anyway. She simply drove on, content that fate would take her where she needed to be.

Reaching behind her into the backseat, she scratched the fur of her dog, Gatsby. He licked her hand, then yawned and went back to sleep. He had the soft tan and white coloring typical of a corgi and the sweet personality to accompany it. She'd rescued him from the streets of San Francisco as a puppy five years earlier, and since then he'd been her best friend.

Though she considered herself wealthy in friendship, she never let anyone get close enough to truly know her. Long ago, she'd learned a valuable lesson about trust. It ended with her understanding that she needed nothing and no one but herself to be content. To be free.

She came around a swooping bend, the towering trees leaning over the road on both sides like a canopy. Her headlights caught the leaves and branches and cascaded over the aged, tired asphalt. As she pulled out of the curve, she spotted a young woman in jeans and a white T-shirt walking on the side of the road.

Before she had a chance to slow down, she passed the woman. One glance in her rearview mirror, and she was gone.

Behind her, Gatsby let out a low growl.

Jackie depressed the brake slowly, then looked to her right. Sitting in the passenger seat was the young woman, her shoulder length blonde hair tangled and in disarray. Her hands were clasped together tightly in her lap, the jeans she wore tattered and stained with blood. A vivid bruise bloomed over the pale white skin on her neck. Haunted blue eyes stared at Jackie in shock.

"Can you see me?" the young woman whispered in a soft southern lilt. She blinked back tears.

Jackie nodded, absorbing the waves of confusion and misery that clung to the girl like an overpowering perfume. She might have been sixteen, maybe seventeen, practically still a child.

"Am I dead?" The girl's question ended on a sob, as if she knew the horrible truth.

Jackie let out a long, measured breath. She turned her eyes back to the road and continued to drive. "Yes, darling."

"I...I don't remember dying."

"People often don't," Jackie told her, sympathy in her voice.

The girl shook her head. "I've been wandering down this road for a long time. You're the first person to see me."

Jackie attempted a smile. "You are not my first."

"There are others?"

"They are all around us." Jackie glanced over at her with bright eyes. "You are not alone, Rachel."

The girl trembled with a visible shudder. "How do you know my name?"

"I read about you in the paper when I stopped in Gainesville," Jackie explained, recalling the quaint diner she'd enjoyed before hitting the road. "A year ago today, you lost control of your car and rolled into a tree."

Tears fell silently down Rachel's face and she rubbed at

her neck. For a long moment, she said nothing. Jackie drove, not minding the company. In the backseat, Gatsby decided the girl was not a threat and fell back asleep.

When Rachel spoke, her voice was hollow with fear. "What am I supposed to do now?"

"I don't know, darling. Maybe seeing your family again will help guide you on."

"Will you take me to them? It's just up the road a ways."

With a kind smile, Jackie nodded. "Of course."

Rachel's face lifted with a small hint of joy at the thought, though sorrow still weighed her down. She tried to reach out and touch Jackie's hand, only to wince as her ghostly fingers passed right through Jackie's solid ones. Another sob built in her throat, but she fought it back.

"So…who are you? How come you can see dead people?"

Jackie could tell the girl wanted to distract herself. "I go by Jackie. I'm a medium, which means I can communicate with spirits."

Rachel shook her head in disbelief. "I can't believe that's real."

"As real as you are sitting here beside me," Jackie mused, eyeing her serenely. "There is so much more to this world than black and white, dead and alive. When we die, we do not just vanish. We live on."

Rachel fiddled with the frayed tears in her jeans. "Have you always seen people like me?"

"I saw my first spirit when I was six years old in my hometown of Saginaw." Jackie smiled, the memory sweet. "I was playing hopscotch with some friends and I saw an older man standing in the street nearby. He was staring around, lost and confused. When I pointed him out to my friends, they laughed at me. They didn't see him. So, I walked up to him and asked who he was. He looked at me much the same way you did, with complete surprise. No one had spoken to him in the twenty years he'd been wandering around the street even though he'd tried to get people's attention. He didn't understand that he was dead until that moment. Then he thanked me, turned around and disappeared."

"How did he die?" Rachel's eyes were on her, filled with wonder.

"He had a heart attack while crossing the street in 1970. He was dead before he hit the ground."

"Did you start to see more of them?"

Jackie's hands tightened on the steering wheel. "Many, many more. I saw children at school raising their hands and never getting called on. At the little market where we bought fresh eggs, I saw a young woman crying in the corner. I even saw spirits in my own home; a young boy and his father. They were killed in the 1940s when a fire broke out and destroyed most of the home."

"Did you talk to them?"

"The boy became somewhat of a friend to me," Jackie said, that old ache returning to fester in her heart. Not a day went by that she didn't miss him. "His name was Henry. He shared my room and we would play hide-and-go-seek together, share secrets, tell stories…"

Rachel managed a smile. "That sounds nice."

Jackie nodded, though a lone tear fell from her eye. Her hand came up to grasp the small, silver cross she wore around her neck. "It was for a while. Until my father found out."

"What did he do?"

Her fingers tightened around her necklace, the points of the cross digging into her skin. "He tried to exorcise me."

Rachel blinked. "Like, from a demon?"

Jackie let out a long breath, her hand finding the steering wheel again. "Yes, but that came later, when I was thirteen.

You see, my parents both came from very long and very old bloodlines of strict Catholics. Italian on my father's side and Spanish on my mother's side. When I was very young, my mother died of cancer. I was an only child. From that point on, my father raised me to be the model of Catholic perfection. Of course, his idea of perfection did not include speaking to the dead. Or, as he believed, speaking to demons."

Rachel's hands tightened in her lap. "Demons?"

"They exist, though at the time I was not in contact with any," Jackie explained, shrugging. "I was simply a child delighted with a gift that, in my eyes, was bestowed upon me by God."

"Did you try and hide it from your father?"

Jackie laughed, though it held little humor. "I should have, but no. I was too curious, too naïve. It wasn't until he pulled his belt on me one evening after catching me talking to Henry that I considered ignoring my gift. But even after the beating, I couldn't resist. The dead continued to call on me for help, for guidance. I suppose I wasn't strong enough to say no to them. Over the years my gift grew stronger, and with each additional beating my father grew more and more aggravated that I wasn't getting better. He started locking me in my room, keeping me away from outsiders. He was ashamed and frightened of me. He reached out to our priest for guidance, suggesting an exorcism. Fortunately for me, the priest evaluated my case and determined there was no evidence of demonic possession. He refused to perform the exorcism."

"That's good."

An old, familiar pain hit Jackie's heart. "It was. But *un*fortunately for me, my father decided to attempt the exorcism himself."

Rachel's face went slack with horror. "That's awful."

"Exorcisms can't be performed by just anyone. You have

to be a priest and have permission from the church itself. My father was just a tailor with no experience in rituals as damaging as an exorcism."

The memories flooded back, blindingly hot and real. She saw herself as she had been at thirteen, wild dark hair and slender, coltish body. She'd been tied to a chair in the basement, her hands bound behind her back by twine with more of it wrapped around her chest, pinning her arms to her sides. Her legs had kicked helplessly until he bound those too.

She remembered pleading with him, begging him to leave her alone. His face had flushed red with indignation, with hate. He'd crossed her forehead, then himself, angry tears in his eyes.

Be gone, devil! he'd cried and splashed holy water on her face. He'd thrust the wooden cross of his beloved heirloom rosary before her, as if eager to see her flesh burn from the holy image.

Except it hadn't because she wasn't possessed. Words could not convince him, leaving her helpless and at his mercy. Instead of showing compassion he only ramped up his efforts.

In his right hand, he'd clutched the *Rite of Exorcism*, a book filled with the prayers needed for the ritual. He'd read them off fervently, feverishly, nearly mad in his attempt to free her from the Devil. To free her from her gift.

Therefore, I adjure you every unclean spirit, every specter from hell, every satanic power, in the name of Jesus Christ of Nazareth, who was led into the desert after His baptism by John to vanquish you in your citadel, to cease your assaults against the creature whom He has formed from the slime of the earth for His own honor and glory...

"What happened after?" Rachel asked, bringing Jackie back to the present.

"He looked me in the eyes and asked me if I was myself again," Jackie replied, remembering distinctly how there was more revulsion in his expression than concern.

"What did you tell him?"

"I said I had always been myself." She wiped away a tear that fell down her cheek. "So, he left me there and went to talk to the priest again. When the priest found out what he had done, he rescued me from the basement and threatened to contact the police if my father attempted to harm me again."

"Did he?"

Jackie brushed back a strand of hair that the wind had tossed into her face. "He kept his promise because he had to, but that didn't stop him from forcing me to pray and fast, which the priest recommended. He spread blessed salt around my room and burned blessed incense and candles all hours of the day, consumed by his belief that I was still under the influence of Satan. We didn't speak to each other for months.

"I had a very strict curfew. I was only allowed to leave the house for school and church, and as a result I had few friends and no one I could trust. The only consolation was that I still had Henry and the other spirits, and they kept me hopeful that my future was brighter than my father's prison."

"I'm sorry." Rachel bit her lower lip, unsure what else to say.

Jackie's mouth curved. "Don't be sorry. I'm not. My experiences shaped and empowered me. By the time I ran away from home at sixteen, I was stronger than I ever imagined I could be."

"So where did you go?"

"I had a little bit of money stashed away, enough to get me on a bus south. I went as far as I could go and ended up in Toledo. I found a local Catholic church and offered to clean toilets and sweep floors in exchange for a place to stay. They took me in and helped me get work organizing books at the local library.

"But I couldn't stay in Toledo. I had to keep moving, to get as far away from my father as I could. A few months later I'd saved up enough money to take a bus down to Louisville where I got a job waiting tables with a room to stay in above the restaurant. It wasn't much, but I was free."

"Did your father ever find you?"

Jackie shook her head. "No. I don't know if he even tried. I imagine he was happy to be rid of me."

"But you were still his daughter, despite everything," Rachel argued, brows creased. "He must have loved you still."

"I think in the beginning he thought of me as his daughter, but after all the years of trying to beat the demon out of me, I could see the love fade from his eyes. When he looked at me he only saw evil. It came to the point that instead of trying to save me, he was just trying to protect himself *from* me."

"Do you think he's still up there in Michigan?" Rachel asked. Her eyes widened as a second thought hit her. "And when he dies, will you see his spirit? Then he'll know you were telling the truth all along."

Jackie laughed. "Not every spirit lingers, darling. Only those with a purpose to fulfill, or with a stain on their soul that holds them back. He may simply move on to his intended place."

Rachel looked uneasy. "Wait, do you think there's a stain on my soul and that's why I haven't moved on?"

"No." Jackie turned to face her, sincerity in her eyes. "I can tell you are not stained, Rachel. You have a purpose left to fulfill."

"To say goodbye to my parents?" Rachel wondered, sadness passing over her face.

Jackie nodded. "Most likely."

"Okay." Rachel took a deep breath, somewhat relieved. "We're almost there, just a few more miles."

Jackie's eyes passed to the dashboard clock and saw it

was nearly three a.m. Rachel's parents were likely asleep, still grieving over the loss of their daughter. Hopefully, soon they would see Rachel in a dream or hear her voice and take comfort that she was okay.

"So, what happened after Louisville?"

Jackie smiled. "I saved up again and continued south until I reached the Gulf. I stayed in New Orleans for just over a year, waiting tables, making friends. I guess I really found myself there.

"I was eighteen when I met The Gypsies. That's what they called themselves, anyway." She laughed and her heart filled with a warm, quiet ache. "There were three of them, teens like myself that came from bad homes and were in search of freedom. They'd wafted into town in this tired old Volkswagen bus and I ran into them one day on Bourbon Street. Dominic was strumming his guitar and Hannah played her sax, while Bobby had this lovely old bass guitar that he'd inherited from his grandfather. As I was walking past them on the street, something stopped me. It drew me to them, like a moth to a flame. So, I sat down and just listened, and Dominic began to sing to me. He looked into my eyes and I knew I'd found a familiar soul. A week later, I joined them on the road."

Rachel sighed wistfully. "Did you love him?"

Jackie blinked then let out a quick laugh. "Dominic? No. I've never been in love. Though I guess you could say what we shared was as close to love as anything I've ever known."

"Did he love you?"

Jackie shot her a knowing look. "What I've learned is that romance is never the fairytale you want it to be, Rachel. In real life, it's much more complicated, chaotic, and painful."

Rachel's brow furrowed. "So, then what did you mean by familiar soul, if not soul mate?"

"I meant I saw in him the same things in myself that I'd

always thought were abnormal. He couldn't see spirits the way I could, but he did occasionally see auras and he had the most poetic, troubled heart. Unfortunately, as the years went on, he fell into self-abusive habits to cope with the emotional pain he felt, and I had no choice but to distance myself from him."

"You didn't try to help him?"

Jackie sighed. "There was no helping him. His demons were buried so deep, embedded in his very bones. One time, he opened himself up to me spiritually and I witnessed the events that happened in his childhood that damaged him so greatly. He'd been abused by his uncle, not just once, but continuously over the course of seven years since the age of six."

Rachel's face fell. "That's horrible."

"It was," Jackie agreed, extending her hand outside the open window to coast the air. "I didn't stay with The Gypsies for very long, as fate took me down other paths. Every once in a while over the years I found my way back to them but never permanently. At some point they all split off, landing in different corners of the country. I heard Bobby died last year of an overdose in San Francisco, and Hannah is married with kids in Salt Lake City, living the white-picket-fence life."

"And Dominic?"

"He wanders, as I do. Last I heard, he was in Massachusetts somewhere near Salem."

"Have you ever been there?" Rachel asked, looking wistful again. "I always wanted to visit Salem."

"I've been lucky enough to see most of the country and many other places. I dated a guy once who let me tag along while he backpacked through Europe. I've lived out of hostels and motels, and when I eventually had the chance to buy this Jeep, I lived out of it for a while."

Sadness darkened Rachel's eyes. "Doesn't it get old? Don't you ever want something, like, *familiar* to come home to every day?"

"This life is not for everyone, but for me, it's perfect. I guess you could say I'm a wanderer with perpetually itchy feet, taken by the wind."

Rachel sighed. "You lead a fascinating life. I wish I could have the same chance…"

Jackie looked at her kindly. "There are great things to come for you, darling. You are not finished just because your physical body has died."

Rachel nodded, though she didn't look convinced "I hope so."

"I know so." Jackie turned her attention back to the road as it swooped around another bend and came upon a lone house in the wilderness. Rachel pointed to a small dirt driveway noticeable only because of the bright blue mailbox beside it.

"That's it. My house." Rachel's hands wrung together in her lap as Jackie pulled to the side of the road. They met eyes, and Rachel shivered. "What do I do?"

"You'll know." Jackie's eyes brightened as she took in the worried looking teen beside her. "I hope I didn't bore you with the story of my life. I don't make a habit out of telling people about my past."

"No, it helped. It really did." Rachel let out a rush of breath, the moonlight glowing over her hair and ghostly pale skin. "You made me feel better. I felt so lost, so afraid, before."

"Just remember that you are not alone."

"Where will you go now?" Rachel asked.

Jackie shrugged. "The wind carried me to you. Now it will take me to someone else who needs my help."

Rachel looked past Jackie to her parents' house, a bittersweet feeling coming over her. "You know, this one time my parents took me on vacation to this cool coastal town in Massachusetts. I think you'd like it there."

"What's it called?"

Rachel's eyes shifted back to hers. "Mad Rock Harbor. I don't know what made me think of it, but for some reason I have a feeling you're needed there."

Jackie reached behind her to pet Gatsby, her lips curving in a smile. "Then that is where I shall go. It's been a while since I've seen Dominic; maybe I'll stop in on him."

"See, it *is* fate." Rachel beamed, pleased she had contributed in some small way to Jackie's mission. She twirled a piece of her blonde hair around her finger, biting her lower lip. "Well, I guess this is goodbye."

"No goodbye is ever permanent. We will meet again, if not in this world then the next."

Rachel reached out to lay her hand over Jackie's on the steering wheel. The ghostly chill sent tingles through Jackie's skin. "Cool. See you."

Their eyes held and when Jackie blinked, Rachel was gone. The tingling feeling remained, and she rubbed at her skin. She was pleased to help the girl find her purpose, though departing was always bittersweet. She would continue on her path, while Rachel would move on to her intended place.

In the backseat, Gatsby yawned and let out a polite bark.

"I know, I know." Jackie laughed and reached back to help him into the passenger seat. He hopped over and smiled up at her, tongue lolling out. "How does Mad Rock Harbor sound, my love?"

He barked again, stamping his front two feet excitedly.

"I agree." Jackie pulled onto the road, tossing back her hair to let the wind rush through it as she picked up speed. "I feel like something special awaits us there."

As Jackie headed northeast toward the rising sun, a doctor five hundred miles away was receiving a late-night phone call that would change her life forever.

And in Seattle, a ghost hunter awoke from a strange dream, the name of a woman he'd never met on his lips. *Grace*. He fell back asleep and forgot the dream, but fate had done its job. Soon he and his partner would hit the road on the hunt for the paranormal.

Four strangers were unknowingly en route to each other, bound for a tiny, seaboard town in Massachusetts.

To a house that had claimed the life of a sparrow.

"We are all wanderers on this earth. Our hearts are full of wonder, and our souls are deep with dreams." –Gypsy Proverb

So Fell the
SPARROW

KATIE JENNINGS

Sapphire Royale
publishing

ORIGIN

*For death is no more than a turning of us
over from time to eternity.*
—William Penn

PROLOGUE

October 1865

Mad Rock Harbor, Massachusetts

For Sally Lockwood, time moved slower than it had *before*. Clouds lingered, frozen in the sky. The indigo water of the harbor lay unnaturally calm. Dry leaves clung to the spindly branches of towering elms, the wind unwilling to shake them free. Sparrows no longer sang. Stray dogs refused to bark.

It was as if the world itself had come to a standstill, though her young mind could not comprehend why.

How could she understand? Her death had been too sudden.

Sally's family home stood comfortably on its generous plot of land—its white colonial columns and blue siding set against the backdrop of a quaint and quiet Eastern Seaboard town. The house and the town were all she knew; all she had seen of the world.

In her short five years of life, she had been sheltered from many horrific things. A Civil War that pitted brother against brother. The brutal destruction of entire towns. The slaying of over half a million men in the name of equality. The assassination of a prolific president.

It was five years that would change the course of history, years she witnessed with the innocence of a child.

Safe within the confines of her home, she skipped down the upstairs hallway. A carefree smile brightened her porcelain face as her blonde curls danced. The lacy white dress she wore billowed at her knees, the movement fluid and graceful. She felt lighter and less clumsy, the skinned knee and bruised elbow from a previous fall now miraculously healed. The inexperience of youth kept her from wondering how or why.

The wooden floorboards creaked beneath her bare feet, the only sound to penetrate the silence. She paused for a moment in the doorway of her parents' bedroom. Her smile faded when she saw it was empty. No bed, no armoire, no vanity with a dressing stool where her mother sat and powdered her nose. Concern rushed into her mind briefly, then flew away like a little, lost bird.

She wandered to the stairway, her hand tracing the banister of the second-floor balcony. It dropped off abruptly where the banister was broken, the wood sharp and splintered. She peered nervously over the edge and down to the first-floor entryway. A sick feeling washed over her. On instinct, she backed away and continued to the stairs. She wanted to find her mother and listen to her play the piano.

As if she could already hear the sweet music, Sally began to hum.

She made her way down the stairs, her feet thudding on

the wood with each step. Hazy sunlight poured in through the windows and filled the entryway with light. Out of habit, she twirled to the right at the bottom of the stairs and headed for the room where her parents kept the piano.

Something stopped her dead in her tracks. Her gaze locked on a dark, spreading stain. It marred the wood floor underneath the second-floor balcony where the banister was broken. Coldness settled over her, along with a feeling of dread and discomfort she didn't understand. In the blink of an eye, she saw a vision of her own body lying crumpled and lifeless over the stain. For a fleeting moment, she saw her death with clarity. As rapidly as it appeared, it vanished. The cold feeling escaped with it and she continued on as though nothing had happened.

The lack of furniture in the living room stopped her again, and her tiny brow creased with worry that she had been abandoned. What if her parents had left her there all alone? She heard the slamming of the front door and immediately followed the sound, calling out for her mother. Her cries fell on deaf ears, as the living rarely hear the pleas of the dead.

Shoving aside the lacy curtains of the parlor window, she watched her parents approach a horse drawn carriage. She beat her hands against the window pane, begging them not to leave her. Not to abandon her.

As her father secured a trunk to the back of the carriage, her mother took a final, long look at the house. Her eyes fell on the window and seemed to capture, for one last time, the image of her angelic daughter's face.

Mrs. Lockwood shook her head and climbed into the carriage, tears spilling down her cheeks. The carriage pulled away, never to return to the house that had claimed the Lockwoods' only child.

Sally crumpled to the floor, heartbroken, and spotted the leather case holding the tintype photograph her father had always carried of her. It sat forgotten on the lowest stair.

She pulled her knees up to her chin and began to cry. Though tears fell, they did not exist, for she was nothing more than a lost specter. A lonely spirit. A ghost. Fated to drift within the shadows and lose herself in the house. The Sparrow House.

It would be hers for all eternity.

ACT 1:

SHADOWS

Dying is a wild night and a new road.
—Emily Dickinson

He has outsoared the shadow of our night;
Envy and calumny and hate and pain,
And that unrest which men miscall delight,
Can touch him not and torture not again;
From the contagion of the world's slow stain
He is secure...
—Percy Bysshe Shelley

CHAPTER ONE

October 2012

Upstate New York

G race was a woman who knew death. She had witnessed it, tried desperately to prevent it, and comforted those about to succumb to it. But even with all that, death was a thing she had never truly understood.

Until now.

They say the death of a parent is one of life's inevitable tragedies. It was often something she said to others as they accepted the news of their own parent's passing. Now she realized how worthless that rationalization really was. It didn't lessen the blow or soothe the pain. It didn't provide justification. It was nothing more than useless words used by people who didn't truly understand.

She didn't want to hate them for trying to comfort her, but part of her did. Because she hadn't lost just one parent—she'd lost both. No words could justify or make sense of such waste. It was simply a tragedy; one she still had trouble coming to terms with. Trouble accepting.

So, instead of facing it, she was running away.

She rolled down the window of her black Mercedes as she tore through the backwoods of New York, craving fresh air. It whipped in and prickled her skin with an icy chill, sending her shoulder length waves of russet hair flying around her face. On the radio, Jim Croce was telling an operator about his broken heart.

For a moment, Grace let her eyes close. She wanted nothing more than to absorb everything surrounding her; to find relief in the wind, the lilting guitar, the lonely stretch of rain-dampened highway. She knew she must be somewhere near Albany by now, halfway to her destination. Until she got there, she'd simply try and enjoy the drive. At least while driving she couldn't give in to the pain and cry. She could be alone but not feel alone. Not with the other cars passing her on the road, few as they were. It troubled her that complete strangers provided more comfort than her own friends, colleagues, or fiancé had. Well, ex-fiancé now.

The bastard.

But none of that mattered. She escaped Chicago, leaving her job behind. The three-month leave of absence had been forced upon her by her superiors, men who had known and trusted her father. Men who grieved nearly as much as she did.

The medical community was a tight-knit one.

She was Dr. Grace Sullivan, only daughter of the esteemed Dr. Allen Sullivan and his beloved wife Marie. May God rest their souls, or however they said it.

Ever since the car accident, everyone around her had done nothing but talk about God, saying her parents were at peace now in Heaven. It was all nice, but it literally meant nothing to her.

She didn't believe in God. It was pretty hard to when you were raised with science; educated on the importance of medicine and the human ability to survive the impossible. In her eyes, it wasn't God who granted miracles. People made their own way in this world and created their own fate. Except for unfortunate accidents. Those were simply an unavoidable part of life.

Funny how that had never seemed so cold to her before.

She shook off the chill and rolled up the window, irritated. She had promised herself she wouldn't think about it. It was too soon, even if three weeks had passed since the accident. Her parents were cozily buried in the earth, beside each other in death just as they had been in life.

Though her drive to Massachusetts would take her within a few hours of her parents' final resting place, she didn't have the heart to visit them. Instead, she was headed for some house her father had owned—one he'd never told her about. A house five hours from her parents' main residence in Manhattan.

She'd only found out about the home because her father's will gave her sole ownership of the property. A house he'd kept secret, one she'd never visited, in a town she'd never heard of, was now hers.

At first, it had seemed crazy to make the drive from Chicago to see this mysterious house. But somehow, she'd found herself packing her bags, breaking out her GPS unit, and climbing into her car. She'd arranged for her neighbor to watch her cat and hastily blocked her ex-fiancé's phone number from her cell. The last thing she wanted was for him to come looking for her. Or for anyone to come looking, really. She had no surviving family members, though her co-workers and friends at the hospital had all tried to console her. Had pitied her. It had been enough to drive her crazy within twenty-four hours of the accident.

Everyone has a different way of grieving. Hers was paved with a truckload of denial, indifference, passive-aggressiveness, and a hell of a bitchy temper. It was best for everyone involved that she simply leave, get some space…and find out why her father had left her a house in Mad Rock Harbor, Massachusetts.

From her brief Google searches, she determined that Mad Rock Harbor was nothing more than a speck on the map. A tiny Eastern Seaboard town with little more than a splattering of pre-Civil War era homes and one main street that linked the east side with the west side. The west side had what looked like a few businesses—a diner, a pharmacy, a veterinarian. A small local market seemed to be the biggest place in town, second only to the courthouse and the paltry sheriff's station.

The east side of town held most of the homes, many of which lined the harbor with tiny docks built on the water. Her father's home—*her* home—was one of these. She'd looked at it suspiciously from the comfort of her computer, unsure what to make of it. It didn't look special. It certainly wasn't a vacation home she would ever spend money on.

Just why he had bought it, she had no idea. She liked to believe her father had never had an affair, but maybe this was a nest for an unknown mistress. If not, and her mother had known about the place, then she'd done an excellent job of hiding it from her only daughter.

Which made Grace wonder what *other* secrets her parents had kept from her. Many of them she would likely never know.

A tear slipped unexpectedly from her right eye, alarming her. She brushed it away callously and turned her full attention back to the road. No more daydreaming. She was only four hours away; she had to keep driving. Driving toward a future that seemed uncertain save for one, simple truth.

Loneliness would be her new best friend.

* * *

Clouds rolled in, heavy with rain, as Grace pulled up to the house. She shut off the engine and stared out the window. Around her, the tidy suburban neighborhood was eerily still and quiet.

The house looked just as she expected —two stories, colonial-style with pale blue siding and white trim. A wide, covered porch shaded a navy blue front door flanked by a collection of windows on both sides. A white picket fence lined the property, the paint beginning to flake and peel. Weeds grew among the wild grasses in the yard, complemented by scraggly rose bushes along the porch. There was a much smaller house to the right, almost like a companion to the main house. Grace wondered if it was part of the property, though the lawyer hadn't mentioned it. Beyond the side of the house she could see the harbor, the water calm in the cool evening air. A man in a tiny metal fishing boat cut through the gray-blue surface, sending ripples out to the shore.

Grace looked back at the house, uncertainty warring with her curiosity. What if she found out something about her father that she wasn't prepared to learn?

Not that it mattered. He was dead. It wasn't like he could explain himself. All she could do was try to piece together this strange puzzle he had left for her.

Climbing out of the car, she grabbed her purse and the key she'd gotten from the family lawyer. She cast an instinctual glance at the trunk where she'd stowed her suitcase and beloved cello. She had to stop and remind herself that she wasn't in Chicago anymore. People didn't just break into cars on quiet, residential streets in Podunk little towns like this. People in small towns had manners and morals…didn't they?

Feeling ridiculous, she rolled her eyes, hoisted her purse onto her shoulder, and pressed the lock button on her key ring before making her way up the shabby brick path to the house.

She was a tall woman, willowy of figure with surprisingly strong and capable hands. They were her greatest tool as a doctor; second only to her sharp mind and iron composure. Although these days it felt more like tin foil, easily torn and crumbled.

Eyes like the grayest skies could fill with both resolve and sympathy, but rarely were they prone to tears. She'd learned long ago how to shield herself from emotion. In her line of work, it was a matter of survival.

As a result, she was quite the cynic. Though, as with her iron composure, she felt her hardiness weakening with each day that passed. Each day that the truth became more real to her.

Her designer heels nearly slipped through the cracks on the porch stairs and her weight had the wood creaking. She grimaced as she realized if the porch needed fixing, who knew what else needed to be repaired. She paused before the entrance, key out and ready. Her eyes fell upon a small, wooden sign nailed into the siding just to the left of the door.

It read: *Welcome to the Sparrow House.*

She suppressed a laugh. Where had her father come up with that? With a disheartened sigh, she shoved the key in the lock and opened the door, surprised it didn't groan as loudly as the stairs had. Maybe the house wasn't as dilapidated as she assumed.

The entryway was high-ceilinged and airy with stairs to the right and a wide hallway leading to what looked like the living room straight ahead. To the left was an open doorway that led into the kitchen and dining room, and to the right before the stairs was what she assumed to be the parlor.

There was no furniture, no belongings, no curtains, no

rugs…not even a speck of dust. The house was spic and span with white plastered walls and an ancient looking wooden floor, carefully polished. Grace wondered who had been taking care of the house as she made her way down the hall.

Her eyes took in every aspect of the first floor hungrily, as if searching for some clue, some evidence to explain why her father had purchased this home. She had expected to find *something* of his here—maybe a photograph, a book, some silverware. Instead, she found nothing. The cherrywood kitchen cabinets were vacant, the smooth white and gray marble counter free of crumbs. The old fridge was empty and unplugged. A butcher block island filled the middle of the kitchen, its surface weathered and worn. She wondered who had used it for so many years.

Beyond the kitchen was the spacious living area, the long wall covered with windows and a set of French doors leading to the back porch. Through the glass, she could see a beautiful view of the harbor, growing dark in the dimming light. She even spotted the little dock, sitting boatless in the water. It looked as lonely as she felt.

"Who are you?" A voice barked from behind Grace, startling her. She whirled around to face the intruder.

A short, older woman was standing inside the living room with her hands resting on her generous hips. Her brown eyes were mean and distrusting, and she had a frizzy mass of gray and white curls atop her head. Wrinkles fanned out from her eyes and lined the grooves of her face and her mouth was set in a glower. She wore faded jeans with weathered work boots and a loose brown and white plaid shirt with the sleeves rolled up to the elbows. From the dirt on her knees, Grace imagined she'd been working in a garden somewhere.

"This house isn't for sale, if that's why you decided to just wander on in," the woman said with a derisive sniff.

"I own this house," Grace informed her, regaining her wits. She stared down at the woman. "Who the hell are you?"

The woman's eyes narrowed. "Dr. Allen Sullivan owns this house. I don't know who you think you are."

"His daughter."

The woman's face softened. "Oh. I see. Is Dr. Allen here?"

Grace imagined a fist squeezing the blood from her heart, draining it dry. "He's dead." Now the woman looked completely devastated. Grace took a moment to relish it before she spoke again. "He left this house to me. Who are you, exactly?"

"My name's Nellie. I live in the little house next door." The woman ushered forward and stretched out her calloused hand, eager to shake Grace's. When they did, their eyes met and held. "I'm so sorry to hear about your father. He was a wonderful man. And your mother, too."

So, her mother *had* known of this place…

"Unfortunately, she's also dead. Car accident." Grace released her hand from Nellie's as she turned away. She walked to one of the windows and stared out at the water.

"Oh no," Nellie murmured. "God bless them. You know, they told me all about you."

"Did they?" Grace asked, though she found she didn't really care. All she wanted was to be left alone in this empty house—one that bore no memories of her parents. Had she been hoping it would?

"Dr. Grace. Your father was so proud of you. After he retired, he said he missed being at the hospital with you."

"How often did my father come here?" Grace continued to watch the harbor, her arms crossed defensively. She realized then just how cold it was inside the house.

"Not often. Once or twice a year, maybe." Nellie ventured forward to stand beside her. She watched Grace through troubled eyes. "Your father loved this place. That's why he asked me to take care of it for him."

"If he loved it so much, why is it empty?" The question seemed hollow, much like the house itself.

Nellie's face creased with pity. "I don't know, child."

Grace gritted her teeth, clutching her arms tighter to ward off the chill she felt from discussing her parents. She tore her eyes from the harbor and looked around the house. "I suppose I'll have to go find a hotel. I honestly thought there'd be some furniture," she said with a tired sigh.

"Why don't I call up Johnny Hayes? He owns the antique furniture store in town," Nellie offered with a smile. "He may have a bed frame you can use. And I'm sure we can hunt down a mattress. No need to go to the hotel. This is your house. You should stay here."

"I need more than just a bed. The damn fridge isn't even plugged in. I have nowhere to sit, nowhere to eat, no towels, no television…"

Nellie rested her hands on her hips again. "Don't you get all 'woe is me,' city girl. You clearly haven't been in enough small towns to know that people like to help one another out. I'll make some phone calls and get you what you need."

She left before Grace could argue, leaving her speechless. The woman went from rude to comforting to sassy so fast her head was spinning. Nellie had managed to squash Grace's negativity with her old-fashioned hospitality.

Grace stared at the front door, shaking her head. There was no way she'd have a bed by nightfall. Much less sheets, blankets, and food. "Better look up the hotel," she muttered to herself, grabbing her cell phone from her purse.

She made her way into the kitchen and felt behind the fridge for the cord. She may as well plug it in—if the electricity was even turned on.

It hummed to life as power shot through it, and she flipped

on the kitchen light. A pale-yellow glow filled the kitchen. Staring at her cell phone, she realized the battery had died. She slapped the device down on the kitchen island. Why shouldn't her cell be dead? Everything else in her life was a mess.

It was like they always said—when it rains, it pours. And she had her own personal storm cloud.

* * *

The self-absorbed and distrustful nature of city dwellers had long since hardened Grace's outlook on humanity; however, she couldn't deny that the people of Mad Rock Harbor came through for her.

Nellie dragged Johnny Hayes from his well-worn sofa at home and persuaded him to call his three best employees to help haul an antique, wrought iron bed frame, mattress, and an oak dining table set over to the Sparrow House. Then she rallied together a few of the neighborhood wives to contribute linens, cookware, plates, and food, which they brought over in waves of welcoming smiles, chenille sweaters, and flowery perfume. One of them thought to bring over a bottle of Merlot to Grace's enormous relief. After the day she'd had, she desperately needed a drink.

"There." Nellie beamed as she laid the last casserole dish in the fridge, labeled with baking instructions on the lid. She faced Grace with a pleased smile. "See? Didn't I tell you I'd get you what you needed?"

"Thanks." Grace nodded absently and uncorked the Merlot. She fought back a tired yawn as she poured herself a glass.

Nellie looked around the room as if to assure herself she hadn't forgotten anything. "Think nothing of it, child. Now, you get some rest in that nice new bed of yours, and I'll be by to see you tomorrow."

Grace leaned against the counter, wine glass in hand. "Let me know what I owe you for the bed and the table."

Nellie waved her hand in the air. "Consider it a welcome home gift."

Grace pondered the word 'home' and wondered why it irritated her. "You really don't have to do that."

"Shut your mouth and accept the gift," Nellie stated flatly, eyes bright with humor. "See you tomorrow."

Sipping her wine, Grace watched Nellie turn to leave. The woman paused in the doorway and faced Grace. "Welcome to the Sparrow House. You're going to love it here."

Grace held onto the words as Nellie left, an odd feeling settling over her. She drank more wine and closed her eyes, more tired than she'd ever been. Even the long hours at the hospital didn't compare to the overwhelming feeling of exhaustion that now plagued her.

It wasn't just physical, but emotional, too. Her soul was lonely, her mood dark. It grated against her insides and crept into the recesses of her mind, burrowing to fester like a disease.

Depression *was* a disease. One that she'd never experienced before. She regretted all those times she'd tried pathetically to talk others out of depression. It wasn't something you could switch off. It was *internal*. And it was now a part of her.

Much like the house was now a part of her. She knew she should just put it on the market, take the money, and vacation in the south of France. That's what the old Grace would have done. Before *it* happened.

Now everything had changed. What would she do with the house, if not sell it?

Never had her future felt so bleak and out of focus. She felt lost in her own skin, unable to find her purpose. How could she cope with the mortifying blow that life had dealt her?

Her eyes stung as she imagined her father's face, laughter lines fanning out from his brilliant blue eyes. He had been her rock, her protector, and her hero, all wrapped into one; by far the greatest man she had ever known.

She could almost picture him walking toward her in the kitchen of the Sparrow House with a good-humored smile, salt and pepper hair neatly combed. He would reach out and cup her face in his gentle, comforting hand, and tell her she would be okay. Tell her the world wasn't so bad, that it wasn't actually out to get her.

If only he'd known he would be taken from her so violently, so pointlessly. Maybe then he would have realized that the world was bad, and that it was always out to get everyone. That was just how it worked. That was life.

Feeling bitter, she downed the last of the wine. She grabbed the bottle and stormed out of the kitchen and up the stairs, furious at the tears that burned in her eyes. The last thing she wanted to do was cry. She knew once she got started, she'd be unable to stop.

She tore into the master bedroom, ignoring her new wrought iron bed. Instead of choosing the comfort of fresh blankets and pillows, she stumbled into the corner of the room and collapsed onto the floor. Setting aside the wine, she pulled her knees up tight against her chest. Her body trembled as she wrestled with her grief, unwilling to let it win.

Moonlight crept in through the open window, casting strange shadows along the wood floor. Her cello lay in its case in the corner, neglected. Since the accident, she hadn't been able to play. It reminded her too much of what she had lost.

Outside, she heard nothing. Silence. It was a cold, lonely contrast to the city that had been her home all her life.

At that moment, Grace had the harsh realization that coming to Mad Rock Harbor was a grave and terrible mistake. If she had thought she'd find comfort, she was wrong.

She only felt haunted.

CHAPTER TWO

The sparrows woke her. They flew and sang in the trees outside her window, cheerful despite the gloomy fog that spread its greedy fingers over the town.

Grace opened her eyes, only to shut them again and wince as pain pounded in her head. She groaned and regretted polishing off the bottle of wine. It had been stupid, *really* stupid, but she'd been in too desperate a mood to do anything else. Alcohol had never been a crutch for her. Then again, her parents weren't dead before. Things were different now. *She* was different now.

With a groan, she sat up, her mood sour. She glared out the window, irritated with the birds. What right did they have to be so chipper?

She rose unsteadily to her feet and grabbed the wine bottle, taking it with her as she headed downstairs. In the kitchen, she found a mug and loaded the coffee maker Nellie brought the night before. Once it was brewing, she leaned against the counter and shut her eyes.

Her entire body ached from sleeping on the floor, and she knew she'd need an Excedrin once she ate. She also needed a shower and desperately needed to shave her legs. Thankfully, Nellie confirmed that the upstairs bathroom was updated with modern fixtures and that everything worked. Otherwise, she'd be hightailing it over to the hotel after all. Dealing with no furniture was one thing. Living without decent plumbing was another.

The second there was enough coffee to fill the mug, she poured it, not even bothering with sugar or creamer. She sipped at the piping hot liquid and left the kitchen, heading for the living room windows that faced the harbor. The fog hindered her visibility, but she found its presence soothing. It was dark and dreary, which suited her mood perfectly. Blue skies and sunshine were for happy people. She wasn't a happy person.

On impulse, she stepped out the French doors onto the back porch and breathed in the cool scent of the sea. Through the haze, she watched a pair of small boats coast by through the water, too far away to notice her but close enough that she could hear their engines groaning and the men talking.

Except for the boats and the birds flitting in the large, leafless elms scattered on the property, the world around her was jarringly quiet. The wind whistled in from the ocean and shivered along her skin.

Her eyes wandered to the lonely dock hovering in the water down the embankment about twenty yards from the house. She lost herself in thought as she stared at it, unable to look away.

Something about it disturbed her, though she wasn't sure why. More than likely it was the hangover.

Rolling her shoulders to shake off the bad vibe, she wandered back inside. She polished off her first mug of coffee and went to the kitchen to pour another, taking it with her as she began to explore the rest of the house, starting with the upstairs. There hadn't been time to do so the night before, not with all the locals dropping by the house.

She found four bedrooms upstairs, one of them slightly larger than the rest. That was where they had put the bed, so it would be her room for the time being. It wasn't as if she could move it by herself even if she wanted to.

The other three rooms were hollow and vacant; lifeless without even curtains or wallpaper. Part of her wondered if children had once lived in the house, but she shrugged off the thought. What difference did it make?

The bathroom upstairs was small but practical with a clawfoot tub fitted with a shower head on the wall and surrounded by a gauzy curtain. A toilet and pedestal sink flanked the opposite wall, with a mirrored medicine cabinet built in over the sink. She eyed the tub wistfully before making her way back downstairs, pausing as she stepped into the entryway.

On the wall below the stairwell was a small door she hadn't noticed before. She approached it with both curiosity and confusion. Before her hand could grasp the door knob, she froze. A wave of nausea swept over her. Her heart began to pound and her palms suddenly felt clammy. Grace frowned and shook her head to clear the unusual sensation from her system.

She blamed it on the wine and grabbed the knob to pull the door open. She stared into a darkened stairwell that led down to the basement, irritated that her hands were still shaking.

God, she hadn't had *that* much to drink. More than likely she was just dehydrated and worn out from the drive. She knew that kind of combination could illicit such symptoms in a person.

Ignoring the feelings, she began to climb down the steps, her hand trailing along the wall searching for a light switch. She found one at the bottom attached to an electrical box that was probably installed long after the house had been built. She flipped it on and a single incandescent bulb hanging by a wire from the ceiling burst to life.

What she saw made her eyes widen.

The room was spacious but musty, with concrete block walls and a hard-packed dirt floor. Sheets white as snow covered large mounds stacked together in the center of the room. Along the far wall were cardboard boxes and a trunk.

Grace didn't hesitate as she rushed forward and slid the sheet off the closest mound, revealing a beautiful, handcrafted wood loveseat with royal blue upholstery.

"You've got to be kidding me." She reached for the next sheet and snatched it away to reveal a glossy mahogany coffee table with inlaid floral designs. A few more sheets revealed an end table, a few lamps, and a stunning matching mahogany grandfather clock.

She stared at the towering clock in bewilderment. "And here I thought they'd just left me an empty house." Her hands trailed over the carved wood, admiring the precision and care the creator must have taken to make such a masterpiece. The face of the clock was inlaid with gold, the dials ornate with intricate floral patterns. It was one of the most beautiful things she had ever seen.

"I don't even *like* antiques," she muttered, surprised by her reaction to the clock. Something about it charmed her in a way that her absurdly overpriced designer furniture back home never had.

A smile spread over her face as she stepped back and admired her discovery. She didn't know why her father had left these things in the basement, but she had every intention of bringing them to the surface. They were beautiful; amazingly preserved despite their age.

"And now they're mine." Excited for the first time in weeks, she hurried upstairs to get her phone. She had a favor to call in.

Within the hour, Johnny Hayes and two of his men arrived at her house, ready to hoist the furniture up from the basement. Grace talked with him as he carried one of the lamps down the hallway. "I appreciate this. Let me know how much I owe you. I have cash." She carried the other lamp in her arms as they walked.

"I'll let you know after we bring that clock up," Johnny replied easily. "Gotta be careful with antiques like that."

"I understand. Whatever it takes, just get it up here." Grace set the lamp on the dining table, admiring the loveseat that had already been brought up. Johnny set the lamp he carried beside hers and wiped his forehead with the back of his gloved hand. He was a young man, early-thirties with chestnut hair and kind blue eyes. He was exactly what she imagined most small-town men were like—faithful, well-mannered, simple-minded.

And, naturally, a wealth of information.

"The whole town's talking about you," he told her with a toothy smile. "The newest Sullivan to come to Mad Rock Harbor."

Her left eyebrow shot up. "I've barely been here a day."

"Word spreads fast around here." He leaned against the kitchen island, lifting his ball cap and running a hand through his hair. "Everyone's curious if you're gonna be a permanent fixture or not."

"Well, I'm not. You can tell that to all your bar buddies so they can tell their wives, and then you can all get over your little fascination with me." Grace crossed her arms. "Now, go get my clock."

"Yes, ma'am." Johnny tipped the bill of his baseball cap and grinned, leaving her to brood in silence. She was irritated at having her privacy shattered. All she wanted was peace and quiet, and as generous as the townspeople were, she still wasn't ready to make that trade just yet.

Perhaps it was best if she kept to herself from now on.

* * *

Hours later, Grace stood before the grandfather clock in the living room, wine glass in hand. She had just finished setting the time, and was busy watching the minute hand tick closer and closer to the twelve. If it still worked and she'd set it right, the hour strike should chime at six o'clock. She mentally crossed her fingers as the minute hand inched closer. Enraptured, she awaited the telltale gong as the hand slowly but surely met its fate.

The doorbell rang as the hour struck, causing Grace to nearly jump out of her skin. She gripped her wine glass to keep from spilling red liquid everywhere, cursing under her breath as her heart galloped from the shock. Annoyed at both herself and the intruder, she stalked into the entryway. The sound of the gong quieted as she opened the door.

Nellie stood on the other side, a large, round dish in her hands and her smile bright. "I brought you some dinner."

"I can see that." Grace sighed, eyeing the dish. "What is it?"

"Beef stew." Nellie lifted the dish to show it off. "You're too skinny, child. You could use some meat on those bones of yours."

Grace snorted. "I'm a vegetarian."

"Not tonight." Nellie pushed past Grace and made her way into the kitchen, cheerfully setting the dish down and grabbing two bowls from one of the cabinets. When Grace followed her, Nellie nodded at the dining table. "You sit down. I'll bring it to you."

"What service," Grace grumbled sarcastically. She tossed herself into one of the dining chairs and watched Nellie dish out the food and bring it over.

"Be careful, it's hot," Nellie warned. She handed Grace a fork before taking a seat across from her. Grace only stared at the bowl with a questionable look on her face. Nellie sighed. "It's not poisoned."

"It's red meat."

"So what? You're a carnivore, aren't you?" Nellie snapped, though there was humor in her tone. "Now eat it and be grateful."

Grace sniffed at the bowl of stew. It'd been years since she'd eaten beef, but it did smell incredible. Her stomach rumbled, low and hollow. She shoved aside her uncertainty and dug in.

The first bite actually made her groan. All thoughts of slaughter house animals, injected hormones, and coppery blood disappeared the instant she savored the incredible flavor.

Across the table, Nellie looked pleased with herself. "Not so bad, is it?"

Grace groaned again and scooped up another bite. Her mouth full, she met her neighbor's eyes and shook her head. "I don't eat meat."

"So you said."

She swallowed. "Why am I still eating this? I can feel my arteries clogging."

"Shut up and stop being so dramatic." Nellie chuckled and took a bite of her own stew. She wagged her fork at Grace.

"If you know what's good for you, you'll polish off that bowl and let me serve you seconds. Then you'll enjoy a nice glass of wine before turning in for the evening. No wonder you're so famished. You've been eating nothing but carrots and that tofu crap. That's no way to live."

Grace laughed despite herself. "I eat more than carrots and tofu."

"Oh sure, and I'm a belly dancer from India. Keep eating, I'll get you some more wine."

Grace scooped up the last of the stew before shoving it across the table. Her hands fell to her stomach, satisfied yet hating herself. "I'm so full. I'm never going to eat again."

"Yes, you will." Nellie poured more wine into Grace's glass then corked the bottle and took her seat again. "So, tell me about your life in Chicago. Do you enjoy being a doctor?"

Grace toyed with her wine glass as she gave it some thought. "It's in my blood. My grandfather and my father were both in the medical field."

"Yes, but do you like it?"

"I guess. It's rewarding."

"So they say. What about a boyfriend?"

Grace grimaced. "Not anymore."

Nellie's face fell. "Oh. What happened?"

"I don't want to talk about it." Grace met eyes with the older woman, her temper smoldering just beneath the surface. "Why did my father buy this house? He must have told you."

Nellie blinked in confusion. "Buy the house?"

"Yes." Grace leaned forward, resting her arms on the table. "What was the point of this place? My parents had a townhouse in Manhattan and they never mentioned vacationing here. So why did he buy it?"

"He never told you about the Sparrow House?"

"No," Grace snapped. The wound of knowing her father

had kept something like this from her was still fresh.

Nellie sighed. "Well, that explains why you're so confused." She reached across the table to grasp Grace's hand firmly. "Your father didn't buy this house—he inherited it. It has been in the Sullivan family for over a hundred years, since 1865."

Hearing that only made Grace angrier. "Then why is this the first time I've heard of it? That doesn't make any goddamn sense."

"I don't know." Nellie shook her head sadly. "It's been many years since any member of your family lived here permanently. They all seem to prefer to keep a distance."

"Then why not just sell it? Why hold onto it?"

"It's been rumored that the house is an addiction your family can never shake. They try to run from it, but they always come back, generation after generation. And now you're here." Nellie tried to smile, though her expression was oddly haunted.

Grace's eyes narrowed. "You want me to believe that my father was *addicted* to this house, and that's why he didn't sell it?"

Nellie nodded. "It's not unheard of. Many people become attached to places and things in ways they can't explain."

"That's stupid," Grace retorted, more than a little frustrated. "That still doesn't explain why he kept this place a secret."

"Maybe he wanted to save you from the same addiction he had." Nellie shrugged, rising to her feet to clean up the dishes. "Either way, you ended up here, didn't you? I'd say that's fate."

Grace paused, absorbing the woman's words carefully. She realized then that she had barely even hesitated before making the trip to Mad Rock Harbor. The old version of herself would have gone overseas to Paris or to the hills of Tuscany. But instead, she'd come to some inconsequential town in Massachusetts. Why? What had pulled her there?

Absolutely nothing, except a desire to know the truth,

Grace decided, feeling foolish. She was letting the old woman's superstitions cloud her judgment. She'd come to Mad Rock Harbor to feel closer to her dead parents, and there was nothing odd about that at all.

But something still prickled at the back of her neck, causing her skin to crawl with uncertainty.

"I'll be going now. You enjoy the rest of that wine," Nellie said suddenly, appearing beside Grace with her coat over one arm and the empty pot in the other.

Grace looked up at her, blinking. "Oh, okay. Thank you for the red meat."

Nellie smiled. "You're welcome." She glanced around the room, taking in the antique furniture. "These old things really look lovely in here, don't they?"

"Didn't you know that furniture was down in the basement?" Grace asked, turning in her chair to stare at Nellie. "Seems odd that you didn't mention it."

Nellie hesitated. "I don't go down in the basement. Fear of the dark."

Grace sensed the older woman's discomfort. "Right. Well—"

The gong resounded from the grandfather clock as it struck seven, the noise startling them both. After the seventh gong, Grace sighed. When she noticed that Nellie's face was white as a sheet, she got immediately to her feet.

"Are you okay?"

Nellie's eyes shot from the clock back to Grace, her hand fluttering over her heart. "That startled me, is all." She tried to laugh, though she looked around the room nervously.

Grace folded her arms and gave the clock a cross look. "I may have to disconnect the gong. It's too loud."

"Don't you feel that?" Nellie asked in a murmured whisper, rubbing her free hand over her arm as if to ward off a chill.

Grace frowned. "Feel what?"

Nellie said nothing for a moment, then shook her head. "Nothing, child. Goodnight."

She left before Grace could respond. Grace stared after her, more than a little confused, then turned to the clock again. "Stupid clock," she muttered, though part of her oddly missed the sound of the gong now that it was gone.

* * *

Grace decided not to disable the hour strike on the old grandfather clock. Part of her hoped she would get used to the sound in time.

She regretted that decision when the clock struck three a.m., and violently shook her out of a deep sleep.

Gong. Gong. *Gong.*

Each slam of the pendulum was a fist pounding viciously into her chest, square over her heart, knocking the wind from her lungs. Her eyes flew open from the horrid pain, wide with terror and wet with unshed tears. Sweat beaded on her face, cold and slick, matting strands of her dark bangs to her forehead.

She fought to catch her breath as the echoing of the final gong drifted into oblivion. The sheets were tangled up with her legs, constricting her as she fought to free herself.

What the hell was that? A dream? A nightmare?

Her head began to pulse with a dull pain. The pressure in her chest faded as her senses came back to her.

She stared around the quiet bedroom, lit only by thin streaks of moonlight that came through the window. The branches of a nearby tree left twisted, spindly shadows along the wooden floor. They looked like crooked, deformed arms, stretching and reaching out to grab at her like some malevolent monster. When the breeze outside shifted them, it broke her trance and jolted her back into awareness.

"Get a hold of yourself," Grace whispered, rubbing her face

and exhaling a heavy, burdened sigh. She fought to convince herself that nothing was out to get her, that the nightmare had simply been a result of too much stress and a little too much wine.

Her depression wasn't helping either. The black cloud followed her wherever she went, hanging over her head like a bad omen. A scar. A blemish on the beautiful person she once was.

Grace knew she would never be that person again.

A soft sound permeated the darkened house, alarming her. Her ears perked as she strained to listen, hoping to hear it again. When she did, her hands tightened on the sheet she held.

It sounded like…crying?

Unable to resist, she slipped from her bed quietly, reaching for the pepper spray she carried with her everywhere. She tiptoed over the floor, wincing each time it creaked and groaned beneath her.

When she reached her doorway, she stared into the darkness of the hallway. Ahead was the banister and the stairwell, open to the moonlit entryway. Her eyes strained to see in the pale blue light but caught no movement.

Grace loosened her death grip on her pepper spray, realizing how stupid she was being. There wasn't anyone in the house. How could there be? And if there were, what reason did they have to be there? She had nothing worth stealing. No flat screen television, no valuable jewelry. Unless they were there to hurt her. But if they were, why were they crying?

Resigned that she was being pathetic, she started back into her room. The return of the soft crying stopped her dead in her tracks. It sounded like it came from downstairs in the entryway. Curiosity gave her courage as she stalked forward with purpose, this time flicking on the light in the stairwell to illuminate the space.

She stepped down the stairs, eyes shooting from one corner to the other, searching for the source of the sound. If she wasn't mistaken, it sounded like a little girl. But how was that possible?

When she found nothing, she shook her head and decided she really *was* being stupid. And probably losing her mind, too. It had most likely been a bird or a cat outside, or perhaps she was just imagining things to get upset about. That's what Rick seemed to think. Every time she got mad at him or felt anything other than joy he seemed to think she was exaggerating and creating chaos for herself.

That was the *last* time she'd ever date a psychologist.

Even though she tried to let her cynicism over her disastrous relationship harden the pain, she failed miserably. It all came back like a rushing tidal wave, and it took all she had to not crumble to her knees.

She clutched at her chest and frantically climbed the stairs, desperate to lie down. The dizziness slowed her, and her vision blurred as she stumbled into her bed.

Crawling under the covers, she pulled them over her head and waged war with her emotions. But the fury could only carry her so far as images of her parents, smiling and happy, flashed through her mind. Of Rick, irresistible with that boyish grin, proposing to her on the rooftop of Willis Tower. Her friends and coworkers surprising her with a lavish party for her birthday several months ago. It all flew by her like a movie reel, and it was impossible to make it stop.

Until it turned on her. Painful, horrible memories replaced the good ones, overwhelming her with a harsh, brutal ache. The phone call that had delivered the news of death. The caskets that held her parents being lowered into the ground. Discovering Rick in bed with her best friend on the day of the funeral. Succumbing to the grief on her last day at the hospital. The humiliation of falling apart in line at the grocery store. The compelling urge to run—run far away and never look back.

Wasn't that what she was doing? She had run to Mad Rock Harbor to escape it all. Did she intend to ever return to Chicago?

Grace found she had no answer to that question, not at the moment. Instead, she inhaled deeply, her throat aching and her head pounding with pain as exhaustion claimed her. She settled into it, accepted the relief it promised, and plunged into a restless sleep.

Downstairs, the tearful sounds of sorrow faded into the night.

CHAPTER THREE

A full week passed, and Grace found herself missing the city less and less. There were some things she longed for, like Starbucks and city lights and her favorite hole-in-the-wall Italian bistro, but she was learning to live without them. Just as she was learning to live without her parents—her father, in particular. She was slowly coming to terms with the fact that she would never hear his voice again or laugh over a bottle of Merlot at Christmas while her mother fussed over decorations no one but them would see.

This year she would celebrate alone, which wasn't a celebration at all. The idea of boycotting the holiday and spending it somewhere it wasn't celebrated crossed her mind. Just the sight of a Christmas tree might push her back into that dark hole of misery.

Or she could just remain at the Sparrow House and

barricade herself inside with gallons of chocolate ice cream, murder mystery novels, and barrels of wine. That was a perfectly respectable way to spend the holiday.

She bundled her coat around her, watching the harbor from her seat on the back porch. Even though it was chilly and the mid-morning fog still hung in the air, she felt content. In this moment, she could reflect, and simply *be*.

Over the course of the week, she'd accomplished quite a lot. At least more than she'd figured, given her current state of mind. She'd walked the entire property, admiring the tall, leafless trees and sandy shoreline with its lonely dock. The dock itself was precarious; rickety on its pilings and weathered from the salty sea air. She had only managed a few steps on it before turning right back around, certain it would collapse under her at any moment.

She'd driven into town for supplies, visiting the local market that carried an impressive amount of produce and quality fish. It pleased her to know she wouldn't be stuck eating Nellie's beef stews and pot roasts every night, delicious as they were. No one should eat *that* much red meat.

Some of the locals introduced themselves to her as she wandered around and checked out the local diner, the library, and the wharf where the fishermen brought in their daily catch. Out of habit, she was short tempered with most of those she met. She didn't want to come across as too friendly. They might expect her to stick around or make her feel sorry for leaving when the time came. Besides, if she made any friends then they'd be stopping by all hours of the day like Nellie was prone to do. Grace could only handle one intruder for the time being.

As it was, her solitary retreat had turned into a safe house with her the one to be saved and Nellie the one doing the saving. It was unexpected, yet not entirely unwanted.

"I made some hot chocolate to warm those bones of

yours," Nellie announced as she stepped onto the porch with two steaming mugs in her hands.

Grace snickered. "Hot chocolate? What am I, five?"

"Don't you know how to say thank you?"

Grace accepted the mug, then looked down at it with a laugh. "Check it out, I even get some marshmallows."

"You're never too old for hot chocolate and marshmallows," Nellie chided. She sipped from her own mug as she gazed at the harbor. Her gaze grew wistful while she enjoyed the view.

Grace warmed her hands over the mug, eyeing her neighbor thoughtfully. "Nellie, are there any children living on this street?"

"No, it's mostly just retired folks. The Sampsons three doors down are in their forties, but they don't have any children. Why do you ask?"

"Well—this is going to sound really stupid—and honestly, I don't even know why I'm bringing it up except it's been bothering me," Grace began, suddenly irritated with herself. "I've been hearing what sounds like a little girl—crying, laughing, talking. I thought maybe one of the neighborhood kids had been playing near the house. It's the only rational explanation."

When Nellie said nothing, Grace felt anger sweep over her. "Or maybe I'm just crazy. I know I'm depressed, but crazy? I guess anything's possible at this point."

"You're not crazy, child. It was probably just your imagination. Old houses give off all sorts of weird vibes."

Grace's eyes narrowed. "You look like you're not telling me something. What is it?"

"Nothing." Nellie bristled, her lips pressed into a firm line and her earlier humor gone. "Excuse me, I have things to do."

She turned and went back inside, leaving Grace stewing on the porch. She pictured Nellie going to the nearest phone and calling up everyone to inform them that the newest Sullivan in town was certifiably crazy. A Grade-A lunatic who should be committed for absurd delusions bordering on schizophrenia. Hell, maybe she'd commit *herself* if the voices kept up...

A sharp scream and crash echoed from inside, startling her. She set down her mug and bolted through the door, her heart pounding as she found Nellie standing in the living room. Hot chocolate and shards of porcelain lay at her feet, marshmallows dotting the wood like flecks of snow.

"What the hell happened?" Grace demanded. She stared around frantically for an intruder, a spider, *something.*

Nellie shook like a leaf, her hands clutched against her chest as if she were having a heart attack.

Grace sighed and went to the older woman, concern in her eyes. "Are you okay?"

Nellie nodded, taking deep breaths to calm down. "Yes, I'm fine."

"What happened?"

"Nothing." She leaned over and started to clean up the mess, grabbing the larger pieces of porcelain while her hands continued to tremble.

Grace frowned and crossed her arms. "It doesn't look like nothing. Why won't you tell me?"

"It was her," Nellie whispered.

"Who?"

"Her."

"Is there someone in the house? Do I need to call the police?" Grace asked impatiently.

Nellie got to her feet and glared at Grace with angry tears in her eyes. "That won't solve a thing, child, and you know it. You've heard her. Now I just saw her. She's made herself known to us."

"Wait, what?" Grace blinked, her eyebrows shooting up in

disbelief.

"Your father had mentioned seeing an apparition of a little girl in the house. He said he saw her nearly every time he came to visit. I've never seen her until now." Nellie pointed over to the hall that led to the entryway, the stairwell visible. "She was standing right there, plain as day. One minute she was there, the next she was gone."

"My father claimed he'd seen a...a *ghost*?" A skeptical laugh bubbled out of Grace's throat as she shook her head. "You're messing with me, aren't you? You thought it'd be funny to tease me for hearing voices."

"Don't be an idiot," Nellie snapped, irritation hardening the lines of her face. "Do I look like I'm making this up? I saw what I saw and I'm not ashamed. Not like you are."

"So, you believe in ghosts?"

"I do now."

Grace rolled her eyes. "Right. You realize how ridiculous that is, don't you?"

Nellie sighed and rubbed her temple tiredly. "I have things to do. Excuse me."

She left, leaving Grace standing amidst a pool of hot chocolate and marshmallows. She stared down at the mess, annoyed. Great, now she had insulted her neighbor. It hadn't been her intention, but the whole idea of there being a ghost in the house was simply laughable.

She went to the kitchen for a towel and knelt to clean up the chocolate, sopping up marshmallows with it. She tilted her head and looked at the antique sofa beside her, concerned when she noticed part of the fabric on the arm was tattered and scratched.

Had the movers done that when they brought it upstairs? she wondered, examining the damage carefully. It didn't look fresh, but rather worn from age. The royal blue fabric was even faded and fraying in spots, damaged as though by sun exposure.

If it had looked that way before, she hadn't noticed it. Shrugging it off, she rose to her feet to wash her hands of hot chocolate and the entire notion of ghosts.

* * *

A couple of days later, Grace felt ambitious enough to head back down into the basement and tackle the stack of remaining boxes. It took her a while to muster up the strength for what she knew would be a difficult task, but the weight hanging over her felt lighter and her mood was oddly cheerful for once.

It could have something to do with the neighborhood tabby cat that had wandered over that morning, greeting her with a cheerful meow and rubbing his forehead against her hand. She missed her cat Charlie back home in Chicago more than she realized, and the encounter lifted her spirits. Though it was odd the way the cat tensed up after greeting her, eyes on the front door with its ears bent and a warning hiss on its breath. She'd looked around for the source of its anxiety but saw nothing. By the time she'd turned back, the tabby had fled.

She shrugged it off, not wanting to let it bother her. Instead, she slipped into comfortably faded jeans and a black T-shirt, tied back her hair, and took her coffee with her into the basement to get some work done.

On her way down, she flicked on the light. As her feet hit the solid-packed dirt floor, she took a moment to take in the room around her.

Without the old furniture, the basement appeared much larger. The vacant spots left behind by the sofa and tables were marked by grooves in the dirt, leaving only the boxes to line the cement block walls. Grace counted ten aged, cardboard boxes and one large antique trunk the color of blueberries. She rubbed her chin with her free hand, pondering where to begin.

Since the trunk seemed to be the most accessible, she started there. She set her coffee aside on a nearby box before pulling the trunk away from the wall and into the center of the room where the light was best. As she knelt beside it, she flipped up the latches and lifted the lid, letting it fall back on its hinges.

In the dim yellow light of the single bulb above her, Grace found herself staring into a trunk filled with photographs. Hundreds of them, all black and white and weathered by time. From the styles, she figured they spanned decades.

Beneath the photographs, she discovered a few albums and old camera equipment, along with reels of negatives. Intrigued, she opened one of the reels and pulled out the spool of film, holding it up to the light.

Pictures of women and children, the Sparrow House, the harbor—most likely taken by her relatives. Memories of them were long gone, yet they still lived on in the photographs kept secret in the trunk.

She replaced the negatives in the trunk and sat down on the dirt floor, reaching for a stack of photographs. Flipping through them, she looked for identification on the back. A few were labeled, though she didn't recognize the names. Her father had never told her the history of her family and she'd never asked. Now she wished she had.

Now she was on her own to solve the mystery of her past. The mystery of the Sparrow House.

Grace held the photographs carefully, her capable hands reverent of the history they held. Part of her worried they might fall apart and she'd lose this little piece of her family she had found. This treasure trove of times past.

One photo was of an elderly man and woman standing arm-in-arm on the dock outside the house. From the clothing they wore, Grace guessed the date to be just before the Great Depression.

Were they her great-grandparents? She squinted at the image, trying to see some part of herself in these strangers. The names on the back labeled them as Howard and Ethel Sullivan. Who were they?

Feeling lost, she set the photograph aside and lifted the next one. An infant, dressed elegantly and lying among black blankets. It took her a moment to realize that this was a picture of death, common in the late 19th century. The child had likely died within the first few months of birth, and this was the only photograph ever taken of him or her. Seeing it made Grace shudder. What a morbid tradition.

She set it with the others as she heard Nellie come through the front door and call out to her.

"I'm down here, Nellie," Grace replied, shaking her head to rid herself of the morose feelings.

Nellie stood in the doorway to the basement, her silhouette blocking the light. "Child, what in the world are you doing?"

"I wanted to go through these boxes," Grace explained, glancing around at the photographs. "Though all I've done is sour my mood."

"Well, why don't I come down and help you," Nellie offered, taking the first couple of steps into the basement. Grace watched the older woman stop abruptly, almost as if she'd run into a wall. She teetered back, trying to regain her balance, then shook her head as if to clear it. When she tried to step forward again, she stumbled backward and nearly toppled over onto the steps. "Good Lord!"

"Nellie?" Grace watched her friend stumble back up the steps, clutching her chest and wheezing before disappearing into the hallway. Her initial thought was that Nellie was having a heart attack. She took the stairs two at a time and found Nellie leaning weakly against the wall.

Grace held Nellie's shoulders in a firm grip, her iron-gray eyes filled with concern. "Breathe, Nellie. Do you feel pressure in your chest? Any pain?"

Nellie let out a strained breath that ended in a laugh. "I'm not having a heart attack if that's what you're thinking."

"Are you sure? I have a bottle of aspirin upstairs."

Nellie batted Grace's hands away and turned into the living room to get some space. "I'm just spooked."

"Does this have something to do with your fear of the dark?" Grace asked. "Because if it is, then—"

"No," Nellie retorted, still trembling. She looked around nervously, as though something was going to jump out and grab her. "It's not that."

Grace walked to the older woman, turning her around to face her. "Why are you acting like this? You've been strange ever since I mentioned hearing voices. I'm getting tired of whatever little game you think you're playing."

Nellie bristled, both shame and anger playing over her face. "There's no game. I felt what I felt and I saw what I saw, and—"

Her gaze flicked over Grace's shoulder to the basement door, and her face drained of all color. Her mouth fell open as she froze like a rabbit in front of headlights that promised death.

"What now?" Grace whirled around and saw nothing but the entryway, lit with peaceful morning light. "Right. Nothing. Christ, Nellie, get a hold of yourself."

"How did you not see it?" Nellie stammered. She sucked in air with heavy, frantic gasps, her eyes still wide with fear. "It was right there, by the door."

"Well, what happened to *it*?" Grace asked, unwilling to let the terror on Nellie's face alarm her.

"It was a shadow...i-it *slid* along the wall. Then into it," Nellie said almost in disbelief.

"The shadow did," Grace stated flatly, crossing her arms. "Are you on any medication? Diazepam? Amitriptyline?"

"Damnit, there is something evil in this house!" Nellie

asserted, snapping out of her fear. "You are so closed off to the world that you can't see, but the girl is speaking to you. You hear her. I've seen her, and I've felt the evil that has somehow found its way into this house. I don't know where it came from, but it wants to harm you. It weighs on this house like a dark shroud. Don't you feel it?"

Grace didn't know what to say. The sincerity in the other woman's expression and statement worried her. She didn't believe it, and yet she couldn't deny that Nellie definitely believed what she was saying. "No, I don't feel it," she admitted.

Nellie let out a frustrated breath. "I'm going to get someone who can help. You're in denial, but the house is not. It's only going to get worse unless we do something."

"This is *my* house," Grace reminded her. "Just what the hell do you think you're going to do to it?"

Nellie softened, reaching out to grasp Grace's shoulder. "I know you're grieving, child. I know you don't want any of this, but that doesn't change anything. I want you to be happy in this house, to stay as long as you can. If we don't fix this, in time the house will not be habitable."

Grace wearily shook her head. "I'm going back to bed. I need to be alone."

Nellie let her hand fall lamely to her side. She nodded, saying nothing as Grace fled to the sanctuary of her bedroom.

Once upstairs, Grace started to shut her bedroom door, only to pause when she heard footsteps directly outside in the hall. Exasperated, she threw back the door and leaned out of the doorway. "Nellie, I—"

There was no one there. The hall was empty. Downstairs, she heard the front door click shut as Nellie left.

Confused, she tried to rationalize how Nellie could have been right outside her bedroom and then out the front door in a matter of seconds. Had she even heard the old woman follow her up the stairs?

"Who's there?" she called out, assuming someone else must have come in. Silence met her question, which only made her doubt her sanity even more. Feeling ridiculous, she stepped back into the room, shut the door, and turned around.

Her bedroom window was wide open. A tiny brown sparrow sat on the windowsill, eyeing her curiously. She blinked, struggling to remember if she'd opened the window earlier that morning. Shouldn't she remember if she had?

The sparrow fluttered outside, joining its companions in the trees. Grace let out a rush of breath and walked over to shut the window, closing the latch on it. She stared at the birds accusingly as if they'd left the window open and made the footsteps right outside her bedroom door.

Because, as much as she wanted to deny it, she knew it hadn't been Nellie.

CHAPTER FOUR

D id you die in this room?"
    ...we all did.

"Were you tormented by the doctors, the nurses? Did they drive you to kill yourself? Or were you murdered by one of them?"

Silence saturated the halls of the once great Bellhurst Institution, but what the human ear could not detect, Ian Black knew his digital recorder would. Haunted souls craved acknowledgement, and he was more than willing to listen. Given the strange events that had already happened that night, he had a gut feeling they'd captured some dynamite evidence. He couldn't wait to review it once the investigation was over.

Until then, he'd ask his questions of the lost souls and the damned that he knew remained in the old asylum. He could feel them, could sense their presence. It chilled his skin with goose bumps and lifted the hair on his arms. He felt like there were eyes on him, though he could see no one. Such was the magic of the supernatural.

He was, by profession, a ghost hunter. A teenage obsession with horror flicks and haunted houses turned quickly into real life adventures with some truly frightening encounters. It was in his mid-twenties that he founded Great American Paranormal with his childhood best friend, leaving behind a career as a trained chef and focusing everything he had on investigating the paranormal. Now at thirty-one, it was everything to him. And by some stroke of either genius or luck, he had managed to capture worldwide interest in his investigations and offers for TV deals were being thrown his way.

None of that mattered to him, though. At least not as much as his commitment to finding rock-solid evidence of life after death. He'd go to the ends of the earth for it, breaking down doors others were too afraid to touch, opening himself up to a world beyond his own.

It wasn't just his job—it was his life.

The temperature suddenly dropped several degrees in pockets of air around him. His Mel Meter showed fluctuations that were frankly impossible. Drastic and sudden temperature drops like that could only mean one thing. The ghosts had found him.

"Dude, I feel that. Do you feel that?"

Ian didn't bother looking at his partner as he continued to walk down the hallway, holding his recorder in one hand and the Mel Meter in the other. "Yeah, man."

Alex Gallagher grinned toothily and shifted the professional-grade camcorder he held on his shoulder. He kept the lens focused on Ian, the world around him cast in the green glow of night vision. "Check out that doll on the floor to the left, missing its legs and shit. Creepy."

"There were children that were patients here, too," Ian said, repulsed by the thought. "Left here to rot by their families."

"The world was a cruel place back then."

Ian glanced over his shoulder with a dark grin. "Still is."

Alex nodded, panning the camera to the doll as Ian checked the EMF readings surrounding it.

When Ian didn't get anything out of the ordinary, he turned away and continued to ask questions aloud to whatever spirits may be present. "Why were you sent here? Did your family abandon you?"

Alex scratched his shoulder blade, feeling uncomfortable in his own skin. It was a common side effect for him whenever the air chilled and quieted to an impossible void of nothingness. He wanted to scratch his nose, but fought back the urge in order to keep the camera steady. They were trying to get some good footage to show the TV producers, and the last thing he wanted was to drop the camera because of an itchy nose.

Thinking of being on TV got his blood pumping with excitement. He was dying to take Great American Paranormal to the next level, and he knew that they were good enough to make some serious waves in the paranormal community. Hell, they already were. Paranormal groups all over the country emulated what he and Ian showcased on their popular YouTube channel. It was only a matter of time before they had the whole country—the entire world—watching them hunt down ghosts.

Plus, they made a good team. Ian was practically his brother; his best friend since they were kids growing up in Seattle. Where Ian was the more intensely-serious-brooding one, Alex liked to think of himself as the wildly-intelligent-and-nerdy-but-still-good-looking sidekick with a heart of gold. How could that *not* make great television?

The chills that ran up his arms began to dissipate, signaling the end of their encounter. He ran a free hand through his sandy blond hair, his grass-green eyes landing on Ian. "I think they've moved on. Where to next?"

"I want to check out the old infirmary. Nancy said that's where she saw the shadow figure." Ian took the next right and made his way into the asylum's hospital wing, his eyes well-adjusted to the darkness as the hour approached two a.m. He deftly avoided the debris littering the grimy linoleum floor, his ears perked for any sound.

"Remember what that old guy said?" Alex asked, dodging an ancient typewriter that lay mangled in his path. "About patients who misbehaved having their teeth ripped out in that dental chair? We need to find it and do an EVP session."

Before Ian could reply, a resounding crash of something heavy and metallic penetrated the silent darkness in echoing waves.

"Holy shit!" Alex cried out, the camera shaking as he faced the direction of the crash. "What the hell was that?"

"I don't know." Ian faced the camera, his adrenaline pumping hot with the thrill of the hunt. "Let's go find out."

Alex let out an unsteady laugh, embracing the rush. "Great American Paranormal: investigating unexplained crashes and bangs since 2007."

Ian brushed back his dark, shoulder length hair. "Somebody's gotta do it."

They hurried toward the hospital wing, bursting through the doors and into a high-ceilinged room lined with broken beds and tattered sheets. Wide windows covered one wall, though the cloud cover outside prevented any moonlight from shining through.

In the center of the dilapidated room sat a large metal chair, the legs mangled and the backrest bent over the seat. The dirt that layered the floor surrounding it was marred, as though the chair had recently scraped over it.

Alex froze. "Dude, that chair wasn't there before."

"No, it was in the back corner, I remember," Ian recalled, approaching the chair cautiously. "Something must have thrown it across the room."

"No fucking way." Alex focused the camera on the chair and the disturbed floor around it. "Let me check the static camera I set up in here."

While Ian continued to inspect the chair, Alex raced over to the camera set up on a tripod in the corner of the room. He immediately let out a loud curse and seriously considered kicking the equipment. "The battery's dead!"

Ian looked up from the chair. "How is that possible? It was a brand-new battery."

Alex grunted with frustration as he examined the camera with a flashlight. "Whatever it was that threw that chair must have drained the energy out of this battery and used it as fuel."

"Maybe it was trying to get our attention." Ian glared around the room, letting the adrenaline take over. "You wanted us in here, didn't you? Now we're here. Show yourself! Throw this chair again. Use my energy!"

Alex abandoned the dead camera and returned to filming Ian, biting his lower lip anxiously as he looked around the darkened room. Although he didn't hear anything, he sensed a sudden humming of electricity along his skin. He gritted his teeth in a hard smile. "It's here, buddy."

"I know." Ian held his arms out, welcoming the same sensation. In his right hand, he held his digital recorder. "Did you kill people here? Were you one of the sick, twisted motherfuckers that hurt innocent children?"

...can't kill what does not live.

"Why don't you hurt me? If you're so tough, lift that chair and smash it over my head." Ian eyed the chair in challenge, willing it to move. "C'mon!"

In that instant, he both heard and felt an ominous, otherworldly whisper rush at him from behind. He jumped and whirled around, eyes wide as he scanned the darkness. "Did you hear that?"

"Nope. What was it?" Alex asked, still filming as he walked closer. "A voice?"

"A whisper." Ian shook off an icy chill, feeling suddenly lightheaded. He swayed, gripping his head with both hands.

"Dude, you okay?"

"I'm fine," Ian assured him. "Just drained."

"You did tell it to use your energy," Alex joked, patting his friend on the back. "C'mon, let's go find that dental chair."

Ian nodded, glancing back at the broken metal chair as they left the room. He tried to make sense of what the voice had said to him. He could have sworn it said the word *doctor*...

* * *

Hours later, they left the abandoned asylum and embraced the morning sun.

"I could use a big stack of pancakes and a mountain of bacon right about now," Alex announced cheerfully, suppressing a yawn. They wandered to their black utility van with its large lime green and orange Great American Paranormal sign on the side and opened the back door. "Better yet, sausage wrapped with pancakes wrapped with bacon, covered in syrup with a side of fruit. Gotta stay healthy."

"You act like that fruit will save your arteries."

"Since when do you care about my arteries?"

Ian shrugged. "I don't."

"Good. Because we're going to Denny's after we drop this stuff off at the hotel."

"I want to go over the recording from the hospital wing, see if I can make out what that voice said," Ian said before he skirted around to the front of the van and climbed into the driver's seat.

Alex sighed as he slammed the back door shut and slid into the passenger seat. "You're gonna make me wait to eat? After a ten-hour investigation?"

"Yep." Ian shot a look at his friend. "You'll live."

Alex reached into the backseat and grabbed a half-eaten bag of nacho cheese Doritos. "You're lucky I have a stash."

"You're lucky I don't leave your ass here," Ian grunted as he pulled onto the lonely, tree-lined road that served as the entrance to the asylum.

"That's not a very nice way to talk to your best friend." Alex grinned before shoving a handful of chips into his mouth. In between chews and crunches he smiled again. "You wouldn't have even gotten into ghost hunting if it wasn't for me. It was my hobby first."

"Keep playing that card, see where it gets you." Ian chuckled, his anticipation building. "I think we caught something good last night."

Alex nodded and fought back another yawn. "Dude, that chair…talk about freaky."

"Something wanted our attention." Ian's hands clenched on the steering wheel. "It wanted to speak to us. That's why I have to listen to that recording. I need to know."

Alex tossed the empty chip bag into the backseat. "We will. I have a feeling it's going to change things big time for us. Voices like that don't get captured very often."

Ian nodded. "Those TV producers wanted more proof of what we can do. I think this will be a good start."

Half an hour later, they settled into their cramped hotel room and broke out Alex's laptop. They brought up the recording and skipped ahead to the time they were in the hospital. Ian preferred listening to EVPs through the speakers versus on the device itself as it came through much clearer. He wanted his first impression of whatever they caught to be perfect.

Alex clicked the play button, and immediately Ian's voice filled the room.

"...*one of the sick, twisted motherfuckers that hurt innocent children?*"

Alex began to say something, but Ian held his hand up as he caught the warped whisper of another voice. "Wait, play that back."

"Okay, one sec," Alex skipped back a few seconds on the recording, bumped up the volume on the speakers, and hit play again.

"...*hurt innocent children?*"

"...*can't kill what does not live.*"

"Oh, shit," Alex muttered, his hand tightening on the computer mouse. He looked up at Ian, their eyes meeting in a moment of brilliant discovery. "That was a—"

"Class-A EVP," Ian finished, slapping his partner on the back. "Make note of the time on that, then skip ahead to the voice I heard."

Alex did and when he hit the play button again, they both waited in anxious silence.

Ian's challenge to the spirit echoed out of the speakers. "*C'mon!*"

There was a brief pause of absolute silence followed by a dark, raspy grumble. "*Go to...the good doctor...*"

Ian sat down on the edge of the bed, hands clenched over his knees. He stared hard at the lines of sound waves on the computer screen. "Play it again."

Alex complied, and they listened to the voice three more times before turning it off. Alex looked to Ian curiously. "What the hell is that supposed to mean? The good doctor? You mean there was one that *didn't* torture and kill little children?"

"Maybe," Ian replied thoughtfully, staring off into space.

Alex shut his laptop and rose to his feet. "Either way, it's an awesome piece of evidence. I'd say this means we deserve breakfast."

Ian rubbed his forehead, still brooding over the ominous voice. "Yeah, yeah. I know that stomach of yours is going to eat itself any minute."

"Damn right it is." Alex forced Ian off the bed and dragged him to the door. "Don't act like you're not hungry, too."

Ian scowled but said nothing as they made their way to the van. Within the hour, they were in the restaurant digging into breakfast.

Alex smiled happily as he forked up a bite of pancake and sausage. As he chewed, he eyed his partner across the table. "That food's not gonna eat itself."

Ian looked up from toying with the scrambled eggs on his plate, his eyes distant and unfocused. "What?"

Alex sighed. "Dude, let it go for now, okay? We'll do more work after we eat and get some sleep. You're running on empty here."

Ian frowned and took a sip of his coffee. "You know how I am when I hear something like that. I can't let it go until I make sense of it."

"What's there to make sense of? It was most likely a residual voice, anyway. It's not like it was telling you to actually go find the 'good doctor.'"

"What if it was, though?" Ian wondered, still working over the mystery in his head. "There's no way a residual spirit caused that crash."

"Maybe it wasn't the same one."

"No, it was too powerful. It was definitely the same spirit," Ian said, his eyes lit with confidence. "We need to ask some more questions, look back into the history of the asylum. There must be some doctor there that tried to save the patients. Some doctor that has gone unrecognized all these years."

"Or we could just take our evidence and head on home," Alex suggested, downing the last of his orange juice. Before Ian could reply, Alex's cell phone rang. He glanced down at the caller-ID and answered with a grin. "You've reached Alex—dashing, courageous seeker of all things paranormal. We hunt ghosts so you don't have to."

"*You are such a moron.*" Alex's sister and Great American Paranormal manager, Cassie, laughed on the other line.

Alex winked at Ian. "A damn handsome moron."

"*Ew, dream on. Anyway, I have a new lead for you.*"

"Where are you sending us this time, little sis?"

"*Massachusetts. A woman out there called and said there's an evil spirit haunting her house. She needs you guys to check it out, see what can be done about it.*"

Alex nodded to Ian. "Lady out in Massachusetts needs our help."

Ian grimaced. "No."

"Why not?" Alex asked. He didn't wait for an answer before speaking back into the phone. "What happened to her?"

"*She says she's seen shadow figures, an apparition of a little girl. She's also been shoved by an invisible force and almost fell down a flight of stairs.*"

"It's attacked her?" Alex frowned, eyeing Ian again. "We have to help this lady, Ian."

"Our plan was to go to Nevada to check out that old mining town," Ian reminded him, shaking his head and sipping more coffee. "I don't feel like heading east."

"It'll only take a couple of days," Alex protested, standing firm. "C'mon, don't tell me you're not a little bit curious."

Ian rolled his eyes and said nothing, which Alex took as a yes. "All right, Cassie. Send me all the info and directions on how to get there and tell her we're on our way."

* * *

"You don't know what you're talking about, man."

"Actually, I do."

"Just admit that you're wrong on this."

"Nope."

Alex shot a disparaging look at his partner. "You're telling me you *seriously* think Jason has a cooler mask than Michael Meyers?"

Ian fought back a smile and kept his eyes on the road as he drove them the last few miles to their destination. How he'd gotten suckered into driving so Alex could tinker with his new infrared device, he had no idea. But he certainly had no intention of losing this argument. "Jason is by far cooler, period. *And* he has a machete."

"Jason is lame, dude. So lame."

"You wouldn't say that if he had his machete to your throat."

"It wouldn't matter because I'd go Michael Meyers on his ass and slash his throat first." Alex beamed triumphantly.

Ian only shook his head. "Good luck with that. Jason would have you flat on the ground in shreds before you even knew what hit you."

"Regardless of how dead I would be, that doesn't change the fact that Meyers has the better mask. It's a freaking face. You just can't compete with that."

"Anybody can put on a face mask and scare people. It takes skill to wreak havoc in a hockey mask," Ian insisted, tapping his hands on the wheel in time to AC/DC's *Highway to Hell*. "Just admit that I'm right."

"The day you're right is the day Hell freezes over and starts selling ice cream," Alex fired back with a daring grin. "We both know I'm the brains of this outfit."

"If you're the brains then what does that make me?"

"The brawn. Though, I pretty much have that covered, too."
Alex turned back to toying with his new gadget, his excitement
building the closer they got to the coast. "You know, we'll be
within a couple of hours of Salem. We'll have to stop in and see
Aubrey and the guys."

Ian nodded, pleased with the idea. "It has been a while,
hasn't it?"

"At least a year or more." Alex gave up and tossed the
device on the backseat carelessly. "And Halloween is coming
up. You know what that means…"

"Witches and magic and *ghosts*…" Ian smiled. "We can do
a few extra hunts while we're out here, get some more footage
and evidence for the show."

"Took the words right out of my mouth." Alex beamed.
"See, I told you this trip was a good idea. Admit I was right."

"No."

"Aw, c'mon."

"Nope." Ian pulled off the highway at a weathered off
ramp leading them past an old fashioned wooden sign that read:
Welcome to Mad Rock Harbor. You'll Want to Call It Home.

Alex eyed the sign curiously. "Who the hell came up with
the name for this place?"

"Probably the same person who named your dog back in
high school."

"Elvira is an awesome name for a pet," Alex defended as
they continued on a winding, forest road leading toward the sea.
"You're just jealous because I thought of it first."

"Yep. That's definitely it." They drove past a small, fifties-
style diner on the left. A huge flashing sign above it read *Nora's
Cafe*. There were several cars parked out front, including a
bright red Jeep with a smiling corgi sitting patiently in the open
front seat.

Alex continued to stare at the Jeep as they drove past,

wondering how the owner got the dog to stay put like that.

"We're almost there," Ian announced, glancing at his GPS unit. "A couple miles more."

Alex faced the road once again with an eager grin. "Let's go find us a B.G.G. Bad Guy Ghost."

Ian sighed. "This better be worth our time."

CHAPTER FIVE

Her obsession with the boxes from the basement consumed her.

Grace didn't know if it was her mind's way of shoving aside the grief she'd been trying to ignore for weeks, or if she was just going crazy. Because no sane person obsessed over a few boxes of old trinkets and pictures.

Even though the rational side of her brain told her to let it all go and head home to Chicago, the desperate, lonely side fought with all its might to keep her in Mad Rock Harbor. To keep her in the Sparrow House. At the moment, that side was winning the battle.

She spread out on the sofa in her living room, one of the boxes from the basement on the coffee table. She attempted to organize the photographs, grouping them by date, people, and location. Whenever a common thread was spotted, she latched onto it as a possible clue to explain what happened at the Sparrow House. Why no one had ever wanted to live there. Why they wouldn't sell the place. It made no logical sense to her.

If only her father were still alive…but if he was, then she would have no knowledge of the house. So what difference did it really make?

"None at all," she muttered to herself. The pain of remembering him choked her with grief and she forced it away. She withdrew a slim, weathered leather case from the box. It was roughly the size of a postcard and folded open like a book, revealing an old-fashioned tintype photograph. Her own reflection stared back at her in the metallic, silvery image of a little girl.

She was young, less than five years old. There was no date or inscription, but by the lacy white dress she wore, Grace estimated the date as mid to late 19th century. The girl's soft blonde hair framed a cherub face, innocent and lovely. Vivid eyes stared back at her, colorless in the grayed image. Somehow, Grace knew they would be blue.

A bright, happy blue.

Was *this* the child her father supposedly saw inside the house? The one Nellie claimed to have seen beside the staircase and that she had been hearing in the dead of night for days?

Grace shook her head and set the photograph aside, irritated at the thought. There was no little girl ghost parading around the house, crying in corners, and laughing on the stairs. It was ridiculous. She knew better than to let herself get caught up in Nellie's paranoia and superstition. But the chill she felt stayed with her even as she distracted herself with more photographs from the box.

There was a sudden, cheerful knocking on the front door, causing Grace to jump. Irritation filled her as she glanced over at the entryway.

She set aside the photographs and wandered to the door just as the persistent visitor knocked yet again. "Really?" Grace grumbled, her eyes aflame as she threw open the door. She stared at the two men on her porch. "Yes?"

"Hey! How's it going?" the man on the left said with an overtly friendly grin and a wave of his hand.

She leaned against the doorjamb and crossed her arms. "Can I help you?"

The man gave her a blank look, and she frowned as she took in his carefree sandy hair and nerdy good looks, as well as his bright yellow *It's On Like Alderaan* T-shirt and faded jeans, both a little loose on his tall, lanky frame.

The man next to him clearly took himself *way* too seriously. He had the strict, tough-guy stature of a soldier, yet there were silver skull rings on his fingers and tattoos on his arms visible beneath his black T-shirt.

She stared at her own reflection in the mirrored aviator sunglasses he wore, puzzled by the bored, irritated look on his face.

"You don't know who we are?" Alex asked. He glanced at Ian, who shrugged indifferently.

One of Grace's eyebrows slid up. "Should I?"

"You called us. Well, you called my sister, and she sent us to help you."

"Are you sure you have the right address? I know street names and house numbers can be confusing," Grace mocked, feeling more amused than annoyed. She hadn't had the chance to break out her sarcasm in a while. It felt good.

The other man's jaw visibly tightened, but he said nothing.

"Aren't you Nellie?" Alex stuffed his hands into his jeans pockets. He continued to smile, in good spirits despite the confusion.

An annoyed look crossed Grace's face as understanding

hit her. She looked past them and spotted their black van. As she read the logo, she laughed. "You've *got* to be kidding me. What're you, the Ghostbusters? Did she call you? You know ghosts don't exist, right?"

"I take it you're not Nellie," Alex confirmed, surprised by Grace's reaction. Ian let out a frustrated grunt and immediately stalked back to the van, leaving Alex alone on the porch.

Grace watched him go. "Might want to reign in the temper on your stallion there, buddy."

Alex sighed, then flashed a charmingly crooked grin her way. "Excuse me a moment."

He took off after Ian, catching up with him as his partner started to climb into the van. "Seriously? What are you doing?"

"I don't have time to waste on skeptics," Ian growled. The woman had the sarcastic sass of an entitled socialite and he wanted nothing to do with her.

"We came all the way out here, we can't turn back now," Alex reminded him, grabbing Ian's arm firmly and forcing their eyes to meet. "Take that chip off your shoulder and make some dip, okay?"

"What the hell does that mean?"

Alex shrugged. "Who cares. Now let's go back and apologize to the nice lady."

"Nice, my ass," Ian grumbled under his breath. After a moment's hesitation, he shut the van door and trudged after Alex to the front porch where they found Grace still leaning against the doorframe.

Ian watched her closely as they approached. He noted her casual, white blouse with rolled up sleeves, black tights covering long legs, and bare feet. She'd tied back her dark hair, leaving strands of it free to frame her angular face. He figured she would be considered beautiful by some, if she didn't look so sour. Cool gray eyes regarded him with similar scrutiny as he came to a stop before her.

He grudgingly held out his hand. "My name is Ian Black. I'm the founder of Great American Paranormal. This is my partner, Alex Gallagher. We're here to check out reports of paranormal activity within your home and try and help you if we can."

"You're ghost hunters," Grace stated flatly, accepting his hand for a brief shake. She eyed them both with a mixture of sympathy and amusement. "I'm Grace. And just so you know, my house isn't haunted, so you can run along now and hunt ghosts elsewhere."

"Nellie says it is," Alex insisted. "Is she home?"

Grace sighed. "She's my *neighbor* and has no business calling you people to snoop around my property."

Ian removed his sunglasses and stared her down. "You haven't experienced anything unusual in the house?"

She met his cobalt eyes and winced at the restrained anger she saw in them. God, did she offend people so easily these days? "No, I haven't. I'm just out here on 'vacation,'" she made quotation marks with her fingers, "and would love to be left the hell alone. I don't know why she called you."

"Because there's an evil spirit in that house," Nellie interrupted as she charged up the steps. She smiled brightly at Alex and Ian and reached out to shake their hands. "Thank you both so much for coming. Please, come inside."

Alex followed her in. Ian hung back and studied Grace. He found it odd that Nellie shoved Grace so easily aside, especially with her temper. He pushed past her and entered the house, his thoughts returning to ghosts.

The first thing he noticed was the staircase. It was long and narrow with a second-floor balcony open to the entryway. He eyed the balcony curiously, his gaze drifting to the ancient wood floor at his feet. It was beautiful—knotted and weathered and filled with history. He imagined a hundred years of feet pacing over the wood planks, leaving behind traces of energy. He could almost see it trailing throughout the house; glowing lines like freeway headlights following the paths of the past. He had every intention of following those same paths and rousing the energy that lay within them.

In the living room, Nellie was busy explaining in great detail to Alex what she had witnessed. Ian casually listened in as he toured the first floor on his own, noticing that Grace had made her way to the sofa and was busying herself with a box of photographs. He watched her as he wandered through the kitchen, sensing her refusal to believe.

He'd come across skeptics many times in his career, and she was as hard-nosed as any of them. Convincing her to go along with an investigation might be tricky. Then again, she seemed beholden to the old woman. He wasn't sure what their relationship was, but he was more than happy to exploit it to get the evidence he needed.

"Hey, Ian." Alex waved him over, a mile-wide grin on his face.

Ian approached, nodding politely to the older woman. "So, what's the story?"

"Nellie saw an apparition of a little girl standing by the stairs over there," Alex pointed to the entryway. "And she also saw a shadow figure run along the wall over by the basement door."

"It came out of the basement following me and Grace," Nellie added, her hand on her chest as if the memory gave her heart palpitations. "It walked right back into the wall when I noticed it."

"She was also pushed by an invisible entity on the upper steps of the basement staircase, so hard that she had the wind knocked out of her."

Nellie nodded furiously. "Grace thought I was having a heart attack. I was frozen with fear. I'm surprised I was able to stumble to safety."

"Anything else?" Ian asked, arms crossed as he worked over the details in his head, already plotting out what equipment he wanted to use and what locations to use it in.

"Grace has heard her…the little girl," Nellie blurted out.

All eyes turned to Grace, who muttered something distasteful under her breath and tried to ignore them.

"When did you hear her? What did she say?" Alex asked eagerly.

"What I *heard* was an animal making noises. A bird or a cat or something. It wasn't a little girl," Grace insisted.

Alex smiled kindly. "I know it's natural to want to rationalize stuff like this, Grace. But that's why we're here. We want to find out if what's been happening is paranormal, or if it is just animal noises and imagination. That's our job."

Grace held his eyes for a moment, all her years of medical school and science courses playing over in her mind. She shook her head slowly, bemused by him. "You *really* believe this stuff, don't you?"

"Of course I do," Alex declared, the first hint of heat flavoring his voice. She saw a temper simmering beneath his easygoing demeanor, and felt her hackles rising to challenge it.

"Well, I'm sorry to break this to you, but you're wrong."

"You have to understand, boys. Grace is a doctor of science. She finds all of this very hard to swallow," Nellie quickly added.

Ian sighed, convinced this wasn't going to be an easy investigation. "We have to consider the possibility that what we're dealing with here is demonic. It may be wise to bring in a medium after we do our investigation to cleanse the house. Get rid of the bad energy."

Unable to contain herself, Grace started laughing.

"Demonic? Really?"

"I know you claim you don't feel it, child. But I do," Nellie charged, her usual sass back in her voice. "You just sit down and shut up and let these boys do what they do. Not like you have anything else going on."

Grace blinked, momentarily speechless. Ian tried not to laugh at the flabbergasted look on her face. Clearly, she wasn't used to people turning her rudeness back on her.

When she recovered, she said, "Fine. But you're wasting your time." She returned to the photographs in her lap and continued to thumb through them, sorting them into piles.

Ian stared at the photographs, an idea hitting him. "Where are those from?"

"The basement," Nellie supplied with a shudder.

He walked over and lifted a stack of photos, including the tintype of the little blonde girl. He opened its case and eyed it curiously. "Good. We'll use these as trigger objects."

Grace's brow creased with suspicion as she stared up at him. "I don't know what the hell a trigger object is, but you do not have my permission to use these photographs for any ghost experiment. I won't let you damage them."

A cocky smile spread over Ian's lips. "Calm down, Doc. I won't hurt your pretty photos."

Alex sensed a fight brewing and jumped in. "A trigger object simply means an item we place in a room to try and attract a spirit who may remember it from their mortal life. We will take good care of them, I promise."

Grace rose to her feet and snatched the photographs from Ian's hand, gathered the other pictures, and stuffed them back into the box. She lifted the box into her arms and clutched it against her chest protectively. "No."

Ian was taken aback by her behavior. He watched as the fiery distrust in her eyes faded to some lingering, deeply rooted misery. He would have berated her some more, but found he couldn't. Not when faced with that. Christ, the woman had some major baggage hidden in those gray eyes of hers.

"All right, how about I make a deal with you," he began, changing tactics. He needed to level the playing field and meet her on ground he figured she could appreciate. "We spend tonight in the house and do an investigation. You can stay or go, whatever you want. If we find nothing then I will personally apologize to you, renounce the ghost business for good, and declare that ghosts aren't real. But if we *do* find something, then you agree to let us investigate further until a solution and better understanding of what's going on can be established." He paused, pleased he had her attention. "Our track record of uncovering spirits and assisting occupants with cleansing their homes is impeccable. I will not fail you if you give me the chance to help."

Grace eyed him doubtfully. "You'll really renounce ghost hunting for good if you don't find anything?"

"Yes."

"You're just that confident, huh?"

"I am."

Grace admired his arrogance while at the same time pitied him for it. It made him strong, fearless. It also made him pathetically stupid.

She reached out to shake his hand, keeping her other arm safely around the box. "Okay, then. You have a deal."

He accepted the handshake, his eyes intent on hers. "I look forward to shattering your perception of life and death, Doc."

Grace snorted. "I'm sure you do."

"Cool, so it's settled then." Alex clapped his hands together happily, smiling at everyone. "We'll go get our equipment so we can get started." He left the room, patting Ian on the back as he passed. Ian shot one last look at Grace, amusement softening his features.

Grace watched them go and wondered if she'd made the right decision. Regardless, she looked forward to seeing the ghost hunter give up his life's work. The thought alone was enough to lift her spirits.

It wouldn't take long. It wasn't possible to hunt something that didn't exist.

* * *

Grace stood at the parlor window and eyed Ian and Alex suspiciously through the curtains. They were busy sorting through equipment in the back of their van—black duffle bags and metal briefcases. She didn't pretend to have any idea what kind of stupid devices they used while "investigating" a location.

It didn't matter. Her house wasn't haunted. Period. And once they realized they were wasting everyone's time, they would be gone. She wanted so desperately to be alone again.

"This is for the best, child," Nellie said, resting her hand on Grace's shoulder. She stared serenely out the window at the men, looking very much like someone who got exactly what they wanted. It irritated Grace more than she wanted it to.

"They're not going to find anything. You shouldn't have called them."

Nellie sighed. "I called them because I'm worried about you. Whatever it is that's in this house needs to be taken care of so you can have some peace and quiet."

"I'm not staying forever," Grace mumbled, crossing her arms tightly over her chest. "What difference does it make?"

"If you do stay, it will make all the difference in the world."

Grace caught Ian's eye as he looked her way, and he offered her a polite nod. She merely frowned. "I want to stay tonight while they do whatever it is they're going to do."

"Oh?" Nellie looked up at Grace curiously. "You may get more than you bargained for."

"I want to make sure they don't cheat." Grace turned away from the window, feeling the strong urge for a glass of wine. Instead, she'd settle for tea.

She left Nellie in the parlor and headed into the kitchen. Before she could help herself, she started hearing her ex-fiancé's voice in her head calling her an idiot for even playing along. Rick didn't believe in any of this nonsense. So why was she allowing herself the headache of dealing with it?

Grace paused before filling the kettle with water, shutting her eyes tightly. She reminded herself that Rick didn't control her life and what he thought didn't matter. That part of her life was over. For now, this was her reality. An old abandoned house, a nosy neighbor, ghost hunters, disembodied voices…

It all seemed so far from the life she had lived previously. Long nights at the hospital, saving lives, dinner and drinks with friends, romantic weekend getaways with Rick. Before, she had filled her days with the pursuit of life.

Now it seemed she pursued nothing but death. The death of her parents, the long dead Sullivans who came before her to the Sparrow House, the death of her old self and the life she used to call her own. She may as well plunge into the harbor and end it all.

Grace shook off the thought. Suicidal? Not quite. Manic depressive, lonely, and a bit delusional, yes. But not on the verge of taking her own life.

Would she really get to that point? Was she getting worse instead of getting better? The thought troubled her. Instead of dealing with it, she shrugged it off and finished making tea. One day, one hour, one *minute* at a time.

Her next few hours would be filled with ghost hunters and creaking floorboards. Surely that would be enough to distract her.

Not like she had any choice.

CHAPTER SIX

When Ian and Alex returned to the living room, Grace swallowed the urge to laugh. She stood in the kitchen with her cup of tea, resting her hip against the counter. "You boys really are the Ghostbusters," she joked, admiring their camera equipment and Alex's black backpack. "Where's the laser beam thing to nab the slimy bastards?"

"Left the Proton Pack at home, sorry," Alex replied with a crooked grin. "But I *did* bring along this puppy that you should find equally as impressive."

Grace resisted the temptation to roll her eyes and humored him. "You mean there's something better than a Proton Pack?"

He whipped out what looked like an oversized remote control. It had a screen at the top with two numerical readings on it. "This is called a Mel Meter. It detects EMF—electromagnetic field—fluctuations and ambient temperature changes. Ghosts are made up of energy, and when they pass near the meter these little lights at the top will go off, giving us a good idea when they're around. Of course, we usually feel it first. Don't we, Ian?"

Ian shrugged, busy messing with the settings on his camcorder. He glanced down impatiently at his watch, noting it was nearly eight o'clock. "It's still relatively early, but we can take some base readings and do an EVP session. Let's hit the basement first since most of the activity seems to be down there." He set his camcorder on the dining table and grabbed his digital recorder.

Grace's eyes narrowed. "EVP session?"

"Electronic voice phenomena. Spirit voices," Alex supplied. "That's what the digital recorder is for. We often catch disembodied voices speaking within the white noise."

"Is that right?" Grace decided not to mention radio interference and other more logical explanations, deciding it wasn't worth the wasted breath. "What do they usually say?"

A smile spread over Alex's face. "More than you'd expect."

His answer intrigued her despite the cold, hard science that proved "spirit voices" to be nothing but baloney.

"Let's go." Ian nodded to Alex and headed for the basement door.

Grace immediately followed him. "Don't mind me. I'll be sure to stay out of your way."

Ian stopped mid-stride and faced her. "You're staying here?"

"Well, duh. Someone rational has to stick around and make sure you don't cheat or steal anything." She lifted her chin, the movement both distrusting and amused. "Plus, I will admit that I'm a little curious."

"Just keep your mouth shut and don't move around too much," he shot back, irritated that she was going to be hanging around. He'd hoped she would take off for a few hours, give him some room to breathe. As it was, the weight of whatever baggage she carried on her back was stifling the very air in the room.

"Lead the way, boss." Alex motioned toward the basement, allowing Ian to brush past.

He opened the basement door carefully, holding his breath as he listened. The house was silent as death. In his left hand, he held his digital recorder, turned on and ready to go. He started down the steps into the dark basement, feeling around for the light switch near the bottom. Behind him, Alex held the camcorder and closely monitored the Mel Meter, looking for EMF spikes and odd temperature changes.

Grace followed them, her footsteps heavy on the planks of wood. She slurped her tea and fought back a laugh at Ian's exasperated sigh.

"I thought I told you to shut the hell up?" he barked, glaring up at her.

She only shrugged. "Oops."

Alex chuckled and continued down the stairs, reaching past Ian to flip on the light switch. A dim light illuminated the room. They all stared at the nearly empty space for a long moment.

"Feel anything funky?" Grace asked with a sly smile as she watched Ian scan the room. He ignored her question and stepped onto the hard-packed dirt, taking in the sights, smells, and sounds of the space.

It was cold and musty like most underground basements. The concrete block walls kept the heat out, but also gave off an industrial scent that permeated the air. The boots he wore barely made impressions in the floor as Ian made his way around the room, feeling the walls and searching. For what, he wasn't sure. But he would know when he found it. He always did.

"I'm getting some weird readings under the stairs," Alex

called out. He held the Mel Meter under the stairwell and it started to shrill loudly, announcing a spike in the electromagnetic field. Green lights flickered on and off at the top of the meter. "Temperature was 68 degrees coming down the stairs. Now I'm getting 66.6 and the thing is going off like crazy."

Grace stood on the last step and leaned against the wall, looking bored. "666. There's your demon, boys."

...you will pay.

"Actually, that is pretty freaking strange," Alex murmured as he stared at the device. "It's never done that before."

"It could be a coincidence." Grace lifted her tea for another sip, but paused as she watched Ian tense like an animal suddenly detecting a predator. His face hardened as he froze, as if reaching out with all his senses. She would have laughed at him if she wasn't caught off guard by the swift change of mood in the basement. It went from amusing to anxious like a cloud covering the light of the sun.

Ian slowly held up his digital recorder. "Talk to us. Did you make our Mel Meter read 66.6 degrees?" He went quiet for a moment as his eyes met Grace's. He saw the skepticism on her face but also spotted the intrigue. His mouth curved in challenge. "Grace thinks you're a demon. I think otherwise. I think you just wanted to get our attention."

Alex was focused on the Mel Meter, monitoring it as Ian spoke. Suddenly, the readings on the device went back to normal. They hovered in silence for a few moments, the heaviness in the room lifting. He glanced up at his partner with a grin. "That was weird. I think you insulted it."

Ian let out a whoosh of breath and flipped off his recorder, running his free hand through his hair. "Maybe."

"So...what happened, exactly?" Grace asked, clutching her mug between her hands tightly. She didn't even realize she was doing it.

Ian looked pleased. "There was a definite presence here. I'm going to play back the recorder and see if we caught anything."

He turned the volume up and played back the last few minutes. As they listened, Grace heard her own voice come out of the recorder.

"*666. There's your demon, boys.*"

She frowned at how mocking her tone was, momentarily distracted as Ian suddenly turned off the recorder, rewound it, and played it again. He did it twice more before he and Alex looked at each other in triumph.

"Did you hear that?" Ian asked, a fire in his eyes that had nothing to do with anger.

Alex nodded excitedly. "Yeah, man. It sounded like 'you will pay' or something like that."

"That's what I heard, too."

Grace shook her head. "I didn't hear anything."

"That's because you don't know what to listen for," Ian began, walking forward and handing the recorder to her. "Hold it up to your ear this time and *listen.*"

She rolled her eyes but did as he requested, hitting play and holding it by her face. Her lips pursed as she listened to her own voice yet again. After her words faded and just before Alex's voice piped in she heard a low mumbling noise mixed with the static. Her forehead creased with doubt as she shut it off and handed it back to him. "I just heard grumbling and static. That could be anything. Hell, it could be your stomach for all I know."

Ian tried to hold on to what little patience he had left. Damn skeptics. "When I get this on the computer and amplify the sound you'll be able to hear it clearer. Either way, this is a great EVP and I feel it warrants more investigating."

"Well, seeing as your little ghost friend hightailed it out

of the basement, maybe you should head upstairs," Grace suggested with a dry smile. "I'm still not convinced, but I'll give you another chance to prove it to me."

She started up the stairs, leaving Ian to brood. Alex patted him on the back. "That old lady was right. There's something in this house."

"I know," Ian agreed, staring after Grace. "The problem is convincing Dr. Cynic to give us free reign of the house to do a proper investigation."

"She did get really touchy about those old photographs. I don't know how much she'll let us do."

Ian focused on the space beneath the stairs, pondering the 66.6 reading and the EMF spikes they got. There was bad energy in the basement, most particularly near that area. But why?

"She's not going to have much of a choice," Ian decided. He turned to his best friend with a hard smile. "I'll tie her down if I have to. Whether she likes it or not, we're doing a full investigation."

Alex chuckled. "You attract more flies with honey, my friend."

"Who the hell wants to attract flies?" Ian winked before making his way upstairs.

Alex followed close behind, shaking his head. "A spider."

* * *

They did a quick sweep of the upstairs, finding nothing but hollow rooms and creaking floorboards. Ian was convinced that the activity was centralized in the basement and the first floor by the stairs where Nellie had her encounters. The spirits appeared to have an attachment to the lower half of the house, and he was determined to find out why.

He found it interesting that he had made intelligent contact with a spirit in the basement with very little provocation. What kind of response would he get when he kicked it up a notch?

Grace grew increasingly skeptical as the night wore on, so Ian made a point to explain things to her before he and Alex left for the local hotel. He'd already made up his mind that he wasn't going to let her stand in his way, but it was more polite to reason with her. At least, that's what Alex suggested and Alex was better with people.

Where Ian could be a steamroller, Alex was a convincer. It didn't take much for people to side with Alex once he had the chance to lay on the charm. Unfortunately, though, that charm didn't seem to be working very well on the doctor.

"What do you think you're going to find tomorrow that you didn't find tonight?" Grace asked impatiently. She poured a glass of Cabernet in the kitchen and lifted her glass in a mock toast. "I gave you what you wanted. It failed. Shock. Now it's time for you to move along and leave me alone."

Ian gritted his teeth but Alex only smiled. "We got our base readings and know the house better now. Give us the chance to come back with some more advanced equipment and go all out. We'll set up cameras throughout the house, take some infrared photos…"

Grace sipped her wine, unimpressed. "And use 'trigger objects' or whatever the hell you called my photographs?"

"Exactly." Alex clapped his hands together. "I know you think your neighbor is crazy, Grace. But the EMF readings, the EVP, and the temperature fluctuations we got down in the basement prove otherwise."

Grace frowned as she lifted the aged photograph of the little girl off the counter and held it in her hands. She'd been looking at it earlier while they roamed around upstairs. She stared into the girl's colorless eyes, her thoughts drifting to her father. Would he have allowed a couple of fanatical ghost hunters to poke around the house? Or would he have told them to take a hike like she desperately wanted to do?

She closed her eyes, absorbing the pain that hit her. Sorrow draped over her body like a cloak. Like an impending storm.

When it eased, she opened her eyes and met Ian's resolutely, her decision made.

"Fine. You can do your full investigation. But if you don't find anything, then we're done here."

Ian nodded. "I told you I won't let you down, Doc."

Grace downed the last of her wine and poured another glass. "All you've done is fight me on this." She turned away and faced the kitchen sink, feeling lost and tired. "Please go."

Alex grabbed his backpack and motioned for Ian to follow him out. "See ya tomorrow, Grace."

She didn't bother to answer. The sound of the door shutting behind them was like a final gunshot to the heart. Her misery crept back in, kept at bay only long enough for her to watch them drive away out the window. As their headlights faded into darkness, she felt her knees weaken and her heart thud helplessly. Unable to do more, she abandoned her fresh glass of wine, wanting only her bed and the solitude it promised. The dark, welcoming shroud of nothingness.

Yet as she passed by the stairwell beneath the second-floor balcony, she could have sworn she heard a faint, whispering voice. A little girl's voice.

I am the sparrow.

"Damn you." She squeezed her eyes tight in disbelief and fear. It just wasn't possible.

She raced up the stairs, taking them two at a time, and slammed her bedroom door shut behind her. There would be no more ghostly whispers, laughter, or weeping tonight.

If there were, then she had definitely let her sorrow drive her crazy.

* * *

"Don't you want to listen to it?" Alex asked, plopping down on one of the queen size beds in their hotel room and breaking out his laptop. He plugged in the digital recorder and began downloading the EVP they had captured.

"No," Ian replied quietly, his thoughts elsewhere as he

started unpacking his suitcase. He pulled out his toothbrush and toothpaste and stared down at them for a long moment, distracted.

Alex glanced up at him. "You okay, man? You were really quiet on the drive over."

Ian blinked, then shook his head. "Yeah. Go ahead and pull up that EVP. I want to take a quick shower."

"You don't look like a guy who just got some insane evidence of the paranormal," Alex observed with a frown. "In fact, you look depressed. What gives?"

"It's nothing," Ian snapped as he went into the bathroom.

"Bullshit," Alex called through the shut door. He sighed and went back to downloading the EVP, knowing his friend would talk when he was ready. At that moment, he was brooding and Alex knew better than to bug him. Not unless he wanted the business end of the bull to take him out.

In the bathroom, Ian tossed his toothbrush aside and rested his hands on the counter. He let his head fall and shut his eyes, needing a moment to collect his thoughts. Part of him desperately wanted to get the hell out of Massachusetts, to get away from that house and away from the woman that lived there. The heavy feeling he'd felt in the house had followed him, hanging over his shoulders like a dark, gloomy cloud. He wanted to shake it off, to chase it away, but he couldn't seem to.

Just as he couldn't get the image of her misery out of his mind. What had happened to Dr. Grace Sullivan that marred her that way? He didn't want to care, didn't see how it was any of his business. But for some reason he couldn't let it go.

He decided he needed to speak with her alone. He had to find out what she knew about the house that she wasn't telling him and why those photographs were so precious to her.

Once he knew, maybe he'd also learn the reason for that storm cloud she carried around with her.

CHAPTER SEVEN

G race grabbed a mystery novel and made herself at home on the front porch. She had to drag the chair from the back around to the front of the house, but it was worth it. She was sick of looking at the harbor.

Something about that dock bothered her. She couldn't quite put her finger on it, but it made her uneasy. It felt like something *bad* had happened there, something long ago. Which was completely ridiculous. What the hell could have possibly happened on a dock that was so malevolent?

Regardless, she felt happier on the front porch. Less distracted. At least for the time being.

Soon the ghost freaks would be back, and she'd have to stay out of their way while they set up strange cameras in her house and ran wires everywhere. Alex had called her that morning to explain the details, how they would come by for a couple of hours to set up and take a few more readings, then they'd go home, get some sleep, and be back fresh the next night at nine o'clock to start the investigation. He also asked her to write down what little she knew about the house, including some of the names she'd read on the backs of the photographs from the basement.

She was also supposed to pick out the photographs she felt most "connected" to and leave them on the dining table for the guys to use as trigger objects. She wasn't sure what it felt like to be "connected" to an inanimate object, so she'd just grabbed the first few photographs from the stack and boxed up the rest.

She'd humor them for now, but that didn't mean she believed in what they were doing. Though she did make sure to leave the photograph of the little girl in the stack. Despite her skepticism, she believed her father *had* seen the girl. He may have been intoxicated—though he didn't drink—or high on painkillers, which was doubtful. But if Nellie was telling the truth and he had admitted to seeing a ghost, then it must be true.

Her father had never been a liar. He may have not always told the *whole* truth, but he never lied. If she had discovered the house while he had been alive and approached him about it, he would have confessed to her. How could he not? He had the worst poker face. That's what made him such a compassionate doctor. He was never cold, distant, or aloof. He felt each and every death, illness, and diagnosis as though it were his own.

It was a skill she'd always tried so hard to emulate. Unfortunately, she was a natural cynic. She got it from her mother, who was a pessimist of the worst degree. Everything was always going to hell in a hand basket in her mother's eyes. That was why her parents had made such a strong couple—her realism balanced out his idealism.

By contrast, Grace's ex-fiancé Rick was a hardcore realist. He claimed to see everyone exactly as they were—no fluff, no circumstance. Just *people*. The good, the bad, and the ugly. And then he'd gossip about them. He thrived on dissecting the ins and outs of peoples' lives. That's why he'd gotten into psychology. He was fascinated by the demons that lived within people's hearts and minds.

He was especially fascinated by Grace. She never really discovered why, but he was always trying to interpret her. To read her. To *know* her. It was the most frustrating and exposing thing she'd ever been through.

Unfortunately for her, his obsession with the human mind took him into the arms of another. She could only prove the one indiscretion—the time she walked in on him sleeping with her whore of a friend Veronica—but she was sure there were others. Hell, he may have been cheating on her the entire time. That wasn't really what bothered her, though.

The kicker was that he betrayed her on the day of her parents' funeral, while she stood at their grave, turning the engagement ring he'd given her over and over on her finger, desperately wishing he was there. What a fool she'd been. What a stupid, pathetic fool.

But that was over with. Yes, she wasn't as trusting these days but who wouldn't react the same way? She'd been betrayed by the one person who was supposed to save her.

Now the plan was to somehow pick up the pieces. The key word being *somehow*…

She woke from her reverie as the black van pulled up to the curb in front of her house. She let out a breath to steady herself, fighting back the nasty feelings of loss and regret that flooded through her. Determined not to show any of it, she slipped on a wry smile and nodded at Ian as he stepped from the van.

"I forgot to ask which one of you is Dan Akryod and which one is Bill Murray," she called out, her feet casually propped up on the porch railing. She leaned back in the chair, cozy with her book.

Ian shook his head as Alex rounded the back of the van. "There's no question. I'm definitely Bill Murray."

"How the hell are you Bill Murray?" Ian asked as he opened the back doors to the van.

"He's the cool one. Ergo, that's me." Alex accepted the duffle bags Ian handed him and made his way up the small pathway toward Grace.

She felt blinded by that smile of his, but was getting used to it. Did that guy ever have a bad day? Though she had to admit, his optimism was oddly infectious.

"I agree, you're definitely the cool one," Grace told him with a wink as he passed by with Ian in tow.

Ian gave her a long look and a sly smile. "You just don't know me well enough yet, Doc."

Her eyebrows shot up at his comment as he went inside, and she stared after him curiously. "Is that an invitation?" she murmured.

He was most certainly an asshole, but then again, so was she. She was also *not* in the mood to deal with another man. Much less a man who believed in Big Foot and the Loch Ness Monster and who knew what other wild things created for scaring five-year-olds.

With a sigh, she got to her feet. That cocky smile of his was a distraction she really didn't want. At least, she didn't *think* she wanted it.

She followed them into the kitchen where they were spreading out equipment on her butcher block island and dining table. A part of her winced at seeing the butcher block covered in something other than fresh vegetables, but she beat back the urge to jump down their throats. She had to try and play nice.

For now, anyway.

"I see you found the photographs," she said conversationally.

She crossed her arms and leaned against the doorway to the kitchen.

Ian thumbed through the stack. "How long did it take you to pick these ones out? Two seconds?"

"Hey, I spent a lot of time looking through those," she lied. Was it that obvious? "Those are the photos that *spoke* to me."

He glanced up, amused. "Is that right?"

"Totally. That one of the old man sitting on the porch. He's definitely a relative."

"Funny, I don't see that photo here. You must've shoved it back in the box with the others." He flipped through the stack again, then set the photos aside. He leveled his gaze with hers. "Look, I know you feel this is all ridiculous. Maybe it would be better if we went somewhere you don't feel so defensive so we can talk."

Oh great, another man who wanted to analyze her. Grace was immediately affronted. "I'm staying right here. Ask whatever you want while I still have the patience."

"There's a diner down the road. Let's go there."

"Why?" Grace asked, stiffening. "What do they have there that we don't have here?"

"A decent cup of coffee. A burger. I don't know. What kind of shit do you like to eat?" he asked exasperatedly. Why was she being so stubborn?

"Things they don't sell at a *diner*."

"I see. So, you're too damn prissy to eat at a diner?"

"No, but up until recently I was a very strict vegetarian. I may have a weakness for Nellie's beef stew but I'm not prepared to scarf down a burger dripping with hundred-year-old diner grease."

He shook his head. "Whatever. C'mon, we're going to get coffee."

"You're not my boss."

"No, but I want to get to know you better." He enjoyed the shock that flashed over her face with a cocky smile. "Does that surprise you?"

She recovered, feeling like a complete moron. Like hell if she'd show it, though. "Nope. Not at all. I'll go get my purse." She stalked off, leaving Ian feeling triumphant.

Alex looked up from unpacking camera equipment. "You think she's cute."

"Shut up. I'm only doing this to smooth over the investigation."

"Hey, you don't have to explain it to me. I'm not judging."

"Just shut up." Ian left without another word and went to wait in the van for Grace.

* * *

Nora's Diner was a packed little building on the best corner in town. It had cemented itself as a town landmark after over thirty-five years in business.

A large neon sign above the roof flashed all day and night in fluorescent pinks and blues. White stucco walls covered the outside, cluttered with wide windows and the town bulletin board. Any and all news related to the happenings in Mad Rock Harbor were displayed proudly there, mostly put up by Nora herself. She was a short, capable woman with a ready smile and the town's biggest heart. If anyone in town had a problem, Nora would gladly lend an ear or a shoulder to cry on.

The one time Grace had met her, she'd tried her hardest not to like the woman. Making friends was not high on her priority list, and yet she couldn't help but be fond of the woman's smile. She reminded her a lot of Nellie, only softer, kinder. Then she'd learned that Nellie and Nora were sisters, and suddenly it all made sense.

Nora was busy behind the counter when Ian and Grace strolled in. She glanced up and shot them a sunny smile and a wave, which Grace attempted to awkwardly return. She wasn't used to the small-town treatment yet. In the city, life was fast and anonymous. In Mad Rock Harbor, Grace found the world relaxed and welcoming. And *everyone* noticed when there was a new face in town. The man beside her was no exception.

"Great, they're all going to think you're my boyfriend or something." Grace scowled as she noticed the curious stares they were receiving from all corners of the room.

"Why do you care what they think?" Ian asked, settling into one of the white and red vinyl booths by a window.

She sighed as she sat down across from him, eyeing the cars that passed by outside on the highway. "I don't know."

He draped his arms over the backrest with a hard smile. "I can tell you haven't been in this town for very long, Doc. What's your story?"

"I don't really see how that's relevant." She folded her hands in her lap and avoided his eyes.

"It could turn out to be the most relevant thing in the world," Ian insisted, interrupted as Nora came by to take their order. They both ordered coffee, black. As Nora walked away, Ian turned back to Grace. "If you don't want to tell me the whole story, I get it. It's not my business. But at least give me something to go on. I need to know if there's something about you that brought these spirits out. Nellie says she experienced nothing in the house until you arrived. Ergo, you are in some way, shape, or form, the crucial piece of the puzzle."

Grace's eyes flicked to his with a cold stare. She fell back on her old defenses, not wanting his pity, his comfort. She didn't want him to know just how broken and damaged she really was. And so, she decided to lie. Or, at least, not tell the whole truth.

"I came out here for a vacation and for some alone

time. That's all there is to it."

"I get the feeling that you're running from something," Ian ventured as Nora dropped off their coffee. He took a sip from the ivory white mug, eyeing her in that intense way he had.

Grace laughed and passed her own mug back and forth on the table between her hands, not in the mood to drink it. "Just what do you think I'm running from? Since you seem to know so much about me already, surely you have it all figured out."

"I think you're running from yourself."

She blinked, then rolled her eyes and drank some coffee to hide the tremor that shot through her at his words. "You make this sound like a *Lifetime* movie."

"Something bad happened to you, Grace. I don't know what it is, but you have it written all over your face." His humor faded as sincerity replaced it. "The cloud that hangs over you may be what's attracting these spirits. They're drawn to you because you're in a weakened emotional state."

"Weak," she scoffed, insulted and stunned at the same time. Could it be? "You make it sound like I'm having a mental breakdown."

"Aren't you?"

She started laughing, then brushed aside her bangs in an attempt to shrug off the acknowledgment that she actually *was* as fragile looking as she felt. If a complete stranger who had only been in her presence for a number of hours could read her like a book, then what did that say about her?

Overwhelmed, she said her next words without thinking. "I heard the little girl last night after you left. She said, 'I am the sparrow.' What does that even mean?"

A tear escaped her eye and she wiped it away, hoping he didn't notice. She cleared her throat and tried to laugh off her admission. "But that's stupid, right? You have to use that recorder to hear ghosts. If they even exist. Which they don't."

Ian stared at her intently and leaned forward in his seat. "She wants you to hear her. And so you have."

Grace frowned, her head spinning. "This is ridiculous. I can't believe I'm even humoring you."

Anger flashed in his eyes. "You're *humoring* me because even though you say you don't believe it, part of you does. That denial you carry around like a shield is only going to get you so far. Eventually you'll have to accept the impossible."

"Accept the impossible?" she repeated, darkly amused. "Who has time for that? The world is a scary enough place as it is without believing in goddamn ghosts."

He sat back in his seat and sipped his coffee. "You should try it on for size, Doc. It's a lot less *damaging* than you think."

"Yeah, right." Grace sighed, toying with her mug again. Suddenly, she felt a tap on her shoulder.

"Excuse me."

Grace turned around and eyed the dark-haired woman behind her irritably. "Yes?"

The woman's teeth flashed in a serene smile. "The man next to you would like you to pass the pepper."

Grace's eyes narrowed as she looked back at Ian, who shrugged. Deciding the woman was probably out of her mind, she ignored her and returned to her coffee.

She heard the woman sigh sadly. "He's been waiting fifty years for someone to pass him the pepper. Poor soul."

The woman turned back around and left them alone. Grace

snickered, not sure if she should feel sorry for the woman or prescribe her some antipsychotic meds. When Ian suddenly got to his feet, Grace nearly spilled her coffee mid-sip. "Where are you going?"

"One sec." He brushed past her and took a seat across from the crazy woman. Grace whirled around and watched as he struck up a casual conversation with her as though they had known each other for years.

"You've got to be kidding me," Grace muttered, facing forward again. She tried to eavesdrop, though it was difficult to hear over the peppy Motown music playing on the radio.

"That's amazing," she heard Ian say, an odd sort of eagerness to his voice. Grace felt jealousy rise up and take a bite out of her chest. Who the hell was he to ask her out for coffee and then just abandon her at the first sight of some strange hussy?

She was so busy cursing men for being bastards that she missed the rest of the conversation. Seconds later, Ian returned to her booth and had brought the crazy woman with him.

"Grace, this is Jackie," he introduced, beaming like a second-grader at recess.

Grace pretended to be too busy taking a sip of coffee to shake hands. "Hi."

Jackie smiled and her hand lifted in a little wave as she settled into the seat beside Ian. "Greetings. Oh, what a divine scarf you're wearing."

Grace stared down at her gauzy white and gold scarf with a dispassionate grunt. She hadn't even paid attention to what she'd grabbed on her way out the door. "Thanks, I guess."

She glared at the woman, taking in her draping, colorful clothing and layers of beaded jewelry. Wild waves of rich, ebony hair fell around Jackie's shoulders, a few strands woven into braids. Skin the color of dusted gold covered an exotic, gypsy face, complete with warm, dark eyes and full, unpainted lips.

"Jackie is clairvoyant. A medium," Ian explained, ignoring Grace's irritation. "She says there's a ghost sitting right next to you."

Grace instinctively shifted over in her seat then realized she was being stupid. "Ha ha, very funny."

Jackie tilted her head slightly and focused on the empty air to Grace's left. "Actually, he's quite friendly. He's just dying for some pepper for his soup. No pun intended."

Ian broke out into laughter and Grace gawked at him. He didn't laugh like that when *she* said something witty.

She didn't even try to reign in her attitude as she frowned at Jackie and her flashy attire. "You are aware that it's not Halloween yet, aren't you?"

Ian bit back a grin, amused by Grace's obvious jealousy. He found it incredibly entertaining.

Jackie propped her elbows up on the table and sipped at her fragile white and blue tea cup. She stared into Grace's eyes wistfully, as though seeing right through her. "I always say there's a shortage of color in the world," she mused, her eyes drifting up and sideways as she stared around the diner. "This town is fascinating. Everyone is so...*small*."

Grace's hand came up to knead her right temple as she shook her head. "Do I dare ask what you mean by that? Or do you believe the town is being overrun by midgets?"

Jackie sighed contentedly. "There's no large worries here, nothing from the outside affects this place. It's as if a bubble covers the whole town. It makes everyone small and inconsequential, like tiny figures in a snow globe."

Ian continued to watch Grace, enjoying the range of emotions flash over her face. Amusement to confusion to disbelief. *That* he also found fascinating.

"I'd say that makes sense," he put in, tilting his head to look at Jackie. "Grace here lives in a haunted house."

"You don't say?" Jackie perked up, eyes wide with intrigue.

Grace shot Ian a dark look. "Ian *thinks* my house is haunted, but really he's just looking for something to do with his trivial, pointless existence."

"We're doing an investigation tomorrow night. If you're not busy, you should come by," Ian said to Jackie.

She smiled at him. "Do we have to wait till tomorrow?"

"Nope." Ian winked at Grace. "You don't mind, do ya, Doc?"

Grace imagined strangling him and let that image put some cheer into her voice. "Of course not. Strangers are always welcome in my house."

"That's the spirit." Ian set down his empty coffee mug and pulled some cash out of his pocket. "Why don't we get going?"

Jackie rose smoothly from the booth, her every movement easy and languid. "I'll follow you in my Jeep. I have Gatsby with me."

"Oh, really? Jay Gatsby's hanging out in your car? Is Daisy with him?" Grace snickered.

"That would be amusing, but no," Jackie replied, seeming to have missed the sarcasm. "Gatsby is my Corgi."

"A dog." Grace's smile fell. She hated dogs.

"He's very well behaved," Jackie said as she walked past, the vivid sapphire, gold, and burgundy of her skirt flowing behind her. Grace mumbled under her breath as she got to her feet, avoiding Ian's eyes.

His face broke into a smile as he followed her out, sincerely looking forward to seeing more of that angry heat color her face. It gave her back some of that life he knew she must have had in spades before whatever twist of fate rendered her broken.

* * *

Alex expertly hooked up the last camera in the corner of Grace's bedroom. The small, portable radio beside him was tuned to the only classic rock station he could find. Black Sabbath poured out in a haze of electric guitar and Ozzy Osbourne's signature voice wailed about paranoia.

He tapped his foot to the rhythm, completely in his element. Anytime he had the opportunity to tinker with wires and camera equipment he was in heaven. He had the mind of an engineer and the patience of a surgeon, two of the three things required to be a good video and audio tech. The third was, of course, luck. His luck ran out at the last location, but he was determined not to hit the same snag this time.

He flipped the power switch on the wires he'd run throughout the upstairs, not wanting to take the chance of the batteries dying again. Since there was an available power source, he'd use it.

Turning on the camera, he adjusted the lens so it got as much of the room in view as possible. The sound of the front door opening and closing echoed through the house, punctuated with Grace and Ian's bickering.

"Can't we all just get along?" Alex muttered to himself, shaking his head. He never understood why some people enjoyed arguing so much. He'd always labeled himself as a lover, not a fighter. Anger and grudges just weren't his style.

Continuing to stare at the camera's tiny screen, he made a few more adjustments. When someone suddenly walked through the door and into the room, he caught a flash of sapphire and burgundy and looked up to face a stranger.

For a moment, he thought he was seeing things. She wafted into the room as though on air, her movements graceful and unhurried. Her hand trailed over the walls, her dark eyes serenely taking in the room. When she spotted him she smiled, yet said nothing as though it were perfectly normal for her to be there.

"Hi," he greeted, unable to say more. He cursed himself for

being tongue-tied at such a crucial moment. She was, without a doubt, the most stunning creature he had ever seen.

Jackie paused in front of the wide windows to stare out at the harbor. "Hi there."

Alex attempted to swallow the lump in his throat. "Are you a psychic? I've always wanted to have my palm read," he blurted out, immediately wincing at his stupidity. Why the hell did he just say that?

"Me too," she replied easily, turning to face him. She wandered over, eyeing the camera equipment and the wires. "Though I value the mystery of not knowing my future."

He shrugged, unable to do more as she breezed past him, the rich scent of sandalwood invading his senses. "Are you a friend of Grace's?"

"Are you hoping to catch a ghost?" Jackie asked as she ran a finger down the side of the camera, fascinated.

Alex grinned. "That's what I do. I'm a ghost hunter."

"You are?" Her eyes met his and held for a long, quiet moment. Then she broke the gaze and drifted back to the window. "I love the view from up here."

Alex watched her, unsure whether to be amused or nervous. Before he could make up his mind, he heard Ian and Grace arguing loudly as they came up the stairs. Both looked ill-tempered when they came into the room.

"You better unplug this camera tonight, buddy." Grace pointed an accusatory finger at Alex, her other hand on her hip. "This isn't a free peep show."

Alex laughed. "Point taken. Can I ask what she's doing here?" He nodded in Jackie's direction.

Ian perked up. "Alex, this is Jackie. She's a medium that we met at the diner."

"*Ian* was gracious enough to invite her over," Grace put in bitterly, crossing her arms. "Though I think there's enough crazy people in my house as it is."

"Cool." Alex grinned at Jackie. "Welcome aboard."

Jackie continued to stare out the window as though she'd heard none of it. "That dock is a lonely little place. Death claimed someone there long ago."

They all fell silent and stared at her. Ian and Alex looked eager, while Grace was mortified. She gaped at the other woman, her heart faltering. She wouldn't have cared so much if she hadn't thought the same exact thing about the dock. Did that mean she was right? Had something horrible happened there?

"How can you tell?" Ian asked, whipping out his digital recorder so he could capture her response on tape.

Jackie looked over her shoulder at him. "It's stained black with pain. With death."

Grace shivered, the woman's words disturbing her. She wanted to shrug them off, but instead they festered in her mind as panic rose like a slippery snake into her throat.

Without a word to the others, Grace left the room. Her pulse hammered beneath her skin as she stumbled down the stairs and out onto the front porch. The chill of the misty evening air blasted her face, and she embraced it with relief as she fell onto the front steps. She pulled her knees tight against her and bowed her head.

She fought to control her breathing, to stabilize her heart rate. The last thing she needed was to start having panic attacks, yet she had no control over it. She knew she had all the symptoms.

Something about the dock and the idea of dying there horrified her. It brought all her personal demons to the surface to trample over her grief-stricken heart.

A hand touched her shoulder, cool and comforting. Someone sat down and wrapped an arm over her.

"Be still, child," Nellie murmured, her strong and solid

presence soothing. "You're taking so much on at once."

"You didn't give me a choice," Grace replied wearily, lifting her head to meet her neighbor's soft brown eyes.

Nellie smiled. "Because there is no choice to make. The spirits must be banished from the house before you can know peace here."

Grace shook her head, filled with resentment. "I still don't believe that. I can't."

"You will." Nellie patted her shoulder then rose to her feet. "Such things don't always come easily."

Grace watched her leave, considering her neighbor's words. Nearby, Jackie's dog lay calmly in the grass, tongue hanging out in a happy smile. As Nellie approached, a sudden change came over him. A low growl rumbled from his throat, his ears flicking back as he bared his teeth. He stared up at Nellie, inching backward as though threatened. A bark flew from his throat, a sharp yelp that echoed around the empty street.

Nellie ignored the dog and kept walking. Grace stared at him irritably, wondering what had gotten into him.

"Stupid dog," she muttered under her breath. It reminded her of the tabby cat and its equally sudden switch from friendly to hostile.

But once Nellie was gone from sight, Grace noticed Gatsby settle back down onto the grass. He sent a doggie grin her way, completely at ease.

* * *

An hour later, she uncorked a fresh bottle of wine in the kitchen. As she poured it, Jackie wandered down the stairs and joined her, looking calm and politely curious.

Grace could hear Ian and Alex upstairs packing up before they left for the night. They would be back in twenty-four hours to begin the investigation.

Jackie came over to the kitchen island, resting her elbows

on it as she relaxed. Gatsby trotted around at her feet, then plopped down beside her. She rubbed his back with her bare foot as she admired the butcher block wood, her fingers tracing over the scars and grooves from times past.

"Would you like a glass of wine?" Grace offered, feeling oddly sociable.

Jackie glanced up, a smile lifting the corners of her mouth. "That would be lovely."

Grace said nothing as she poured an extra glass and brought both over to the island. She handed one to Jackie and attempted a smile. "I apologize if I've been…rude."

Jackie sipped at the wine, savoring the taste. "I don't blame you."

"Well, thank you," Grace mumbled, fighting back the urge to roll her eyes. "So, what are you doing in this Podunk little town?"

"The wind blew me here," Jackie replied, humor lighting her face. "What about you?"

Despite everything, Grace laughed. "The same."

Jackie drank more of her wine and glanced around the room. "You're not quite at home in this house yet."

"I've only been here a couple of weeks." Grace followed Jackie's gaze, feeling sentimental. "I won't be here much longer."

Jackie set her wine glass down on the island before wandering into the living room, admiring the antique furniture. She came to a stop before the grandfather clock, reaching up to touch the glass covering its face.

"Do you feel anything off about this place?" Grace asked.

Jackie let her hand fall. "The doctor is very sad to see you here."

Grace stiffened. "Did you talk to Nellie? Did she tell you to say that?"

Jackie shook her head slowly. "I spoke to no one but you, Ian, and Alex."

"Tell me more, then. What else did this *doctor* say?" Grace snapped angrily, setting her now empty glass aside to join Jackie in the living room. She saw the sorrow pass over Jackie's features, the empathy. It made her stomach turn over hideously.

"He says this house is a burden you shouldn't have to bear."

Grace felt sick and immediately sat down on the sofa. She buried her face in her hands and let out a long, slow sigh, struggling to make sense of everything. Jackie *had* to be lying to her about not talking to Nellie. There was no other possible explanation. Except that the woman hadn't left the house since arriving, and Nellie had not been by to see her since she had comforted her on the porch.

She heard Ian and Alex come into the room and lifted her head. She struggled to keep the sharp sting of doubt and misery from showing in her expression. The last thing she needed was anyone else's pity.

Ian's eyes found hers, and despite her best efforts, he saw the pain she felt. It darkened the storm gray of her eyes, creased her forehead, and softened the curve of her mouth. In that moment, he saw why so many others would consider her beautiful. She had the haunting frailty of a woman who had seen a lifetime's worth of suffering.

It was amazing how well she hid it most of the time.

"We're going to take off," he said quietly.

Beside him, Alex shifted one of the empty duffle bags on his shoulder, then bent over to rub Gatsby's belly. He nodded to Jackie. "You'll be back tomorrow? We just remembered it's going to be Halloween. Should make for an even better investigation."

Jackie smiled and looked down at Grace. "I don't have any plans. If I am welcome, I'll be here."

Grace simply nodded. She knew Ian was still watching her, but she didn't have the courage to face him again. It bothered her that he could read her so easily.

"Well, goodnight." Alex left, Jackie and Gatsby following him. Ian hung back, unsure why he felt obligated to do so.

He couldn't help but feel as though she shouldn't be alone.

Grace glanced at him, her face a cold, emotionless mask. "Aren't you going?"

He hesitated, warring with the conflict inside of him; the desire to help and the instinct to mind his own damn business. Knowing the latter was the best for his sanity, he nodded at her. "Goodnight, Doc." He turned and left, shutting the front door quietly behind him.

Grace listened for the sound of their cars leaving. When she knew they had gone, she closed her eyes and sucked in a deep, shuddering breath. All at once, she felt an invisible shroud settle over the room, weighing down upon her head like a wet blanket. It suffocated her and seemed to darken the light, as though attempting to extinguish it.

Fearing she was having another panic attack, she shot to her feet and grabbed her purse and car keys, desperate to free herself of the house. She had to get outside, out into the open where it couldn't harm her anymore.

She left the front door open and stumbled out to her car, her hands shaking as she unlocked it and threw herself inside. Within moments, she was out on the open highway, the windows rolled down to let the cold night wind explode into the car.

The haunting lilt of Stevie Nicks' voice warbled out of the stereo, lamenting dreams of loneliness and thunder.

Tears began to roll down Grace's face, though she had no idea what was wrong with her or what was happening.

The image of the little girl's face flashed in her mind, blinding her with a hard, shocking pain. She slammed on the brakes and squealed to a stop on the side of the road, her breath coming out in ragged gasps.

"The sparrow," she whispered, her heart breaking into two, horrible pieces.

After a few moments of sitting in shattered silence, she got back onto the highway and turned around. She didn't know what, or why, or how, but something pulled her back.

There would be no leaving the Sparrow House.

ACT 2:
SPIRITS

*He was exhaled; his great Creator drew His spirit, as the
sun the morning dew.*
—John Dryden

*And what the dead had no speech for, when living, they can
tell you, being dead: the communication of the dead is tongued
with fire beyond the language of the living.*
—T. S. Eliot

CHAPTER EIGHT

Jackie drove through the night, her headlights barely cutting through the heavy fog. The air swirled around her, the open top and sides of the Jeep exposing her to the elements. She could have put the cover on and protected herself, but she didn't mind the feel of the mist on her skin. It was part of what she enjoyed about east coast towns like Mad Rock Harbor.

The town was a far cry from the temperamental midwestern storms she'd long ago forsaken, her perpetually itchy feet carrying her elsewhere. Anywhere but there. She was a woman who called no particular place home. Instead, she brought her sense of home with her everywhere she went.

She had seen the sun set on the bluffs of the California desert, walked the well-traveled city streets of New York, and dipped her toes in the warm waters of Florida. She'd taken a lover in the heady splendor of Barcelona, kissed the blarney stone in

Dublin, and sipped tequila in the tropical heat of Mexico.

She lived her life by the mantra that not all who wander are lost.

She'd never once felt lost, not in all her travels. Instead, she considered every step she took to be one more rung on destiny's ladder. She trusted her every whim, her every desire, to fate. For fate had never once let her down.

It was fate that had led her to Mad Rock Harbor. She wasn't sure why, but she was certain that the hauntingly lovely Grace and her ghost hunters were a part of it.

And that house…Lord, what she felt there deeply concerned her. The confliction of emotion, both living and dead, was almost more than she could handle. But she had learned long ago how to conceal the immense feelings her sight gave to her. All it seemed to do was frighten those around her, or persuade them to doubt her sanity. While she was never one to let the opinions of others hurt her, she still held on to her instinctual self-preservation.

One can never be too careful.

She pulled up to the quaint, early 20th-century colonial house she was staying in and shut off the engine. Her lips curved as she looked down at her dog.

"Today has been an exciting day, my darling," she said, scratching Gatsby playfully behind his ears. His tongue lolled out lovingly as he leaned into her hand, his auburn and white fur soft beneath her skin.

She glanced up at the house, noting it was one of the few on the street glowing with light and teeming with sound. At this late hour only the creatures of the night thrived and danced as the demons do in Hell. But these were her people, her crowd. These were the misfits of society—the lonely, downtrodden, and forsaken. She always found herself drawn to those who defied convention and lived true to their nature, preferring freedom of restriction to conformity.

She herself had long since broken away from the rigidity of such a life. Never again would she be bound by its chains.

Unbuckling her seat belt, she slipped from the car and grabbed her emerald green, beaded purse. Gatsby hopped out on cue, following her as she made her way up the short walkway to the front door. She considered slipping in the back instead, but knew she was more likely to run into Dominic if she did so. For reasons she couldn't explain, she needed to be alone.

As she entered the house, a wave of smoke, acoustic guitar, laughter, and loud voices hit her. She shut the door and went straight for the stairs, avoiding the living room where several people lounged, high on more than just life itself.

Before she could take the first step, she felt an arm wind around her waist and pull her close against a long, lean body she had known for more years than she could count. She felt his breath on her neck as he nuzzled against her, the scent of Jack Daniels invading her senses.

"I need to rest, Dominic," she began, already attempting to pull free. "Please leave me be."

He grinned lazily, the haze of whatever high he'd ventured into that night clouding his eyes. "You rest too damn much, Jackie. Life should be lived, moment by moment, second by second."

They'd been on and off again lovers, always ending with her goodbye and beginning again with his hello. They tended to wind up in the same places, though she didn't always attribute that to fate. She just knew he possessed a lonely heart and a lost soul beneath all the tanned skin, tattoos, and needle marks.

She started up the stairs, dragging him along like dead weight. Gatsby charged ahead of her, ears flicking back and forth uneasily. As little as he was, he'd take a bite out of Dominic if he tried anything unseemly.

"I agree, but I've drained my energy for the day," Jackie told him as she approached the bedroom they temporarily shared. She turned to face him, her eyes softening as she reached to cradle his cheek in her hand. She worried about him even though they were more friends than lovers these days. His path had and always would be a dangerous one. "Good night."

He let her go, his long arm returning to his side as she slipped into the room. Once inside, she leaned up against the door and shut her eyes. Her hands came up to rest over her heart, and its gentle beating soothed her, centered her. She used its rhythm as an anchor to bring her back to reality.

Samhain, All Hallow's Eve, was upon them. She sensed the spirit world writhing with renewed vigor, eager for the chance to mingle with the living. Soon they would get their wish.

Every year she was bombarded on that day, her senses flooded with the voices of the dead. This year would be no different. In fact, she had a feeling it would be much, much worse.

The spirits within the Sparrow House were already thriving. Upon Samhain, they might just take over the entire place.

* * *

When she pulled up to the Sparrow House the next evening, Jackie made sure she had her protective charms with her. She did one last check of her skirt pockets, feeling for her tiny bundle of sage, her vial of holy water, and her satchel of salt. Her hand came up to touch the tiny, silver cross necklace she wore specifically for days like this. Days when the break between the living and the dead was even wider than usual.

Satisfied that she was prepared, she slipped on her peacock feather masquerade mask and admired herself in the rearview mirror. Fixing a serene smile on her face, she left the car and approached the house.

The light breeze caught the ends of her sunny yellow skirt,

sending it billowing around her legs. Her ebony curls hung loose down her back, nearly to her waist.

She spotted Grace sitting on the front porch steps, arms crossed and an anxious look on her face. When Grace noticed her, dry amusement replaced the anxiety.

"Aren't we a little old to be dressing up?"

Jackie continued to smile. "When we feel we are too old for the little things, then we surrender to the boring and the mundane."

Grace rolled her eyes. "Whatever. I guess the look suits you."

Jackie settled onto the step beside her, removing the mask and setting it aside. She let her arms drape lazily over her knees, and the faint glow of the dying sun caught the silver of her numerous rings.

Around them, the neighborhood was oddly quiet. Most people had settled in for the night. Since no children lived on the street there was no reason to celebrate Halloween. A few had porch lights on just in case, but most were treating the night like any other.

Jackie knew better than to assume this night would be normal.

"There is motion in the air tonight," she mused, staring around the yard. "We are not alone."

Grace frowned. "You can drop the act with me. I won't rat you out to the guys, I promise."

Jackie glanced over at her, an innate curiosity and humor brightening her face. "Then you can drop your act as well, darling. I promise not to rat you out, either."

"What act is that, exactly?" Grace asked, meeting the other woman's eyes directly. Up close, she realized that Jackie's features were not nearly as perfect as she had earlier thought them to be. There were soft lines of heartache, pain, and even suffering written into the planes of her face and burrowed in the depths of her eyes. Instead of making her less beautiful, however, it only made her beauty more compelling.

But what did that pain and suffering say about the woman? How could she seem so aloof and carefree if she had known great heartache in her life? Grace desperately wished she knew the answer. She could use some advice in that department.

"You have built a wall around you for protection. It hinders your sight," Jackie explained, her voice taking on a wistful, ethereal tone. She stared off into the night sky, her lips upturned in a knowing smile. "You peek over your own wall constantly, wanting to be a part of what's happening around you, but fear holds you back. Let the wall come down and things will make themselves right again."

Troubled, Grace looked away and rubbed at her temple, feeling a headache coming on. And the night had only just begun.

"That's all very philosophical of you, but I know my own mind. And rationalizing the paranormal is something I just don't have the energy to do."

"Life is more satisfying when we accept that we do not know everything," Jackie told her, watching as the moon began its slow ascent over the trees. "Tonight, there will be more things you won't understand than things you will."

Before Grace could think of something to say in response, Ian and Alex both emerged from inside the house. Alex brightened instantly at the sight of Jackie.

"Hey! I was wondering when you'd be back," he greeted, reaching for her hand to help her up. She rose to her feet, holding the peacock feather mask in her hands.

Without a word, she slipped the mask over his head, fastening it in place. She stepped back to admire him with a smile. "Marvelous."

Alex looked to his partner. "Ian, I think this should be the new look for our show."

Ian coughed, horrified by the thought. "No."

"Why not?" Alex reached over and casually draped an arm over Jackie's shoulders. "We could be the masked ghost hunters. Say that they keep us impervious to negative energy so no evil spirits follow us home. It's brilliant."

"Oh, my God." Grace buried her face in her hands and broke into laughter, while Ian sighed.

"Can we just get on with the investigation?"

"We have to eat first," Alex protested, removing the mask. "I will not be forced to go hungry again."

Jackie giggled as Grace looked up at him. "I wasn't notified that I have to feed you people."

Ian sighed. "You don't. We can go get something and come back."

"I know how to make a splendid tortilla soup," Jackie suggested.

Alex beamed at her. "That sounds amazing. Let's do that."

"With what ingredients?" Grace pointed out. "I don't really cook. Nellie brings me food."

"Then run over and ask Nellie for the ingredients," Ian told her, running with the idea. "I could make us some tacos, too. I'll make a list and you can go get everything."

He disappeared inside and Alex and Jackie followed him in, excitedly talking about the soup.

"Oh, sure. I can go get everything. And then you can shove it up your ass," Grace grumbled to herself as she got to her feet. She was being outvoted and overrun in her own house. The old her would have never put up with it.

Then again, the old her wouldn't have heard strange voices in the middle of the night, either. Nor would she have humored ghost enthusiasts in their hunt for evidence.

No, the old Grace would be too important and busy to give an ounce of her time to any of it.

But even she wouldn't have turned down a bowl of homemade tortilla soup.

* * *

The scent of poblano peppers and tomatoes filled the house, blending with the hot spices of Ian's signature carne asada. Grace made herself useful by chopping up tomatoes, onions, and cilantro, while Alex toyed with his camcorder at the dining table. Ian and Jackie bustled around the kitchen, silently building a masterpiece.

When they all sat down to eat, Grace eyed the carne asada warily.

"You're really going to make me eat this, aren't you?" she asked Ian, lifting a thin piece of meat between her fingers.

He flashed her a proud smile. "You haven't lived till you've tried my carne asada, Doc."

"I suppose I won't live much longer *after* trying it, either." She sighed, then bit hesitantly into the piece of steak. As she chewed, her eyes narrowed and held his.

"Well?" He filled a corn tortilla with meat and crisp green cilantro as he watched her.

Her chin lifted imperiously. "It's okay."

"Why can't you just admit you like it?"

"Because I'm stubborn." She grabbed a tortilla and piled more carne asada onto it. "Take my going for more as confirmation that I enjoyed it well enough."

"I could eat this every day," Alex piped in cheerfully, already through one taco and halfway done with a bowl of soup. He smiled at Jackie. "Both talented and beautiful. Are you sure you're real?"

Jackie sipped at her bowl of soup, forgoing a spoon. "Are we ever one-hundred percent confident of what is real and what isn't?"

"Grace thinks she is," Ian said, earning an icy stare from her across the table.

"The human mind is capable of all kinds of fallacies," Grace replied, lifting her glass of wine as she fell into her element. "Paranoid schizophrenics can hear voices. Focal seizures in epileptic patients can elicit visual hallucinations. Dementia can cause psychosis and bring on aggression. So, the statement that we are not one-hundred percent confident of reality is certainly true for many people. Not all, but many."

"What did you specialize in as a doctor?" Ian asked, his blue eyes intent on hers.

"I'm a surgeon. I work at the most prestigious hospital in Chicago, just like my father and grandfather before me."

"You work with your dad? That must be cool," Alex said.

Grace froze, realizing the slippery path she was heading down. Her heart rolled over in distress, torn by that perpetually gaping wound. She fought back the feelings and looked to Alex with a forced smile.

"Not anymore." She rose from her chair and began gathering their plates, taking them into the kitchen so she could clean up. She was grateful that they didn't push her further about her father.

"Well, it's almost nine o'clock," Ian announced, checking his watch. "We might as well get started."

Jackie swept into the kitchen to help Grace while Ian and Alex went upstairs to double-check their equipment. As she began washing plates in the old farmhouse sink, Jackie tilted her head to smile at Grace. "The doctor is your father," she said quietly, sympathy in her eyes.

Grace's lips pursed in anger as she dried off the plates that Jackie handed to her. "I don't see how it's your business."

"He sent the ghost hunters to help you."

Grace sighed. "You know, I want to like you. I really do. But if you piss me off, don't be surprised when I kick you out of my house."

Jackie cleaned the last dish and looked at Grace as she handed it over. There was no hostility, no judgment in her eyes. Only empathy. "You come from a rough world. You've seen more death than most will ever see in a lifetime. A five-year-old boy died on your operating table just days before you lost your parents."

Grace's eyes widened. "How…"

"Your wall has all kinds of inscriptions upon its surface, Grace."

Deeply disturbed, Grace turned away, unable to look at the woman any longer. She fought to catch her breath, the memory of losing the boy that night coming back to her. She'd almost forgotten about that, had lost it under the heavier weight of her parents' deaths. But now, reliving the experience of having to deliver the news to the boy's parents was crushing down on her like a hundred-ton boulder.

Her arms clutched her torso, the pain too great to bear. She sat down in one of the dining chairs and shut her eyes.

Jackie said nothing as she sat beside her, reaching for Grace's hand with a comforting squeeze.

When Grace felt she could speak again, she tried hard not to cry. "Is this all real?"

"It is real if you want it to be," Jackie said quietly, sorry to see such pain. She wished she had the power to relieve Grace of all the darkness that plagued her. "If you can't handle it, then you don't have to. You can leave this house."

"No, I can't," Grace choked out, eyes on fire as she looked up from the table. "I tried to leave, but I was pulled back here by something. I don't know how, or why, but it wouldn't let me go. *She* won't let me go."

Jackie nodded, understanding. She squeezed Grace's hand again. "Then you must learn to accept what you cannot control, what you cannot rationalize. It is the only way to see this through to the end."

"What happens at the end?" Grace wondered aloud, feeling helpless and lost.

"No one knows." Jackie's eyes drifted to the grandfather clock and became unfocused, misty. When she spoke again, there was great sadness, and even a hint of fear, in her voice. "There are monsters here."

Grace found she had nothing to say in response. Instead, she simply held Jackie's hand, not realizing just how badly she had needed the comfort the gesture offered.

Just then, Ian and Alex came down the stairs. Alex hoisted his professional grade camcorder up onto his shoulder, while Ian grabbed his digital recorder and Mel Meter. Alex had a small backpack with other equipment in it that he slung over his other shoulder. They turned to face the women, looking determined and focused.

Ian's mouth spread in an adrenaline-charged smile. "We're ready."

* * *

They turned off all the lights in the house and armed themselves with flashlights. Alex instructed Grace and Jackie to leave the flashlights off unless it was absolutely necessary. Grace held hers like a weapon, not appreciating having to walk around in the dark. It made it easier that some faint moonlight trickled in through the windows.

"I'm going to start filming now," Alex told them. He stood back and focused in on the others, watching them through the screen of his camcorder as he hit record.

Ian faced the camera and began his introduction, giving a brief background on the house and on Grace and Jackie. He explained some of the experiences that Nellie had, and named off the key locations where they had set up static night vision cameras to capture any activity both upstairs and downstairs.

"The most important area is the basement, so we want to focus most of our attention there," Ian continued, nodding to Jackie. "Jackie, will you lead the way and give us an idea of what you see and feel?"

Jackie waved graciously at the camera and approached the door to the basement, focusing her senses. Despite the darkness, her vision was alive. Earlier, she had noticed things— shadows—slithering over the walls, but had ignored them. Now, she purposely sought them out and found they weren't the only energy pulsating within the home.

There was misery like molten lava oozing over the floor, sliding through the rooms of the first floor like a plague. It shifted like a living, breathing thing, black as coal. A shiver ran across her skin, an effect of witnessing such an unnatural entity. It was compiled of residual energy and dark, dark pain. An old suffering that had lain dormant in the house for a very long time.

She considered this as she tried to put into words what she was seeing. "There's a dark energy on the floor...some of it slithers up the walls." Her eyes drifted upward to the ceiling light in the living room. "It's pouring out of the light bulb like rain..."

The others were silent as she continued to gaze around, trying to make some sense of what she was witnessing. That was always the hardest part for her. Most times, the spirit energy she observed was so chaotic, so extraordinarily frenzied, that it was difficult to judge the source or the meaning behind it. Then other times, there was a direct point of origin for what she experienced, and a spirit would make themselves known to her personally. Those were the most emotionally and mentally draining of experiences, as they required so much of her focus and energy. But she knew they could be helpful when trying to determine what kind of turmoil resided in a home.

As it was, she saw nothing of that sort on the first floor. It was time to venture underground.

"The basement…" she murmured, half in a trance as she turned back to the basement door, hand extending toward the knob.

Alex came up beside her to film her face, to capture her every reaction to what was happening around them. Suddenly, he saw her freeze as though hit by an icy wave.

"Jackie?" He reached out to touch her shoulder to comfort her. She had the most incredible look of pain and alarm on her face. "What's wrong?"

"Oh my," she whispered, her eyes focused on something about waist level next to him. A shudder visibly ran through her body, and Alex nearly interrupted whatever she was witnessing just to rescue her from it.

Before he could, she let her hand fall from the knob as she kneeled. Compassion filled her eyes and a single tear fell down her cheek.

"I understand," she said to no one in particular. At least no one the rest of them could see.

"Jackie, what do you see?" Ian interrupted, impatience getting the better of him. He held out his Mel Meter, startled to see it spike to absurd levels and shrill loudly. There was something there. Something very strong.

"She's just a child," Jackie told him. "She's upset and doesn't want us to go into the basement."

"Why not?" Ian asked.

Jackie looked up at him, the camera catching the haunted dread in her eyes. "She's afraid we'll let him out."

CHAPTER NINE

Him?" Grace's voice lost all confidence, but she stood tall regardless. Despite what Jackie said earlier to her about the little boy, Grace still wasn't convinced this wasn't an act. After all, there was no way to explain it using a rational mind and proven science, so how could it be true?

Doubt swirled in with the fear that had taken home in her gut, settling in like a hissing snake. "Can I just say, for the record, that I have been down in that basement several times and have *never* seen or heard anything unusual."

Ian turned to her. "That doesn't mean there isn't something there."

Grace frowned. "So, you're just going to take her word for it? We don't even know her. She's probably making all of this up."

"Have a little faith, Doc." Ian dismissed her with a wave as he focused back on Jackie. "We need to go into the basement."

Jackie rose to her feet, sadness still etched in the lines of her face. She lifted her eyes to meet his while Alex continued to film. "Unfortunately, what she's afraid of has already found its way into the house. It isn't confined to the basement any longer."

"Good, so there's nothing stopping us from going down there," Ian affirmed, reaching for the door himself and pulling it open. He didn't wait for a response as he charged down the steps, ready to wage war on whatever entities were there.

He felt along the wall as he descended the stairs, stopping as he felt his feet hit the dirt. His eyes stared purposefully into the darkness. "Alex, hand me the Spirit Box."

Alex followed him and reached into his equipment bag for a small, black device with a speaker on it. He handed it to Ian, then stepped back to film. In the opposite corner, one of the static night vision cameras was set up.

Jackie and Grace stepped down into the room, both looking wary.

Then Jackie doubled over in brutal agony. She cried out, but raised her hand to keep Alex and Grace back, not wanting them to help her. She sucked in air through gritted teeth as she absorbed the pain, the shock of it being transferred into her by the spirits present.

One of them wanted her to know how it felt to die.

Images flashed over her eyes of a young woman chained to a chair, writhing in fear as a man inflicted great pain upon her. Torture of the worst imaginable kind. He beat her with a leather strap, the whoosh of it cutting through the air, deafening as airplane engines. She felt the contact of the strap on her face, her chest, her legs. The pain was impossible to work through, impossible to comprehend. It triggered something dark and buried deep within her, demons that festered. They threatened to explode out of her, to overtake her senses.

Everything became a nightmare.

She forced her eyes open and fought with all the energy she had against the pain, needing to see what force brought this on her. She spotted it, skittering like a hunched over gremlin along the walls. Its shadowy mass vibrated with pure evil, its eyes glowing like fiery embers in the dark.

Her heart clenched with fear as she gaped at it, mortified. Never had she seen something of this magnitude, of this concentration. The only explanation she could surmise was that it was the coalescence of one man's dark hatred and morbid nature. It was the sum of all his vile acts, thoughts, and desires. His malevolence was so awesome in power, so vile against the laws of nature, that it had broken free of him and manifested itself into the form of this *thing*. This creature that wreaked havoc on the living and represented a lifetime of horrendous torture.

"What are you seeing, Jackie?" Ian asked, troubled by her reaction and equally as concerned when his Mel Meter soared to impossible levels, sounding off the alarm in the presence of spirit energy. The temperature reading bumped up to 66.6 degrees. He thrust it at Alex so they could catch it on film.

Jackie swallowed the bile that rose in her throat, trying to cope with the onslaught of emotions, bad energy, and threats that came her way from the spirits around them. It wasn't just the creature that plagued her. The basement was filled with dark voices, with lost stories of suffering never told. They strained against the confines of the walls like prisoners trapped by a sheet, desperate to get at her. Desperate to be heard.

Samhain had given them this much, and the desire to walk among the living powered them like rabid hounds.

"A young woman was tortured here," Jackie began, her eyes unfocused as she tried to get more information from what she was witnessing. It was all so frantic, like a Ringling

Brothers Circus. The creature scurrying over the floor, the bodies attempting to push through the walls, the images of the woman being violently tormented, and the sound of her screams.

Her eyes drifted to the staircase, and she saw something beneath it, something violently unstable. Death—old, brutal death—hung in the air over the dirt like a deformed, warped cloud.

She felt suddenly faint, her knees buckling under her. She staggered back, her hand flying out to balance herself against the wall. Nausea hit like a punch to the gut, and she realized hysterically that she had to get out of the basement. Any longer and she would be overwhelmed to the point of insanity.

Without another word, she stumbled up the stairs and left the others. Alex immediately tossed his camera at Grace and raced up after her, his panic a vice contracting his insides. When he burst out of the basement, he found her crumpled to the floor.

He hesitated, then gathered her into his arms. Tears of grief fell in streams down her face.

"What happened?" he asked, shocked as she buried her face into his chest, clinging to his T-shirt like a woman who'd just narrowly escaped tumbling off a precarious cliff.

Jackie squeezed her eyes shut, willing away the demons that had nearly claimed her. Her voice cracked as she spoke, but she fought to get the words out. "I think there's someone buried in the basement."

"Wow," Alex managed, unable to do anything but hold her as he digested her words.

* * *

Back in the basement, Ian faced off with the spirits. "I'm going to turn on this device and I want you to speak into it," he ordered, holding up the Spirit Box. He shot an intense look at Grace. "Keep that camera on me."

Grace gaped at him, unsure what to do. The only light

source came from the camcorder's screen, and it glowed over her face as she lifted the camera. Ian filled the screen, visible in the green light of night vision. "All right, I got it. I think."

Ian flipped on the Spirit Box and immediately a loud, static sound poured out of it. He held it out and turned slowly, his eyes searching the dark. "This device emits radio frequencies. It passes over several stations a second. Use this to speak to me."

Grace didn't realize she was holding her breath, but she let it out slowly as she watched him. The static sound echoed deafeningly off the cement walls, grating on her senses and disorienting her. It didn't help that worry and doubt over what happened to Jackie was nagging at the back of her mind.

On the screen, Grace watched Ian turn to face her, his eyes lit with adrenaline. "I can feel cold spots all over. I've got goose bumps on my arms, the hair the back of my neck is standing up. What about you?"

Grace shivered, though she tried to shrug it off. "No, I'm okay."

Ian's lips curved in a knowing grin. He turned away from her and spoke out loud to the darkness. "Did you torture a young woman here?"

A man's voice warbled almost instantly out of the device. *Certainly.*

"Shit," Ian cursed, jumping at the sound of the voice. He glanced over at Grace, just able to make out the shock in her eyes. "Why did you do it?"

Control.

Nothing in the world could have prepared Grace for that voice. As much as she wanted to tell herself that it was some pre-recorded nonsense that Ian had put into the device to say just the right things, she almost believed that less than the idea that it was real.

That it was an actual ghost.

"Ian..." Grace called out, distressed. "I can't stop shaking."

"You're scared. Embrace it," Ian declared boldly, enjoying his own rush of fear and exhilaration. His voice took on a darker tone as he addressed the spirit yet again. "Why are you still here? Why won't you move on?"

A few seconds passed with no response. Ian started to ask another question only to freeze as a different voice came through. It was still a man, but somehow softer, less aggressive.

The good doctor.

Ian stared immediately at Grace, astonished by what he had just heard. He shut off the Spirit Box then let his arms fall to his sides.

Grace frowned as she lowered the camcorder. "What's wrong?"

He shook his head. *"You're* the good doctor."

One of her eyebrows shot up as he suddenly went to turn on the light. The single bulb burst to life above them, and the alarm in his eyes truly frightened her.

"What does that mean?" Grace stammered, rubbing her arm with her free hand. She felt singled out and vulnerable, especially under the weight of Ian's intense stare. He was looking at her like he was seeing her for the very first time, like she was a stranger.

"I've heard those words before. In fact, we heard them in an EVP we captured the day before we came here," he explained, still not sure what it all meant. His brow furrowed as he rubbed his face.

"Just because I *happen* to be a doctor doesn't mean this 'ghost' is talking about me," Grace reasoned, not willing to believe a single word of it. "This is ridiculous."

With fire in his eyes, Ian called out once again to the dark spirits residing in the basement. "Grace doesn't believe you. Do something to prove that you meant her when you said those words."

Grace let out a shaky laugh, but it was cut off as the door to the basement suddenly slammed shut with a resolute bang. The camcorder slipped from her grasp as a scream caught in her throat, terror exploding through her like dynamite.

Ian wasted no time and grabbed her arm. He dragged her toward the staircase, pulling her up the steps.

"Ian?" They heard Alex's voice from far away then the sound of his footsteps pounding over the wood floor.

When they reached the door, Grace tried to push it open, but found it stuck. "Oh, my God," she gasped, forcing all her weight onto it. Ian shoved her aside and tried it himself, only to fall through the doorway as Alex opened it from the other side. He stumbled through with Grace right behind him.

"What the hell happened, guys?" Alex asked, shutting the basement door once again.

Grace fled to the living room where Jackie was sitting on the sofa, a cup of tea in her hands. Grace collapsed beside her and buried her face in her hands.

When Jackie attempted to touch her, Grace pushed her hand away. "Don't."

Jackie nodded. She looked at Ian and Alex as they came into the room. "You look like you've seen a ghost."

"Heard one," Ian corrected her, brushing back strands of his dark hair restlessly. He panted, out of breath from the struggle and the rush of panic he'd felt from the door slamming. Never had he experienced something of that magnitude.

Alex patted him on the back. "Why don't we call it a night. I think we're all a little shaken up."

Ian grimaced, not wanting to give up. The night was still young. But even he couldn't deny that there was no way he'd get any of them to go back into the basement just yet. In fact, he didn't think he could even manage it.

"Whatever's in this house is way worse than anything I could have imagined," he said to Alex, shaking his head. "And whatever it is, it led us here."

"How's that?" Alex's eyebrows lifted in surprise.

"Remember that EVP we got at Bellhurst that said *the good doctor*?"

"Of course."

Ian's face tightened. "I just heard it again downstairs out of the Spirit Box. A similar voice, most likely the same spirit."

Alex sat down on the armrest of the sofa in shock. "Do you think it followed us here?"

Ian nodded. "It's the only thing that makes sense. And I think Grace is the doctor the voice referred to."

"No way," Alex turned around to look at Grace, who was still collecting herself in silence. "That's cool. So maybe we were meant to come here."

Jackie smiled up at him. "Always trust in fate."

* * *

While the others continued to discuss what happened, Grace wandered to the wide windows of the living room. She opened each of them, shoving the oak-lined glass panels up in a fevered attempt to let in the night air.

Or, perhaps, to let *out* whatever it was that had slammed that door.

She stood in front of the windows, embracing the rush of chilled wind that came in from the harbor. It caressed her skin like ice, frigid and shocking, but she absorbed the tremors it gave her and let it awaken her senses. She needed some semblance of reality to wake her from this nightmare. Surely, that's what it was. Just a horrid, dreadful nightmare.

Behind her, Jackie was explaining in detail what she had witnessed. Hearing the words brought back Grace's cynicism, her skepticism. None of it could have *possibly* happened the way Jackie was describing it. How could it? Gremlin-like creatures and bodies pushing themselves out of the walls...it was like something out of a horror movie.

It wasn't real life.

"The creature is a manifestation of this cruel man's violent nature and his evil deeds," Jackie said. She sipped her tea peacefully from her perch on the sofa. Grace envied her ability to recover so quickly from what appeared to be a traumatic event. Then again, it only gave credence to her deeply rooted suspicion that Jackie was nothing but an elaborate, imaginative liar. "Whoever he is, he is the spirit the little girl is afraid of. Something released the creature from the basement, but I don't know what..."

Ian frowned and scratched his chin. He looked over at Grace, lost in thought. Then it hit him. "Hey, Grace. Have you brought anything up from the basement besides those boxes of photographs?"

She let out a tired sigh, but didn't turn to face him. "The furniture. It all came from the basement."

Jackie nodded. "That's likely the cause."

"You think the spirits were attached to the furniture?" Ian asked, running with the thought. "That would explain why the activity started when Grace came to the house and not before."

"I believe they are thriving on Grace's energy, as well," Jackie continued. "They are using her emotions to build their strength."

Grace's hands shook with one, quick tremble as she turned around. "That's ridiculous. I told you, I haven't felt anything in this house."

Jackie eyed her curiously. "Nothing?"

Grace crossed her arms defensively, images of her own depressive breakdowns flashing in her mind. They had only gotten more frequent since she'd come to the Sparrow House, but the more plausible explanation for it was that she was simply *depressed*. Which was a perfectly normal condition given the circumstances.

Then there was the furniture. She had noticed scratches on the surface of the coffee table, and more aging on the sofa, but shrugged it off as being there before. But what if it wasn't?

"Nothing," she answered flatly.

Anger hardened Ian's face as he rounded on her. "Are you seriously going to stand here and act like what just happened to us was *not* the work of paranormal forces?"

A chilly frost settled over Grace as she met his eyes. "Honestly, I'm still not convinced. Sorry."

"What the hell will it take to convince you, then?" he demanded, throwing up his hands. "Because if you're going to be this fucking blind, I'm not going to waste my time helping you."

She winced at his words. "I didn't ask for your help. Nellie did."

"That's right, because Nellie isn't an idiot. I can't say the same for you," he snapped, his temper getting the better of him. When he saw both shock and grief flare within those storm gray eyes of hers, regret swam in to join the anger he felt.

Grace visibly trembled and clutched her torso even tighter. She felt, yet again, like she was being singled out. She despised him for making her feel that way. "Do you call all people who disagree with you idiots?" she asked coldly, lifting her chin. "Or just those who fight back?"

Ian sighed, tossing up his hands in exasperation. "I'm sorry, Grace. That was out of line."

"Yeah man, it was," Alex agreed, eyeing Ian strangely.

Grace softened her stance, though her expression remained cold. "Apology accepted. So, what do we do now?"

"There's a body buried in the basement," Jackie piped in,

earning stunned looks from the others.

"How do you know that?" Grace asked.

"I could sense it."

Alex looked deeply concerned. "Jackie mentioned it to me after she came out of the basement."

Ian considered this for a moment, then turned to Grace again. "We need to dig it up."

Alarm flashed over her face. "Excuse me? Last I checked this was still *my* house. You don't get to call the shots around here, I do. And I say no digging."

"But if there is a body down there, that could explain the activity," Ian began impatiently. "We could end this once and for all if we remove it from the house."

"I don't care. I won't let you excavate my property just because some crackpot ghost whisperer thinks she *sensed* a fucking body," Grace fired back. "I can't believe I'm even listening to this."

"Open your goddamn eyes, Doc," Ian growled. "The solution is staring you right in the face."

"Yeah, well, you're just going to have to figure out a different way." Grace stood firm.

Ian kept his mouth wisely shut, while Alex turned to Jackie.

"Is this man, creature, *thing*, dangerous? Maybe Grace should come stay at the hotel for a while."

Jackie nodded. "He is very dangerous."

Grace's eyes widened. "I can't leave the house."

"Maybe you should consider it," Ian decided.

"No," Grace shot back. "I won't."

"Why not?" he asked, concerned at the terrified look that came over her face.

A laugh bubbled out of her throat, though she felt no humor. Only a manic form of distress. "I don't know, but I can't leave. I tried, I can't."

Ian's brow creased as Jackie suddenly spoke up. "I'll stay."

They all looked at her.

"You'll stay here?" Alex asked, before turning to Ian. "Maybe we should stay, too."

"Oh, no." Grace shook her head. "This is not a sleepover." Ian rolled his eyes. "Shut up. We're staying. We won't leave you in this house alone."

She blinked at the finality in his voice, wondering when she had lost all authority over her own house. "I don't have beds for any of you."

"We have sleeping bags. Jackie'll take the couch," Alex decided. "Loosen up a bit, Grace. It'll be fun."

"Maybe a glass of wine will help?" Jackie ventured, rising to her feet. She smiled warmly at Grace, her hand extended in an offering of peace.

Grace let out a frustrated huff of breath, unsure why she felt so relieved at the thought of not being alone anymore. Since when had that been the case?

She accepted Jackie's hand and let herself be guided away. As she passed by Ian, she sent him a warning glance.

"This is still my house, buddy. If I decide you have to go, then that's it."

Ian cracked a smile. "You won't."

She rolled her eyes and cursed him for his ability to both get on her nerves and charm the hell out of her at the same time.

CHAPTER TEN

Her dreams horrified her.

Grace saw the things Jackie claimed to see and more. Faceless men and women forcing their way through the walls, shadows scuttling over the floor like giant spiders, hands reaching up for her from under the bed.

Everywhere she looked, some part of the house was attacking her. Claiming her like a possession to be taken, not embraced. Forced, not welcomed. It was a beast hell bent on swallowing her whole, and she had no chance of escape. No hope of survival.

Her imagination went wild, riding on the fear and the stress of having strange people barge their way into her life. People she was forced to trust with her property, her time, her well-being. Her options had only narrowed in scope the longer she stayed in the Sparrow House. The longer she let the house grab hold of her and tighten its stranglehold grip.

She tossed and turned in her bed, the nightmares extraordinarily vivid. The shadow of a man stood in the corner of her room, black as night and just as sinister. He—*it*—rocked side-to-side in an eerily threatening motion, as if preparing for the instant to strike.

The instant to kill.

Grace bolted awake, her eyes flying open. Tears tracked hot lines down her cheeks. She clutched at her throat, choking back the scream that strangled her. Her eyes shot to the corner of the room and saw nothing. Relief flooded through her, loosening her tightened muscles and soothing her aching heart.

With a heavy, cleansing sigh, she fell back against her pillows and tried desperately to relax and forget the nightmares. They had been so real. If there was any ounce of truth to Jackie's claims, then it was amazing the woman wasn't mad. Or maybe she was, and she just had a terrific way of concealing it.

Because Grace knew if she had to walk around every day witnessing those *things*, she would rather die than live another second. It was too horrible to bear.

After a few minutes of trying to fall back asleep and finding it pointless, Grace shoved aside the twisted blankets and sheets and got out of bed. There was milk in the fridge and she knew it would help calm her. It was an insomnia remedy her father had always sworn by.

As she got to her feet, she noticed that the window was open. Like before, there was a sparrow perched on the sill, watching her.

She froze, her eyes on the bird as it angled its head, its beady eyes shining in the moonlight. It continued to stare at her silently, almost like a sentient guardian come to protect her. When she moved toward it, the bird flew off into the night.

Unsure what was happening or why, Grace shut the window and latched it again, then rubbed her eyes. Once she could rationalize as her own forgetfulness. But twice?

She didn't want to give the event more meaning than it deserved, so she pushed it to the back of her mind. Most likely, one of the others had left the window open at some point during the day and she just hadn't noticed.

She clung to that possibility as she left the room and tiptoed down the stairs, trying not to wake the others who were fast asleep in the living room. She heard manly snores and shook her head, annoyed that they could sleep so soundly. It wasn't fair.

She flipped on the kitchen light, hoping it wouldn't disturb them, and carefully opened the refrigerator door to get the milk. As she poured herself a glass, she heard footsteps behind her.

She jerked around with a small yelp, only to see Ian standing in the kitchen.

"Boo." He chuckled, approaching her and reaching over her head into the cabinet for a fresh glass. He pried the milk carton from her hand and poured some into her glass and his.

Grace sighed, still anxious after seeing the sparrow. "I couldn't sleep."

"Not surprising after what went on earlier this evening," he replied, returning the milk to the fridge. He grabbed his glass and sipped, then leaned his hip comfortably against the counter. "Are you doing okay?"

"Define *okay*." She tried to keep her voice down so as not to wake the others. "I have three strangers in my house, ghosts in the basement, furniture that's possessed, and an increasingly overactive imagination that refuses to let me sleep."

"We *strangers* are only here because we want to help you."

She tilted her head to the side. "Right, because you aren't getting anything out of this investigation but charitable feelings."

"We live to give."

When he smiled, she sipped her milk and tried to casually get a good look at him. He'd slipped on a nicely fitted black T-shirt and blue flannel pajama pants, giving him an unusually relaxed look. Paired with his lightly mussed length of hair and sleepy blue eyes, he was almost handsome. Almost *normal*.

Grace caught herself, and bit her lower lip as she considered this new revelation. Though she hated to admit it, she was attracted to him. As much as he pissed her off and got under her skin, it was a welcome relief to at least feel *something* other than misery and desolation.

She knew she should enjoy it while it lasted. Soon they'd all be gone and she would need to pick up the pieces of her life.

"So, what's your story? How did you get into chasing after ghosts?" Grace asked.

"Alex and I have been into the paranormal for as long as I can remember." Ian shrugged. "I didn't think of it as a career until my life took me down that path. I witnessed something that changed my perception of everything, and the next day I quit my day job and focused all I had on hunting down evidence of what I saw."

"What did you see?"

Sentiment brightened Ian's eyes. "I saw the ghost of my grandfather walking through his home, just days after he died. He passed right in front of me in the hallway, then disappeared. I think he was searching for my grandmother, but she wasn't home." He paused, running a hand through his hair with a heavy sigh. "It was the most incredible thing I have ever witnessed."

Grace stared at him, searching his face for any sign of doubt, any hint that he was lying. She didn't find it. Instead, she saw more honesty and passion in him than she had ever seen before.

Shaken, she looked away from his face. Instead, she reached for his right hand and admired the tattoo over his fingers. He had the letters G.A.P.C. in bold black letters, one on each knuckle. Great American Paranormal Crew.

"You're very dedicated to this stuff," she mused, tracing her thumb over the ink that marred his skin. "But I think you take yourself too seriously."

He didn't realize he was holding his breath, paralyzed by the feel of her touch. She had such strong, capable hands, not delicate like he had expected. He got the impression that before coming to Mad Rock Harbor, she had lived each day saving lives with those hands.

The corner of his mouth lifted as she glanced up at him, and he subtly inched closer to her. The soft yellow glow of the kitchen light brightened her eyes, chasing away the clouds in all that gray. The beauty of it caught him completely off guard. "I take myself seriously because I expect the best of myself."

"Perhaps humility would soften you up a bit," she said, her heart skipping at the dark intensity that sparked in his gaze.

"You should be giving yourself that same advice."

He was surprised when she laughed, a real smile blooming over her face. He marveled at it for a moment, unsure why it pleased him. Unsure why it mattered to him that she shouldn't lose herself to sorrow.

She studied him closely. "I suppose you and I are not so different."

His teeth flashed in a smile. "It's not rude if it's true."

"My sentiments exactly." She nodded, only to realize she still held his hand. She released it and lifted her glass of milk again to distract herself from what was happening between them. She hadn't meant to flirt with him, or be friendly, or whatever it was she was doing. It would only make her want his company more than she already did.

"So, it's only fair now that you tell me your story," Ian decided, crossing his arms casually. "You have some secret you're not telling me."

Grace pursed her lips, irritated that he'd turned the tables on her. Though she couldn't blame him for being curious. She decided to give him as much of the truth as she was willing to divulge. At least for now.

"On the worst day of my life, I walked in on my oh-so-brilliant-and-charming fiancé cheerfully banging my best friend in my bed." She smiled cynically, her face hardening as she recalled the scene. "It was late afternoon, pouring rain outside, and this asshole was cozy in bed with my younger, sexier, but incredibly brainless friend. Why he did it, I'll never know."

"Did you kill him?"

She grinned. "God knows he deserved it, but no. I just threw them out, naked, onto the street, locked my door, blocked his phone number, and turned Alanis Morissette on full blast so I could drown out his pathetic pleas for forgiveness."

Ian chuckled, admiring her fiery side. "I'd say you showed him."

"Well, it helped, at least." She sighed, though there was still laughter in her eyes. "Anyway, I came out here to take some time away from him and regroup."

"Regroup in a haunted house."

"If that's what you want to call it," she replied, her humor slowly fading. "Sometimes I think I'm just going crazy. None of this is real. It can't be."

His mouth quirked in a cocky grin. "Let me assure you that I am one-hundred percent real."

She started to laugh but was cut off by Alex's chipper voice. "We're all real, baby."

He wandered into the kitchen, Jackie at his side. They both leaned over the kitchen island, looking right at home. Grace tried to get over how weird it felt.

"Sorry if we woke you," Grace said, attempting a smile. "I

couldn't sleep."

"I conked out." Alex shot a look at Jackie. "Even with all the pretty ladies in the house, you couldn't keep me from my beauty sleep."

Jackie leaned into him and her teeth flashed in a warm, lazy smile. "The house is calm now. They're letting us rest."

"They have us right where they want us," Ian realized, meeting eyes with Alex. "We were brought here for a reason. It's important that we finish this the right way."

"Do we have to talk about it right now?" Alex stretched and yawned, his left arm slipping around Jackie's waist casually. "Let's enjoy this. You got anything other than wine in that fridge?"

Grace turned and opened the fridge door, grabbing a bottle of silver tequila. She eyed it strangely, wondering who brought it over. "Looks like I do."

"Break out the glasses, let's toast to something," Alex decided, glancing down at Jackie. "What should we toast to?"

Jackie considered his request as Grace passed out glasses and Ian poured a double shot of tequila into each one. When she spoke again, she looked to Grace and held up her glass. "To new friends. And soon, to new beginnings."

"Amen to that," Alex cheered, tapping his glass against the others and knocking back the shot.

Grace swallowed and set her glass down, distracted by how close Ian was standing to her. It worried her that she liked it so much. She knew it was a dangerous path to take, one she had no business pursuing.

"I have a deck of cards," she suggested, shrugging it off even as Alex and Jackie perked up excitedly. Even Ian nudged her with a knowing grin, pleased to see her attempt to enjoy herself.

"Good way to practice that humility, Doc," he murmured

with a wink as he brushed past her to take a seat at the dining table. She stared after him, the tequila loosening her reserve.

Hell, maybe a little fun wouldn't hurt. Didn't they always say that life was short?

* * *

The sun rose over the harbor and beat back the fog. It filtered in through the haze and lit up the living room, glowing over Jackie's eyes. She inhaled slowly, deeply, as she awoke, her lips curving at the sound of Alex's snores. The inner peace and comfort she felt flowed over her, encasing her in a welcoming cocoon. She felt right in this place, with these people. She may not be like them, but somehow, she felt connected to them. Like she was meant to be in the Sparrow House.

Within moments, the peace was disturbed like a ripple in a pool of water. She felt a presence beside her and opened her eyes.

The little girl stood beside the sofa, dressed all in white with her golden hair curled around her cherub face. Jackie felt no fear, no apprehension. She only felt curiosity and intrigue.

Jackie sensed the girl's insistence, her desire to show something to her. She sat up slowly and allowed her to lead the way through the house.

They walked into the entryway, and the girl paused beneath the balcony. She stared up at the banister, and Jackie followed her gaze. That was when she noticed the ghostly mirage of broken shards of the railing as though someone had fallen through. Her eyes drifted to the floor, and she saw the spreading pool of blood accompanied by the broken body of a tiny girl.

Sorrow pierced through her heart as she regarded the girl beside her. She understood how the girl had died, and now the pain, the grief, the misery that flowed through the house all made sense. She could feel the panic and disbelief the mother had felt upon finding her daughter. The anger and despair of the father as he listened to his wife's cries of anguish.

It all rushed at her in pulsating waves, nearly bringing her to her knees. But she fought to stand strong, to stay in her own mind and body, as her gaze swept the entryway around her.

The walls were covered, floor to ceiling, in large, scribbled writing that repeated itself over and over. It said: *My Little Sparrow.*

The words glowed white over darkened walls as though imprinted on the surface by a whisper, by a source of light in a world of darkness. Jackie looked back down at the girl and saw tears flowing down her cheeks. She said nothing, but Jackie understood that the girl knew it was her father who had left the messages for her. Her father who came to the house searching, desperate to be reunited with his daughter.

But something stood in their way.

Heartbroken, Jackie knelt and met the girl's eyes, attempting a smile. This was why she was here, to save the child from the monster.

"Jackie?" Alex stepped into the room, worried to see her crouched in the entryway alone.

Jackie looked at him, and her smile faltered as fresh tears fell from her eyes. Before she could speak, spots swam over her vision, making her dizzy. Her legs gave out, dropping her to the wood floor.

As she crumpled, Alex rushed forward to help her. "What's wrong? Are you okay?"

She nodded, but sobs ached in her throat and her body weakened from the rushing onslaught of grief. The grief of parents who had lost their only child, and the torment of the daughter who desperately wanted to find them in death.

She was suddenly grateful for Alex's presence. For his acceptance. Never had she met anyone who accepted what she was, and what she saw, so easily.

Her voice was breathy, anxious, as she spoke. "I know what happened."

"Tell me." Alex loosened his protective grip on her arms, concerned at how the visions weakened her and sorry there was so little he could do to help.

Jackie sighed, releasing the worst of the emotional energy from her body. She brushed aside the tears and met his eyes. "The little girl died right here after falling from the balcony. Her father has been searching for her for so long. He writes his pet name for her on the walls, hoping she will see it. But the monster is keeping them apart..."

Alex instinctually stared at the walls, though he could see nothing but white plaster. "What does it say?"

"My little sparrow, over and over again..." Jackie said softly, reaching up with her right hand to lightly touch Alex's face, to turn him back to her. She needed the physical contact to bring her back to reality, away from the little girl's nightmarish existence.

The urge to kiss him flooded her senses as she stared into the soothing grass green of his eyes, and she realized it was the perfect solution. "Don't read too much into this, please." She leaned in and pressed her lips to his, craving the distraction the kiss offered. Her intent had been one of innocence, but she realized her mistake the instant he responded to her.

At first, only shock registered in his brain. Then urgency blasted through it, taking the lead. He framed her face with his hands and deepened the kiss, his mouth roaming over hers with a vibrant heat and eagerness she hadn't been expecting.

All thoughts successfully fled her mind as she held onto him, embracing the thrill like it was her last. For all she knew, it could be. And she was never one to not enjoy a thrill when it presented itself.

When he released her, her eyes fluttered open lazily, her

lips still parted. He thought she looked like a beautiful, stunning miracle. His mouth spread in a crooked grin. "I think we should do that more often."

She burst into laughter, shaking with it as she rested her head against his shoulder and savored the feeling of his arms around her. It was such a comfort to be with him, unlike anything she had ever experienced. Part of her wished it never had to end, but in her heart, she knew it did. Nothing was ever permanent in her life, except her faith and her own spirit. People came and went, that was just how it was. He would be no different.

For that reason, she knew she had to keep things casual.

"I'm going to make breakfast, and then we can talk about Sally."

"Who's Sally?" Alex asked as Jackie rose to her feet.

She smiled at him, her eyes still wet with tears. "The little sparrow."

* * *

"She died in the house?" Grace frowned, fork filled with scrambled eggs held just before her mouth. She lowered it, suddenly not feeling hungry. "That's…morbid."

"It was a tragic accident," Jackie affirmed, slathering jelly on a piece of wheat toast. "But a tragedy nonetheless."

Ian looked thoughtful. "If we can find out more information on who these other spirits are then we might figure out what they want and why they're here."

"Yeah, we need to figure out who the woman was that got tortured in the basement," Alex added. "And who the bastard was that hurt her."

"Well, we can look through those photographs again and see if we find anything," Grace offered, earning an appreciative smile from Jackie.

"That's a splendid idea."

Ian eyed her curiously. "This is strange coming from you.

Are you sure you're feeling okay? Did you hit your head?"

Grace shot him a heated look. "Humility, remember?"

He looked impressed and patted her hand cheerfully. "Good. Well, I think you and I should take a trip down to the local courthouse and see what records they have on the house and who lived here. We have one name now, Sally. Let's find out more about her."

She nearly choked on her eggs. "Seriously? That sounds like a lot of work."

"What, do you have something better to do?"

She swallowed with a frown. "I figured you guys would want to do another investigation or something."

"We will, but not today. I want to learn more about the house before we go any further."

Grace sighed, but felt herself giving in. "Fine. Just let me go shower." She got up from the table, dumped her plate in the sink, and disappeared upstairs.

Ian noticed Alex watching him with a goofy grin. "What?"

"You really are hot for the doctor, aren't you?"

Ian's eyes narrowed as Jackie giggled. "I'm hot for the investigation. And just because we're friends doesn't mean I won't kick your ass."

Alex held his hands up in peace. "Hey, I'm just calling it as I see it."

"Sure, you are." Ian got up and left the room, irritated that it was so obvious. What the hell was wrong with him? She was a hot mess of problems and ridiculously high maintenance. Not to mention she was the queen of skeptics, in denial about anything and everything that was happening to them. How could he ever enjoy the company of a woman like that?

But the truth was, he did. He didn't like to admit it, but he knew there was something about her that drew him in, snared like a worm on a hook. Which was probably exactly what he'd be if she sunk her claws into him. The woman was insane, out of her mind delusional and riddled with more emotional problems than an episode of Dr. Phil. No one had time to deal with someone like that. Much less him.

He waited for her in the entryway, brooding in silence. When she eventually came down the stairs, he glanced up and faltered at the sight of her. The sun poured in from the windows, glowing over her face and bringing out the chestnut in her hair that hung loose to her shoulders. She'd slipped into faded jeans and a comfortable, white button up top with the sleeves casually rolled up. Gray eyes regarded him with the slightest hint of insecurity, of hesitation.

In that instant, he realized that she really was beautiful. A troubled, haunted sort of beauty, but beauty all the same.

Damn her for it.

Grace came down the last step, one eyebrow lifted. "What's your problem?"

"Nothing. Let's go."

He tried not to touch her as he opened the front door and ushered her through, grumbling under his breath as they headed to the van. Grace climbed into the passenger seat and folded her hands awkwardly in her lap, unsure what to do with them.

When he hopped into the driver's seat, he seemed to lighten up a bit.

"If you're nice, maybe I'll take you out to lunch," he told her as he started up the van and pulled out onto the street.

Grace tried not to smile and failed. "Don't you mean if *you're* nice, I will *let* you take me out to lunch?" She shifted in her seat so she could see him better. "Don't forget that I can still pull the plug on all of this."

"But you won't," Ian replied confidently.

"Once again, you sound so damn sure of yourself," she mused, poking him in the shoulder with her index finger. "That head of yours is so big I'm surprised you fit in the car."

"Coming from the woman with an attitude the size of a city bus."

She smiled. "I have no regrets."

He looked at her, more amused than he wanted to admit. "I have a feeling you'll turn that attitude around once we get some answers on the house."

"If we even find anything."

Moments later, they pulled into the parking lot of the courthouse. She eyed the ornate government building in irritation, part of her hoping their search proved fruitless just so she could shove it back in his smug face.

Ian parked the van and hopped out, making his way up the steps without even waiting for her.

She scrambled out of the vehicle and slammed the door shut, her temper sparking as he raced off. "Why'd you even drag me along if you're just going to leave me behind?"

Ian pulled open the large wooden door of the building, motioning for her to get inside. "Hurry up."

She shot him an annoyed look as she passed over the threshold, upset that he could mess with her temper that easily.

"Where to?" She eyed the high-ceilinged, grand hall of a room that had a small reception desk off to the side and several doors lining the beautifully painted walls.

Ian asked the receptionist for directions and then took off again, leaving Grace to race after him. They ended up inside a library with historical town records stored in small file cabinets and in books on numerous wooden shelves. In the middle of the room was a row of empty tables.

Without a word, Ian went to a specific shelf and began pulling down oversized books, handing them to Grace. She awkwardly tried to balance them in her arms and ended up toppling them onto one of the tables.

With a grunt, she sat down and waited for Ian to join her. At last, he took a seat and reached for the first book.

"These are the property records. It should show the transfer of the title on the house over the years, who owned it originally, and who it was passed on to," he explained, thumbing through the pages eagerly.

Grace rested her chin in the palm of her hand and watched him, sarcasm in full swing. "Fascinating."

Ian ignored her as he found the right page and scanned the addresses. "Here it is."

"What does it say?"

Ian's eyes narrowed. "First evidence of title was in January of 1860 when the house was built. A man named Francis Lockwood owned it. Then in June of 1866 the property was transferred over to a man named Carter Sullivan."

Grace blinked. "That's my last name."

"Odds are it was a distant relative of yours who tortured that woman in the basement," Ian theorized, watching her closely. He expected to see denial flash over her face, but instead she only sighed.

"Well, let's find out who this bastard is, then." Grace reached for another of the books marked as death records and began skimming through it, searching for her last name. Minutes later, she found out that Carter Sullivan had died in 1889 of tuberculosis. His wife died not long after of pneumonia.

Out of curiosity, she checked the records from 1865 to 1866. When she found the name Sally Lockwood, her heart fluttered with recognition and emotion. Was this the little girl who had died in her home? The girl who, according to the others, still resided there?

She started to show Ian, but instead closed the book and set it aside. She wasn't sure why, but she didn't want to talk about Sally at that moment. In an odd way, the subject was personal to her. Sharing it would only make it more real, and that thought terrified her.

She opened another book filled with scanned newspaper articles and tried not to let Sally's face creep into her mind.

An hour passed as they both did their own silent searching. When Ian suddenly tensed across the table, Grace perked up with interest. His hands gripped another book filled with newspaper clippings that the receptionist had suggested.

"What'd you find?"

Ian ignored her for a moment longer as he hurriedly scanned over the article, dated October 1912. Then he slapped the book down on the table and looked at her in triumph. "I think I found our tortured girl."

"Seriously?" Grace grabbed the book and skeptically read the headline of the article herself. "*Father and daughter disappear under suspicious circumstances. Police have no leads.*"

"There is no record of either of them being dead," Ian added, pointing to the death records book he had just referenced.

"Ray and Mercy Sullivan," Grace murmured, reading the names from the article. She looked at him. "Maybe the record just got lost."

"Unlikely." He flipped to another article written twenty years after the disappearances and began to read out loud. "*The greatest mystery to ever descend upon Mad Rock Harbor... Sparrow House remains empty, still no clues as to what happened to Ray Sullivan and his daughter, Mercy. The Sullivan family, in understandable fashion, avoids the house.*"

"So, what? You think he tortured and killed her in the basement, buried her, and then fled?"

Ian tossed the book aside. "That's a possibility. And when he died, he became trapped in the hell he had forced her to endure in life."

She shuddered involuntarily, the heavy weight of it all closing in on her. "*If* this is true, then what are we supposed to do to fix my house?"

A dark smile tightened his face. "We call him out by name, and we force him out."

Grace opened her mouth to speak, only to pause as Nellie entered the records room with a cheerful smile.

"I was wondering how long it would take you to come here," Nellie said brightly as she approached their table. She looked comfortable in her usual faded jeans and plaid button up shirt.

Seeing her neighbor cheered Grace more than she would have expected. "Ian thought we should do some research on the house and my family."

Nellie nodded approvingly at Ian. "That should be helpful. How did the investigation go last night? I've heard Halloween can be a flurry of activity."

"It can and was." Ian shut the book he was looking at and watched Nellie closely. "I'd hoped you'd come by and help us."

"Oh, I don't know what kind of help I'd be." Nellie waved the comment off with a laugh. "Besides, I didn't want to intrude on all the fun you young people were having."

One of Grace's eyebrows shot up. "Oh yes, fun," she mumbled sarcastically, though she caught Ian's eye and he grinned.

"Boatloads of fun." He rose to his feet and began gathering up the books. "But it's probably time we head back. I think we found what we came here for."

"I'm just heading to the market. Why don't you come with me and get something nice to cook for dinner tonight?"

"Are you going to come by for dinner?" Grace asked, rising from her chair to help Ian with the books.

Nellie shook her head. "Oh, no. I have so much to do at

home."

Grace's face fell, but she pushed aside her disappointment. "Okay. Hey, have you heard the story about Ray and Mercy Sullivan?"

"Of course, child. It's been a hundred years, but most of us in Mad Rock Harbor have heard that story."

Ian replaced the books on the shelves and came up beside Grace. "What's the story?"

An odd eagerness brightened Nellie's features. "They say he used to beat the poor girl senseless after her mother died. No one wanted to intervene, so they let her suffer for ten long years. Then one day, they both disappeared into thin air. Neither of them were ever seen again."

"What do you think happened to them?" Grace crossed her arms, feeling a sudden chill.

Nellie smiled sadly. "Can't say. But one thing's for certain...they're both dead now." She patted Grace on the shoulder and left the room.

Grace released a long, tired breath, and looked up at Ian. "Does something seem off about her to you?"

He shrugged, his expression troubled. "Not really. But I don't know her as well as you do."

"And even I don't know her very well," Grace agreed, still feeling cold. She rubbed her arms and started for the door. "Whatever, let's go back. At least we have something to go on now."

CHAPTER ELEVEN

S o, where are you from?"

"Earth." Jackie tossed a tennis ball across the grassy area behind the Sparrow House, smiling as Gatsby chased after it on short, stubby legs. He kicked up dry leaves as he went, releasing the scent of autumn into the air. Nearby, the cool water of the harbor lapped ashore, the hazy rays of the afternoon sun shimmering over its surface.

"Oh, that's funny, I thought you were a fellow Martian like me." Alex tucked his hands into his jeans pockets, unable to take his eyes off her. Her body was draped in a cotton dress that hugged her waist and tied at her neck, her shoulders and arms covered in a burgundy wool sweater. Though they were surrounded by autumn on the Eastern Seaboard, the cerulean blue color of her dress reminded him of the warm waters of the Caribbean. As did her exotic scent of burnt sugar and the dark honey of her eyes that seemed to stare right past the skin of his face and into the recesses of his mind.

She smiled at him, and he got the sense she knew exactly what he was thinking. "Would you like me to be a Martian?"

Gatsby bounded up to her and dropped the ball at her feet. She bent down for the ball and tossed it again, her laughter filling the air as she watched him dart off.

Alex watched the dog get distracted by a bird, leaving the forgotten ball behind. "Do you have a job? A family? Friends?"

"You're my friend, aren't you?" she asked, winking at him before suddenly kicking off her shoes and bolting toward the harbor. She laughed as she dipped her toes in the water, enjoying the sharp, frigid bite and the shiver it sent along her skin.

Alex let out an unsteady breath as he watched the sun flicker off the rippling water, setting her aflame with light. She'd floated in like a renegade leaf riding the wind to more exciting places than the tree she must have once called home. Why he was obsessed with learning the truth about her past, he wasn't sure. Perhaps he knew it would validate her existence somehow, prove that she was human and not a mirage that would soon slip through his grasp.

A mirage that radiated joy, spontaneity, mystery...

Jackie returned to the shore, embracing Gatsby as he joined her by the water.

Alex approached, unwilling to let her dodge his questions again. "What's it like to see spirits everywhere?"

Jackie's smile softened, and she rose to her feet as she considered. "Chaotic."

"How so?"

She bit her bottom lip, wondering how she could explain it. "I suppose it's like being at an amusement park. There's this rush of people going every which way, lost in their own minds, their own agendas. Some of them stand around motionless, caught in the moment, others press onward even though there's no place to go. There's the pushy vendors, vying for your attention, desperate to make contact. They know they can get something out of you if they can just catch your eye. And then there's the rides, and the helpless screams of the people trapped on them. Sometimes it's impossible to make sense of anything else with all the screaming..."

Sadness shadowed her face, a lifetime of experiencing death's despair weighing down upon her. She tried to brush it off, but it radiated off her.

Alex reached out, pulling her into his arms. She welcomed the warmth he offered, even as she regretted it couldn't be more.

"You are the most fascinating person I have ever met," he said quietly, trying to put humor in his voice to keep the situation lighthearted. But he knew she could see past his act. Her emotions, her words, troubled him more than he cared to admit. How she remained so carefree and compassionate despite the horrors she must see every day astonished him.

Jackie let the soft cotton of his shirt caress her cheek, the top of her head barely reaching his chin. He smelled of warm pancake syrup and Old Spice, a combination she assumed most people would associate with home. For now, she could pretend that she did too.

She tilted her head back to look at him and placed a soft kiss on his lips. It was meant to be friendly, but what she told herself in her head negated what she felt in her heart.

When he pulled her in closer and crushed her mouth with his, she felt her limbs go weak with the exhilaration of it. The madness. That stunning spark of lust, of joy, of romance that she craved the way a drunk yearns for that hot kick of whiskey. She'd never been shy to the art of chemistry, of attraction. When she wanted someone, she made no secret of it.

She didn't know why part of her screamed that this time

it was different. This time was not going to be as simple as the others. Alex could never be simple. But maybe that was what she desired the most.

She whispered his name, her hands trailing up to take hold of his shirt and clutch him against her possessively. Her mind spun with wild ideas of his warm, naked skin against her own and of the feel of his hands claiming her.

She knew she could have that. It would be easy, effortless. But would it be right?

She broke the kiss, but kept her eyes on his as she pulled away. A smile curved over her lips, teasing and lighthearted. "They raise good kissers in Washington," she said, distancing herself from him as casually as she could and tossing the ball once again for Gatsby.

Alex watched her wander off, stunned by the abrupt change of mood. As the shock wore off, delight at the challenge took its place.

She wasn't going to get away so easily. He wouldn't let her. He didn't care if he had to beg, borrow, and steal his way into her heart.

It was going to happen, one way or another. His mother hadn't raised a quitter.

* * *

That evening, Grace disappeared upstairs to change into more comfortable clothes. She could hear her new friends through the poorly insulated floor—Jackie's lilting laughter, Alex's punchy jokes, Ian's dry comebacks.

She closed her eyes, enjoying the sounds and the feeling of having people with her who knew nothing of who she was and nothing of what had happened to her. Jackie claimed to know, but she hadn't mentioned it again so that was as good as not knowing.

It was comforting to not have to pretend to be okay. To

not have people looking over their shoulders at her, waiting for her to burst into tears or shatter like a broken vase. The three strangers downstairs didn't expect that of her.

All they wanted was a chance to help her; a chance to learn the truth about her family. It was still odd to her that anyone would bother helping the way they were. Even though Ian and Alex had something to gain by investigating the house, they were still spending more time there than they needed to. They could have just left the first night with their EVPs and strange temperature readings and called it quits. But they didn't. They stayed.

And Jackie and Nellie…neither had any business bothering with her. They could have simply continued with their lives as if Grace didn't exist. Certainly, Grace had tried to convince them both to do just that.

But they hadn't. Did that make them true friends? She considered the people she called friends back home, those who felt so lost to her now. She hadn't contacted any of them in weeks, hadn't even thought about them. The memory of that life seemed so foreign to her, as if it was someone else's past and not her own.

This house, these people, this town…this was her life now. As were the *ghosts* that apparently haunted her.

With a heavy sigh, she slipped on comfy black pajama pants and a faded Led Zeppelin T-shirt before making her way downstairs. As she came into the kitchen, she spotted Ian at the stove with Alex and Jackie standing hip-to-hip at the kitchen island, Gatsby asleep on the floor nearby. She watched curiously as Jackie ran her hand lazily up Alex's back, the move flirty and affectionate. When Alex tilted his head down to look at her, the spark in his eyes said it all.

Grace pondered this as she walked over to Ian, feeling uncomfortable. Alex was a really nice guy. Didn't he see that

Jackie wasn't the kind of girl that stuck around? It was obvious to Grace that the second the wind blew in Jackie would drift away. If Alex got his feelings tied up in her he would only be left to disappointment.

Then again, why the hell did she care? It wasn't her problem.

But part of her envied the easy affection they had for each other. And the other half of her pitied them for it. Love, lust... it only led to heartache. That little lesson she had learned many times over.

When she came up beside Ian, she fell out of her thoughts and back into reality, her eyes meeting his. The corner of his mouth lifted into a sly smile, and she caught herself enjoying the look of it way too much.

"What're we having?" she asked, peering into the pot he was busy stirring.

"Gumbo." He spooned up a small amount and held it for her to sip.

She leaned closer and blew away the steam, her gaze intent on his.

His breath caught in his throat as he watched her cautiously take a sip, her eyes fluttering closed as she savored it.

"Oh," she managed, straightening. She smiled wistfully, biting her lower lip as she met his eyes again. "Now *that's* incredible."

"Glad you like." He resisted the urge to touch her and instead went back to stirring. "Why don't you grab some bowls?"

She nodded and shot a look over at Alex and Jackie, who had somehow managed to get even closer to each other, their faces nearly touching as they laughed and murmured things she couldn't hear.

Ian saw what she was staring at and leaned to whisper in her ear. "Alex may be a geek, but he's always been a ladies' man."

"And her?" Grace wondered, disapproval creasing her brow. "It just seems so…juvenile."

Ian shrugged. "We need her. If the only reason she sticks around is him then I'm all for it."

"She's going to break his heart," Grace realized, unsure why the thought bothered her so much.

"He'll be fine. He's a big boy." Ian turned back to the stove, once again battling the desire to touch her. She had that sad, troubled look in her eyes again, the one that meant she was overthinking things. But he knew there were more important problems to worry about than Alex's crush on Jackie.

Grace grabbed four bowls from the cabinet, setting them beside Ian so he could spoon soup into them.

"I wonder if Ray knows that we're onto him," Alex said to Jackie.

She seemed less amused than he was. "He most certainly knows."

A series of long footsteps echoed from upstairs, thudding hollowly over the ceiling above them. All eyes shot upward as the footsteps came to a sudden halt near the second-floor balcony.

Gatsby awoke with a start and growled. Ian looked to Alex for a quick confirmation that they had both heard it and, without a word, both men darted toward the stairs. Grace hovered by the stove, unable to move as uncertainty froze her in place.

Jackie stayed by the island, her hands twisting together in front of her. "He's angry." Her eyes closed as she absorbed the vibes coming from the spirit. Vibes of malicious intent. Fear licked at her insides as she fought the urge to panic.

Grace looked to her anxiously. "It was probably just old pipes rattling around."

Jackie released an unsteady breath. "Something bad is

coming..."

Ian and Alex came back into the kitchen, both looking agitated.

"We didn't see anything upstairs. Nothing that could have made the sound," Ian said, running a hand through his hair. His blood was pumping a mile a minute, making him restless and uneasy.

"It could've been the pipes," Grace repeated, clinging to the explanation like a life raft.

Alex leaned over the kitchen island again. "All I know is that I mentioned Ray's name and then bam! There were footsteps. Some coincidence. Huh, Grace?"

She frowned at him, clutching her chest to ward off the cold she felt. "Whatever, let's just—"

Gatsby let out a panicked bark, then a low whine. A second later the old grandfather clock burst to life, despite having been disabled days earlier. It gonged six times to announce the hour. They all stared at it, wide-eyed, as the bellowing sound resonated throughout the first floor.

Jackie felt a tickle on the back of her neck, and shifted her eyes from the clock to the entryway. A startled yelp burst from within her throat.

Alex jolted as though hit by a spark of electricity. "What is it? What do you see?"

She pointed, though she knew they wouldn't see what she saw. At least, she didn't think they would. Her eyes were glassy with shock as she tried to find her voice. "She's being chased! He's going after her!"

She ran out of the kitchen and followed Sally, Gatsby bolting after her. The world seemed to move slowly, as though surrounded by an invisible shield of water. She wasn't meant to interfere, and the shadowy mass that flickered menacingly in the air behind Sally wanted to remind her of that. It abruptly abandoned its pursuit of Sally and made a dash toward Jackie.

Gatsby started barking and growling, though nothing could deter the monster. Both Ian and Alex saw it this time now that its intention was to hurt the living. Alex grabbed Jackie and forced her to the floor, while Ian jumped out of the way and let the shadow shoot past him and straight into the basement door.

Grace burst into the room, alarmed. "Are you all right? What happened?"

Ian was leaning up against the wall, panting. He shot her a dark look. "We just got a glimpse of Ray."

"All three of you?" Grace gaped, watching helplessly as Alex helped Jackie stand up. Gatsby whimpered beside her.

Alex nodded in her direction. "Yep. Dude, that was intense."

Ian patted him on the shoulder as he met eyes with Jackie. "Are you okay?"

Jackie nodded, shaking as she lifted Gatsby into her arms. "Sally managed to get away. That's what matters."

"Where did she go?" Alex asked.

"Into the walls…she's learned how to hide from him."

"We should have recorded that." Ian slapped his hand against the wall angrily, cursing himself for not thinking of it before. "That was one of the clearest shadow figures I have ever seen."

"We weren't expecting it," Alex reminded him. "It'll be back. Right?"

He looked down at Jackie, who nodded solemnly. "He's not done with us yet."

Grace crossed her arms, unsure what to make of the situation. How come she hadn't seen this shadow? Suspicion reared its ugly head and cloaked her in distrust. "I didn't see anything."

Ian glared at her. "You're not open to it. Until you are,

don't expect to see anything."

"Well, how can I be open to it if I don't see it?" Grace argued, exasperated. "All I've had to go on regarding these *ghosts* are Jackie's hallucinations, the voices out of your devices, and random door slams and footsteps. But all of that can be explained away with reason."

"Reason?" Ian shook his head, still riding on the anger of having missed the opportunity to capture the shadow on film. "You can use your science as a crutch all you want, Doc. But it won't protect you from this. These spirits *will* harm you."

Grace rolled her eyes. "What're they going to do? Give me goosebumps?"

"Nellie was pushed by him!" Ian reminded her, cobalt eyes aflame. "Or do you not believe that happened, either?"

Grace pouted, but stood her ground. "Nellie's an old woman who was probably having a bad case of vertigo."

"Goddamnit," Ian cursed under his breath, turning away from her with his hands in his hair. He knew he had to calm himself before he went after her again. If only she wasn't so insufferably ignorant.

Alex eyed Ian anxiously before looking to Grace. "Why don't we just eat dinner and get some rest?"

"I'm not hungry." Grace pushed past them and went upstairs, angry with herself and angry with all of them.

But, perhaps, most upset that she hadn't seen tangible proof of what her new life revolved around—proof of the paranormal.

* * *

Grace awoke the next morning with the sound of footsteps echoing in her mind. For a split second, she imagined Ian outside her bedroom door, coming to apologize. Or to fight some more, maybe. He was irritated with her, though she didn't blame him. She would be irritated with her, too.

But then she remembered the footsteps from the night

before and fear raced into her system. She jolted out of sleep, sweat beading on her forehead as her eyes immediately went to the door.

The house around her was quiet. The footsteps had likely only been a dream.

A relieved breath rushed out of her lungs and her hand came up to her furiously beating heart. What a fool she was being, succumbing to nightmares. Her entire life that had never happened to her, not even as a child. Was it the house that was doing it? Or was it the depression, the grief?

She had avoided sleeping pills thus far, but maybe it was time to give them a try. Anything to quell the bad dreams, the voices, the footsteps…

Outside her window, the fog pressed in and blocked out all sights, all sound. Even the birds seemed to have taken the day off, and the gentle breeze she'd become accustomed to off the harbor had fled. It appeared the world outside wanted to be as haunted as her home, as her soul.

There would be no escaping it today.

Her body ached from poor sleep as she sat up and stretched, brushing her bangs back from her face. She got to her feet, slipped into her robe, and walked to the window.

She might as well have been looking out at nothing. A blank screen of gray.

The urge for coffee snuck in and pestered her brain, driving her downstairs and into the kitchen to brew a pot. She found the others still sleeping. For a moment she hesitated, eyeing Ian's sleeping form with both regret and insecurity.

Would he forgive her? Why did it matter to her so much that he did?

Emotions stirred within her that only brought misery, so she fought them back and went to work brewing coffee. As it steamed and bubbled out of the machine, she grabbed four mugs and the makings for pancakes. Perhaps she could win them back with food.

When there was just enough coffee brewed for one cup, she poured it and enjoyed it black. The piercing bitterness of it jolted through her system and warmed her.

She got out a mixing bowl and measured out the ingredients for the pancakes. She tried to remain as quiet as she could, hoping to wake them with the smell and not the sound.

Realizing she couldn't have pancakes without some bacon, she carefully rummaged through the fridge and found some. As she straightened and shut the door, she heard a soft scratching noise coming from the French doors that opened to the back porch.

Her eyes shot toward the sound, panic darting through her. When she saw a small sparrow fluttering outside, its wings and feet hitting the glass with urgency, she nearly dropped the package of bacon she held.

Not again. Why wouldn't the sparrows just leave her alone?

She tried to ignore it and shakily sipped some more of her coffee, only to hear the bird scratching once again. Now she was angry. It was going to wake the others before she even had a chance to get food cooking, ruining her plan to make peace with them.

She stepped quietly as she made her way to the door, hoping to scare away the bird. When she was a foot away the bird shot off into the fog.

Grace started to head back into the kitchen, but froze when the fog parted just enough for a glimpse of the harbor and the lonely dock. On a normal day, this wouldn't have alarmed her. But today was not a normal day.

A body slumped lifelessly at the end of the dock, dark and indiscernible. Grace's heart leapt into her throat as she stared at it, squinting her eyes to debunk it as just a jacket or a blanket or an animal…

When she noticed Nellie's gray curly hair, true panic tore through her in one, violent swipe. She gasped and ripped open the door, not caring how loudly it slammed as she ran barefoot onto the grassy slope.

The second she made it to the end of the dock, she stumbled to her knees, her hands on Nellie as she turned the older woman onto her back. One look at Nellie's cold, ashen face, and Grace knew she was dead. On instinct, she checked for a pulse, feeling nothing.

"No." Tears pooled in Grace's eyes as her hands fluttered over Nellie's body helplessly, her well-trained physician's mind searching for a cause, for a reason, for a solution…

But there was none to be found. There were no marks on the woman's body, no cuts, no bruises. Whatever had killed her had likely been internal. Unnoticeable. Likely sudden.

Grief consumed her as she stared down at her friend's lifeless body, the loss bringing back all the pain of losing her parents. It encased her in an icy cocoon of shock, and all she could do was crumble to the soft wood of the dock and let it devour her.

"Grace!" Ian's voice broke through the haze of despair, but she didn't have the strength to address it. Instead, she covered her face with her hands and gave in to the pain.

More footsteps pounded over the ground as Alex and Jackie followed Ian to the dock, the three of them in shock at seeing Nellie's lifeless form.

"I'll call an ambulance," Jackie said before racing back to the house.

Grace knew it was too late for that. Hell, she'd known the second she spotted the body. Death was something she had long been familiar with. Though she'd always thought she was protected from the emotional aftereffects of it—the sorrow, the anguish. Until death had claimed someone she cared about. That was when everything had changed.

That was when *she* had changed.

And this new loss hurt no less than the last one. She hadn't toughened from the experience. If anything, she had only weakened. Weakened into a completely unrecognizable shadow of who she once was.

Ian's arms came around her as he lifted her to her feet. "Let's go inside."

She had trouble getting her feet to function properly, her mind slow and thick. But she held onto him, letting his supporting arms give her comfort. She hadn't realized just how badly she needed it.

While Jackie and Alex dealt with calling the ambulance, Ian brought Grace upstairs to her room. He lowered her onto the bed and sat beside her, slipping his hand into hers.

Soundless tears slid down her cheeks, her eyes wide open and glassy. She stared at the fog out the window, still in disbelief that Nellie was gone. That same, familiar grief trickled back into her soul, destroying her.

One more person she cared about was dead. Lost to the world, lost to her. Even though she'd only known Nellie a few weeks, the woman had made an impression on her. She had burrowed her way into Grace's life as though she wanted to be a permanent part of it.

But now she wouldn't be. Grace realized she was just one death closer to being all alone.

Ian watched her, alarmed by her silence. If she was rioting with emotion on the inside, he couldn't see it. All he saw was the shell of a woman who felt nothing. He thought he knew her better than to assume she wasn't experiencing an explosion of pain.

He could hear the EMTs arrive downstairs and Alex's voice as he showed them outside.

A flicker of pain passed over Grace's face at the sounds, and Ian saw her marble façade begin to crack.

"These things happen," he said lamely, unsure how to help her. He tried squeezing her hand, but she only pulled away and got up, avoiding his eyes.

"I know." She wandered to the window, hoping to see them take Nellie away. The fog had cleared up just enough for her to see the ghosted figures of the men outside, and she gave herself the closure of watching the deed be completed.

Ian rose as well, stuffing his hands into the pockets of his jeans. "Can I get you anything?"

"I'd like the three of you to leave me alone for now," Grace said, the decision instant and final.

Ian nodded. "Okay. We'll go back to the library, do some more research."

"Don't come back." She wrapped her arms around her chest tightly to keep her body from shattering to pieces. Cold settled over her, but she embraced it. It was an old, familiar feeling.

Ian's brow creased in confusion. "Ever?"

She let out a long, slow breath, unable to look at him. "For now. I can't do this anymore."

He started to argue with her, to tell her she wasn't thinking straight, wasn't being reasonable. But he held his tongue, knowing it wasn't his place to force her. If she wanted him gone, he'd go. His pride wouldn't allow him to beg.

"Okay." He slowly backed out of the room, hoping she'd change her mind. When she didn't, he stood in the doorway and fought back the dark feelings of abandonment. "I'll see you around, Doc."

She listened to him go and struggled to convince herself that this was for the best. That being alone was the one and only way for her to survive.

Then the only death she'd have to mourn would be her own.

CHAPTER TWELVE

You have my number. Call me if you need me." Jackie raised her right hand in a salute as she climbed into her Jeep, Gatsby at her side.

"Don't you disappear on me," Alex called out, waving goodbye.

She sent him a wistful smile and a wink as she put the Jeep in drive and took off.

Above, the clouds were ominous in the sky, threatening rain. Ian looked at the oncoming storm, feeling restless. "I got the last of our equipment from upstairs. We might as well hit the road. We can check out of the hotel tomorrow morning."

Alex turned to him. "You're not serious about leaving town, are you?"

"Of course I am." Ian rounded the front of the van and hopped into the driver's seat. When Alex joined him inside,

Ian flipped on the radio and tapped the steering wheel with his hands impatiently. "She wants us gone. So, I'm out."

"She wanted us gone before and you insisted on staying," Alex pointed out.

Ian shrugged. "That was different. Death does things to people; it changes them. She said she wants to be alone, so I'm not going to force myself on her."

They pulled onto the road and drove the short distance to the hotel in silence. When they arrived, they left the majority of their equipment in the van, removing only their duffle bags of clothes.

"I don't know, man. I just don't feel right about it," Alex said as he plopped down on the bed he hadn't slept in for days. He flipped on the television and stared at it blankly. His friend disappeared into the bathroom without a word and, within seconds, the hiss of the shower could be heard over the din of the television.

Ian set out to scrub away all remnants of the Sparrow House, both physically and emotionally. He didn't want to even hear the name Grace for the next few weeks. If he did, he knew he'd picture her face, and that would only irritate him.

He'd made his decision to honor her wishes. That was the gallant thing to do. She should be eternally grateful to him for abandoning an investigation and granting her alone time when there was still evidence to capture and spirits to deal with. God knew she was going to have a hell of a time dealing with it all on her own.

Thankfully, it was no longer his problem. He was determined to saddle up and move on to bigger and better things, and forget all about Dr. Grace Sullivan and those haunting eyes of hers.

Hours later, he lay in bed staring at the popcorn ceiling of the hotel room, unable to rid his mind of her. Alex still had the television on, though he seemed distracted as well.

When Alex spoke, it was clear he wasn't going to let the situation go. "You need to go back there, man."

"No." Ian crossed his arms, shielding himself with pride and anger.

Alex faced him. "Don't tell me you're cool with leaving her all by herself in that house. After what we saw? After what we heard?"

Ian grimaced, guilt seeping through his veins. "Why me? You can go."

"She's closest with you."

"I'd say she never wanted to get close to any of us."

"Will you just go so I can get some fucking sleep?" Alex fired back.

Ian looked at his friend. "Why can't you just let it go?"

"Because unlike you, I give a shit about other people."

Ian gave in to his own temper as he sat up. "If I go over there, I'll just be wasting my time. She wants to be alone."

"Nobody *really* wants to be alone, Ian." Alex shook his head tiredly, laying back on the bed and closing his eyes. "Just go. We'll both feel better about all of this if you do."

"Fine." Ian climbed out of bed and changed into a pair of jeans. "But if she chews me out, I'm blaming it all on you."

"Go for it." Alex waved him off, already falling asleep.

Grumbling under his breath, Ian slipped out of the hotel room and into the night. As he got into the van, a steady rain began to fall.

"Great." He sighed, flipping on the windshield wipers as he pulled onto the road.

* * *

For the first time in weeks, Grace found the courage to play her beloved cello.

She dragged a chair up from the kitchen and dropped it on

the floor of her bedroom, knowing it had to be there. If she was going to break free it needed to be in the one place that felt the most like home.

Outside, the rain turned into a steady downpour, dripping down the window pane like mournful tears. She lit a few candles and scattered them along the floor around her, needing their ambient glow. Somehow, she knew it would inspire the music just itching to be released from her system.

When she lifted the instrument from its protective case, she let her fingers trail over the glossy wood surface lovingly, reverently. She cradled it between her legs as she sat in the chair, one hand tenderly holding the bow, the other clutched purposefully along the strings. Raising her eyes to the rain, she began to play.

Softly, at first. The old, familiar feeling slowly returned to her limbs, her mind recalling the movements. Her arm shifted right and left with a steady elegance that produced the richest, most soulful sound. It sang through her ears like magic, and her broken, damaged heart filled with joy.

She felt a cool breeze circle around her, almost like a draft through a cracked window. Yet it seemed to have a mind of its own as it enveloped her in an almost comforting cocoon of energy, pulsating with life. The hairs on her arms stood up, goose bumps shivering along her skin. She stopped playing as her eyes widened, looking around the room wildly in search of what caused it. She saw nothing, but she certainly felt it.

A soft, childlike hand caressed the bare skin of her shoulder affectionately. She nearly jumped out of her chair, but something held her back, told her it was okay. To not be afraid.

She released an unsteady laugh as she clutched her cello, her heart racing with terror and exhilaration all at once.

When a few strings of her cello were plucked, creating an odd little sound, Grace nearly fainted. "Oh, my God," she gasped, shutting her eyes tight and biting her lower lip so hard it nearly bled. She had to keep from panicking; she had to remain calm.

Hadn't she wanted this? Hadn't she wanted proof?

"Sally..." Grace whispered, opening her eyes and staring around the room. She still saw nothing, but she knew she wasn't alone. She felt a few strands of her hair lift off her head, and tears suddenly spilled from her eyes. "I'm so sorry. So sorry I didn't believe in you..."

She thought she heard the distant sound of laughter and singing, hollow and surreal, and it only made her weep more. Riding on the discovery, on the stunning confirmation of her darkest hopes and fears, Grace poured her soul into the music. She sought the refuge it offered, and somewhere deep inside she knew Sally wanted her to play.

Somehow, she knew that Sally had always loved music.

She gave in to the urgency and played with a vibrant fervor that took her beyond her own body, her own life.

In those moments of such brilliant heartache, Grace became a believer.

* * *

When Ian arrived at the house, he paused before the front door. He started to knock, only to freeze as the door slowly swung open on its own. His eyes narrowed with suspicion as he gently pushed his way through, staring around the empty, dark entryway.

"Grace?"

That was when he heard the music.

He let out the breath he'd been holding, relief coursing through him. He started to leave, figuring if she was feeling up to playing her cello then she must be okay. But something stopped him, pulled him back.

The front door clicked shut as if pushed by an invisible

force. Then he felt something tugging at the bottom of his shirt, urging him toward the stairs. Fear rose in his throat, but he pushed it away, somehow reassured that it would be all right.

All he had to do was go upstairs.

The old wood creaked under his weight as he ascended the steps, consumed by the music. It echoed loudly through the house, deep and vibrant and filled with a sorrow so genuine it tore at his heart.

When he slipped into the bedroom and caught sight of her, he lost the ability to breathe.

Her back faced him as she furiously played, her entire body shifting with the movement as the music poured out of the instrument she held. The light of the candles flickered hauntingly over her skin as the rain pounded against the window.

He had never seen anything more powerful, more graceful, more emotionally charged than what he witnessed at that moment. She embodied all those things, and the fervor of her playing stunned him.

So much strength and sorrow. So much undeniable passion.

Her hair fell over her face as she let her head fall back, completely absorbed in the cello's evocative sound. She vaguely heard the footsteps behind her, and knew instantly it was him. She'd know his presence anywhere. He had returned, after all.

When his hand fell over her shoulder, she slowed her playing to a smoother, more soulful level. She heard Sally laughing once again and basked in the blissful sound of it as she brought the song she played to a close, ending on a soft, sweet note meant as a dedication to the little girl she never imagined she would believe existed.

For a moment, she let her heart and her breathing settle to a quiet calm. Then she tilted her head back and looked at him. "You came back."

The fragility in her eyes said it all.

Ian swallowed the lump in his throat and nodded, unsure what to say to her as she rose to her feet and set her cello against the wall.

"Will you sit with me?" she asked, motioning to the bed. He followed her and sat down, impossibly moved when she reached for his hand. She seemed so calm now, so open and vulnerable. The impact it had on him was extraordinary.

"You play really well."

Grace smiled. "I've been playing since I was a teenager."

"Your parents must be proud."

Sadness filled her, but she embraced the feeling with a growing strength and sense of closure. At last, she knew she could face the truth of what happened without fear of looking weak.

"They were…before they died." She watched the regret flash in his eyes and was sorry for it. She didn't want to burden him with the truth, but she knew he would want to hear it. "That's the real reason I came here. The real reason I left everything I had—everything I was—behind."

"Why didn't you tell me?"

Her gaze shifted to the window to watch the rain. "I didn't want anyone's pity. I had enough of that in Chicago."

He knew he would have felt the same way. "What happened to them?"

"Car accident." She closed her eyes briefly, then faced him unashamed as tears trailed down her cheeks. "They were all I had. Then I came here, and Nellie sort of became my family. And now that she's gone…I have no one."

"You have us," he reminded her, slipping his hand from hers and wrapping his arm around her instead. She rested her head on his shoulder, grateful for him.

For a while they said nothing, both enjoying the sound of the rain. When Grace spoke again, there was a deep regret in her voice. "I'm so sorry I doubted you."

His brows knit together as he gently ran his hand along her arm. "What do you mean?"

She pulled away from him, her eyes searching his. "Sally was in this room with me. She touched my shoulder and my hair, and I heard her laughing…Ian, I was so afraid, but I can't deny what I felt, what I heard. She needed me to believe in her, and now I do."

He smiled. "Welcome to the dark side, Doc."

She laughed even as more tears fell from her eyes. Tears of stunned relief. "I know, I know. I've been so stupid."

"You've been a skeptic, there's a difference." He brushed aside one of the tears, his hand cradling her cheek. "A small one, but a difference all the same. No one blames you for that."

"I do," she decided, leaning against his hand. "I still need some time alone…but I don't want you to leave for good." She pressed her lips softly against his palm, the act one of humility, of tenderness. "Just don't leave me tonight."

"I won't." He helped her lay down on the bed, cradling her in his arms. His mouth brushed over the back of her neck as he spoke. "Get some sleep."

She nodded, exhaustion overtaking her as her eyes fluttered closed. A soothing sense of contentment and relief washed over her, and she rode the wave of it into a deep, dreamless sleep.

* * *

"Where have you been going lately? I haven't seen you at all," Dominic complained, grabbing Jackie by the arm and dragging her against him. He lowered his head to kiss her, but she pushed him away.

"I told you, I'm helping my friends with a bad spirit." Jackie tried to free herself of his grasp but found he wasn't letting go. Her dark eyes shot to his in warning. "Let me go."

Dominic laughed and ignored her request. "You and your

spirits, Jackie. When are you going to give up on that?"

"The same day you throw out your needles." Fire sparked in her eyes, her usually placid temper set aflame. "Now let me go. I need to sleep."

"They kick you out, and you come crawling back here and I'm supposed to just *let* you in? You don't live here." Dominic backed off, wiping his nose with his forearm. He shot her a bitter glare. "You come and go like you've always done, figuring old Dominic will be here when you need me. What am I to you, anyway?"

She frowned, knowing in her heart that he was right. But then again, she was who she was. And she would change for no one.

"You're my *friend*," she began, reaching out for his hand so he would turn to face her. When their eyes met, she fell back on the same old words she always said to him. "I belong to everyone and no one at the same time, darling. You know that I can never stay."

He scowled. "Why not?"

"Because I can't. It's not who I am."

"Then who are you? Hell, we've been friends for years and I feel like I hardly know you, Jackie. You're like these spirits you spend so much time obsessing over. Hollow and nonexistent."

Tears of anger sprang into her eyes at his words. "How dare you."

"Oh, that's right. You don't like to talk about your past." He turned away and went to his dresser where his fix lay waiting. He began to prepare the needle as he spoke again. "Whatever. Why don't you go find a ghost to keep you company? You always preferred that."

She stared at his back, at the tanned skin, the dark tattoos threaded between the scar tissue of pain long past, the length of messy black hair. He had been her crutch in many ways for so many years, her fallback when she craved an anchor. She knew she had abused the kindness he once showed her, the trust he placed in her.

But the truth was she had to be free.

At that moment, however, she needed comfort. Comfort he couldn't give. Grace's dark grief plagued her even though she hadn't met the woman that died. It was the sort of heavy emotion that blasted through her weakened veil and infiltrated her senses, masking anything she may have felt of her own.

There was only one person who could distract her from the pain. Though she knew she would regret going to him and leading him on, she didn't care. He would just have to deal with the future when it came. Until then, she needed him.

She left without a word and fled the house. When she reached the hotel room where Alex and Ian were staying, she knocked lightly on the door and rested her palm over the painted white surface, praying he answered. Praying he was alone.

Alex opened the door, the soft light of the nightstand lamp glowing yellow behind him. The television was on though he looked like he had been asleep.

"Hey." He smiled sleepily, pleased to see her. "Is everything okay?"

Jackie nodded and stepped into the room when he shifted out of the way. "Where's Ian?"

"Went to see Grace a couple of hours ago. Not back yet." He stretched his arms over his head and settled down on the side of the bed. "You sure you're all right? You look upset."

She let out a soft sigh but met his eyes assuredly. "I'm fine. Now."

Without hesitation, she moved forward and cupped his face in her hands, lowering her lips to his. She kissed him lightly, sweetly, running her fingers through his waves of sandy hair. She breathed in the warm scent of his soap, of the beer he must have had before bed, of the minty toothpaste he used. She welcomed it all, everything he was, letting it be her refuge.

He was so kind, so gentle. Unlike anyone she had ever known. No wonder she felt such reprieve in his presence. He had this calming way about him that chased away the demons in her mind, making them cower in the corner like the horrors that they were.

When she was with him there was no suffering. There was only Alex.

His hands came up to grasp her waist, and the quiet strength of them sent her mind reeling with wild ideas. She felt all the grief, the pain, the tragedy slip away like grains of sand, lost to the brilliant spark of desire that replaced it. She brought her legs up and around him as she climbed into his lap, never breaking the kiss. Instead, she held on to him like a lifeline, absorbing the feel of his touch and the taste of his mouth. That was all that mattered now.

"Jackie…" He let her push him back onto the bed, his eyes finding hers. The intensity she saw in them sent shivers down her spine and a beautiful ache bloomed within her heart.

She placed a fingertip against his lips to quiet him, a slow smile curving over her own. Her hands slid under his shirt and urged it off him, revealing the warm skin underneath. She undid the dress she wore, lifting it over her head effortlessly to toss it aside.

He took in the beauty of her body, still in disbelief that this was even real. That *she* was real. Surely, he would wake up and this would all be some incredible dream. It didn't seem possible that she could be there with him as the rain poured like misery outside and his whole future seemed so damn uncertain.

But she was. And he realized he had to make the most of this moment before she changed her mind and slipped away. Away from Mad Rock Harbor, from Massachusetts. Away from his life like some dandelion swept off by the wind. He had to prove that he could be good enough for her. That he *was* enough for her.

Having no words, she relieved them both of what remained of their clothes. Her eyes held his as she took him inside of her, and her head fell back with this unbelievable sense of relief.

As he rose up to wrap her in his arms and claim her mouth with his, she gave in to the wonderful, blissful feeling of coming home.

CHAPTER THIRTEEN

In the days that followed Nellie's death, Grace noticed the
change that fell over the house. It darkened the shadows,
chilled the air, and inspired unknown things to mysteriously go
bump in the night.

She would be lying if she said it didn't terrify her. Suddenly
accepting the reality of the paranormal had done a number
on her psyche, only made worse by the uptick in activity she
experienced. The spirits knew they had her undivided attention,
and they had no qualms about exploiting it.

What was a girl to do? Keep living, she supposed. And
ignore the problem until it refused to be ignored. She was
powerless to combat the spirits, and too emotionally exhausted
to try.

The medical examiner said it was cardiac arrest that took
Nellie from her. Grace couldn't argue with the practicality of that

conclusion, but it certainly didn't make the pain any less horrid. Nellie, much like Grace's parents, had been so full of life. Grace had learned long ago that just because life was perfect didn't mean death wasn't waiting patiently right around the corner.

Like the little boy who had died on her operating table. Or Sally, who Jackie claimed had fallen to her death from the second-floor balcony. An accident caused by a faulty stair rail. An accident that had taken Sally away from her parents, just like Grace's parents had been taken from her. Perhaps that was why she felt so strongly connected to the girl. They were both lost and lonely, orphans not just in life, but in death.

Ian respected her desire to remain alone for a while, though he did call to check on her occasionally. He, Alex, and Jackie were busy at work digging up more information on the house, interviewing those whose family history was tied to the town, and poring over every last scrap of documentation they could find. They hoped to find out more about Ray and his poor daughter Mercy, both as supplemental research for their investigation and for Grace's sake.

One thing that did turn up at the house of an estranged, distant relative of the Sullivans was Mercy's diary, worn and faded with time. Apparently, it was picked up by the relative right around the time that Mercy disappeared, and then forgotten among a library full of books that were rarely read.

Ian said the diary detailed much of the physical and emotional abuse that Mercy had endured at the hands of her father, far worse than anything they could have imagined. Mercy wrote that her father blamed her for her mother's death, that grief had driven him to madness. Though Mercy suggested that evil had always existed in his heart, it took a tragedy to unleash its full fury.

Ian wouldn't let Grace read the diary, for which she was grateful. She already felt bad enough for Sally...she didn't have it in her to mourn over Mercy, too.

Then he told her that Jackie believed the body in the basement—the one Grace still didn't want to believe was there—belonged to Mercy. Though he didn't say anything else, Grace knew he was itching to take shovels to the dirt beneath the stairs and find out for sure.

Something in the back of her mind screamed that it was a bad idea to disturb the basement floor, as if doing so would release even more darkness into the house. She wasn't sure if it was just her own paranoia, or if it was Sally influencing her. Either way, she wasn't ready to allow them the chance. Not yet. Maybe not ever.

As the days turned into a week, and the weeks into two, Grace slowly grew impatient. Impatient for what, she wasn't sure. But there was something that needed to happen that wasn't occurring, and it was causing her sleepless nights and fits of helpless anxiety.

She thought it had something to do with Nellie, though the woman was settled and buried now. Her sister Nora took care of the funeral and Grace managed to attend. She hovered in the background, struggling through cold sweats and panic attacks as images of her parents' funeral plagued her. It was like reliving that awful day all over again.

Then she went home, picked up her cello and played out the pain.

Sally was most interactive with her when she played and part of her craved the company. It still frightened her, but she grew used to the sensation of spirit energy caressing her skin, pulling her hair, laughing hollowly on some otherworldly wavelength of sound.

In other parts of the house, Sally was harder to find. Grace sensed that the girl was often chased away by the darker spirits that resided there, the ones that must have come from the basement. The ones she had unknowingly released when she had the antique furniture brought upstairs, only to witness it deteriorate before her very eyes with each passing day.

She looked down at the sofa now, shaking her head at the sight of it. The beautiful fabric was completely faded, with splitting tears and cigarette burns and stains marring its surface. The wooden coffee table and end tables were cracking, as though water damaged, their glossy surfaces peeling and bubbling. The lamp shades over the antique lamps were tearing, the threads of the fabric frayed and weathered.

The grandfather clock Grace so admired had ceased to operate. Even though she'd disabled the gong weeks earlier, the hands no longer moved and the quiet ticking sound disappeared. Deep scratches appeared down its wooden face as if carved by a knife. How could someone have damaged such a beautiful clock?

Now that the spirits no longer needed their vessels, they began to crumble.

She had yet to point out this phenomenon to the others. From the beginning, it had been her secret. Her personal evidence of the paranormal that almost seemed too odd to be real. She'd never heard of ghosts inhabiting inanimate objects before, but surely there was no other explanation for what she was witnessing with her own eyes.

And as long as she wasn't crazy, which she was still hoping she wasn't, then that left ghosts as the only explanation.

She laughed at herself, though it wasn't with humor. It was just so beautifully ironic that she would find herself attributing something to ghosts. To the paranormal. To what she, for a lifetime, convinced herself was make-believe.

She knew better now.

It occurred to her that maybe it was time to bring back the others, to show them the furniture and finally take action to rid the house of the bad spirits. After all, it appeared she was going to be staying longer than initially planned, so better to improve the house rather than let it deteriorate.

She decided to call Ian after she took a shower. Hopefully, he and Alex would have some idea of what to do now.

As she closed herself inside the bathroom, she slipped out of the robe she wore and turned on the shower at full heat. She wanted the steam to cleanse her of the past. In an hour, she may fall back into her weakened, anxious self, but until then, she was determined to save the house.

Save *her* house.

As she washed her hair, she imagined playing the cello and let the music in her head soothe her. She began to hum, smiling as she popped open the conditioner and poured a dab onto her palm.

Out of the corner of her eye, she caught a glimpse of something dark moving beyond the gauzy shower curtain. It scampered along the floor like an animal hunched over on two legs. She hovered, frozen with fear, her eyes glued to the shadow.

She had seen it before. In fact, it seemed to enjoy bothering her while she bathed. That didn't make it any less terrifying when it showed up again and again, never truly showing itself to her, only existing as this mirage through the curtain.

On impulse, she threw open the curtain, like she always did, and the creature was gone. Vanished into thin air, as though it had never existed in the first place.

She found her breath and gulped in air like a starving woman gorges on bread. Her body shook with uncontrollable tremors, and she knew then that her decision to bring back the others was the right one. How much longer could she go on living like this? Exposing herself to this evil that had every intention of messing with her mind, terrifying her into a cowering mess of fear?

No more. She was going to start fighting back. Starting with leaving the curtain open from now on.

* * *

Alex hunched over his laptop, giant headphones covering his ears. He listened intently to the audio captured by one of the static cameras during their stay at the Sparrow House. It was the camera that had been in Grace's bedroom, and though he hadn't expected to hear much of anything, it was turning out to be one of the most active recordings they had gotten.

Not only had they captured a little girl's laughter and singing voice, the audio also picked up delicate footsteps and faint whimpering sounds. He had a notepad before him with all the times marked down and he scratched his chin as he penciled in a new one.

At 3:08 a.m., a menacing growling sound penetrated the silence. Alex paused the recording and rewound, his eyes searching the video feed to see if anything visual had been captured. He spotted the vague outline of a shadowy figure in the corner of the room, shifting side-to-side like a boxer ready to fight.

"Oh, shit." His right hand shot out to slap around the nearby bed for Ian, his eyes not leaving the screen. He made contact with Ian's shoulder and vaguely heard him grunt through the heavy headphones. "You have to see this, man."

With a sigh, Ian shut off the television and rolled over, nudging Alex out of the way. He lifted the headphones off Alex's ears and propped them onto his own. "What am I looking at?"

"Look in the corner," Alex instructed, rewinding the recording back. When he hit play, his eyes honed in on Ian's face, eager to see his reaction. He wasn't disappointed.

Ian's eyes widened. "Shit."

"Yeah. Shit." Alex grinned, slapping his friend on the back. "We hit the mother lode."

"What time did this happen?"

"A little after three. Why?" Alex reached around for a bag of chips, popping a few in his mouth.

Ian looked sick to his stomach. "Grace was sleeping right there as that *thing* hovered in the corner."

Alex frowned. "Yikes. Hadn't thought about that."

"Damnit." Mind reeling, Ian shot to his feet and ran his hands through his hair restlessly. He paced the floor, gathering his thoughts, creating an action plan. "I should tell her. But if I do, she's going to be terrified."

"Maybe she should be terrified. That could be the thing Jackie keeps seeing at the house. I didn't realize it went into Grace's room."

"None of us did. We thought that room was safe." Ian walked up to the wall and slammed his fist against it. "I've given her enough fucking space. I'm going back over there."

"I don't know if she's ready."

"She's going to have to be ready," Ian declared, shrugging into his black leather jacket impatiently. "Can you send that video to my phone? I want to show her."

"Seriously, don't show her this," Alex pleaded, reaching over to close his laptop.

"She deserves the truth." Ian stood resolute, eyes intense. "Just send it to me, okay?"

Alex sighed. "Okay. But she isn't going to be happy."

"Yeah, well I'm not happy either," Ian growled, grasping at his hair again. "The woman is driving me insane by keeping me out. This is one of the hottest paranormal locations we've ever investigated—she even admits it now—and she *still* won't let us back in."

"Her friend died, cut her some slack." Alex reopened his laptop and tapped away at the keys, preparing the video to send off to Ian's phone.

Ian knew Alex was right, but he was determined to free her from her pain, if only for the sake of the investigation. And because he cared about her. A lot. He rubbed at his face, scared of the way he couldn't stop thinking about her. The lines of her face, the storms of her eyes, the cynicism of her smile. She wouldn't let him go.

All the more reason to get back over there and rid her house of the bad spirits. Then he could go back to Seattle and leave all this behind. She could get back to her life in Chicago, and maybe they could email each other once in a while.

Or not. He didn't want it to matter.

His phone went off in his pocket, and he glanced at the caller ID as he pulled it out. When he saw her name, his pride crumbled fantastically to pieces.

"Hey, Doc."

"*Hey. I need you to come back. Bring the arsenal. There's something strange in the neighborhood, and I'm calling in the Ghostbusters.*"

Despite everything, he broke out laughing. "Only if you sing the song."

"*Fat chance. Now hurry up and get over here before they eat me.*"

She hung up before he could respond and he felt his humor fade to dread at her words. The spirit they captured hovering in the corner of her bedroom looked ready to hurt her, giving him second thoughts about showing her the video.

It may be the one thing that caused her to snap in two, forever broken. Forever afraid.

* * *

Grace tossed her cell phone on the kitchen counter, feeling edgy. She paced back and forth for a moment, her stomach fluttering with nerves.

This had to be the right decision, she told herself. Because once she brought them back into the house, there would be no turning back. No more alone time, no more ignoring the obvious threats plaguing her house. She was ready to face it all without fear.

At least she hoped so.

When she heard a knocking on the front door, her first thoughts were of Ian, though she knew it wasn't possible for him to be at the house so fast. She shook off the jittery nerves she felt and went to the door.

A middle-aged man in a well-tailored gray business suit stood on her porch. "Sorry to bother you. I was told this house is for sale."

Grace bristled with suspicion. "I don't know who told you that."

The man lifted a business card from his jacket pocket. "Man named Allen Sullivan. Nice guy. Met him at a gala in Manhattan a few months ago. He mentioned he had this house up for sale and that I should stop by and take a look if I was interested. So here I am." His smile was friendly but Grace's anger blinded her to his true intentions.

She only saw a man callous enough to intrude on her grief.

Her jaw clenched and without thinking, she snatched the card out of the man's hand and shredded it to pieces. She tossed the remnants to the ground and met his eyes with a fierce look. "I don't know who you think you are, buddy. But this is *my* house and it's not for sale. Not now, not ever. Now, get the hell off my property."

Bewilderment flashed over his face. "I apologize, I didn't realize he had already sold it."

"He didn't," she barked, getting in his face and poking her index finger into his chest. "But it's mine now. How dare you come here and say that name to me? Do you even realize what you've done?"

He staggered back a step, confused by her statement. "I don't know what you mean."

"He's *dead*. They're all *dead*." She threw up her hands dramatically. "This house is full of nothing but dead people so you might as well get the hell away before you get sucked in like I did. Trust me, you don't want anything to do with this place."

He stared at her like she had purple feathers sprouting out of her face. "Okay, okay. Sorry to bother you."

Without another word, he hurried back to his car and drove off. She watched him go, feeling like a fierce guard dog that had just frightened off an unwanted intruder.

Then she realized how crazy she must have looked and panic shot through her. What was wrong with her? Why hadn't she just told the man that the house wasn't for sale? Or better yet, why hadn't she told him to call her up in a month or two and that she would let him know then if she was willing to sell?

Instead, she'd gone after his throat like a rabid coyote, overly defensive and mean. Cruel, even. That wasn't who she was.

Yet, despite her horror over how she had treated the stranger, relief that he was gone sailed in to comfort her. At least she had that. Odds were he wouldn't be back, either.

She stared down at the shredded pieces of her father's business card and a sob built precariously inside her throat. Regretful tears stung her eyes as she knelt to pick up the mangled scraps.

That had been a mistake, she realized as she piled the pieces in her palm and eyed them sadly. Maybe it was only a business card, but it was her *father's* business card. And even though she had a few of them back home in Chicago, maybe even one in her wallet, it didn't change the fact that she no longer had this one.

As she hovered in ashamed silence, Ian pulled up in his van. She looked up when he exited the vehicle, embarrassed at the tears that fell down her cheeks. She wiped them away and rose to her feet, attempting a smile for him.

"I don't see your Proton Pack," she joked, hoping he wouldn't notice how fragile she was.

But he did.

"What's wrong?" He charged up the porch steps. He saw she held something in her palm and, without waiting for her response, he reached over and pried her fingers apart.

The sight of the shredded card confused him. "What's this?"

She stared at him miserably. "Have you ever imagined doing something completely irrational just to see what people will say?"

He released her hand. "No."

"Never?" A laugh rose in her throat, brief and painful. More tears swam in her eyes as she looked down at her hand. "I think it's natural for us, in a civilized society, to hold back our urges. We recognize the damage we can do, the inconvenience we can cause, by following our impulses. We can hurt other people so easily..."

Ian lifted her chin, forcing her to look at him. "Tell me what happened, Grace."

Her lower lip trembled, but she tried to smile through it. "I assaulted a perfect stranger."

When his brows rose she laughed again, patting his arm reassuringly. "Okay, maybe assaulted is an exaggeration. But I did tear his card to pieces and verbally threaten him a bit."

"And why did you do that?"

She sighed. "He thought the house was for sale. Apparently, he met my father a few months ago and they discussed it. The business card was my father's."

Sympathy hit him as he swallowed her words. "I see."

She shrugged, trying to roll the pain and regret off her shoulders. "I overreacted, but what can I say? I was angry and hurt."

"Understandable."

"I told him the house was full of dead people." She smacked her forehead, feeling foolish. "God, he must have thought I'd gone off my Xanax or something."

"Well, it wasn't a lie. The dead people, that is." The corners of his mouth lifted as he urged her to look at him again. "So you scared off some guy, big deal. You don't want to sell the house, do you?"

She shook her head, even as her words contradicted it. "Yes. Maybe. I don't know."

"Are you sure you're not off your meds?"

She smacked him on the arm, a smile teasing her lips. "Shut up. I'm not on any meds."

He looked thoughtful. "Being a doctor, you could probably get your hands on some good stuff. No one would blame you."

"I would blame me," she corrected him, lifting her chin with pride. "I know what the side effects are of pill addiction. Trust me, it's enough to scare you away from them for a lifetime."

"I was joking." He tugged at her hair playfully, his hand lingering to cradle her cheek. "I like you a little bit crazy."

"I'm not crazy." She blinked, startled by the intense look that came into his eyes. Her smile fell as he shifted closer, his other hand trailing around her waist. She found it suddenly very hard to breathe. "But, hey, if you like crazy, I can do crazy."

His teeth flashed in a wicked grin a second before he kissed her, the act demanding and urgent. He couldn't even comprehend what sparked the sudden need for it, but it was there, staring him in the face. Something about the contradiction of frailty and strength warring within her eyes fascinated him. It lured him in until he couldn't take it anymore. He had to have a taste of her, to know what it felt like to have her skin beneath his hands and her breath over his.

He wasn't disappointed by her, nor by the way she reacted to him in an instant like brilliant wildfire. It ignited like a firework and hit them both with a stunning wave of ravenous heat.

He dragged her against him as his fingers dove into her hair, reveling in the rich warmth of it. A strangled moan escaped her throat when he tightened his other hand on her waist possessively. She grasped at his back, fingers clenching over the shirt he wore until he thought she'd rip it to shreds from his very body.

The more feral part of his nature demanded it, while the rest of him just knew he wanted her. At that point, nothing else mattered. The house, the ghosts, the investigation. He'd say to hell with it all in an instant if it meant he could have her.

She gave in to the onslaught of emotions—the chaotic need, the righteous pride, the helpless surrender. The unexpected assault on her senses left her blinded with a desire she hadn't even known she could feel, much less for him. For the man more arrogant than a king and as temperamental as a wild hornet defending its nest. He was capable of kindness, she knew that. But damn it all if she didn't enjoy the fights and the irrefutable heat more.

He broke the kiss, finding his hands lost in her hair and his senses equally lost in the fresh scent of her lavender soap. He pressed his lips to her forehead, needing a moment to brace himself, to regain some clarity of mind. His heart beat like a stallion in his chest, racing against the pounding of hers.

"Christ," he murmured, lowering his hands to her forearms. He pulled away to look her in the eyes, stunned by what he had just done. But in no way was he sorry.

"Christ is right." She released a long, uneasy breath, her eyes wistfully dark and unsettled. "Why…"

"It doesn't matter." He backed away slowly, clearing his throat. "Anyway, I have something to show you—"

A loud slamming noise from inside the house caused them both to jump.

"What was that?" Grace darted to the open front door, peering inside anxiously.

Ian came up behind her. "Stay here. I'll go look."

"Excuse me, this is my house. I'll go." She rushed inside and went straight to the living room, searching for the source of the sound. She heard Ian walking around the entryway and kitchen, but somehow, she knew they wouldn't find whatever had made the noise inside the house.

Her gut instinct proved right as she looked out the wide living room windows and spotted a woman teetering on the edge of the lonely little dock.

"Oh, my God. Who the hell is that?"

Ian approached, suspicion tightening his eyes. "I don't know."

The woman was tall and willowy with long, coffee-colored hair and pale white skin. She faced away from them, her gaze set out to sea. Her body was draped in a Victorian era ivory gown splattered with dark stains. For a horrified moment, Grace wondered if it was blood.

"Was she inside my house?" Grace panicked.

"Let's go find out."

He started out the back door and hesitated when the woman suddenly dove headfirst into the ice-cold waters of the harbor. "Shit."

Both he and Grace ran to the dock, wet leaves and branches crunching under their feet. Ian came to a stop along the shore, his eyes searching the water, while Grace made the more dangerous decision of tackling the crumbling dock.

He called out to her in warning but she ignored him, adrenaline pushing her to the end of the dock. She fell to her knees and stared into the watery depths of the harbor.

"Where did you go?" she whispered, filled with dread as she searched through the muddy water. She noticed there weren't any ripples or bubbles, nothing to indicate that a woman had just jumped in.

Was it an illusion? It seemed so real.

Then she spotted a face within the murky water, and true fear paralyzed her. It swam up out of the darkness, the rest of the body emerging with it. Lanky, pale arms, white legs, blood splattered ivory gown, length of dark hair. The woman's eyes were closed as though she were peacefully asleep.

Or dead.

"Ian," Grace stammered, unable to breathe. Unable to move. Panic rose within her like a furious geyser, destroying her from the inside out. She thought she heard Ian approaching, thought she felt his footsteps vibrating over the shaky wood dock. She wanted to pull away, desperately grasped for the strength to flee, but it floated just out of reach. All she could do was stare helplessly into the water.

The woman's eyes shot open, revealing nothing but pitch-black corneas. Her face twisted in a malicious snarl, lips molded into a scream of true hatred.

Somewhere in the deepest recesses of her mind, Grace swore she could hear the piercing sound of the scream. Or, perhaps the scream she heard was her own.

Ian grabbed her and pulled her back to land, back to safety. He let her cling to him as he led her up to the house. He realized it hadn't been a woman at all. Rather, it had been one of the most stunning apparitions he had ever seen.

Grace struggled for air as he brought her inside the house

and to the sofa. She cried out, afraid of the deteriorating furniture. Instead, she stumbled into the kitchen where he caught her and settled her onto the floor.

"What did you see?" he demanded urgently, framing her face with his hands. "Tell me before you rationalize it and forget it."

Her face was ghostly pale and her eyes darted back and forth, as if expecting a monster to jump out at any moment. He forced her to look at him, and she seemed to calm down.

He repeated his question. "What did you see?"

"The woman. In the water." She let her head fall back against the cabinets behind her. Her breathing became easier as she shut her eyes and focused. She was safe now. The woman couldn't hurt her.

"What did she do?"

"She screamed at me." She rubbed her eyes feverishly, willing the images to go away. Wishing she had never gone out on the dock. "She was so angry, so *violent*...I've never been that scared in my life."

"I don't imagine you have." He watched her thoughtfully, regretfully. He wished he had seen it instead of her. But then again, maybe he didn't want that image emblazoned on his mind. "I bet that was Mercy."

"What?" Grace let her hands fall as she gaped at him. "Really?"

He nodded, running with the thought. "She was the right age, had the right type of clothing on. Not to mention the blood."

Grace swore under her breath as her mind reeled. "Why did she scare me like that? I thought we were supposed to help her?"

"Maybe she's pissed we haven't been here for a while." He settled back on his heels, feeling restless. "Either way, we both saw her, so you're not crazy."

She stared at him, one eyebrow lifting. "Or maybe we're both crazy."

Humor softened the worry on his face and he reached out to brush her bangs away from her eyes. "I told you, I like a little bit of crazy."

"You stupid bastard," she exhaled, too weak to laugh.

He grinned. "This coming from the crazy bitch."

"Touché." She closed her eyes and released a long, slow sigh. The image of Mercy's hollowed, empty gaze hovered just behind her eyelids, refusing to leave. "What were you going to show me before Mercy decided to take a dip in the harbor?"

Ian hesitated. How in the world could he show her the *thing* that haunted her bedroom after what they just witnessed?

"Nothing important." He got to his feet and helped her up, making a mental note to delete the video Alex had sent him.

"Okay." She teetered on her feet unsteadily, flustered when he placed his hands on her hips to help her. She slowly backed away from him and met his eyes. "Well, I have something to show you."

When she brought him to the living room and he saw the damaged furniture, his eyes darkened with concern. He ran his hands over the warped surface of the coffee table, traced the tattered seams on the sofa, and inspected the deep gouges in the grandfather clock. For a few moments, he said nothing as he took in the weight of what it all meant. Understanding the horrific reality they were facing made him sick to his stomach.

"Well, what do you think?" Grace asked, chewing on her thumbnail nervously.

"The damage happened so quickly," he murmured, running his fingers down the cracked glass.

"The spirits did this, didn't they?" She cupped her hands under her elbows, shifting her weight. "You said they were probably attached to the furniture and that was how they broke free of the basement, but did you think they could cause this kind of damage?"

He shook his head. "I've heard of spirits possessing inanimate objects before, but never to the point that their possession *reversed* the signs of aging."

"Only to reverse it yet again when they no longer possessed the pieces."

He faced her, rubbing his chin in thought. "If this is any indication of their power, then we're in trouble."

"Tell me about it."

"It's entirely possible that they are capable of possessing a person as well," he theorized, beginning to pace. "Mercy and Ray are both clearly strong enough to do it."

Grace blinked. She hadn't thought about that. "Wait, you mean they could possess *me*?"

"Any of us." Ian saw the panic in her eyes and tried to backtrack. "Look, since it hasn't happened already I think we're okay. Don't freak out."

"I'm not freaking out." She stared him down defensively. "It's just that I'm already having a hell of a time accepting that I just saw a ghost in the water, and now you're telling me that possession is real and that it can happen, too."

He shrugged. "After everything you've seen, does it really surprise you?"

She considered his words, realizing he was right. "No. I suppose it doesn't."

"I'm going to call Alex. Get him and Jackie back over here."

Grace nodded and wandered to the living room windows while he talked on the phone. She stared out at the harbor, at the dock, and did her best to stand tall. To stand strong.

That little sliver of strength was all she had left to cling to now that the spirits reigned.

CHAPTER FOURTEEN

Jackie took a deep breath as she re-entered the Sparrow House for the first time since Nellie's death. She wasn't quite sure what to expect since Ian said the activity had escalated. Between the possessed furniture and the apparition of Mercy, things had taken a turn for the worse. If Grace was seeing ghosts, then she knew she better prepare for an all-out war with them.

Alex hovered behind her, protective and alert. Her eyes scaled the walls of the entryway, taking in the white plaster. She still saw remnants of Mr. Lockwood's messages and the miserable hope and pain he carried with him each time he visited clung to the words. She released a long breath and forced the emotion out, breathing in deeply again as she shifted her focus to the staircase.

Sally sat on the third step, hugging her knees tight to her chest. Fear radiated off her, flickering like dark shadows across her features. Jackie sent a reassuring smile but knew it did little to help. Until they were rid of Ray's spirit and the others that plagued the house, Sally would be tormented by them and kept from her father.

"What do you see?" Alex asked, his hand falling over her shoulder. She closed her eyes at the warmth of his touch, absorbing the strength it gave her. The peace of mind.

When she reopened her eyes, she looked deeper into the fabric of the home. The negative energy caused by Ray's spirit was like a dark, spreading stain, seeping its way throughout the house. It surrounded them, inching its way menacingly over the floor and up the walls, on the ceiling, and into corners. The staircase was relatively unaffected because Sally's energy was strong there. For now, anyway. The stain was making headway through the house, expanding its reach. Soon it would encompass everything.

And Sally would have nowhere left to run.

"He's growing stronger." Jackie stepped under the second-floor banister and stared up at what had once been a broken railing. The twisted, gremlin creature of Ray's demented evil hung there like a primate, swinging cheerfully back and forth. Taunting her. Daring her to pursue it.

"His shadow creature is stronger as well."

"I've seen it." Grace walked into the entryway, Ian at her side. She crossed her arms and followed Jackie's gaze, though she wasn't able to see the monster this time. "Little bastard likes to watch me shower."

Ian shot her a horrified look, but she only shrugged.

Jackie faced the others, her expression grim. "Things are getting worse. We need to perform a cleansing ritual. Probably more than one." She rubbed her forearms to chase away the chill she felt. The spirits didn't like her talking about rituals. "Unfortunately, I'll need some help. I can only do so much on my own."

"We know some people," Ian said.

Grace scowled. "Oh great. More strangers."

"These are good strangers," Alex informed her, perking up at the idea. "Why didn't we think of this before?"

Jackie smiled at him, though it was lined with sorrow. "The sooner they get here the better." She looked around the room again, eyes filled with terrible images the others couldn't see. "There's more than just one evil spirit in this house."

Grace watched Jackie thoughtfully, her heart filling with a question that seemed so ridiculous, and yet..."Do you see Nellie?"

Jackie shook her head. "No, darling. She has moved on. The spirits here are damned, tormented, and lost to evil. They don't know how to leave."

"Which is why we have to show them the door." Ian wrapped his arm around Grace. "Don't worry, Doc. We'll make this right. I promise."

"I'm going to hold you to that."

* * *

Grace sat in Nellie's old chair on the front porch, pretending to read a book. Inside, Ian and Jackie were preparing dinner while Alex toyed with his Mel Meter at the dining table. She could have joined them, but the urge to be alone for a while had won out over the desire to socialize.

Even though she wanted to be relieved that Nellie's spirit wasn't trapped in the house like Sally, part of her was disappointed. It occurred to her that if Nellie had stayed then maybe her parents had stayed as well. Then she could communicate with them one last time.

But Jackie insisted that wasn't the case. When Grace had cornered her and asked about the time Jackie claimed to have seen the doctor, presumably Grace's father, Jackie seemed hesitant to offer any hope that Grace could reach him in the afterlife.

She said that the spirit world was tricky and that it was like portals. Some spirits possessed the ability to travel, in a sense, from one location to another. Many of them didn't even realize they were doing it. So the odds of contacting her father without doing a full séance, which Jackie discouraged, were very slim.

Grace brought her knees to her chest and hugged them close. Why did she feel jealous? Jackie's…condition was nothing to be envied. If anything, Grace knew she should be thrilled she only saw vague remnants of what Jackie experienced on a day-to-day basis. It was scary enough as it was.

She just couldn't escape the fact that Jackie had seen her father. She'd heard his voice, saying that he was sad to see his daughter in the house. That it was a burden she should have never had to bear. At the time, she hadn't believed Jackie. Now she did and it mortified her that her father had been so close and she had shut him out.

She wondered if things would have been different if she had been open then. Would she have been able to sense him the way she could Sally? Hear his voice, faint and distant as it may be, whispering in her ear?

Tears sprang into her eyes at the thought. She knew there was nothing she could do now to change it. There was no point in dwelling on what might've been.

She spotted a bright-silver BMW cruising up the street heading straight for the Sparrow House. Shock paralyzed her and she could do nothing but sit and watch as the car came to a stop behind Ian's van. She watched as her worst nightmare stepped out of the driver's seat.

Rick saw her sitting there and a concerned look came over his impeccably handsome face. He was purebred Italian with the dark hair and charming hazel eyes his father and grandfather before him had all been known for. He wore his favored gray slacks and crimson red button up shirt, sleeves perfectly pressed and pinned with gold cufflinks. There was nothing casual about his appearance. Instead, he was full of conceit and egotism all rolled into a five-foot eleven package.

He jogged up the pathway, giving her a moment to collect herself. When he came to a stop before her, she tried not to feel any pain. He wasn't worth it.

"What are you doing here?" She lowered her legs, feeling awkward and foolish.

"I can't believe you came all the way out here, Grace. What were you thinking?" Rick frowned disapprovingly. "I've been worried sick about you."

He stepped closer to touch her face but she pushed him aside and got to her feet. "Wasn't blocking your phone number and kicking you out enough of a hint to you? We're done. I don't ever want to see you again."

He grabbed her arm to keep her from going inside. He tried to look apologetic but instead, he only looked irritated. "I told you I was sorry. It was just a mistake."

"A mistake?" She yanked herself free of his grasp, the urge to slap him erupting like a volcano inside of her. Instead, she crossed her arms, knowing it would only make things worse. "Mistakes are innocent. What you did was cruel and you know it."

He let his resentment fuel his sense of control over her, his inherent belief that he knew what was best. "You left me to wander the streets *naked*, Grace. Who does that?"

"Hmm, let me think." She tapped her lower lip with her fingertip, temper sparking. "Oh, that's right. A pissed off bitch does that. And you know what I am? I'm a pissed off bitch."

"Honey, you're letting your emotions get the better of you. You know what happens when you do that, don't you? You end up creating a false sense of victimhood that hurts you more than it helps." He grabbed her again, this time squeezing her upper arms firmly so she was forced to look at him. "Just go grab your things and get in the car. I'm taking you back home."

"I am home," she stated flatly, disgusted by his habit of psychoanalyzing everything she did. God knew why she ever stayed with him. It had been such a weak attempt at a perfect life, like so many of the other things she used to cling to.

She found it amusing how much her perception had changed after dealing with death.

Ian suddenly emerged from inside the house, eyes on fire as he saw Grace pinned against a strange man.

"I heard shouting, what's going on?" he demanded, a dish towel in one hand and a hothouse tomato in the other.

Grace felt embarrassment flush over her face. "Ian, this is Rick. Rick, this is Ian. Rick was just leaving."

Rick let out a light laugh and released her. She rubbed her arms irritably as he faced off with Ian. "This is my fiancé, Ian. I don't know if she told you she was engaged before she let you into her bed, but she is. Now, I'm not the jealous type, so I'm willing to let this slide. But you should probably leave now and forget any of this happened."

Ian's brows shot up. "That's nice. But I'm not sleeping with her."

Rick didn't look convinced. "Maybe not yet. But I can see what this is." He looked back to Grace, shaking his head unhappily. "What happened to the girl I was going to marry? She would have never come all the way out here to a rundown old house to fool around on me. She had more class than that. I'm disappointed in you, Grace. Your parents would be, too."

Grace's hackles rose defensively. "The girl you were going to marry walked in on you *screwing* her best friend."

Rick sighed, impatience simmering along the edges of

his cool reserve. "You're going to have to get over that, honey. We're getting married."

"I don't see a ring on my finger." She yelped when he suddenly reached out and grabbed her hand, lifting it to inspect for the ring.

"What did you do with it? That was a very expensive piece."

"I had it sent to your office, but apparently you've been too busy screwing around to check your mail," she spat, wishing she had thrown the ring down the garbage disposal instead. He'd probably just slip it onto another woman's finger within six months.

Ian stepped smoothly between Grace and Rick, crossing his arms. "I think it's time for you to go."

Alex and Jackie joined them and, without a word, Alex went to stand at Ian's side. He was taller than all of them and nodded with false politeness at Rick.

"What's up?"

Rick looked furious, his façade breaking as he realized he was losing control. "This is ridiculous."

Grace blinked back the surprise at seeing two men standing up for her, men who had been nothing but strangers mere weeks ago. It humbled her in ways she couldn't even comprehend.

"Please go, Rick," she said as she stood beside Ian.

Rick looked her straight in the eye as he evaluated her. When he spoke again, he seemed to have decided she wasn't worth it. "Fine. Goodbye, Grace."

He backed off the porch, holding his head high as he stalked off. Suddenly, he turned back around and called out to her, eager to get one last shot in. "Your father never wanted you to come to this place, honey. He knew it would be bad for you. Clearly, he was right."

Before she could think of what to say in response, he'd

hopped in his car and drove off. She let the finality of it all sink in as she tried to ease the tension in her body.

Ian sighed. "Well, at least that's over."

She nodded, determined to push all thoughts about Rick and his ominous knowledge of the house aside until it had to be faced. Until she couldn't ignore it any longer. "Is dinner ready? I'm starving."

"Yeah. Just about done." He handed her the hothouse tomato and followed her and the others into the house. The door closed with a final click behind them, shutting out all remnants of her past life for good.

* * *

"Where are they now?"

"In the walls." Jackie ran her fingertips over both walls of the upstairs hallway as she retreated backward, facing Alex's camera with a sly smile. Her eyes drifted up and she spoke on a long, measured breath. "On the ceiling."

Alex resisted the urge to look, knowing he wouldn't see anything. Even with the last dying rays of the sun filtering in from the rooms, her gift was hers alone.

Ian and Grace were busy rummaging through photographs downstairs, searching for one that matched the woman they saw on the dock. Alex had seized the opportunity to take Jackie upstairs for a little side project he hoped Great American Paranormal fans would be interested in.

He was going to call it *Confessions of a Medium*. While it would drum up some interest and be a great addition to the footage they were getting of the investigation itself, it also gave him an excuse to be around her.

He turned the camera away and gently pushed her up against the wall, shocking her back to reality with a kiss as tender and easy as summer rain. Her eyes closed as she welcomed him in, her hands sliding up to rest on his shoulders. The feel of his body pressed against her own sent her mind reeling with hopeless need. Memories of what his skilled hands were capable of in the dark flashed over her, shutting out everything else.

She let out a frustrated moan when he pulled back.

His mouth lifted in a crooked grin. "Something tells me you like it when I kiss you."

A breathy laugh escaped her throat as she rubbed at her heart, startled to find it fluttered like a breathless teenager's. He made her feel young and carefree, no longer burdened by the weight of her sight. He gave her something she had never before felt.

True acceptance.

Realizing she was getting dangerously close to falling down a long and damaging road, she slipped out of his grasp and continued down the hall. She shot him a friendly look, crooking her finger. "There's more to see."

He smiled again, not noticing the war she silently waged within her own mind.

"So, what are the spirits doing?"

He focused the camera on her face, capturing every flicker of her dark eyes, every lift of her mouth, every crease of her brow. A range of emotions passed over her features as she absorbed the spirit presence surrounding them. The shock of pain, the grip of fear, the sorrow of lost love. It all existed within the house, and though he could only sense them intuitively, he knew she witnessed them in all their horrific glory.

"They want to break free," she said softly, her gaze unfocused as she watched spirits straining against the walls, trying to claw their way out.

She understood that they were all connected to the house. Former owners, caretakers, nannies, maids...but something kept them tied to the house in death and wouldn't let them go.

Or maybe it was they who wouldn't let the house go.

She shivered involuntarily, and all humor fled from her face. "I understand now."

"Understand what?" Alex shifted the camera.

She froze just before one of the spare bedrooms, unable to speak. What she saw had her questioning everything. A woman fitting the description of the apparition Grace saw by the harbor stood in the corner of the room, surrounded by dark wisps of energy. It flowed around her like smoke, snaking around her feet and from the palms of her hands.

The ivory dress she wore was covered in blood, but Jackie noticed something else. The woman was completely drenched in water.

Jackie's hands began to shake as she continued to stare at the woman, noticing her pitch-black eyes and pale, wet skin. Water dripped down the sides of her face from her mop of wet brown hair, pooling to the floor at her feet. A fishing line dangled from the hem of her dress, a tiny, ancient hook caught in the fabric. Her mouth twisted in a cruel, mocking snarl as she eyed Jackie with contempt.

"She didn't die in this house." Jackie backed away, not liking the waves of fury that rolled off the woman.

"Who?"

"Mercy." Fear gripped her throat until she could hardly breathe. She had to pull at Alex's shirt to urge him back down the hall toward the staircase. There the energy was calmer, more innocent. Sally was waiting for her, her face contorted with sorrow.

"How do you know?" Alex set aside the camera and helped lower her onto one of the top steps. He held her close to ward off the tremors pulsing through her body.

"I just know." She shut her eyes, consumed by the powerful emotions of Mercy's spirit. It was unlike anything she'd come across before. Such a combination of wrath, bitterness, fear, and torment. How one spirit could embody all those things…it could only mean that in life she had, too.

It became clear to her that what they were dealing with was far beyond anything they could have imagined. "I don't think her body is in the basement." She wrung her hands together, her eyes glassy and unseeing.

"Is there a body down there at all?"

She nodded, but said nothing. There was nothing she could say—she was just as disturbed and confused by the revelation as he was. What she really needed was time to think it over, time away from the house.

Alex felt helpless. "Is there anything I can do?"

She shook her head as she rose precariously to her feet. "No. I just need to go clear my head. I'll talk to you later."

She hurried down the steps and out the front door into the daylight. Her Jeep awaited her, Gatsby smiling cheerfully at her from the front seat. She climbed inside and reached for him, letting the feel of his soft fur and adoring kisses soothe her.

As she pulled away from the house, she did her best not to look back. She knew exactly what she would see if she did.

From the upstairs window, Mercy watched her leave.

* * *

Alex went immediately to both Ian and Grace, finding them sitting on the living room floor with photographs scattered around them. He was edgy and restless, something Ian wasn't used to seeing from his easygoing friend.

"What's wrong? Why'd Jackie leave?"

Alex tucked his hands into the pockets of his jeans to keep from pulling his hair out. "She saw Mercy upstairs."

"What?" Grace dropped the photograph she'd been holding, the image of that ghostly, violent face in the waters of the harbor flashing before her eyes. Fear had her imagining that face hovering over her while she slept. "I thought we decided the upstairs was safe."

"Jackie says the bad energy is creeping through the whole house now. The staircase is one of the last calm spots, and it's only because Sally stays there."

Ian's eyes narrowed. "Did she say anything about Mercy? Anything we can use?"

Alex shook his head. "Not really. Other than it might not be Mercy's body in the basement."

Grace frowned. "You mean *if* there's a body in the basement. Which there probably isn't, especially if she's going back on what she said before."

"She's just getting different vibes now," Alex defended. "We made assumptions about it being Mercy, but Jackie never concluded that for sure. I guess something about Mercy told her that she didn't die in the house."

Both Grace and Ian hovered in thoughtful silence, unsure what to make of Alex's statement. If Mercy hadn't been killed in the house by her father, then what happened to her?

"I'm going back to the hotel. I can't focus here." Alex looked to them regretfully. "I'll see you guys later."

"Bye, Alex." Grace watched him grab his camera and take off. They could hear the van drive away, leaving them alone.

Ian ran a hand through his hair tiredly. "This just keeps getting stranger."

Grace shivered. "You can say that again."

"So you're sure none of these women look like the face you saw in the water?"

"I'm sure." She rubbed her eyes, the woman's face burned hideously into her brain. "Trust me, I won't be forgetting it."

He reached into one of the unopened boxes they had dragged upstairs from the basement and pulled out another small stack of photographs, tossing a few in front of her. "Check those."

She began sifting through the aged, glossy images dispassionately. The search was mentally exhausting, especially since she knew she would recognize the face the moment she saw it.

It was one of those things she could never remove from her mind, no matter how hard she tried. No amount of psychotherapy from someone like Rick could convince her that she did not see what she knew she saw.

A real ghost.

She came across a photograph in near perfect condition from the bottom of the stack Ian had given her. She stared at it as her world came to a slow and painful stop.

The eyes were different, not black as night like before. These eyes were lighter, filled with life. But even that life couldn't hide the despair. Dark hair pulled back in a traditional updo framed a plain, emotionless face. Only the eyes seemed to display any sort of feeling, and even that was masked by poor photography and lighting. The dress she wore was lacy and long, not fancy but not paltry either. It covered almost all the skin of her body except for her face and hands. Those hands were clasped in her lap so tight that Grace imagined her knuckles must have turned white.

Ian noticed her staring intently at the photograph and knew instantly it was the one.

"Grace?" He nudged her, bringing her back to reality.

She tore her eyes from the image and handed it to him.

He turned it over, examining the scrawled handwriting on the back. "Miss Mercy Loraine Sullivan, 1911."

Grace suddenly felt sick to her stomach. "Well, now we know for sure."

"Yes, we do." He set the photograph aside, unable to look at it any longer. It unsettled him in ways he couldn't explain. "Why don't we take a break? Put on some coffee or something."

"Or wine." She accepted his hand after he got to his feet. "Wine is better."

He went into the kitchen and pulled out her last bottle of Merlot. "Your stash is running a little low here, Doc."

"Shit." She sighed and leaned over the kitchen island jadedly. "That's the worst news I've heard all day."

"You mean other than your ex knowing more about the house than you did?" Ian poured them both glasses and wandered over to hand one to her. He watched his words sink in as he sipped.

"I was trying to forget about that."

"What were you doing with that guy, anyway?"

She shook her head and downed half her wine, feeling miserable. She set the glass down on the butcher block counter and stared at it sadly. "I don't even know. My parents liked him."

Surprise flashed over Ian's face. "I'm shocked anybody likes him."

She managed a small laugh. "He has his moments, but for the most part he's a bonafide prick."

"Good riddance, then." He stared at her intently, the desire to reach out and touch her again hitting him like a punch to the gut. Since the incident on the dock she had shied away from him. He didn't think he could bear holding back any longer.

She sipped more wine, lost in thought. "I wonder what my father told him about this place. And why he told Rick but not me. That's what hurts the most, really. My father trusted Rick with his secret more than his own daughter."

"Maybe he wanted Rick's help selling the place," Ian ventured, though she shook her head and shot him a dry look.

"Rick doesn't know the first thing about real estate. Most likely, my father wanted Rick's help keeping the house a secret from me. If I ever got too close to learning the truth, Rick could convince me otherwise. He always liked convincing me that what I wanted and believed wasn't what was best."

Anger flared in Ian's eyes. "You're making me wish I had kicked his ass when I had the chance."

She laughed, delighted by the thought. "He wouldn't fight you. He'd just crumple into a fetal position and try and reason his way out of it."

"Unfortunately for him, I'm too bullheaded to listen."

"Ain't that the truth?" She tapped her glass against his before polishing off the rest of the wine. The instant she set it on the counter, he filled it up again.

"So how are you adjusting to seeing ghosts these days? You seem to be handling it better than I thought you would."

"Oh, yeah. It's been a real trip. Loads of fun."

"I'm serious." He looked her in the eyes. "How are you doing?"

She tried to reign back the feelings of anxiety that crept in at his words. "I'm not sleeping. But who would, right? After what we saw…"

"But you still won't leave the house."

She grimaced, knowing he would think she was ridiculous. "I can't leave her."

"Sally?"

"She's a part of me now." Her eyes filled, bright with tears. "She needs me."

The heartache on her face destroyed him. "Then we'll just have to get to work and save her."

For a moment, she said nothing. She only watched him, amazed and frustrated and stunned by him all at once.

"I just don't get it."

"Don't get what?"

She shook her head sadly. "You stand there like you're the answer to all my problems…like you have nothing better to do than to help me. How can that be? You don't know anything about me."

Frustration hardened his features. "I do know you."

"You know that I lost my parents. That I'm a doctor who now believes in the afterlife, and a lifetime atheist who has no choice but to accept that there is something more to this death thing than just death." Her voice cracked, and she brushed away a tear, embarrassed. "You know that I'm a goddamn mess, but not much else. So why do you stay?"

"Why can't you just accept that I do?" He moved closer to her, reaching up to hold her face in his hands. The tears that spilled from her eyes haunted him.

"I'm too literal. I can't just accept something, you know that," she managed, her pulse jumping at his touch. "Accepting you has been the hardest of all…knowing that eventually you'll have to go."

"I won't leave you in this house alone," he told her, needing her to understand that. "Not for as long as you want me here."

"Okay." Relief washed over her as she leaned in to brush her lips over his, her hands rising to take hold of his wrists. Her fingers slid over his skin tenderly, her heart lost in the emotions rioting within her. She felt nearly mad with it, like nothing was the same in the world anymore. It had all changed. And she had changed right along with it.

Now she was with him, teetering on that slippery border of lust and love. It would only lead to heartache…it had to. But she knew it was impossible to go back to what was. To what might have been had she never come to Mad Rock Harbor.

Ian's pulse thundered within him, as consumed as she was. The house was having an effect on them, he was sure of it. Never before had he felt anything so strongly, so fiercely, the way he did at that moment. Yet, despite his fears, he couldn't deny that being with her felt so impossibly right.

Jackie would've said it was fate.

"I want you," he groaned, crushing her mouth with his. She buckled against him, knees weak even as her hands held strong, gripping his arms like they were her only anchor.

He embraced the contradictions of her. The strong and the weak. The cynic and the believer. She was suddenly more real to him than any other woman alive.

His hands slid into her hair and dragged her head back so he could expose her neck. She cried out as his lips trailed along her skin, her fingers digging into the flesh of his arms. When he suddenly lifted her by the hips onto the island, she nearly forgot where she was, who she was. Instead, she lost herself in the feeling of his hands dragging aside her clothes to lay claim of her. To remove all boundaries, all restrictions, that had been keeping them apart.

There would be no more holding back.

She lifted his shirt over his head and kissed him again, feverish to the taste of wine on his tongue and the feel of his bare skin touching her own. Her hands traced over the dark, winding tattoos that lay patterns over the skin of his shoulders and back.

He pressed eagerly against her, shocking her system with a hot, vibrant need. She hadn't realized just how badly she wanted this, how badly she *needed* it. Now it seemed like the only thing left in the world worth living for.

"Please," she moaned, her head falling back as he tore off what remained of her clothing and exposed her.

He wasted no time and drove himself into her, and they fell gloriously off the cliff's edge of sanity and into oblivion.

ACT 3:
SOLACE

*I stay a little longer, as one stays, to cover up the embers
that still burn.*
—Henry Wadsworth Longfellow

Let us go in; the fog is rising.
—Emily Dickinson

CHAPTER FIFTEEN

The cold chills of impending winter blew in as November entered its third week. It was milder on the coast of Massachusetts compared to what Grace was used to in Chicago, but the wind still carried that distinctive, frosty bite. It meant that within no time, snow would crumble out of the heavens and life would recede into a state of unavoidable hibernation.

For now, autumn was still lingering over the Eastern Seaboard. Withered leaves lay neglected on the brittle grass of her front yard and over the walkway. She couldn't muster the energy to bother raking. There were much more important things to do first.

Like exorcise a haunted house.

She sat on the front steps, a mug of coffee in her hand and her favorite black pea coat wrapped securely around her body. Jackie relaxed beside her, less concerned with the chilly breeze in jeans and a red knit sweater.

Both watched the road, anxious for Ian and Alex to return.

"They've been gone for a while." Grace passed her mug between her hands and bit her lower lip impatiently.

"Maybe they stopped and got lunch." Jackie sipped her Earl Grey tea, serene on the outside despite the worry that dragged at her heart. She couldn't shake the foreboding feeling she'd gotten that morning, warning her that something bad was coming.

Something she would be powerless to stop.

Grace set her coffee aside so she could lean back on her hands. She let her head roll over her shoulders and closed her eyes. "These friends of theirs better be able to help us. I don't like wasting time."

"Time is such a relative thing," Jackie replied easily, winding one of her ebony curls around her finger. "A minute for us means nothing to the spirit world. Where they are, time has no meaning."

Grace sighed. "Well, it has meaning here. I've been in this house for well over a month. I don't know how much longer I can stick around."

"I thought you said you couldn't leave?" Jackie turned to her, dark eyes curious.

"I can't…" Grace agreed with a frown. "But if we succeed in helping Sally, then I see no reason why I can't go back to Chicago. Hopefully, whatever hold the house has on me will be broken by then."

Jackie's lips upturned in a warm, understanding smile. "Even if you do go back, it won't be the same. You'll always long for this place."

Grace looked away, uncomfortable. "Will I?"

A few moments of thoughtful silence passed before Jackie spoke again. "I didn't tell you this before because I didn't want to worry you, but I think you should know." She reached for Grace's hand and held it tightly in her own, urging Grace to meet her eyes.

"What could worry me more than evil spirits living in my house?" Grace joked, though her voice held little humor.

"The truth of why your entire family is trapped in this house."

Grace blinked, unsure she'd heard her right. "Wait, my *whole* family? What do you mean?"

"Every person of Sullivan blood is bound to this house in some way. They were in the furniture, now I see them in the walls. They live and breathe within them like the blood in our veins. Some have figured out how to come and go, but they always return. I guess you could say they are just as addicted to the house in death as they were in life."

"Why?" A fist clenched tight around Grace's heart. "What is it about the house that keeps us here?"

Sadness cast a shadow over Jackie's face. "I'm not entirely sure. I think it has to do with Ray and Mercy. Sally, who is not a Sullivan, remains here because her death was sudden and tragic. But she's not why the others stay. I think Ray is holding them here, drawing them in like moths to a flame."

"That's demented." Grace swallowed the bile that rose in her throat. "What does he gain by all this?"

"Power." Jackie's shoulders lifted and fell as she sighed. "Control. I don't really know. All I do know is that we need to remove him and Mercy from the house if your family is to ever know true peace."

Grace absorbed her friend's words, dissecting them quietly. A sob hitched in her throat as the realization hit her. "That would mean my father is here."

"He is here, from time to time," Jackie confirmed. "I didn't want to get your hopes up that you might see him. I don't know if he'll reach out to you."

"Why wouldn't he?" Grace looked behind her frantically, as if she would see him standing in the front doorway. There was nothing there but a few desolate leaves scattered along the porch.

"I would imagine he thinks it will hurt you more than help. He wants you to heal, Grace. Not dwell on his death."

Grace swallowed the pain that came over her, trying to take comfort in that. It was something he would do. He had always been wise that way.

"What happens if we get rid of Ray and Mercy, but nothing changes? What if every time I try and leave, I suffer from the panic attacks again, the anxiety? I don't think I can handle that."

Jackie squeezed her hand comfortingly. "Have faith, darling. God works in mysterious ways."

Grace sighed. She'd always hated that phrase. Then again, much of what she used to think was reality had been turned on its head. What made this any different?

She managed a strained smile as she met Jackie's eyes. "If you say so."

At last, Ian and Alex pulled up in their van, another car trailing behind them. Both vehicles came to a stop at the curb and Grace tried to hide the relief she felt when she saw Ian. He hopped out of the passenger seat, tall and lean and dressed all in black, and she had the crushing realization that she cared about him. A lot. Definitely more than what was safe.

It terrified her, and at the same time thrilled her, a dangerous combination.

Ian avoided looking at the house, knowing Grace was there. It bothered him how much he missed her, even though it had only been a handful of hours. His pride had him grabbing a few things out of the van instead.

He closed the van door and walked to the car that had

followed them, nodding to his friend Aubrey. They went way back to the days when he and Alex had first started ghost hunting. She was a practicing witch, deeply in tune with the spirit world. She'd helped them with research on investigations before, but this was the first time they sought her renowned expertise as a witch.

He didn't know the man she brought with her, but something about him bothered Ian. He couldn't put his finger on what it was, but he had a feeling the man had ulterior motives for wanting to come to the house. Motives other than to be the sixth person they would need for the séance Aubrey suggested they perform.

For the time being, he figured he'd reserve his judgment.

Jackie waved to Alex as he slipped out of the van, and he wasted no time racing up the pathway to greet her.

"My lady." With a slight bow of his head, he extended his hand and pulled her to her feet. Her answering smile was cut off by a quick and affectionate kiss. "I missed you."

She slipped away from him easily, sending him a teasing look. "You never left, in spirit."

Her eyes wandered to where Ian was busy exchanging words with the occupants of the other car. She watched him turn around and walk up the pathway, the other two leaving their plain white sedan behind to follow him.

All at once, confusion and recognition hit her like a brick to the face.

"Are you okay?" Alex asked.

Anger contorted her features, something he had never seen before. "No."

Dominic approached, a sly grin playing over his hard-edged face. "There's my girl. I figured you would be here."

The short, curvy redhead draped in an elaborate black and purple dress beside him began to laugh, the sound more spiteful than friendly. "Oh please, is it any surprise? She goes where the spirits are."

Jackie had the sudden and desperate wish to crawl into a hole and disappear. Instead, she said a quick, silent prayer for strength and faced her rival with as much politeness as she could manage. "It's lovely to see you, Aubrey."

"Wait, you know them?" Alex asked, staring back and forth between Jackie and the others.

She nodded, avoiding his eyes. "Dominic is an...old friend. He and I met Aubrey two years ago when we found ourselves in Salem." She turned to her ex-lover dispassionately. "I didn't realize the two of you stayed in touch."

Dominic shrugged. "I hit her up when I came out this way again. I never know when you're going to come around, Jackie. I had to find someone to party with."

Alex still looked confused as he turned to Jackie. "Wait, is *he* the person you've been staying with?"

She winced at the obvious disapproval in his eyes. "He rents a house nearby. I'm only staying there temporarily—"

"Until you find someone else to leech off," Aubrey declared with a wry smile.

Jackie's cheeks flushed as she glared at the woman who had once been somewhat of a friend. Aubrey had the appearance of a practicing witch and the beliefs to go along with it. While she and Jackie shared a fascination with the supernatural, the kinship ended there. It seemed Aubrey's jealousy over Jackie's gift was something the other woman could never get past.

Ian grimaced at Aubrey, resisting the sudden urge to tell her to take a hike. Friend or not, he wasn't going to put up with childish bickering. "I get that you two don't like each other, but all of us need to try and be friends here so that we can help Grace."

Grace stared Aubrey down with intense dislike. "Something

tells me this isn't going to work out, anyway."

"We will make it work. I'm just surprised, that's all." Jackie insisted, not wanting to let her personal problems get in the way of the investigation. From the look on Grace's face, she wasn't buying it.

"You're surprised that I wanted to see you?" Dominic asked Jackie. He folded his long, tattooed arms over his tattered black T-shirt and shifted his weight, a bit unstable on his feet.

Jackie knew the reason for his instability, knew he'd sought his crutch before finding the courage to come see her. It was his way. He had always been inherently terrified of the outside world. At least until the substances took the fear and turned it into indifference.

It was a quality they both shared, though her vices were decidedly less dangerous.

"I suppose I am." She let her pity for him soften her anger. "I hope that you are up for what awaits us tonight."

Dominic let out a bitter laugh. "I can handle a few ghosts, Jackie. What're they gonna do? Kill me?"

Worry darkened her eyes, but she said nothing.

"Why don't we go inside and fill you guys in on everything?" Grace interrupted, having had enough drama for the day. She looked at Ian, but he only shrugged. He hadn't been expecting this confrontation, either.

Grace sighed and went into the house, Aubrey and Dominic following her with Ian picking up the rear. He shot a look at Alex, silent regret passing between them. If only they had known…

When the others were inside, Alex turned to Jackie.

"What's going on? What is this?"

"Things you couldn't possibly understand." Her shoulders fell as she met his eyes, wanting strength and finding nothing left. Now she knew what the bad omen had been all about. Everything was bound to get more complicated, and fast.

"Like what?" He reached for her, worry chasing away the worst of his anger.

She only shook her head and pulled out of his grasp, forcing a smile over her lips. "Come. While there is still a scrap of peace remaining in this house."

* * *

"This Ray guy sounds like a real piece of work." Aubrey's face lit with anticipation, the light of the old-fashioned lamp over the dining table glittering in her eyes.

"Most definitely." Alex tapped his fingers restlessly on the tabletop, leaning back in his seat. "The emphasis needs to be on getting him out of here. So, whatever you need to do, get it done."

"We should perform a cleansing ritual first, of course," Aubrey began, lifting her cup of coffee to her lips in a dramatic pause. "Then we can do a séance. Speak to Ray, call him out and force him to leave."

Jackie inhaled sharply, disapproval tightening her eyes. "A séance is an awful idea, Aubrey, and you know it."

"Not really." Aubrey pouted, looking to the others for encouragement. "It's the best way to get in direct contact with him. You can use your Spirit Box and your digital recorder all you want, but if you want to talk to him, talk to him through me."

"What does that mean, through you?" Grace asked with a skeptical frown.

"Often, the spirit will communicate through a vessel, through a medium. I will direct him to enter my body and use me to speak."

Grace couldn't help but laugh. "How do we know you won't just fake it and make it all up for kicks?"

Aubrey glared at her. "Because I have integrity. Just ask Ian and Alex. They will vouch for my abilities."

Grace pressed her lips together to hold back another laugh as she glanced at Ian. He sat beside her, arms crossed and stony faced, impossible to read. Alex, on the other hand, looked conflicted, eyes darting back and forth between Jackie and Aubrey.

"A séance will only intensify Ray's hold on the house. Not to mention we risk opening ourselves up to even more spirits, possibly bad ones." Jackie's brow furrowed with frustration, her hands tightening over her cup of tea. "A cleansing ritual is crucial. If all of us participate, then we can weaken him. Then, if we dig up the body in the basement, we should be able to remove Mercy, and hopefully Ray, from the house."

Grace rolled her eyes. "Not the body thing again…"

"Disturbing the grave is the absolute wrong thing to do." Aubrey cut in, eyes on fire. "Don't you know anything?"

Jackie flushed. "I know what I see. The darkest energy is centered on that body. Most likely, it's the catalyst that's making the energy so powerful."

"Then we should dig it up," Alex decided, his hand finding Jackie's knee under the table with a comforting squeeze.

Ian didn't look as convinced. "I'm leaning toward doing the séance before we discuss digging up the grave."

Grace turned to him in frustration. "Jackie says the séance will make it worse. I thought the goal here was to make things better?"

"Look, I can see that as a possibility. However, if we're going to do this right, I feel we need to tackle it head on."

"Ian likes to take the aggressive approach," Alex confirmed with a nod, though he felt uneasy about the whole thing. "But this time it may be too much, man."

Ian looked at him, eyes bright with a sudden rush of adrenaline. "If we set up our cameras down there and break out the infrared equipment, the full spectrum camera, the Spirit Box, imagine what evidence we could capture during a séance like this. When we *know* that there's dark energy down there and spirits that want to communicate with us. They reacted to our provocation before, I think it's the way to go now."

Alex tried to fight back the instinctual thrill he felt just thinking about the potential evidence, knowing that beside him, Jackie was feeling increasingly outnumbered. "Maybe we shouldn't rush this. Let's do the cleansing ritual and wait a day or two and see if it helps. Then we can discuss whether to dig up the body or do a séance."

"I can't wait around that long. I have a life, you know," Aubrey interrupted, finishing off the last of her coffee and rising to her feet. She planted her hands upon the table, the light glinting off the many silver rings she wore on her fingers. "In my professional opinion, we need to do a séance. If you don't wish to follow my advice, then fine. I'll go home. But if you do, then let me know. I'll be outside getting my things for the cleansing ritual."

She tapped Dominic on the shoulder and the two of them sauntered out of the house. Once the door shut behind them, Grace immediately turned to Jackie.

"Tell me honestly. Is this a bad idea?"

Jackie could barely restrain her anger as she pushed out of the chair, immediately going to the old grandfather clock. She stared at it closely, her fingers reaching up to trace over the damage that had occurred to its previously stunning surface. There was corrosion inside the clock face, rotting away at the gold-plated clock hands and turning them blue.

The spirits had done this. They had festered inside the antiques, preserving furniture that had been destroyed a hundred years earlier. If their energy had been strong enough to salvage what was brutally damaged, just what power would they hold if given the chance to strike back?

She had to admit the very thought terrified her. Yet, once again, she was helpless to stop it.

"A séance has the potential to be dangerous. Nothing is guaranteed…but it may work." Jackie turned to face the others, her features calm and composed. She smiled reassuringly. "Now, do you have a broom?"

* * *

They spent the next hour performing the cleansing ritual as night fell. Alex followed Jackie with his camcorder, capturing every graceful movement she made as she went through the timeless motions that had been carried out for centuries.

She held a smudge stick made of white sage, lit to burn like incense. Beginning at the front door of the house, she lifted the dried herbs up and into a clockwise circle. The trail of smoke left a sweet aroma that filled her with peace.

As she spoke, her eyes closed and she put all her faith into the words, knowing they were strongest when she believed in them. "May only those of positive energy be welcome into this home." She moved to the right and into the kitchen, circling the window and drawing bars with the smoke to keep out the negative spirits. "May nothing and no one be allowed to enter."

Alex followed her silently, watching as she sprinkled salt from a small pouch in her pocket into the corners of the living room and near the deteriorating furniture. She moved to the living room windows and followed the same routine, the smoke of the burning sage gathering around her like a white cloud. She spilled more salt upon the window sills and along the floor in front of the back doorway.

"Do you see them around us right now?" he asked, taking a quick glance around the room as if he might see them too.

Jackie breathed evenly, focusing her energy as she waved the smudge stick over the back door. "They're agitated. They don't like what we're doing."

"I bet."

She closed her eyes as she faced him, focused her mind, then opened them again. She scanned the living room, searching the ceiling, the walls, the floor. The dark stain was still there, but it was retreating like the tentacles of a threatened octopus. It recoiled from the salt and smoke, as though nervous. On edge.

Pleasure rushed through her. It was working, at least a little.

A quirk of a smile teased her lips. "We still have much to do, but it is helping."

"Good." Alex shut off the camcorder and set it aside on the coffee table. Without a word, he dragged her against him for a fast, demanding kiss.

A thrill shot through her as she leaned into him, her mouth just as greedy as his. Just as questioning, as searching. Her mind went blissfully blank and she praised God for it.

Alex broke away and held her close, a fire burning within him. His chin rested on top of her head and he breathed in the scent of sage and sandalwood he'd come to know as her. "I want you to come stay with me at the hotel. Ian's staying here with Grace now, so it'll just be us."

Jackie winced, the wings of her freedom flapping restlessly. She tilted her head back to meet his eyes, and slowly shook her head. "I can't do that, Alex."

"Why not?" He eased back, keeping his hands on her shoulders.

She chewed on her lower lip, trying to decide how to explain it. How to break it to him in a way that wouldn't crush him. Either way, she knew he would end up hurt. She had known that from the start…

"We're having fun, aren't we?" She reached up to touch his cheek, a sad smile curving her lips. When he nodded, the smile deepened. "Then let's not complicate it."

He sensed she was fighting some kind of demon she wouldn't share with him, some dark stain on her past that she kept hidden deep inside. Eventually, he would get it out of her, or at least rid her of its binding grip.

Until that day, he would settle for what she was willing to give. As little as it may be.

"Okay."

She watched a playful grin brighten his face and her heart slowly cracked at the edges in a way it never had before.

* * *

Upstairs, Ian had his camcorder focused on Aubrey. The collection of silver trinkets around her neck and wrists rattled together as she moved her arms. Her length of auburn hair fell in curls to her waist, her bright blue eyes determined and empowered.

He knew his viewers would get a kick out of seeing a *real* live witch performing a ritual. Especially since Aubrey was dedicated enough to look every bit the witch she claimed to be.

"I cast thee out seekers of evil. Be gone with you now," she commanded, her voice loud and forceful. In her hands was a smudge stick identical to Jackie's, also lit, and she waved it in the air near the windows and corners of the room. "Let the cleansing aroma repel you. Only the *light* can reside here."

Ian followed her as she moved around the room, retreating to continue her clockwise progression through the upstairs. It would all end at the stairwell, where she would urge the negative energy right down the stairs and out the front door.

As they exited into the hallway, Ian nearly bumped backward into Grace.

"Watch it, Doc." His smile was quick and devious as he winked at her.

Her eyes narrowed. "You're the one who backed into me."

"Make sure you get every corner with that broom. Otherwise, you won't get all the negative energy and you'll get a failing grade."

The broom she held nearly made contact with his head before he ducked out of the way. He laughed and chased after Aubrey to continue filming in one of the other bedrooms.

This left Grace alone with Dominic, who had also been assigned to sweep duty. "I vote we declare mutiny and redefine the words 'sweep duty' to include shoving a broom where the sun don't shine," Grace muttered, earning an appreciative snicker from Dominic.

"That's not a nice thing to say about your boyfriend."

"Who the hell says he's my boyfriend?" she shot back, clutching the broom handle so tight her knuckles went white.

His shoulders lifted and fell impassively. "He's made it very clear that you are off limits."

"Is that right?"

"Yep."

Taken aback, Grace turned away and continued sweeping the hallway. She grumbled under her breath about men and possessiveness and caveman syndrome. But inside, her heart was fluttering like an excited bird.

She didn't know why it mattered, but it did. Ian mattered, so, therefore, his getting protective meant he thought she mattered, too.

God knew it had been too long since someone had cared enough about her to get jealous. With Rick, it had all been his own selfish pride. He'd wanted her back only because *she* had left *him*. His pride had been wounded, and like any man, he couldn't stand walking around knowing that he had been dumped.

Grace wasn't the kind of woman who accepted the excuses of an affair. Despite all his psychobabble analysis of her and her "tendencies," he had been dead wrong on that one. The thought alone brought a vindictive sort of joy to her heart that helped heal that last, lingering wound. Chapter closed, match set. She was over him. And Ian was next up to bat.

She carried that thought with her as she finished sweeping out the negative energy of the house with Dominic, ending at the front door. They brushed the air symbolically, sending whatever bad vibes had plagued the house right out with it.

And despite how stupid of a ritual she thought it was, it made her feel a whole lot better.

Outside, a light rain began to fall.

CHAPTER SIXTEEN

The basement was as dark and musty as ever, yet there was an electricity to the air that Ian couldn't explain. It was simply the anomaly he always attributed to ghosts. He could almost hear it fizzling and crackling, dangerous as a live wire. The hairs on the back of his neck stood at attention, obedient to the chills that marched down his spine.

He couldn't deny that there were highly active spirits in the house. That had been established many times over. The séance could further prove their existence, not to mention make for damn interesting footage for Great American Paranormal.

Not only was he helping Grace, but this entire investigation was yielding some unprecedented evidence. He couldn't wait to compile it all together and get it out there. GAP was already one of the most highly respected paranormal teams in the country, but this could take them to the top.

First, though, he needed to focus on helping the woman he had once despised, then put up with, then cared for, and now... well, cared for was enough. He wasn't ready for more than that just yet, nor was she.

After the investigation was done and her house was saved, maybe he'd give it some thought. Until then, there were ghosts to hunt.

Hours earlier, Alex had set up static night vision cameras in each corner of the basement. He had also put in place a full spectrum camera to detect ultraviolet light, aimed directly at the dining table and chairs they'd dragged downstairs, with the staircase in the background. They hoped to capture shifting variations in brightly colored light which could indicate the presence of a spirit. With the activity the way it was in the house, Ian had no doubt they'd at least get something.

He walked down the last step into the basement, irritated that Aubrey insisted he leave his Mel Meter and Spirit Box behind. She claimed the devices weren't needed to communicate with the dead, not during a séance. Not when she had every intention of letting Ray speak through her.

Behind him, Alex followed with his infrared camera around his neck. With it, he'd be able to snap photographs before and after the séance that could capture hot and cold spots, maybe even in human form.

Ian walked to the table and reached into his pocket for his digital recorder. He flipped it on and set it in the middle of the table to capture any EVPs, just in case.

"We haven't even started yet and I can feel the energy." Alex snapped off a few pictures with the camera he held.

"I know." Ian stared at the dining table, empty except for the recorder. Upstairs, Aubrey and Jackie were busy gathering the rest of the materials they would need for the ritual. He looked up at his friend with a hard grin. "This is it, man. What we've been working for these last few weeks."

Alex chuckled and tweaked a few of the settings on his camera. "You mean while we've been getting distracted by two beautiful women?"

Ian's smile faded. "Other than that." He busied himself with checking one of the static cameras, irritated for reasons he couldn't explain.

He felt a tickle on the back of his neck and turned just as Grace came down the steps. They met eyes the second her feet touched the floor, uncertainty and a spark of heat passing between them.

He saw the fear and tension that bunched in her shoulders. Her storm gray eyes were dark and filled with emotion, though by the stern line of her mouth he knew she was fighting to keep it at bay.

Becoming a believer had opened her up to all kinds of new and unfamiliar feelings and he knew the séance would push the limit even further. She had no idea what she was in for, but he did. And it made him wish he could shelter her from it.

"Why don't you take a seat over here, Doc?" He pointed to the chair beside where he intended to sit and next to where Jackie would be.

Grace nodded, urging her knees not to buckle from the anxiety that boiled like a pressure cooker in her chest. In her hands, she held the photographs of Sally and Mercy. When she sat down, she stared up at him and forced a sarcastic smile. "Some party you dragged me to. Looks like you forgot the booze."

He moved behind her, his hands finding her shoulders for a slow, comforting rub. "Trust me, this will be better than getting drunk."

"I find that hard to believe." But part of her shivered at the thought, both in anticipation and in fear.

He leaned in, his lips brushing over her ear. "I won't let anything happen to you."

"How noble of you." But the feeling of his breath on her neck and his hands kneading the tense muscles of her shoulders sent her mind reeling with images of the night before. His hands, deft and strong, running over her skin. His eyes, blue as the sky nearing nightfall, intense on hers. Never had someone looked at her the way he did, as though nothing else in the world could distract him. When she had his full attention like that, it made her both uneasy and delighted all at once.

"You matter, Doc." He pulled away from her with a friendly pat on the shoulder and took his seat beside her.

Her heart skipped at his admission and she silently cursed herself for the butterflies he sent fluttering about in her stomach. She fought to ignore them as she set the photographs on the table. The leather case holding the tintype of Sally lay open to reveal the silvery image.

Aubrey, Jackie, and Dominic came down the stairs carrying the rest of the supplies needed for the séance.

Jackie held a basket of candles and pouches of salt in her arms which she set on the dining table. She avoided Alex's gaze, knowing he watched her intently from his perch in the corner. Soon they would have to face each other and share an intimacy so few people share.

The intimacy of spiritual contact.

She looked at Grace who sat with her hands bundled together in her lap and an uncomfortable look on her face. Jackie prayed that the séance would go as planned and they would be able to convince Ray to leave the house. If it didn't work, if her worst fears came true…she was too frightened to even think of it.

She put her troubles in fate's hands, in God's hands, and calmed her mind.

Aubrey came up beside her and grabbed three stubby white candles from the basket. "Did you bring a lighter?"

Jackie dug into the basket for a matchbook. "Use this."

Aubrey pursed her lips and set about lighting the candles while Jackie sprinkled salt in a protective circle around the table and chairs. She paused before completing it and looked to both Alex and Dominic who hovered near the wall. "Please turn off the light. Then come inside the circle and take a seat."

Both men eyed her, then each other. The combativeness between them sparked an obvious tension in the air, but she was thankful when Alex set aside his camera and flipped the light switch. They both silently came into the circle.

As Alex passed her, he leaned in to press a soft kiss to her forehead.

She exhaled slowly, the feeling of his lips staying with her as she completed the circle. She turned to sprinkle more salt upon the table. It would help keep unwanted, negative spirits at a distance, should they attempt to bring harm.

The light of the three candles flickered off the cement walls of the basement, casting odd shadows in every direction. She stared around the room, seeing those shadows come to life. The basement was full of spirits, ones that had run from the cleansing aroma of sage upstairs and burrowed themselves below. Now they emerged from the walls, curious and eager to be heard.

Some were residual, others were not. She sensed the dark stain that hovered under the stairs the strongest and it took all she had to not look in that direction. She was afraid of what she may see if she did.

Instead, she sat down at the table and reached for the basket. She removed her quartz crystals, setting them beside the candles. All jewelry had been removed beforehand, no watches, metal earrings, bracelets. Nothing that would negatively repel the spirits.

She rested her hands on the table top. To her right was Alex, to her left, Grace. Both accepted her hands, watching her in anticipation and worry.

Instead of looking at them, she cast her eyes directly upon Aubrey and nodded. This was to be Aubrey's séance, not hers.

"Hold hands, everyone." Aubrey reached for Ian's hand and Dominic's. The candlelight hardened the planes of her face, darkening the pale blue of her eyes. It gave her an almost sinister look and certainly her devious smile did nothing to help. "I will be the only one to speak. Please do not break the circle by releasing your hands and do not get up to leave. There's no turning back now."

She inhaled deeply and let her head fall back on her shoulders, her eyes closing. "Ray, if you are here, make yourself known to us."

Grace held her breath as her eyes darted around the room, expecting the shadow creature to jump out at her at any moment. She thought she could sense it. Thought she heard the telltale skittering sound it made as it scratched over the floor.

Ian squeezed her hand, bringing her back. She met his eyes and tried to relax her body, her mind. His face was unreadable, but she had a feeling he was as edgy as she. He just concealed it better.

"Ray, did you torture your only daughter, Mercy, in this room?" Aubrey continued, her eyes still closed and her body relaxed. "Please give us a sign that you are here. Tap the table. Make a noise."

They sat silently for a long, intense moment. Above them, the old house shifted and settled as the rain fell outside, seeping into the soil. It seemed to permeate into the basement, making the air heavy and damp.

Grace stared at the flame of one of the candles, losing herself in its slow dance. The bright glow mesmerized her, drawing her in until she nearly forgot where she was, what she was doing. Her heart settled and her breathing calmed, and she gave in to this odd sense of nothingness that fell over her. There was nothing but the flame, and the heat beckoned her.

When the fire exploded and crackled like a sparkler, it nearly gave her a heart attack. She jumped in her seat, barely hanging onto Ian's and Jackie's hands as a scream caught in her throat.

Across the table, Aubrey's eyes gleamed. "Ray, thank you. Thank you for giving us a sign of your presence."

A rush of cold descended like fog upon the room, drawing the brilliance from the candlelight and diminishing it. Chills ran over Grace's arms like fervent ants, eager to devour her flesh in one, greedy bite. Her body tensed and froze like a statue as fear made her the frightened rabbit.

Circumstance meant the spirit was the hungry fox.

Aubrey's head rolled over her shoulders and a wicked smile lifted her lips. "We feel you. We know you are with us. Please answer my questions, hear my voice and speak through me. Use me as your vessel."

Grace suddenly remembered to breathe and sucked in air in quick, short gasps. As she did so, she distinctly smelled old, dry leather. The mustiness of it prickled within her nose, itchy and intrusive. Soon, the smell of blood drifted in and had bile rising within her throat.

Coppery and dark, it filled her senses and choked her. She panicked but was frozen in place. There was nowhere to run.

"Blood..." Aubrey murmured, her head falling back again. "Is this what you smelled when you killed your daughter, Ray? Did the scent of her blood sicken you?"

The scent grew stronger and with it came the sudden, shrieking cry of a sparrow. It came from upstairs, beyond the door to the basement. They all turned to face it in shock.

Grace felt sick to her stomach, her thoughts immediately going to Sally. Was she in trouble? Was he hurting her?

"She's warning us," Jackie murmured, shuddering as she looked to Aubrey. Her face was tightened with fear. "We shouldn't have done this."

"Shut up." Aubrey snapped, her eyes open now and filled with anger. "We've made contact. We need to keep pushing. Ray, why did you take your anger out on Mercy? What did she do to you?"

The sparrow's cries faded and the haunting silence left behind echoed around them. Grace watched as Jackie suddenly went still, her eyes glazed over with horror. Concern had her squeezing her friend's hand.

Before she could speak, Jackie's body convulsed in a hard, shuddering jolt, as though a bolt of lightning hit her. Then she went slack and her chin dropped to her chest.

Grace saw Alex's eyes widen with panic, but he didn't break the circle. They all watched with stunned horror as Jackie's head lifted, her face slack and emotionless. Her dark eyes stared unseeingly into the abyss.

When she spoke, her voice was nothing but a whisper. "I did nothing. Nothing. Nothing."

After a moment, Aubrey regained her senses. "Mercy, is that you?"

"Help. Help never came. No one helped." Jackie's lips trembled as the words spilled from them.

"We're here to help you, Mercy. Tell me, is your father in the room with us?"

A shiver shot through Jackie's body, but she remained in her trance.

"Pain. So much pain…the *monster!*" Her voice reached a fever pitch, echoing off the walls.

Shock drained Aubrey's cheeks of color. "W-why are you

still here? Why won't you move on?"

Tears suddenly spilled from Jackie's eyes. "Trapped. Trapped. Trapped."

"Trapped where?"

But Grace knew exactly where. Her eyes shot to the floor underneath the basement stairs where she had long denied a body rested. Maybe this was confirmation that she had been horribly wrong.

Jackie began to rock back and forth, her face contorted with grief even as her eyes remained glassy and unseeing. Grace watched, mortified, as real fear claimed her friend and a scream suddenly erupted from her throat, violent and tortured.

Jackie's head fell back as the scream burst from the deepest regions of her soul, as dark and disturbing as the cries of sinners in Hell.

Upstairs, the destroyed grandfather clock began to chime. Gong. Gong. *Gong.*

The closed door to the basement shook on its hinges as though someone was trying to force their way inside. Then it wrenched open and slammed against the wall so hard, Grace was sure it would break from its frame.

"Don't move!" Aubrey exclaimed, eyes bright and determined. "Ray. Ray, I know you're near us. You're scaring your daughter, but you don't scare me. Stop being a coward. Come down here and face us like a man. Tell us why you won't leave."

The table began to shake as though in an earthquake. But Grace was pretty sure earthquakes didn't happen on the coast of Massachusetts. The candles and digital recorder vibrated, the salt Jackie had poured around them skipping and hopping. Sally and Mercy's pictures stared up at her, shaking in the candlelight.

She bit down hard on her lower lip and closed her eyes, fighting against the fear that told her to run. Run far away and never look back. But she could still feel Jackie beside her, trembling uncontrollably.

"Save me," Jackie whispered, her head rolling back weakly. Grace and Alex both squeezed her hands, looking to each other helplessly.

"Damnit, Aubrey, stop this!" Alex called out, not caring anymore about the séance. He glared at Aubrey with fire in his eyes.

"Not yet!" Aubrey inhaled deeply and concentrated, trying not to think about Jackie and what was happening to her. She wanted to get Ray out. If she didn't accomplish that, then it was all for nothing. "Ray, I command you to leave this house!"

Grace saw something in her peripherals, something dark and ominous. It hovered like a shadowy mist just out of sight. She tilted her head to try and follow it, but it seemed to come and go.

Ian's hand tightened on her own and she knew he saw it too.

Aubrey's eyes flew open. "I see you, Ray. Be gone from this place. Be gone and never return."

The shadow didn't leave. Instead, it circled the table, blending in with the darkness at times and showing itself in others. Grace couldn't believe what she was seeing.

It was like Ray was threatening them. Taunting them.

A panicked look crossed Aubrey's face and Grace realized that the woman had no idea what to do next. Clearly, she had never faced a spirit so strong.

"Do something!" Grace cried out, eyes shooting from Aubrey back to Jackie, whose forehead was covered with feverish sweat. Tears continued to roll down her cheeks, and she tossed her head side to side as if in great discomfort. Strands of her dark curls fell over her ashen face, matted with sweat.

Aubrey took a deep breath and decided that there was

nothing more she could do about Ray's spirit. Instead, she focused her attention back on Jackie.

"Mercy, hear my voice."

Jackie threw back her head and let out a strangled, throaty cry of pain.

Aubrey blanched. "Good goddess."

Grace gritted her teeth. "Jackie, come back to us." She watched her friend suck in quick gasps of air through her nose, as though she were trying to resist the spirit.

Aubrey tried again. "Mercy, I command you to leave the vessel and leave this house at once! Go!"

Jackie tensed like she was having a seizure, her neck straining as her head fell back. Her mouth opened in a soundless scream, her eyes squeezed tight as though she were in unspeakable pain. Her hand squeezed like a vice around Grace's, then seconds later went slack.

The table ceased to shake as Jackie fainted and nearly tumbled from the chair. Alex reached out to catch her, to pull her into his arms. The instant he broke the circle, the candles died, plunging them into darkness.

Grace blinked into the black nothingness, stunned. She heard Ian stand and fumble around the table for the matches. Aubrey cursed under her breath and began to help him, while Dominic let out a sharp scream.

"Something just touched me!" he shouted, and Grace heard his chair fall back onto the floor as he shot to his feet, breaking the circle of salt.

"Shut up!" Aubrey ordered, a fierce sort of panic in her voice.

Grace wrapped her arms around herself, her entire body quaking with terror. She imagined Ray's shadow creeping around the room, hunting them like a lion stalks its prey. She thought she felt fingertips brush her face and jolted as if she'd been burned.

In her head, a dark, otherworldly laughter broke through the haze of fear and vibrated through her very veins. She felt the evil swarm over her like a sea of rabid insects and knew in that moment that Ray was with her.

Ghostly hands trailed around her neck, closing in like icy tentacles. She felt pressure on her throat, the hands primed to strangle the life out of her.

"Ian?" she whimpered, too horrified to move. The scent of blood invaded her senses once again and she nearly passed out from fear.

"It's going to be okay, Doc. Hold on."

She thought she felt Ian brush past her and, within seconds, he flipped on the light switch. The bulb hanging over them burst to life, blinding them all.

Grace shut her eyes instinctively, the icy hands that held her throat retreating from the light. When she opened them again, all hell broke loose around her.

Alex glared at Aubrey, Jackie cradled lifelessly in his arms. "Get out. Now!"

Aubrey blinked, still reeling from the aftermath of the ritual. She nodded and grabbed Dominic, whose face was white as a sheet. They disappeared up the stairs and out the open basement door.

Alex wasted no time and rose to his feet, carrying Jackie. He stared at Ian and then Grace, his expression filled with torment. "We're done here."

Grace watched numbly as he took Jackie upstairs. Her heart thundered in her ears as she turned to Ian, the sensation of those hands still like frost on her skin. She rubbed at it, willing the feeling to go away.

Ian's eyes locked on her neck. She flinched when his hand shot out to touch her skin.

"Christ, Doc."

"What?"

He shook his head, rising to his feet and pulling her with him. "Let's get the hell out of here."

* * *

Jackie stirred, colorful lights flickering behind her eyes. Her head felt heavy, as though gauze had been shoved into every crevice. She thought she felt a hand brush over her forehead, but a wave of dizziness passed over her and muddled her brain.

She fought to open her eyes and to remember what happened. The feeling of soft blankets beneath her brought comfort, as did the hand that slipped into her own and held.

"God, you scared me." She heard Alex's voice and the tender fear in it brought pain to her heart. The memories came back to her, though vaguely. She still didn't know why she was lying in bed.

"I'm okay." Her voice said nothing, but she knew she mouthed the words. Her throat ached miserably as if it had been on fire.

She felt Alex's soft hair brush her hand as he leaned forward, then his lips as they traced over her skin. "Rest, please."

But she didn't want to rest. She wanted to find out what happened. She forced her eyes open, even though the dim light of the bedside lamp in Grace's bedroom stung them. Pushing aside the instinct to recede back into the hole of nothingness, she stared at Alex with as much purpose as she could muster.

"Look at me, Alex."

He did and she saw his charming face contorted with misery. It quite simply staggered her.

Slowly, he reached up to cradle her face in the palm of his hand. "You didn't warn me you could be possessed."

Her breath caught, and she released it on a long, understanding exhale. "So that's what happened."

"Do you need an exorcism performed or something?"

She shook her head, wincing at the word. "It's not possession. The spirit may have channeled through me, used me to speak, but it's not the same as demonic possession. I'll be fine."

He grimaced. "You didn't look fine, Jackie. You looked like you had the Spanish flu or something. I thought you were going to have a seizure and die."

A small smile softened her face and she tried to sit up so she could face him. She winced at how weak her body was.

"Don't worry so much about me, darling." She cupped his hand that held her face, leaning into it. Her dark eyes glittered in the lamplight. "I have seen and experienced worse things."

He didn't look convinced. "You scared the shit out of me."

"For that, I apologize." She sighed, closing her eyes. "Ray is not gone."

"Tell me something I don't know." He pulled his hand away and got to his feet, pacing the room in agitation. "Aubrey and Dominic took off. Grace and Ian have no idea what to do now. It seems you were right…a séance only made things worse."

Jackie pondered his words for a moment, taking in the room around her. "No, I think one good thing came out of it."

"What's that?"

"There's a gaping hole that Mercy's energy once occupied. I think she may have left the house."

"Maybe she's just out of range."

"No, I think she may have left, maybe only temporarily. But the heavy grief, the torment, the anger…it's gone. I only sense Ray's darkness now."

Alex let out a frustrated breath and came to sit beside her on the bed. "So, what do we do now?"

Jackie reached for his hand. "We do another cleansing ritual. It's a must after a séance, especially one like that. After that…well, I guess I'll have to ask Aubrey. She'll know."

"She didn't know anything," Alex snapped, still on edge over Aubrey's insistence to continue the séance despite Jackie's condition. "She kept pushing, she wouldn't help you."

"She wanted to ensure she had done all she could to get rid of Ray." Jackie released her hand from his and sat back, her gaze drifting off thoughtfully. "She knew that if she didn't then it would all be for nothing."

"What if you had died?" His hands dove into his hair as he had the wild thought of finding Aubrey and strangling her.

"I wasn't in any real danger."

"You could've fooled me."

Jackie pouted, tired of his anger. He was no good to her when he was like this. She needed his soothing, positive temperament if she was to gather her strength.

"Come here." She reached out with her hand, tugging on his shirt. He shifted closer as she dragged him against her, her mouth finding his. She poured everything she had into the kiss, weak as she was, and took as much of his light as she could grasp.

He gave in and gathered her close, his fears of losing her chased away by his relief that at least she was safe. His mouth cruised over hers, his hands tangled in the wild mass of her hair. She nipped at his lower lip playfully and he couldn't help the smile that spread over his face.

"You're doing this on purpose."

Jackie nodded, grasping at his shirt. "I need the strength only you can give me."

"That doesn't even make sense."

"Oh, it does." She pressed her face into his neck to settle her heart. It galloped frantically, as if wanting to run from the knowledge that it was perilously close to falling.

She couldn't. Wouldn't. Shouldn't.

"I need to do the cleansing ritual." She got to her feet slowly, pleased that her knees were stronger than she expected. She smiled down at him. "You can film me again if you'd like."

A half laugh escaped his throat as he stood up. "I didn't realize you liked being in front of the camera so much."

"I don't." She reached for his hand, pulling him from the room. "I just need you by my side tonight."

CHAPTER SEVENTEEN

Fear was not enough to keep Ian from examining the footage taken that night, despite the horrors he experienced. After all, he was an investigator first and foremost, and he'd be damned if anything would chase him away from gathering evidence.

He made a mad dash into the basement to grab the cameras, bringing them upstairs to the living room. He hooked them up to Alex's laptop on the deteriorating coffee table and plugged in the digital recorder to upload the recording of the séance.

Earlier, Jackie had performed a final cleansing ritual before Alex took her back to the hotel room to sleep the rest of the night. They were both still shaken up by what happened, so much so that Alex begged Ian and Grace to join them.

But Grace refused to leave. Even though she had visible marks on her neck, red stripes in the shape of fingers, she wouldn't abandon Sally. And Ian wouldn't abandon Grace.

Though the marks were fading by the minute, Grace still constantly rubbed her neck as though she could still feel the fingers pressing into her skin. Ian watched her out of the corner of his eye as she sat beside him on the sofa, wishing she would take his advice and get some sleep.

He reached for her hand, pulling it away from her neck. "You'll be okay."

She met his eyes. "Talk to me when you've been strangled by a ghost."

Guilt shot through him, though he had nothing to say. Instead, he avoided her eyes and turned to the computer. He tapped away at the keyboard, bringing up the footage taken from Camera B, which had been set up in the back corner of the basement facing the table and the staircase. He hit play at the point where they all took their seats and joined hands.

The pale green of the night vision gave everyone on camera an eerie, surreal look. Eyes were unnaturally translucent, skin strangely pale, and the basement that had been cloaked in near darkness was, on camera, completely lit. The flickering of the candle flames added shadows that bounced off the walls.

"I look terrified," Grace commented, chills running down her back.

"You had a right to be."

Ian turned up the sound and Aubrey's voice echoed through the laptop speakers. "*Ray, if you are here, make yourself known to us.*"

They watched closely as Aubrey continued to ask questions, nothing out of the ordinary happening.

That was when the candle exploded.

Grace jumped despite knowing it was coming. On the screen, a dark shroud seemed to slowly descend upon the basement. The light of the candles dwindled and stilled, almost as if a vacuum had sucked all the air from the room.

She wanted to ask Ian if that was normal, but from the stunned look on his face, it clearly wasn't.

The distant cry of the sparrow came through and Grace felt sick watching her own panicked expression. She had been so worried for Sally, but it seemed the little girl had only been trying to warn them.

Because Mercy was busy trying to channel through Jackie.

That was when she spotted what looked like a small, white orb of light hovering just over Jackie's head. It circled, faltered, then dove straight into her.

"Look, see that?" She pointed at the screen, and Ian nodded.

"That must be Mercy."

They watched as Jackie lost herself to the will of the spirit, her eyes and words no longer her own. She trembled uncontrollably and Grace remembered clinging in panic to her hand, helpless to do anything.

Jackie's screams exploded out of the speakers, piercingly loud and tormented, and Grace felt tears spring hot into her eyes. There was so much pain, so much violent anger in that scream. She realized it was the same scream she would have heard from Mercy out in the harbor had there been any sound.

That was when the abrupt, resounding gong of the broken grandfather clock rang out. Followed immediately by the sound of the basement door being thrown open with a loud bang.

Grace's hands shot to cover her mouth, the fear of that moment alive in her heart. A shudder ran through her body as she watched a dark shadow descend the staircase and begin to circle the table.

"Shit." Ian cursed under his breath, eyes glued to the screen as the shadow flickered in and out, morphing in shape as it stayed just outside the circle of salt. Aubrey's commanding voice did nothing to stop it. Instead, it only seemed to grow in strength.

That was when Alex yelled in anger and distress and Aubrey gave up on Ray and turned her attention to Jackie.

The white orb suddenly emerged from Jackie and swirled off, vanishing the second she came back to herself and fainted.

Then the candles went out. In the night vision, Grace could see the way Ian and Aubrey scrambled to find the matches and the frightened way Dominic bolted from his chair after claiming to have been touched. Alex could be seen clutching Jackie in his arms, helpless to do more than wait.

She saw herself sitting vulnerable in her chair as the black shadow appeared behind her. It loomed over her shoulders menacingly, giving her confirmation of what she had felt.

The shadow vanished the second Ian skirted the table and fumbled along the wall for the light switch, relieving them of darkness. Aubrey and Dominic fled moments later and Alex pulled Jackie into his arms.

Ian reached over to shut off the video, completely speechless. He stared at the screen for a moment longer, on the image of him and Grace, alone in that horrid room.

Grace leaned back, wishing she had never watched the video. It was more concrete proof of the paranormal than anything else she had witnessed, a fact that terrified her. How could anyone deny the truth behind what she just experienced?

"Ian?" she managed, tearing her eyes from the screen to look at him.

He rubbed his face with his hands, then looked at her. "Are you okay?"

She nodded in a quick, uncertain movement. "What was that?"

"I think you know." He reached over for the infrared camera then flipped through to one of the images Alex had captured. He handed it to her silently.

When she looked at it and saw the blue and purple figure of a man hovering in the corner, several shades lighter than the walls themselves, her breath caught. "God."

Ian took the camera back from her and patted her on the knee. "We'll figure something out, Doc."

"Will we?" She let out a delirious laugh and got to her feet, unable to stare at the computer any longer. Her hands ran over her neck again. "Maybe I should just get used to living with ghosts."

Ian tapped back into the computer, eager to listen to the audio from the digital recorder. "Whatever. If you want to give up now, it's no skin off my nose."

Grace crossed her arms and shot him a heated look. "Oh, that's nice. You know, this ghost thing wasn't even an issue before you guys showed up. I'm beginning to think all this investigating has made it worse."

"A lot of things made it worse." Ian gritted his teeth and was sorely tempted to slip on his headphones and ignore her. Knowing she would likely hit him over the head with something if he tried, he turned to face her. "Look, we're doing all we can. Yeah, that séance was fucked up and I'm sorry you got hurt. But Jackie says it got Mercy out of the house, so at least we have that. Now we can focus on Ray."

Grace let her head fall back as she sighed. "Fucked up is putting it mildly." She brought her eyes back down to his, her lips pursed in a pout. "And it doesn't hurt, I'm just freaked out."

His shoulders fell, wishing he could have done something to protect her. "I'm sorry, Grace. I really am."

"It's not your fault." She approached him, reaching for his hand. "Why don't we take a break before you listen for ghost voices, okay? I need you."

He blinked. "You need me?"

"Yeah." Her mouth curved slowly, intimately. "If you'll

have me, anyway."

"You want to have sex at a time like this?"

Frustration flashed over her face as she pulled her hand back.

"Damnit, yes! I do." She let out a laugh that was borderline mad and dragged her hands through her hair. "I need something to make me forget all this *death*. I know you could use it, too. You're so on edge, you look like you could tear the head off a Barbie doll and stick needles in its eyes."

He frowned at the visual, but rose to his feet. "All right, Doc. If you insist."

"Well, don't make me pull your arm or anything." Her eyes were filled with frustration even as she bit back a smile. She began unbuttoning her blouse, surprised her hands didn't shake.

"Only if you want to." He closed in on her, slowly walking her backward to the wall. Her shirt slipped from her shoulders and she let it fall to the floor as he tore off his own.

His teeth flashed in a predatory grin, disarming her. Without warning, he pinned her against the wall of the living room, his mouth hungrily finding hers. He lifted her hips so her legs could straddle him, his fingers digging into her skin through the jeans she wore. Her mind reeled from the assault and relief shot through her like a drug. It rammed into her like a searing white wave, and she relished every last drop of it.

Her nails raked down his bare back, a desperate moan escaping her throat as his teeth nipped her collar bone. "You think I'm crazy, don't you? I should be scared, upset, *something*."

He met her eyes, intense and direct. "You're done with that, Grace. Live your damn life already."

She nodded. "Okay."

He captured her mouth again, wanting nothing more than to make her forget it all. To let go. She was more than capable of it, was so much stronger than she realized. He wanted that strength from her now.

He needed it. Craved it.

Almost as much as he loved her.

The realization of it exploded within him and he wasted none of it, riding on its powerful rush. It tore through him with an urgency that blinded, humbled, and alarmed all at once.

Good God, he was in love with her. Which meant that everything suddenly mattered a whole lot more.

Grace's eyes fluttered closed as her head fell to the side, lost in him. Lost to him. He suddenly took on a tenderness she hadn't been expecting, and it rocked her until she was completely senseless. She buried her face in his neck, stunned by it.

Her heart cried out his name, and she fell victim to its command. It was over for her now, there would be no stopping it. She was done for, fallen, helpless.

Joy shot like a dart into her chest and she let its warmth envelop her as he slipped off her jeans, lifted her once again, and took her. Her legs hooked around his hips as her hands clung to his back.

Ian held her against the wall, each movement he made further damning him. Falling for her meant he would never be the same. But he didn't care, because loving her was the greatest drug, the most exhilarating high. It surpassed everything that had come before it.

All that mattered now was saving her.

They both failed to notice the shadows that slithered along the walls around them like living, breathing things. They roamed over the plaster, snaking closer. Watching. Filled with rage. With jealousy and hatred.

They zeroed in on Grace, tormented into a frenzy. Every cry she uttered, every exhaled release, infuriated them. Her heart that beat hot and true with passion and love chased away her grief, her sorrow. It rid her of the pain she'd been consumed by for so long.

The spirits hated her for it. They wanted her miserable, then they needed her dead. Only at that point would she, at last, be truly held captive to the house.

To the beast Ray had created.

* * *

Jackie awoke early the next morning with a blinding headache. It pierced through her temple and shocked her out of a shallow, restless sleep.

She sat up, her palm pressed to her forehead as she looked wearily around the hotel room. For a moment, she completely forgot where she was. It all came back to her when she noticed Alex lying beside her, fast asleep and lightly snoring.

She stared at him, her heart aching. She wanted nothing more than to just curl up beside him and fall back asleep, to forget the world and all its troubles.

It wasn't possible, not now. If she stayed, then he would only get used to seeing her there. She couldn't allow that to happen, for his sake and for her own.

She had no choice but to go.

Moments later, she snuck out of the hotel room dressed in the clothes from the night before. She resisted the urge to look back at him, knowing it would only hurt more. He wasn't going to be happy with her for leaving unannounced, but she knew he would get over it.

Her Alex never held onto anger.

It wasn't until she'd climbed into her Jeep that Alex had driven to the hotel the night before that she realized what she had done. What she had started to believe as truth.

Her Alex? He was no more hers than she was his, and she knew she had to stand firm on that. As much as she may enjoy and appreciate him, it had to end there. There was no other option for her. There never had been.

She drove the three miles to Dominic's house in dead silence, not feeling up to listening to the radio. The roads were slick from the previous night's rain, the clouds still heavy and misty in the sky.

Normally, the damp chill of the wind calmed her. Now it only made her feel hollow, empty. It hurt her skin and dug deep into her lungs to fight its way to her heart. Her heart that told itself it knew better. She couldn't afford to be so foolish where Alex was concerned.

When she arrived at the house, she saw Aubrey's white sedan parked out front. She had a sneaking suspicion she'd find the woman in Dominic's bed, but felt no jealousy. He deserved happiness, even if it was with a callous, heartless woman like Aubrey.

She grabbed her key and let herself in, finding the house still and quiet. It was just past eight o'clock in the morning, meaning no one would be awake for a few hours. She started to go upstairs, but heard a noise coming from the kitchen.

She followed the noise and found Aubrey sitting at the dining table, her hands wrapped around a mug of steaming tea and her eyes haunted.

Jackie stepped into the room. "Is everything all right?"

Aubrey looked up from her tea and gasped, her eyes widening. "Oh, Jackie. I didn't think I would see you again... great Goddess, are you okay?"

Jackie tried to smile but knew it fell short as she took a seat beside her old friend. "I'm right as rain."

Aubrey didn't look convinced. "I tried, I really did. I'm sorry it didn't work. I'm sorry she used you instead of me. You weren't prepared for it, I was."

Jackie waved off the comment. "How could you have known?"

Aubrey frowned, avoiding Jackie's eyes. "I bet the guys

are furious with me, aren't they?"

"No, not at all. They know you tried your best to get rid of Ray's spirit."

"Alex was pissed." Aubrey pouted, embarrassment creasing her brow. "I didn't realize you two were so close…"

"We're not," Jackie countered, rising to her feet to grab a cup of tea for herself. She needed distance from that conversation topic. "We need your advice on what else we can do to banish Ray from the house."

Aubrey looked over at her curiously. "You mentioned wanting to dig up the body. I still don't think that's a good idea, but you never know."

"Yes, but if it's Mercy's body, it may not be enough." Jackie poured hot water from the tea kettle on the stove into a white and black checkered mug.

"I thought you said it *wasn't* Mercy's body, that she didn't die in the house?"

Jackie turned around, dropping a tea bag into the mug. "After last night, after what Mercy said about being trapped… I'm not so sure. Maybe she died outside the house, but Ray buried her body in the basement."

Aubrey sipped her tea as Jackie came to sit beside her again. "Well, you could try a banishing ritual using copper. With the right incantation, it should, in a sense, burn the spirits and chase them out."

"Okay, thank you." Jackie smiled, drinking her tea as she gave it some thought. She had never performed a ritual like that before, but it shouldn't be too difficult. She would just need a necklace made of copper wire, plus the usual trappings of salt, holy water, her rosary, and a mountain of prayers.

She heard footsteps coming down the stairs and watched as Dominic wandered into the kitchen, shirtless and grumpy. When he saw her, he stopped dead in his tracks.

"Jackie." He stared at her as if she were a ghost, then walked slowly up to her and examined her from head to toe. "I thought you'd died."

She sighed. "I am made of stronger stuff than you give me credit for."

He glanced around the room warily. "Did that asshole Alex follow you here?"

"No, why?"

"I don't like him."

"You don't like very many people."

"Yeah, but he's not like us, Jackie. None of them are." A fiery heat came into his eyes as he stared her down. "Don't you see the judgment on their faces? They don't understand us."

Aubrey nodded in agreement. "Total judgment. We had some good times, but they don't get what it's like to be an outsider like we do."

"That hot shot doctor, you think she knows what it's like to be shunned by society for simply being what she is?" Dominic threw up his hands in frustration. "No, she doesn't. Because she's one of *them*, and not one of *us*."

Jackie's head shook as she stared at them in disbelief. "They're good people."

"They're people who will drop you the second they don't need you anymore." Dominic fired back. "They want to use you, and then once they're done, they'll move on with their *evidence* and you'll be left with nothing. I know it's happened to you before."

"I don't want anything from them. I want them to move on," Jackie countered, even as an uneasy feeling settled in her gut. "I won't hold them back."

Aubrey cut in, reaching for Jackie's hand sympathetically. "There's no future with Alex, honey. Girls like us don't wind up with the boy next door. It just doesn't happen. They all think it will be a fun ride for a while, but eventually we get smothered by talk of weddings and babies and white picket fences, and they get frustrated. That's just how it works."

Jackie pulled her hand away, even though she knew Aubrey was right. "I'm going upstairs to take a shower." She fled from the kitchen, leaving them behind with the truth hanging sickeningly in the air.

How had she even let it get this far?

* * *

Alex awoke to an empty hotel room. One look at the clock on the nightstand had him groaning. It was already noon. How had he slept so long?

He sat up and rubbed his hands over his face, urging the sleep from his system. Jackie's purse was gone, and when he got up to peek out the window he saw her Jeep was gone too. What time had she left?

She had left him without a means to follow her. He'd have to call Ian to come and get him, or catch a cab to the house where they had picked up Dominic and Aubrey the day before. Though the very thought bothered him, he knew that was more than likely where she'd gone.

He wasn't going to let her slip from his grasp so easily. They still had unfinished business to take care of, both with the Sparrow House and with each other. She could try to vanish into thin air, but he would find her. He had determination on his side.

He took a quick shower and slipped into comfortable jeans and a green T-shirt, deciding against bothering Ian for a ride. His friend would likely be wrapped up in Grace and he didn't want to bother them.

He phoned a cab and waited impatiently for it to arrive, tapping his foot as he stood just outside the hotel by the curb. When it finally pulled up, he hopped inside and leaned over to give directions to the driver.

The short drive felt like ages. He tapped his hands on his kneecaps, trying not to wonder over the reasons why she may have left without telling him.

It hadn't taken much to convince her to come back to the hotel room with him after she had finished the cleansing ritual. In fact, she'd gone without argument, then collapsed into his bed the second they arrived, exhausted.

If she was angry with him, she didn't show it. So why had she left without at least waking him?

The only answer he could come up with was that she didn't feel she had to. While he understood, being a carefree individual himself, it still bothered him. Probably because he knew she was slipping away from him, little by little. She was placing distance between them to ease herself out of his life.

He couldn't let her. And when he saw her again, he had to make her see that she was it for him. That there would be no one else to compare to her, ever.

He carried these thoughts with him as the cab pulled up to the house. He handed the driver a wad of cash, then jumped from the car and stormed up the walkway.

His fist pounded on the door, a bit harder than he meant.

Aubrey answered, lips parting in surprise as she stared up at him. "What are you doing here?"

"I need to see Jackie." He peered past her into the house, hoping he'd see her. Instead, he saw a few strangers wandering around, lazing on the sofas, eating cereal in the kitchen.

"She's busy right now, but she says she plans to go by the house later today." Aubrey began to shut the door, but his hand shot out to stop her.

"Later today doesn't work. I need to see her now." He pushed past her and wandered around the downstairs. Aubrey shrugged and shut the door, and Alex saw the jealousy on her face as he passed her and went upstairs.

"Jackie!" he called out as he reached the top of the stairs, looking left and right down the hallway. He went left and said her name again, louder this time.

When a door opened slowly at the other end of the hall, he abruptly turned and saw her lean out of it.

"Alex?" Worry darkened her eyes as he approached. "Is everything okay?"

He looked past her into the bedroom, seeing Dominic lying lazily on the bed, fully clothed, smoking a joint.

"I needed to see you." His eyes came back to hers and anger sparked in them. "Please tell me this isn't what I think it is."

Jackie glanced over her shoulder, then realized what he meant. "Oh. No, no it isn't." She closed the door at her back and faced him.

"Good." He pushed her up against the door and kissed her, everything he felt rushing out of him and into the act itself. He felt her yield to him, her knees failing her as she clung to his shoulders. Her breath was ragged as his mouth tore over hers, both jealous and desperate all at once.

She arched against him, then fell limp the second he released her.

"I love you." His gaze bored into her own, burning with flames of green.

She winced, her heart fracturing. "Please, don't." Her eyes closed tight as she fought back the panic, his words destroying her.

Alex frowned, frustration exploding within him. "Don't do what? Admit that I want you? That I need you? That you're the most incredible person I've ever met?"

"You don't even know me." She shivered, her eyes opening even though she avoided looking at him.

"Then tell me everything." He touched her face, his fingers

trailing back into her hair. "Please, Jackie."

"I can't."

"Why let me in at all then? Why let me get close just to turn me away now?" he demanded, urging her to face him. Pain and anger fueled him like kerosene fuels a fire.

A tear slipped down her cheek. "I used you."

"Used me?" He couldn't believe what he was hearing. He pulled away and shoved his hands into his pockets. Disgust filled his eyes as he stared down at her. "I don't know what these people put into your head, but the girl I've been hanging out with all these weeks wouldn't do this. You're different than they want you to believe."

She watched him go and the strings holding her heart together snapped, rendering her useless. More tears fell as she heard the front door slam.

God, she was a fool, she realized with panic. She was letting the best thing in her life walk right out the door. And for what? Because she was too afraid of love, of commitment? Too afraid to let herself be happy when she had gone so long with only having herself?

Alex could change all of that. If she would only let him in.

She made the decision in that instant and raced after him. She passed Aubrey downstairs, but ignored her questions as she tore outside.

Her crimson dress fluttered behind her as she ran, her dark curls tossed up by the stormy wind that smelled of rain. It came down in thick droplets that bounced off her skin and blended with the tears on her face.

Her heart faltered when she saw him walking down the sidewalk, head lowered and hands in his pockets. She called out to him, but he didn't turn around. It wasn't until she reached him and grabbed his arm that he looked at her.

The rain continued to fall, drenching his hair so dark blond strands of it clung to his forehead. Anger hardened his face, but the second she leapt into his arms and kissed him she sensed it slip away.

Her heart thundered in time with the storm above them, and she gave everything she had to the kiss. All the uncertainty, the surrender, the *love*…

"You have my heart," she murmured, pressing her lips to his jawline tenderly. Her hands trailed up to frame his face.

Alex held her tightly, relief soothing the knife wound to the gut she'd given him only moments before. "Then tell me everything. Let me in."

She nodded, backing away and taking his hand in hers. "I will."

Moments later, they sat beneath the protection of a sweeping tree that faced the sea. Rain fell in a steady hum all around them, the waves crashing with continuous fury beyond the rocky shore.

He leaned back against the trunk of the tree, his arm wrapped over her shoulders to keep her warm. She didn't mind the cold, not when he was beside her.

"Tell me from the beginning," he requested, caressing her hand that lay upon his chest.

She let out a hesitant sigh and stared at the ocean. What she was about to tell him was something she had never told another living person. It hurt to tear down her protective veil, but she knew she had to. Knew that if anyone should know, it was Alex. "Jackie is a nickname, not my given name."

He stiffened against her. "What's your name, then?"

"Mary Jacqueline Hart."

"Mary…" He tried out the name, deciding it didn't suit her. "Jackie is better."

"I agree." She tilted her head back to kiss his cheek, a soft smile curving her lips. "I was born in Saginaw, Michigan. My father was a tailor, my mother a school teacher."

"Sounds pretty normal to me."

"I suppose it was in the beginning." She turned her attention back to the sea. "My parents were devout Catholics. We spent so much of our time with the church, in the church, thinking of the church. When my mother passed on, my father took over my upbringing with what most would call a heavy hand."

"He hit you?"

"Never with his fists…he had a belt he preferred instead." Her eyes became misty as the memories flooded back to her. "I suppose that's why seeing Mercy's torture affected me so badly. Though my own experiences weren't as horrific, it still hurt to relive the lash of a belt."

Alex cursed under his breath, furious at the thought of her being whipped with a belt wielded by her own father. He and his sister had enjoyed such a comfortable childhood by comparison.

"I saw my first spirit when I was six years old," she continued. "When I told my father, he believed I was possessed by a demon. He tried to beat it out of me, and when that didn't work, he asked our priest to consider performing an exorcism."

Alex cringed, mortified.

"I didn't know then that the best thing I could've done was hide my gift. Instead, I let my curiosity get the better of me and I continued to explore it. When he would catch me talking to a spirit, or in his eyes talking to the Devil, he would panic. He didn't want his only daughter to succumb to evil. It got to the point where he wouldn't let me leave the house, or even my room. He locked me away, afraid for me. Afraid *of* me." Her fingers tightened over Alex's shirt as she forced back the waves of resentment. "When our priest refused to perform the exorcism, my father took it upon himself to do so. I was thirteen."

Alex was silent for a long moment before he asked a

question he couldn't resist. "What was it like?"

Jackie's eyes closed, her father's words from all those years ago echoing hollowly in her mind. *Depart, then, transgressor. Depart, seducer, full of lies and cunning, foe of virtue, persecutor of the innocent...*

"It...changed me." She pulled her rosary from her pocket, stringing it between her fingers. Staring at the tiny silver cross gave her strength. "Despite the ritual, I still had my gift. I understood then that God had given it to me not to do evil, but to do good. My whole perception of life changed the moment I accepted myself. While the exorcism distanced me from the church, I never lost my faith. I swore I would never let anyone get close enough to imprison me the way my father had."

"Did he ever accept you?"

She sighed. "No. I ran away from home when I was sixteen and never went back. I haven't seen him since. It took me a long time to forgive him. And in many ways, I suppose I still haven't."

Alex pressed a soft kiss to her forehead. "Has he ever tried to find you?"

"I don't know. I've done my best to stay hidden all these years...even went as far as to go by a name he would never think to call me. I never stay in one place longer than six months, just enough time to get a job waiting tables and save some money."

"Sounds lonely."

Her hand roamed over his chest, a smile blooming over her face. "Not always. I've met so many people, seen so many places...have you ever been to New Orleans? Seen the Mississippi river at night and watched the fireflies dance?"

He shook his head, enjoying the happiness that brightened her eyes.

"It's the most magical thing. Well, almost as lovely as this one place out west, where the mountains are jagged and white as shark teeth and this glorious river cuts through the trees..."

He chuckled, and she looked up at him curiously. "What?"

"Nothing. I just enjoy the way you describe things."

Her face flushed, and she looked away from him. "My freedom is everything to me. I need to be able to go where fate takes me at a moment's notice. I will never be restricted again. Do you understand?"

"Is there any reason why I can't tag along?"

Excitement at the possibility shot through her, wondering if he meant it. But then, he was a man with roots—a family, friends, a career. She could never make him leave all that.

"I don't want you to, Alex," she decided, sitting up so she could face him. She ran a hand through his wet hair, her smile sad. "Just know that you have my heart and let that be enough. I'll be around, but I won't always stay. If you can accept that, accept me as I am, then I will give you as much as I am able to give."

He considered her words for a long, quiet moment, wondering if it could be enough. Maybe it would have to be.

"Deal." He pulled her in for a slow, tender kiss, his hand trailing over her neck. When he pulled away, he noticed the rain had stopped. "Maybe we should head back to the hotel room."

A sly smile lifted the corners of her mouth. "I'm actually very fond of this little spot." She pushed him until he lay back on the soft grass and crawled over him. Her lips traced the lines of his face, her heart singing, filled with joy. "Tell me again, darling. Tell me you love me."

He brushed aside her hair as his eyes met hers, grass green into gypsy brown. "I love you."

She smiled, then covered his mouth with hers in a hungry, devastating kiss. His hands ran over her back, holding her close. Welcoming her home.

Relief flooded through her at having her past exposed, out in the open. There were no more secrets between them, no demons digging their claws into her heart. She was free of it all and free to love him.

And, Lord, did she love him.

CHAPTER EIGHTEEN

Cello in hand, Grace sat beside her bedroom window and began to play. Her mind filled with hopeful thoughts of Sally and Mercy, and darker, more hateful thoughts of Ray.

Though the marks of his hands were gone, her loathing for him remained. She hated that her desire to help was outweighed by her inability to do anything substantial. It seemed there was no end to the suffering that plagued the Sparrow House.

Sally needed her. Mercy was tormented. And Ray was pure evil. How in the world had she gotten herself involved in any of this?

Because she knew the answer was beyond her comprehension, she gave in to the one thing she had. The one constant, unrestrained comfort. The cello.

Ian watched from the bed, silently reverent of her. The sunlight came in through the window, giving her ivory skin a surreal, angelic glow. Strands of her hair fell over her face as she tossed her head back, lost in the music she played. The very image of it, of her in this intense moment of vulnerability, humbled him. Just as it had the first time he'd seen her play.

His realization from the night before troubled him. He didn't want the complication of loving her, and yet there it was. Staring him in the face like a blazing, neon sign. Somewhere along the way, he'd developed feelings for the doctor. For the woman who grated on his nerves like sandpaper and did nothing but complain and argue with him. What sick twist of fate was this?

But he didn't try and ignore its effect on him. In fact, he knew he couldn't.

Probably because at that moment, he wanted her. He wanted all the baggage, all the grief, all the cynicism and sarcastic remarks. He would take every poisoned dart she threw at him with pleasure if only because that was when she was most alive. In those moments, she wasn't plagued by grief. She was simply the clever, witty, fun woman he'd come to know. *That* was the woman he loved. And he would accept everything else if only to be with her.

He didn't want to think about what the future held for them. It muddied the waters of his optimism and he wanted no part of that. His goal was to stick by her side until the house was rid of the spirits. Until they reached that milestone, he would ignore the uncertainty wallowing in his gut over whether or not they would even remain in the same damn city after all was said and done.

He figured they'd cross that bridge when they came to it.

When Grace slowed her playing and rested on a long, haunted note, Ian smiled. "Bravo."

She looked at him, her eyes wet with unshed tears but her smile playful. *"Grazie."*

He patted the bed, inviting her to join him. She rose to her feet and set aside her cello before crawling in beside him. Their legs intertwined under the sheets and he kissed her forehead tenderly.

She pulled back and met his eyes. "Hi."

"Hey." His mouth found hers, not wanting to talk. He had other things in mind.

He gripped her waist, holding her against him. She softened under his touch, her body curving into his.

With a movement that was both urgent and nimble, she pushed him back against the bed and rose over him with a wicked smile.

She ran her hands along his bare chest, the urge to tell him how she felt roaring through her. Empowering her. The words were on her lips, eager to be spoken. They frightened her, and yet there they were. *I love you.*

But uncertainty had them retreating like scalded hands from a boiling pot of water. How could she say them when so much of what was happening between them was because of the house and the ghosts?

More likely than not, none of this meant anything to him. And in her current state of mind, hearing him say so could shatter her. Ruin her. God knew she'd been there before. With Ian, somehow she knew it would hurt even more.

It was best to ignore the fire in her heart. She had no desire to dwell on what the future held, so instead she would focus on this moment. On the man before her, the hunter of all things she had never believed in before.

Her hand found his and she kissed the tattoo on his knuckles, the symbol of his life's work and his ambition. What she once found to be foolish she now adored. Somewhere along the way, the entire situation stopped being one big joke and became horrifyingly real.

"Stop thinking." He reached up with his free hand and pulled her face down to his, his mouth teasing hers. Their eyes met and held, and he saw a spark of humor in all that gray.

"Good point. If I think too much I'll realize what a mistake this is."

"Or you'll realize you're in love with me, and then we'll have big problems."

She laughed, trying to hide her uneasiness. "*Very* big problems."

He kissed her again, riding on the feel of her body over his. The scent of her lavender soap hit him as his hands combed through her hair, and her answering groan sent his mind reeling with a dark, hungry need.

To hell with it, he thought wildly. Just tell her the truth.

He murmured her name, the words that followed nearly tumbling to freedom. They would have been spoken, had it not been for the resounding crash that exploded downstairs.

Grace jumped, her eyes flying open in shock. "What was that?"

Ian frowned, pushing her aside. "Stay here."

He got out of bed and tugged on a pair of jeans, leaving her behind as he ventured to the stairs. Within seconds, she was behind him, a robe tucked around her body.

He glared over his shoulder at her, but she only shrugged. "Don't go all caveman on me now. You might need me."

"I might need you to stay the hell away from whatever just made that noise," he grumbled, though he turned away from her and made his way downstairs. His eyes scanned the entryway, then peered into the kitchen and living room as he got closer.

Nothing. No shadow, no apparition. No intruder.

Then Grace screamed.

"No!" She bolted toward the grandfather clock, which had been wrenched from the wall and thrown onto the floor. Glass and shards of wood lay scattered and mangled, and Grace knelt before them in shock and horror.

A thing of such beauty. Destroyed.

"How?" She uttered the word despite knowing it was useless. She knew the clock hadn't just fallen over on its own. It had been dragged, forced from its sturdy location and hurled onto the floor with such ferocity that it was demolished.

It would never run again. And although it had already been deteriorating, Grace felt the loss like a searing knife slicing through her very heart.

Ian continued to stare around the room uneasily. He felt sorry for her, but knew the clock was the least of their problems. Ray was clearly up and about, ready to start a war, and it wasn't even past breakfast.

"Call Jackie. We need to stop this. Tonight," Ian ordered, only to whirl around as the front door burst open and Alex and Jackie stumbled in.

"What the hell was that?" Alex ran into the living room, eyeing Grace and the ruined clock warily. "We heard that from the street."

Jackie came up beside him, her arm encircling his as her eyes took in the scene. "The creature did this. It's in the corner, laughing at us."

Ian ran his hands over his face and grunted. "What can we do? Please tell me you figured something out."

Jackie nodded, lifting the necklace of intricately woven copper wire for him to see. "Aubrey passed on this necklace and an incantation to me. I may be able to make it work."

"Good. Let's do it."

"I still feel we need to dig up the body," Jackie added, looking around at the others. "If we can free Mercy's mortal form from its prison, perhaps Ray will follow her."

Alex looked down at her worriedly. "Are you sure?"

"I'm afraid we are running out of options."

"Okay. So we'll do that, too." Ian looked down at Grace. "That okay with you, Doc?"

Angry heat flared in her eyes, her hands filled with shards of the broken clock. "I just want that bastard out of my house."

Ian's lips spread in a dark grin. "Good. Now find us a shovel."

* * *

From the palpable tension vibrating in the air, it was clear that Ray was not pleased.

Jackie felt his rage. It pulsated behind the walls of the basement as though hundreds of fists were pounding all at once against the concrete. She watched the tenuous weave dividing the spirit world and reality bend with each violent hit, closer and closer to breaking. Soon, there would be no divide at all. The house was perilously close to being swallowed whole by the monsters.

If that happened, then all was lost. They had no choice but to act fast and act well.

She watched as Ray's shadow creature scampered along the edge of the wall, eager for a chance to cause mayhem. Through eyes that burned like embers, it glared at the necklace she held.

Knowing it detested the copper pleased her. It gave her hope that Aubrey's suggestion would work. She said a silent prayer just in case and turned her attention to the dark stain of death beneath the stairs that covered a body. Mercy's body.

She watched as Alex placed a static camera in the corner. In his hands, he held the Mel Meter and the Spirit Box while Ian carried the shovel Grace found in a shed out back. Grace hovered beside him, arms crossed and a strained look on her face. Coming back into the basement was not an easy task for any of them.

The anxiety in the air was contagious and Jackie let out a

soothing breath to try and combat it. She had to remain vigilant and strong. Any sign of weakness would make her vulnerable to Ray's spirit, especially if unearthing the body of his daughter riled him up even more than he already was. She had to believe that removing the body, the bones, would usher his spirit out of the house.

Her hand tightened over the braided copper necklace and she willed it to protect her. To protect them all.

Ian lifted the shovel. "We ready?"

She nodded then watched as he drove the shovel forcefully into the hard-packed dirt beneath the stairs. The initial impact sent shockwaves throughout the basement, rippling like heat waves over the floor. A dark smoky substance began to spill from the freshly disturbed earth, one only she could see. It seeped out of the ground like a sickly black oil, bubbling and churning. The sight of it sent shivers down her spine, a warning sign that something was off. Something was horribly wrong.

The more strikes Ian made to the dirt exposed what lay beneath. He was out of breath, sweat beading on his forehead as he uncovered the first yellowed bone in the shallow grave. It protruded from the musty earth, barely recognizable as the curve of a skull.

A shattered one.

Jagged edges lined a gaping hole in the surface of the bone. As Ian knelt and began to brush away the dirt with his hands, he revealed the rest of what had once been a face.

"Christ." Grace covered her mouth with her hands, mortified.

Jackie began to shake. "Something's wrong."

"What is it?" Alex reached for her, finding the skin of her forearm ice cold.

She shook her head as Ian began to expose more of the remains, seemingly too large to be those of a young woman.

The black oil that spilled from the ground spread out toward their feet, and Jackie backed away from it in fear. Her heart beat frantically as she tried to make sense of it, to understand how she could have been so stupid.

"I was wrong." She trembled uncontrollably as sudden and violent visions blinded her. Ray's spirit emerged, freed from the grave at last, and showed her everything. He exposed the truth he was unable to show before.

She saw his death with horrifying clarity, the unexpected blow to the head so powerful it cracked through bone and splattered blood and brain. There had been so much hate behind the act. A vengeful, righteous sort of hate that spurred its host to pick up an axe and kill.

And then his killer had dragged his body down into the basement and buried him beneath the stairs where no one would find him for a hundred years. His fury behind the circumstances of his death thundered around her, the fists pounding the walls growing louder and more powerful. Cracks appeared as they started to break through the cement, and the shadow creature raced around the room furiously.

The others stared at the walls in horror. Dust began to drift down from the ceiling above them, shaken free by the spreading cracks.

"What's happening?" Grace stammered, instinctively pulling Ian out from under the stairs. He stood beside her, brows knit together as he stared around the room.

A single, mortified tear fell from Jackie's right eye. "That's not Mercy."

"Who the hell is it, then?" Ian demanded.

"Ray." The word was said on an exhale as her eyes rolled back and she gave in to another blast of vision. Ray showed Mercy walking out to the edge of the lonely dock, a bag of bricks in her arms and her face emotionless. She tied the bag to her waist with a rope then, without hesitation, took the plunge into the icy depths of the harbor.

She had murdered her father then took her own life. Jackie wanted to believe that a desire for justice compelled her to kill. But it became horrifyingly clear that Mercy embodied nearly as much evil as her father did.

She was the one keeping Sally from her father out of jealousy. *She* was the one terrorizing the house and wreaking havoc, posing as Ray, leading them to believe a lie. Her suffering at the hands of her father was real, but her final act of revenge and self-destruction had tarnished her spirit. It had damned her soul. And although Aubrey had managed to banish Mercy's spirit from the house during the séance, her *creature* remained. The mindless culmination of violent hate and explosive evil that plagued the house was in fact not Ray's at all.

It was Mercy's.

The light of the single bulb hanging from the ceiling began to flicker and the Mel Meter shrilled loudly. The sound of it reverberated off the walls, almost like a war siren. Get out, it seemed to say. Take cover.

It shook Jackie from the clutches of the vision. She met Alex's eyes, fear paralyzing her.

"Are you okay?" he asked, his hand grasping her shoulder.

She forgot the words to the incantation she needed to use and her mind flailed about helplessly. Her hand gripped the necklace as her eyes were pulled to the area beneath the stairs.

She saw Ray standing there, dressed in a Victorian-era suit. His dark hair was long and scraggly, slicked back from a lean and gaunt face. Blood ran in rivulets down the side of his cheek, the wound that brought his death a gaping hole above his right temple. Eyes dark as coal housed beneath a heavy brow regarded her with amusement, then shifted focus on Grace.

Rage sparked a fire around him and he lunged. *Mercy!*

Understanding had Jackie crying out in warning. "He thinks you're his daughter!"

The others witnessed a shadowy mass rise from the bones and rush at Grace. She braced her arms over her face and turned away from the attack, unable to do more.

A white mist rapidly formed between her and Ray's dark spirit, acting as a shield as it blocked his advance. He retreated into the shadows and Grace eyed the white mist in shock as it formed a protective barrier around her.

"Ian?" She called out anxiously, staring at him through the mist. "What's happening?"

His jaw clenched. "I think it's Sally."

She swallowed a lump in her throat. "Oh. A ghost bodyguard. Okay. That's totally normal."

Jackie let out a relieved breath but watched as Ray continued to prowl in the shadows. The shadow creature hovered beside him, eager to harm. To destroy.

She lifted the necklace up like a talisman as the words of the incantation came flooding back to her. She had the spirits right where she needed them. Soon it would be over.

Beside her, Alex lifted the Spirit Box with a fierce smile. "Let's see if he has anything to say."

He flipped it on and static poured out, bouncing off the walls. Within seconds, a voice came through, warbled and deep.

"Fuck you!" Hysterical, high-pitched laughter followed.

Jackie's breath caught in her throat. She snatched the Spirit Box from Alex's hand and shut it off. Alex looked at her in confusion. Before she could explain, the shadow creature rushed out of the darkness and propelled itself straight into his chest.

It hit like a bull to a matador, violent and untamed. It stole the very breath from his lungs and stopped his heart.

Alex stumbled back from the force of the blow, his face

pale and his eyes glassy with shock. He reached out weakly for Jackie, his fingertips grazing her arm as he tumbled backward and fell to the floor lifelessly.

Jackie watched him crumple and her heart split hideously in two. One half grieved, while the other half raged. She whirled around to face the spirits and held the copper necklace up high.

"You are not welcome here! I cast you out that your spirit be burned. Let this copper serve as my torch. Let its energy scorch your presence. Only the power of love and light is welcome here!" Her voice thundered over the basement walls, echoing mightily. The spirits exploded, shadows writhing with screams of pain and submission at her words. The power behind them forced the darkness and evil from the confines of the house and into oblivion. They fled, every last member of the Sullivan family. Then there was nothing left.

The walls ceased to tremble. The light bulb steadied. The sound of Ray's screams faded out as if sucked into a black hole. The heavy shroud of darkness that plagued the house lifted, fleeing toward the sky as though chased by the light of a rising sun.

All went silent. All went still.

For a moment that seemed like an eternity, Jackie absorbed the emptiness. The loss of spirits. The house was no longer home to them, the bond broken. Only Sally remained, but her shackles were released. Mercy no longer held her prisoner.

Relief knocked at the door of her heart, but Jackie refused to answer. Instead, she turned around and fell to the floor beside Alex. He lay still, not breathing. Strands of his hair splayed over his forehead, his eyes closed as though in sleep.

If only.

Grace was already on top of him, performing CPR. She forced his mouth open and breathed air into his lungs, then sat back to pump his chest with her hands. "C'mon, Alex. Come back to me."

Ian knelt beside her, all color drained from his face. "You can't die on me, Alex. Wake up."

Jackie reached into her pocket for her rosary, tears spilling from her eyes. Please God, she prayed silently. Please don't take him.

She reached for one of Alex's lifeless hands and squeezed it tight, then closed her eyes and began to pray aloud in a hurried whisper. She fell back on the old traditions of her childhood, on the faith that had never left her. "Our Father who art in Heaven, hallowed be thy name…"

Grace forced more air into Alex's lungs and resumed chest compressions.

"Thy kingdom come. Thy will be done. On Earth as it is in Heaven."

Ian met eyes with Grace and saw the determination she felt. She wasn't going to give up.

Jackie's voice faltered as pain swallowed her heart. She continued to pray. "Give us this day our daily bread, and forgive us our trespasses. As we forgive those who trespass against us."

"Damnit, Alex." Grace's vision blurred with desperate tears as she pinched his nose and blew more air into his lungs, knowing the clock was ticking. The longer he didn't breathe the more likely it was that he never would again.

"Lead us not into temptation, but deliver us from evil. For thine is the kingdom, the power, and the glory. Amen." Jackie crossed herself and lifted Alex's hand to her lips, pressing a shaky kiss to his knuckles.

Grace sat back and wiped away the sweat on her forehead, out of breath and heartbroken. For a long, haunted moment, she believed he was gone. She had failed to save him.

Jackie held Alex's hand to her face, murmuring her love for him over and over again. She prayed he could hear it. The words that had been too hard to say before were now so clear it stunned her. How could she have been so blind?

And now, it was too late.

Suddenly, Alex's eyes flew open and he sucked in a huge gulp of air, his body shuddering with it. His head fell back as he struggled to breathe, delirious from the lack of oxygen.

Ian's mouth twisted in a hard grin. "Good, buddy. Keep breathing."

Grace let out a frantic laugh. She checked his heart rate and the dilation of his pupils. "Relax. You just came back from the dead."

"What?" Alex managed, blinking as he tried to focus his vision on the three faces peering down at him. He caught Jackie's eyes and smiled weakly. "Hey, beautiful."

An unsteady laugh fluttered from her lips, tears staining her cheeks. "Thank God."

He continued to smile and looked at Ian. "Dude, did that shadow thing attack me?"

Ian nodded, still in shock. "I'm sure we caught the whole thing on camera."

"Sweet." Alex closed his eyes, focusing on the glorious beating of his own heart. "Now I can add 'ghost attack survivor' to my resume."

Grace rolled her eyes then looked over her shoulder apprehensively. "I don't know what the hell happened to you, but it scared the crap out of us."

Jackie continued to hold his hand tightly, unwilling to let go. "The creature attacked him. I knew it was dangerous, but I had no idea just how powerful it had become."

"Is it gone now?" Grace asked.

Jackie nodded. "The copper spell worked, though as a precaution we should still remove the bones. Ray, the creature, and the other spirits have all fled."

"And Sally?"

"She's still here, but she's free. Her father will be able to find her now."

Ian got to his feet, holding out his hand to help Grace stand. "Good. I'd say she saved your life, Doc."

Grace managed a weak smile, still in disbelief. "Yeah. She did."

"When Ray saw you, he mistook you for Mercy," Jackie explained. "Even though he knows she's as dead as he is, his rage got the better of him and he tried to hurt you." She helped Alex up, his arm winding around her shoulders. "Sally did what she could to protect you."

"Well, I'm lucky she did." Grace chewed on her lower lip, realizing it could have been her lying on the floor of the basement instead of Alex.

Ian pulled her close and nodded to the others. "Let's get the hell out of this basement. For good this time."

CHAPTER NINETEEN

I'd say this was a good investigation."

Ian shot Alex a humored look. "You almost died."

"So?" Alex crunched on a handful of potato chips, cheerful despite the near brush with death. He pointed a salty finger at the computer screen. "Look at me. I'm like James Bond facing off against Goldfinger. Only instead of a gun, I had a Spirit Box."

"Yeah, and you got your ass kicked."

"Bond always gets back up. So does Alex Gallagher."

"You're just lucky there was a doctor in the house."

Alex shrugged, though he glanced over his shoulder to where Grace was standing on the back porch with Jackie. The outdoor light glowed orange over their faces as they laughed about something he couldn't hear. Beyond them, the harbor lay still and quiet in the dead of night.

"I had help from both sides. Practical and spiritual."

Ian followed his gaze, noting the way Jackie slipped her arm around Grace's waist. Despite a million reasons not to be friends, they had found a way. Go figure. "What are we going to do with them?"

"The girls?" Alex asked, turning to his friend.

Ian nodded, tearing his eyes from Grace and back to the computer screen. "Never mind."

"No, really. What did you mean?"

"Nothing." Ian replayed the footage they had captured that night, though his eyes glazed over as he stared at the screen. He was too distracted to watch it.

Alex nudged him with a pointy elbow. "I get it, dude. You care about her. What's wrong with that?"

Ian said nothing as he rubbed his face with his hands. He decided he wasn't ready yet to have *that* conversation. "Hand me those headphones. I want to listen to the audio again."

Alex obliged him, then got to his feet and stretched his arms over his head. "Damn. Nearly dying really zaps your energy."

Ian slipped the headphones over his ears. "You probably just faked it so you could get Jackie to admit she loves you."

Alex patted his friend on the shoulder. "Worked like a charm, didn't it?"

He wandered out to the back porch, leaving Ian to brood. The audio should have served as a viable distraction, except hearing Grace's voice and seeing her face on the screen only made things worse.

There was a truth he couldn't escape. A reality that wouldn't let him go.

Now that the investigation was over and the ghosts were gone, what was left keeping them together?

Where would they go from here now that there was nothing left to accomplish? No goal left to reach? He supposed she would probably go back to Chicago, free of the house for good.

And he would head off to the next haunted location in search of the paranormal.

Would their paths have ever crossed if it hadn't been for the Sparrow House? He knew the answer was no. They were two very different people from two opposing walks of life. She had her science and he had his ghosts. Sure, they'd found a sliver of common ground over the last few weeks. But was it enough to bridge the gap that divided them?

He rubbed the bridge of his nose and closed his eyes, haunted by what he knew was coming.

He had to either forgo his pride and ask her to be with him, or let her go. He had no other option.

* * *

Jackie shifted away from Grace as Alex stepped onto the porch.

"Hey, ladies." Alex grinned, pleased when Jackie went immediately into his arms.

She breathed in the scent of his soap, fresh from the shower he had taken only an hour before. The shower they had taken together. Her head fell back as she trailed her lips along his jawline. "Hi."

He held her closer, nuzzling her nose with his own. "I should put my life in danger more often."

Jackie poked him in the ribs, laughing at his surprised grunt. "You shouldn't tempt fate. Next time you may not be so lucky."

"Well, I'm already the luckiest guy in the world, Jackie. I have you."

She blushed and rose on her toes to kiss him. "My heart, darling. You have my heart."

Grace tried to ignore their blatant affection. She wanted to be happy for them, and was, but jealousy ate away at her. They seemed to have it all figured out, while she was lost in nothing but a mess. It was downright maddening. "So, did the camera catch anything good from tonight?"

Alex pulled away from Jackie and faced Grace. "Yeah. You can see the white mist that protected you and the shadow that hit me. It's pretty intense, we've never seen anything like it. At least not so interactive. I think we've made ghost hunting history in this house."

Jackie smiled up at him. "The Sparrow House is finally at peace. There's only one thing left to do."

"Sally," Grace murmured, sadness passing over her face. "What can we do to help her?"

"Her father will come back. It could be hours from now, or days, or years. I don't know. When he does, she'll be able to move on." Jackie reached over to take Grace's hand in her own, sympathy in her eyes. "You'll miss her."

Grace laughed, trying to brush off the truth behind the statement. "How do you miss a ghost? If anything, it'll be nice to finally get back to my old life."

"Will it?" Jackie mused, releasing her friend's hand with a squeeze. She looked up at Alex. "I'm feeling rather tired. Let's go back to the hotel."

"You guys can stay here if you want, I don't mind." Grace cut in, attempting a smile. For reasons she couldn't explain, she wanted to avoid being alone with Ian. "It's already past midnight, no reason to leave."

"Thanks, Grace. We will." Alex wrapped his arm over Jackie's shoulders and led her inside. He shot Grace a curious look. "You coming?"

She shook her head, arms crossed protectively. "No. I need a bit more fresh air. You guys go."

He nodded and they disappeared inside, leaving her alone with her thoughts. She sat down on the top step of the porch and folded her arms over her legs. Around her, the night came alive.

Crickets sang as barn owls swooped in for prey and field mice scurried away in fear. The moon hung low and heavy in the hazy night sky while a blanket of fog rolled in from the sea.

A chilly breeze blew by her. She bundled herself tighter in her coat, her eyes drifting toward the lonely dock. She could barely see it in the moonlight, but its outline was apparent over the smooth water.

Her thoughts filled with Mercy and she could almost see the young woman standing on the edge of the wooden planks, arms filled with a bag of bricks tethered to her waist.

Jackie's description of what had befallen the woman disturbed her. She'd explained that when a person commits suicide, their spirit remains caught between the worlds of the living and the dead. Which meant, of course, that Mercy was still out there somewhere. While her father had been forced to move on, Mercy would be unable to.

Grace wondered whether the young woman deserved such a horrific fate. She had been a tortured, miserable, rightfully hate-filled woman in life. In death, she was even more so. Her jealousy over Sally's loving father drove her to stand between their reunion. Her malice against her own father had created a monster that wreaked havoc on the living and had nearly killed Alex.

Where Ray was filled with nothing but sin, Mercy was driven by a very human vengeance and jealousy. She had done everything she could to terrorize Grace and the others, leading them to believe her actions were her father's. In reality, Mercy was behind it all. The shadow figures, the threatening EVPs, the disembodied footsteps, the creature. And, worst of all, the hands that attempted to strangle Grace after the séance. For that, Grace found herself unsympathetic to Mercy's fate.

Jackie said she believed Mercy's goal had been to lure in the ghost hunters to successfully banish the spirits from the house, thus breaking the bond that tied her to her father for good.

In the end, Mercy got her wish. But where was she now?

Grace shivered at the thought, disturbed. She started to wonder over her own role, and Nellie's as well, in Mercy's plan, but was distracted as she heard the door open behind her.

"Come inside, Doc."

Despite everything, her heart warmed at the sound of Ian's voice. She willed herself not to give in. Slipping on a sarcastic smile, she rose to her feet and went to him. "You miss me already?"

His lips spread in a wry smile as she passed him through the doorway. "Like I'd tell you if I did."

She laughed. "Heaven forbid you say how you feel, macho man."

With her back to him, she didn't catch the pain that flashed in his eyes or the words he whispered soundlessly under his breath.

If she had, it would have floored her.

* * *

She awoke to the sound of voices. They wafted in from the entryway, low and incoherent mumbles. At first, she thought it was Ian and Grace speaking.

Jackie opened her eyes and saw Alex fast asleep beside her. His face was buried in his pillow and he was lightly snoring. A smile teased her lips as she watched him, soft morning light bringing out the faint dusting of freckles on his nose. Her heart did one, slow tumble, and relished in the knowledge that it loved.

The voices drifted in again, causing her to sit up and face the entryway. She strained to listen, unable to discern what was being said. She was confident it wasn't Ian and Grace when she heard the soft, lilting voice of a child.

Sally.

Jackie pushed aside the blankets and got to her feet, tiptoeing lightly over the wood floor toward the entryway. She heard Alex rouse behind her but continued in her pursuit of the voices.

Her lips spread in a warm smile as she caught a glimpse of the staircase, and the man and child standing beside it. He knelt before the small girl and held her in his arms.

Outside, a light rain fell from the heavens.

Jackie marveled at the sight of father and daughter reuniting at last and her eyes took in the high walls of the entry. They were still covered with Mr. Lockwood's desperate messages. The little girl looked up at them as well, then beamed at Jackie.

I'm the sparrow.

"I know you are," Jackie whispered, her hand lifting to cover her lips as they trembled. She felt Alex come up behind her, his free hand sliding over her shoulder while his other hand held his camcorder.

He aimed the lens directly at her face, catching every compassionate quiver and poignant smile.

"He came for her, didn't he?"

Jackie nodded, biting her lower lip as she smiled. "I've never seen anything so beautiful."

"Tell me."

She watched as Mr. Lockwood straightened, his hand remaining tight around his daughter's. He was stately and handsome in his tailored-gray frock and black vest decorated with silver buttons. Delicate round eyeglasses shielded eyes of pale blue that looked upon her with misty gratitude. He had the same curly blonde hair as his daughter.

His head dipped in a thankful nod and Jackie smiled in return.

"He's overjoyed, grateful," she explained, her gaze falling back to Sally, who hugged her father's leg devotedly. The little girl stared up at her with big, blue eyes. "He says her mother is waiting for them. He's going to bring her home."

"Where is home?"

Jackie slowly shook her head. "The place only the dead know."

Upstairs, Grace watched in silence. She could only see Jackie and Alex, but she sensed Sally's presence. It was that familiar chill she'd come to know so well while in the house, the chill that was more calming than it was discomforting.

She sat on the top step beside the balcony, her arm winding around the same banister that had broken the day Sally died. Tears fell down her face, but she made no move to wipe them away. The sorrow was real, as real as anything she had ever felt.

She would miss Sally, after all.

Jackie blinked as she watched Sally race up the stairs to say goodbye to Grace.

The two women met eyes and Grace let out a shaky breath, embarrassed and moved all at once. When she felt the ghostly hand trail over her arm, she shut her eyes tightly and more tears fell.

Strands of her hair lifted from her head, one of Sally's favorite ways to play with her. Grace wished she could reach out and touch the spirit, but she didn't know how. She longed for nothing more than to see Sally, to have visual confirmation of what she knew in her heart to be true.

Sally existed and loved her. Just as she loved Sally.

When she opened her eyes, she nearly fainted. For the briefest of moments, she witnessed Sally as she had been in life. Young, innocent, and alive. Not just a ghostly chill or a mist. But a full-bodied apparition as real as her own flesh.

"Good God," Grace stammered, her hand tightening over the stair railing as her eyes widened with both wonder and fear. Sally smiled prettily and blew her an affectionate kiss. Then she danced off down the stairs and her apparition slowly faded into nothing.

Grace hovered in stunned silence, incapable of breathing. Her eyes were transfixed on the stairs, where she had just seen a child disappear into thin air. Her mind reeled and she thought she should feel sick, and yet she didn't.

"Grace?" Ian reached down and gently pried her fingers from the railing. "Are you all right?"

"She just saw Sally." Jackie beamed from downstairs, clapping her hands together happily.

Ian reached out for Grace's chin and tilted her face, coaxing her eyes to meet his. When they did, he saw the indescribable awe she felt. "Say something, Doc. Or did seeing a ghost make you mute? It's probably for the best. You talk too much, anyway."

A hysterical laugh burst from her lips and snapped her out of her reverie. The laugh quickly turned into a sob and she had to cover her face with her hands as she broke down and wept.

"Whoa, whoa. I was only joking." Ian pulled her into his arms, startled by her reaction. He shot a worried look at Jackie and Alex. They both eyed him curiously. "Let's get you back to bed."

"No." She battled the hysteria as he helped her to her feet. Without hesitation, he lifted her into his arms and hauled her back to her bedroom, tossing her onto the bed.

She glared at him through blotchy, angry eyes. "I said I don't want to go to bed."

"Yeah, and you're also hysterical," he countered, sitting down on the side of the bed and patting her leg affectionately. "You need a few moments to calm down and come to terms with what just happened. What better place to do that than in a bed?"

"Well, if you'd just give me that moment, maybe I'll calm down." She batted his hand away and fell back against the pillows with a heavy sigh, her mind a whirlwind of emotion. She shut her eyes and focused on breathing, knowing that she had to settle down if she was to even *try* and revisit what had just occurred on the stairwell.

After a few moments of silence, she opened her eyes and stared at Ian. "I just saw a ghost. Again."

"Full-bodied apparition," Ian corrected. "The only time I've seen one that up close and personal was my grandfather."

Grace nodded, remembering his story. "Did it scare you?"

"Damn right it did."

She smiled. "I thought you weren't scared of anything, tough guy?"

He reached out and tweaked her nose, his face softening. "It gets easier, but the fear never really goes away."

She sat up, not wanting to lay in bed like an invalid. She was perfectly fine. "So, good job, Ghostbuster. You finally got rid of every last ghost."

His arm draped over her shoulders as he pulled her in close. He pressed his lips to the top of her head, knowing she hid her grief behind wisecracks and humor. "It's okay to admit you'll miss her. In a way, you loved her. And she loved you."

"She's dead."

"She was always dead. That didn't stop you before."

Grace let out a long, uneasy breath, knowing he was right. "I just don't know what to do with myself now. It's over. There's nothing keeping me in the house anymore."

Ian tensed. He didn't know what to say to her.

She continued, her eyes glassy as she stared into space. "I didn't realize how unprepared I was for this moment. Now it's here and I feel even more lost than before."

"Just do whatever you think will make you happy," he said lamely, knowing it was cookie cutter advice. His heart told him to seize the moment and tell her how he felt, offer her the chance to change her life and come on the road with him.

But his pride told him he would only be stung by her inevitable rejection. She was a doctor, for God's sake. She had a life to get back to. Who was he to keep her from it?

Silently, he got to his feet and closed her bedroom door. When he walked back to the bed, his eyes met hers with a fierce intensity she wasn't expecting. He looked like some brooding, wild wolf, torn between slaughter and compassion for the prey he hunted. It made her blood heat and her pulse race despite the gloom dragging down her heart.

Here was a distraction. Here was lust, maybe love, but at least *something* tangible she could find release in. His eyes spoke the request he didn't utter, his movements beckoned the permission she didn't have to give. She was his, and would be for as long as he'd have her. There was no questioning it.

"Ian." Her arms wound around his neck as he pushed her against the bed, claiming her mouth with his. A moan echoed in her throat as his hands shoved aside the nightgown she wore and raced over the tender skin beneath. Aching for him, she lifted off his shirt and raked her nails down his back. Her teeth nipped at his lower lip as she unbuttoned his jeans.

He pressed against her impatiently, unwilling to admit to himself that he could lose her. That he was days, hours, minutes away from having to say goodbye.

Damnit, it hurt. He grunted her name and plunged himself into her, lost in everything she was. The scent of her drove him mad and he knew it always would. He would never forget the taste of her lips, the feel of her skin, the lilt of her laugh. It would plague him for the rest of his life.

Her hands cradled his face, her forehead touching his as her eyes fluttered closed. He could feel her breath mixing with his own, could hear her voice sighing his name. His anger over their situation made his movements fierce, while the love that plagued him brought out a tenderness he'd never known. He kissed her, impossibly drawn in by whatever spell she wove. By whatever twist of fate rendered him helpless to her.

"Don't leave me," she whispered the words, but he heard them loud and clear. He rode on them and wished she truly meant it. Surely, once she had a chance to think, she would take them back.

"You're already gone." He drove into her one last time, their eyes meeting for a long, crushing moment. He saw the flush of pleasure, the shock of pain, and the brilliance of her beauty all at once. The sight of it staggered him.

Her haunted gray eyes watched him, her lips parted as she fought to catch her breath. Dark strands of her bangs clung to her forehead, and he resisted the urge to brush them aside. Instead, he rolled off her and covered his face with his hands.

Grace stared at the ceiling, unable to move. His words rang out like an alarm in her mind, blaringly loud and obvious. It was true, then. He didn't want it to continue. He wanted her to go. Pain seared through her heart, but she refused to cry. She'd be damned if he knew she didn't agree one-hundred percent with his logic. If he could be the practical, mature adult in this scenario, then so could she.

Forcing a smile on her face, she rolled over to run her hand down his arm. "I've enjoyed this, Ian. I have. I'll miss you when you go."

She got to her feet and slipped into her robe. She stepped

out to take a shower, abandoning him to his dark, self-loathing thoughts.

* * *

After her shower, she made her way downstairs. Ian was in the kitchen making lunch. She ignored him and walked over to what remained of the antique furniture she had once pulled from the bowels of the basement.

She'd done her best to clean up the grandfather clock, but there hadn't been much time the day before. Most of the splintered wood and broken glass had been swept into a pile, while the larger pieces still laid on the floor. She stared down at them sadly, her heart broken. It was her favorite piece.

She turned to look at the rest of the furniture, the tattered love seat and the crumbling coffee table. The lamps were weathered almost beyond recognition, the skeletons of the lamp shades visible with only scraps of fabric left to cloak them.

There was no way she could hold on to the furniture any longer. Even though she had yet to decide if she was staying in the house permanently, she knew she couldn't leave the pieces there. They represented something dark and sinister that no longer resided in the house. As far as she was concerned, it could all burn.

She placed a quick call to Johnny Hayes and requested his help hauling the furniture to the dump. He sounded surprised to hear it, considering the furniture had looked brand new when he helped bring it up from the basement several weeks earlier.

Grace assumed he thought she was crazy. Not that it mattered, though. As long as he showed up with a couple of guys and a truck to take it all away, she would be content.

She also called up the local sheriff's department, informing them of the hundred-year-old bones in her basement. She needed them to come and excavate the body properly and determine the cause of death. They were irritated that she'd already partially dug up the bones, but she had an excuse ready. She told them she was planning on remodeling the basement and, in the process, discovered the bones.

After she hung up the phone, she wandered back into the kitchen. Ian set down two plates on the dining table, filled with turkey sandwiches and chips. He nodded to her and took a seat.

She chewed on her tongue, wondering if this was some sort of peace offering. She sat across from him warily. "Thanks."

"Welcome." He bit into his sandwich, watching her. He tried to figure out her angle, her motive, as she continued to play off her anger with him. Clearly, she was upset. It would take a blind man not to see it. But she only half-smiled at him and avoided eye contact, falling back on a passive-aggressiveness that grated at his insides. "Are you going to get new furniture?"

"I don't know yet." Grace crunched into a chip, her eyes drifting to the antiques. "I guess once I decide if I'm staying here or not, I'll know what to do."

He hesitated, his sandwich halfway to his mouth. "I thought you wanted to go back to Chicago?"

She sighed. "I do. Sort of. I don't know, I'm still such a mess."

"What about your job?"

Her shoulders lifted and fell. "They need me to come back. I know they do."

"Then you should go."

Their eyes met. For some reason, hearing it from him made it more real than before. She caught herself before the pain hit, knowing it was stupid. "Not like it matters to you, anyway. I'm sure you're excited to get the hell out of this place and find other ghosts to hunt."

Anger flashed in his eyes, and he fought to keep his hands steady. "Not like it matters to you, right?"

She rolled her eyes and got to her feet, taking her empty

plate with her. "True. Thanks for the sandwich."

He watched her drop the plate in the sink and escape upstairs. All he could think was that he couldn't leave her like this. He couldn't let this argument be the last they ever had.

If he was going to have to let her go, it had to be on good terms.

CHAPTER TWENTY

Jackie watched Alex load all his equipment into the back of the van. She helped carry out a few duffle bags from the hotel room, the last of his and Ian's belongings.

She'd retrieved her own suitcase and clothes from Dominic's house earlier that day and brought her belongings and Gatsby over to the hotel. She'd also arranged to have her Jeep shipped to Seattle so she could join Ian and Alex on the cross-country drive.

Alex was chipper and in good spirits, and she fought back the instinct to feel trapped. She loved him; that she knew for certain. There was no reason to assume he would smother her spirit or hold her back from the things she loved. He knew her terms and had agreed to them.

If she wanted, *needed*, to go, then he would let her. Then again, it was becoming harder to think of anyplace she would want to go without him by her side. In fact, soon she wanted to take him down to New Orleans to see the fireflies and experience the wealth of ancient spirits that roamed there. It was a magnificent place for a ghost hunter.

She only wished Grace would join them, as impossible as she knew it was. Of course, fate had a funny way of fulfilling the unexpected. She had a feeling that Grace's role in her life had not yet come to an end.

With a smile, she lifted Gatsby into her arms and turned to Alex after he shut the van doors. She kissed his cheek, and he ran his hand over Gatsby's fur.

"You ready to go?" he asked, slipping on his sunglasses with a crooked grin.

She tilted her head to the side. "Where is our next adventure taking us, darling?"

"Nevada, I think. I should probably call my sister," he added as an afterthought, scratching his chin. "We'll figure it out once we grab Ian."

"He's saying goodbye to Grace." Jackie pouted before climbing into the passenger seat of the van, Gatsby nestled comfortably in her arms.

Alex frowned, passing a hand through his hair. "Damn."

He had nothing else to say as he hopped into the driver's seat and drove the short distance to the Sparrow House. Above them, storm clouds moved in from the sea, roiling with impending thunder.

Jackie stared up at them, worry in her eyes. She said a silent prayer and reached for her cross necklace, grasping it tightly in her fingers.

"Man, where did that storm come from?" Alex wondered aloud as he pulled up to the house, eyeing the clouds through the windshield.

"A very sad place." Jackie released a heavy sigh and

pushed open the door.

Alex said nothing as he joined her, her words troubling him.

They walked up the pathway to the front door just as the first drops of rain began to fall. Alex knocked, feeling uneasy. Something bad was in the air, though he couldn't put his finger on what it was.

The door opened, revealing Grace. She attempted a smile, but her mind was clearly on other things. "Hey. Come in."

They followed her inside and found Ian packing up the rest of the camera equipment in the living room. He barely spared them a glance and a dispassionate grunt as he continued to meticulously wind up cords and strap down expensive camera gear in their protective cases.

"Looks like a bad storm's coming," Grace commented, making her way to the wide windows of the living room, her arms crossed. "You guys be careful on the road."

"Yeah. We will." Alex hated the tension in the air, caused by two of the most stubborn people he'd ever known. He considered jumping in and forcing the two of them to make a compromise, but before he could, he felt Jackie's hand on his arm. He looked down at her, and saw her shake her head slightly.

He was about to ask her why, but Ian cut him off. "Help me take the last of these bags out to the van."

Alex grabbed two of the bags and went outside with Ian. To his dismay, Ian left no room for questions or conversation. He was as closed off as any man faced with such a situation could be. It only confirmed how difficult this was on him and Alex had to wonder why Ian wasn't fighting for Grace. Why he wasn't even trying.

He had just given up.

Inside, Jackie ran into the same brick wall as Alex had with Ian. Grace had built an iron fortress around herself with no hope of entry. There would be no getting through to her. Though Jackie knew she still had to try.

When Alex and Ian came back into the living room, Grace turned and faced them, forcing a smile. "Well, I guess this is goodbye." She clutched her hands together awkwardly, not sure what to do.

Jackie made it easier when she wrapped Grace in a tight hug. "This is not goodbye. Our paths will cross again."

Grace sniffed, irritated that she was so emotional. She didn't want to cry. "I hope so. I'll miss you."

Jackie pulled back and placed her hands on either side of Grace's face, a kind smile softening her expression. "Love knows not its own depth until the hour of separation, darling."

Grace's eyebrows drew together as Jackie backed away and Alex replaced her. He dragged her into a tight hug. "Bye, Grace." He patted her shoulder as he drew back, a goofy smile lighting his eyes. "You know where to reach us if you ever need anything. I'll show up on your doorstep with my Proton Pack, ready to rumble."

She laughed, honestly grateful for him and his easy humor. She punched him playfully in the arm, one eyebrow cocked. "Like I'd call anyone else."

Alex chuckled, then shot a look over his shoulder at Ian. One silent nod from his friend and he knew it was time to go.

"C'mon, Jackie." He wrapped his arm around Jackie's shoulders and waved goodbye to Grace one last time. The two of them disappeared out the front door and into the rain.

Grace watched them go, desperately wishing this moment hadn't come. She wasn't ready for it. She faced Ian and tried to stay strong. "I want to thank you for everything. You saved this place. All three of you did."

He nodded, his eyes intent on hers. "We got some great evidence."

A small smile lifted the corners of her mouth. "I look forward to seeing you on television someday, racing around in the dark chasing after ghosts. You'll make all the girls swoon. Then again, you probably already do that."

He snorted, his jaw tightening as he stepped closer to her. His hands came up to frame her face and she placed her own over his wrists.

"You're an incredible woman, Doc. Don't let some asshole make you forget that." He pressed a tender kiss to her forehead, his eyes closing briefly as he savored her scent one last time.

Her knees weakened as tears sprang hot into her eyes. "You've seen me at my worst and you still think that?"

"Yes." His mouth found hers, hopelessly, helplessly.

A sharp pain stabbed into her heart as she kissed him, knowing it was over. Never had it hurt this much. When he broke the kiss, she managed a weak laugh. "Too bad I can't travel the country with you. Hitch a ride in the ghost mobile, see the sights."

"Why not?" He asked the question before he thought about it, before he realized the weight behind the words. Her reaction was as he expected. She laughed it off as though it were ludicrous. And really, maybe it was.

"Please. Can you really see me living out of a van and running around with that little recorder thing to catch EPVs or whatever you call them?"

"EVPs," he corrected, passing a hand through his hair. "And no, I guess I can't."

"So really, this is the best thing for both of us." She managed a smile and held out her hand. "It's been fun. I mean it. I hope you'll call me sometime and let me know how you're doing."

He accepted her hand numbly, torn and broken. "Yeah. Maybe I will."

"Good." She awkwardly closed the distance between them and kissed him one last time, wishing that things could be different. "Goodbye, Ian."

"Bye, Grace." He backed away from her, his eyes haunted. He gave her a casual salute and made his way out the front door.

Her eyes didn't leave him until he shut the door with a definitive click, slicing the string that tied them together once and for all. With it, her heart broke neatly in two.

She heard the van start up and take off down the street, and as it faded away, a low rumble of thunder replaced it. It trembled through her body, and she shut her eyes tight against the onslaught of regret.

For the next few hours, she wandered around the empty house. The old furniture was gone thanks to Johnny and his guys. Soon the bones would be removed by officials from the state. There was nothing left there for her. Without her friends, without the ghosts, the house felt like a vacant tomb.

The very next morning she drove back to Chicago. The only part of the house she took with her was Sally's photograph.

* * *

Two weeks passed by in a blur after she arrived home.

She found herself in a pathetic state watching reruns of *The Golden Girls* on television with a full glass of Pinot Noir in her hand. Her cat Charlie lounged beside her on the sofa, cleaning his soft, white fur.

She reached over to scratch his chin, her gray eyes meeting his bright green ones. "We're gonna be okay, aren't we, baby?"

Charlie yawned and settled in for a nap.

Grace sighed. Even the cat was bored with her.

She had gone straight back to work, eager to fall into her old routine. Her friends and coworkers were ecstatic to see her, but she saw the concern behind their kind smiles. They thought she might break at any moment, crumble to pieces the way she had before she left for Massachusetts. Apparently, a leave of absence wasn't enough to convince them that she was okay.

Everywhere she went, she was reminded of her father. She saw him in the faces of those who had known him, in the rooms of the hospital they had shared, in the numerous plaques and awards lining the halls. His presence was strong there and, while she loved seeing his legacy live on, it was bittersweet.

She was over the worst of the grief. Accepting the afterlife had, in many ways, comforted her. It made her understand that her father was still out there watching over her. She recalled what Jackie mentioned all those weeks earlier about her father leading Ian and Alex to the Sparrow House. And then Ian's insistence that *she* was the doctor spoken of by the voice he caught on his recorder long before they even met.

If it was true, then her father had given her the most amazing gift—two ghost hunters and the medium that saved her from herself. Three strangers who had become friends that taught her how to breathe again. How to live.

Missing them was a daily struggle. Regret was an hourly plague, and loneliness a second by second reality.

When asked how she'd spent her time in Massachusetts, Grace lied. The entire story of ghosts remained a closely guarded secret. She kept the leather case holding Sally's photograph in the drawer of her nightstand, and often found herself waking in the middle of the night to look at it. To remember how it felt to see the little girl, to see proof of life after death.

What would her friends think if she described what happened in Mad Rock Harbor? Would they believe a single word?

Doubtful. In fact, they'd probably encourage her to see a psychiatrist, maybe go on medication. And then what?

Grace sipped her wine, disillusioned. She knew

without a shadow of a doubt that she had fundamentally changed since her stay at the Sparrow House. The lightning fast pace of her old life disoriented her. How had she ever kept up with such a hectic, packed schedule?

Exhausting nights at the hospital. Frantic surgeries in the E.R. Congested city streets and hour-long commutes home. A never-ending thrum of traffic noise and sirens out her bedroom window.

All these things were maddening to her. They piled on top of one another to form a heavy weight that brought her to the floor, anxious and afraid. How could she live this way, as she once had? It seemed impossible now.

Despite everything, she longed for the Sparrow House. Even though she knew it was empty, she missed the way she'd felt when she was there. In many ways, she'd left her heart behind.

Part of her wondered if it was time she went back for it.

The buzzer sounded, announcing someone waiting to be let up. The sound caught her off guard and she jumped, the red wine in her glass sloshing precariously. She set the glass aside and went to the intercom.

"Yes?"

"*It's me.*"

She rolled her eyes. "What do you want, Rick?"

"*I need to talk to you. Please, let me up.*"

"I really don't feel like doing this right now."

"*It's about your father, Grace.*"

She froze, her heart plummeting into her stomach. After a moment's silence, she pressed the button to let him in. She waited by her front door, then opened it slowly when he knocked.

"Hi, sweetheart." Rick smiled at her, but she saw the

anxiety that lined his tired face. He hadn't been sleeping. His body was draped in an expensive black coat and she noticed he was lightly dusted with snow. She wondered if he had walked there.

Without a word, she stepped aside to let him in and closed the door. He wandered over to her sofa, sat down, and tried to pet Charlie. To Grace's pleasure, the cat hissed at him and ran away.

Rick shook his head and rested his hands on his knees instead, his back rigid. His eyes found hers as she took a seat beside him. "I heard you were back in town, so I wanted to get this off my chest, once and for all."

Grace's eyes narrowed. "What is it?"

Rick sighed. "About a week before Allen died, he came to see me. He said he had this house in Massachusetts he needed to sell immediately and that he would sell it to me for way under market value. Said I could use it as a rental, or fix it up and resell it, turn a profit. Either way, it was too good an offer to refuse." He rubbed at the black stubble lining his jaw, distracted as he recalled the memory. "I flew out to see the house and wasn't disappointed. It needed some yard work, but the place had potential. I could easily double my investment on it had I purchased it."

Grace's stomach rolled over, making her sick. "So, why didn't you?"

His eyes shot back to hers, dark with concern. "A woman, the neighbor, harassed me the second I set foot on the property."

Grace's lips parted in surprise. "Nellie."

He grimaced. "She actually shouted at me that I couldn't buy the house, that I didn't belong there. Said she'd call the police and have me arrested for trespassing. She was like some rabid dog, snarling and spitting at me. It was more than enough to convince me that I didn't want the place, so I flew back home and told your father I couldn't buy it."

"I wonder why she did that." Grace thought back to the way Nellie had reacted when they first met and how hostile the woman had been until discovering Grace's identity. Then it had been like flipping a light switch—aggressive to welcoming.

"I don't know, but no wonder your father wanted to get rid of the house." Rick reached for Grace's wine glass and took a long sip. When he set it back down, he met her eyes again. "Allen made me promise that I wouldn't tell you about the house. It seemed like he was intimidated by it. Makes me wonder why he ever bought it in the first place."

"He didn't; he inherited it," Grace corrected him. "I found out that it's been in my family for a hundred years."

"I see. In the end, he left you the house anyway. Imagine my shock when I found out where you'd run off to. After all of Allen's talk about keeping you away from the house, he gave it to you in his will."

Grace chewed fretfully on her lower lip, saying nothing.

"I don't know what changed his mind, but now you know the truth." He reached out to take her hand, urging her to look at him. "And now you're home, so everything is as it should be."

She pulled her hand away, shaking her head. "This isn't my home anymore."

"What?" Rick gaped at her as she rose to her feet, a gleam of discovery in her eyes.

"It all makes sense now." She threw up her hands with a giddy laugh, her mind churning over all the new information. "He tried to get rid of the house to spare me, but quickly realized he couldn't. No Sullivan could ever get rid of it; it's like an addiction. So instead he gave me the tools to save the house once and for all, to make it a place I could call home."

"That doesn't make any sense, Grace." Rick pulled her back down to the sofa, slipping into psychiatrist mode. "You think the house is *addictive*? And what are these tools he gave you?"

She nodded, not caring what he thought. "It *was* addictive, anyway. And he sent ghost hunters to help me."

"Ghost hunters?"

She waved off the remark. "You wouldn't understand."

He pursed his lips thoughtfully. "Okay…what about that neighbor? She didn't give you any trouble?"

Grace's chest tightened. "She died."

"Oh, I'm sorry to hear that." Rick feigned sympathy, but she knew he was delighted. "What happened to her?"

"Cardiac arrest." The memory of it brought back the wave of grief, but this time she embraced it. It was simply a part of her journey now. "She was such a giving woman, compassionate and stubborn. She never let me feel down about myself, despite everything that happened. She opened my eyes to a danger I was too closed off to notice, and in turn helped me see."

"See what?"

Grace smiled, tears in her eyes. "Sally."

"Who's Sally?"

"It doesn't matter now." Grace reached for her wine, polishing off the glass. She fondled it in her hands as her thoughts drifted back to Nellie. "My father asked Nellie to take care of the house in his absence. That's probably why she was so defensive when you met her."

"Defensive is putting it mildly," Rick countered, anger tightening his mouth. "The woman was insane. Frothing at the mouth crazy. If she'd come to me as a patient, I'd have put her on anti-psychotics in a heartbeat."

"I don't get it; she wasn't like that with me." Grace set her wine glass aside and faced him. "She was a bit overbearing at times, but not crazy."

"So why go to such great lengths to scare off a potential

buyer of a house that's not even hers?"

Grace pondered this, realizing she didn't have an answer. Why *had* Nellie react that way? It was almost as if she didn't want anyone but another Sullivan to come into the house. As if she knew the house would only accept the bloodline that thrived within its own walls.

But Nellie claimed she'd never seen the ghosts, nor believed in them, until Grace arrived, so how could that be true? Unless she lied. Grace sucked in a sharp breath as she ran through the events again in her mind. It did all seem rather convenient to her, in retrospect.

Nellie said Grace's father had told her about seeing Sally. So why did it take Grace's arrival for Nellie to see the girl herself? It seemed timed perfectly so Grace would witness her horrified reaction and begin to question everything.

And after the dark shadow supposedly pushed her on the basement stairs and then disappeared into the wall, instead of placing the blame on normal things like vertigo, Nellie immediately ran off to call in ghost hunters. As though that had been the plan all along.

Had it been? Had Nellie purposely sought to convince Grace to allow paranormal investigators inside her home to rouse the spirits and remove them? If so, then why hadn't she just been straight forward about it?

Grace knew she wouldn't have accepted it outright, but still. Surely staging everything had been more work than a simple discussion on the matter. Why all the theatrics?

She thought back to what Ian told her right after they saw Mercy jump off the dock. He suggested that the spirits could possess not just furniture, but people. At the time, she'd been worried for her own mind. She hadn't even thought about Nellie's...

The image of Mercy's screaming face flashed before her

and along with it came a seemingly impossible realization. Had it been Mercy all along? Had Nellie been Mercy's catalyst to get the ghost hunters into the home, ultimately breaking the bond that tied her to the house?

Her mind started running with the possibility, insane as it sounded. It occurred to her that every contact she or the others had with Mercy happened *after* Nellie's death and not before. It gave credence to the idea that Nellie had not been Nellie at all. Instead, she had been possessed by a spirit with a motive to free herself from the clutches of the house. To sever the ties her father had created and at last send him where he belonged. In Hell.

And once the task was complete, the spirit ended the possession and brought the host back to her original state, vulnerable in the midst of a heart attack. Without the spirit to sustain her, Nellie died, alone on the very dock where Mercy had taken her own life.

Then Mercy returned to the Sparrow House and ramped up her efforts, becoming the terror Grace and the others thought for sure was Ray.

"God," Grace murmured, burying her face in her hands.

Beside her, Rick shifted uncomfortably. "Everything okay?"

"No." She let her hands fall and stared at them. She remembered holding Nellie's lifeless body, mourning the death of a woman she apparently had never even known. "I was used. I fell right into her trap."

"Whose trap? The neighbor's?"

Grace tilted her head to look at him. "The ghost's."

* * *

Ian cursed under his breath as he weaved in and out of traffic on the highway, bound for Mad Rock Harbor. He drove in silence, unable to listen to the radio. He pushed the rental car to its limit but still it didn't go fast enough.

Grace's ominous voicemail from the day before echoed painfully in his mind. *Come back to me, Ian. To the Sparrow House. I can't face this alone.*

Every attempt he made to call her had failed. She must have turned off her phone.

His pride despised the power she had over him, that she knew he would come running to her at the drop of a hat. Then again, if she truly needed him, how could he refuse?

He loved her. He'd always love her.

His mind raced with fear and uncertainty over what he'd find once he made it there. Was she suicidal? Had she fallen back into a deep depression? Was she still trapped in the house despite having rid the place of spirits? Any one of those scenarios frightened him. What if he couldn't help her?

When he saw the sign for the off ramp he needed, his heart kicked up in speed. Palms damp with sweat gripped the steering wheel as he drove the car off the highway and barreled down the quiet streets of Mad Rock Harbor.

It wasn't until he pulled up in front of the Sparrow House that he began to breathe again. He tore out of the car and raced up to the front door, ignoring the snow that began to fall. After knocking and receiving no answer, he tried the handle. It was locked.

"Damnit, Grace." His breath formed visible clouds as he ran down the porch steps and rounded the side of the house, peering in the windows. He saw nothing.

Then he turned toward the harbor and saw her. She sat on the edge of the dock in nothing but a thin cotton dress as gray as her eyes, facing the icy water. Flecks of snow dotted her hair.

He wasted no time hurrying toward her, calling out her name. He nearly slipped on the ice-slicked ground, but nothing could stop him. Nothing could keep him from her.

She turned to face him, eyes wide and startled. His name fell from her lips as she rose to her feet. Within seconds he was with her, throwing his arms around her and pulling her close. She gave in to the dizzying relief and held on to him.

When he accepted that she was unharmed and whole, he shrugged out of his coat and threw it over her. "What the hell are you doing out here?"

She managed a weak laugh as she bundled up in his jacket, though there was little humor in it. "Boy, do I have a story to tell you."

"Let's go inside first."

"No. It has to be here." She backed away from him, shivering despite the warmth of his coat. She rubbed her hands together to fight back the chill. "It's about Nellie. Or should I say, Mercy."

Ian frowned. "What are you talking about?"

She turned her eyes back to the water, to the place where she had once seen Mercy's face. "Did it ever seem strange to you that Nellie seemed to know all the right things to say to get you guys to come here? To get you to investigate this place?"

He shrugged. "Not really."

"What about the fact that she avoided Jackie like the plague? Wouldn't you think she'd be interested in speaking to a real clairvoyant about the spirits she claimed to see?" When he said nothing, she continued. "It's because she knew Jackie would see right through her charade."

"Charade?"

She turned back to him, face pale and eyes huge. "And what about when she ended up dead right here on this very dock, the same location that Mercy took her life?"

"Where are you going with this, Doc?" Ian crossed his arms, concerned even as the wheels of his mind began to turn.

"Rick told me that he came to see the house long before I

ever showed up here. He said Nellie chased him off. Why would she do that? And then I show up and she slowly puts it in my head that there's ghosts in the house. Then she calls you guys in to investigate, and she suddenly takes off. Jackie comes in and Nellie stays far away from the house. Then Nellie mysteriously dies and we start seeing Mercy."

"This is all very strange coming from you," Ian admitted, running a hand through his hair. "Then again, it's not completely irrational."

"No, it isn't. Because it's the truth." Grace cupped her hands under her elbows, feeling sick. "Jackie told me that Mercy's goal was to get you guys to banish the spirits from the house and break the bond holding her. So, Mercy possessed Nellie and used her to convince me that the house was haunted so she could bring you guys in."

Understanding flashed over Ian's face. "It was Mercy all along. She used Nellie and created just enough chaos to keep us here, until we found a way to finish it. Getting her spirit out of the house wasn't good enough. She needed the bond that tied your family to the house to be broken. And we did it."

Grace nodded. "But she tricked us, Ian. She tricked *me*. She made me care for a lie and then she took it away from me."

Sympathy softened his features. "We all fell for it. There's nothing you can do about it now."

She shivered, knowing he was right. "Either way, at least she's gone. I don't even want to hear that name again."

"You and me both." He reached for her, dragging her against him. He breathed her in and exhaled, his eyes closing. "God, I missed you."

"I missed you, too." She buried her face in his neck, savoring the warmth he offered. It soothed her frigid, brittle bones and quieted the icy rattle of her heart. "Thank you, by the way. For coming. I wasn't sure if you would."

"You scared the shit out of me with that message," he admitted, pulling away to meet her eyes. "Don't do that again, okay?"

She laughed, the sound breaking as a sob built in her throat. "I won't. I need to tell you something even scarier though, so don't be mad. Just take it like a man."

"What's that?" Amusement flickered in his eyes as he brushed aside her bangs, his hand coming to rest just below her jaw.

"I love you." Her lips curved in a relieved smile, and he marveled at it.

"Is that right?" He ran his thumb along the curve of her lower lip. "That is pretty scary."

"Isn't it? I must be crazy." She shivered from his touch, leaning closer to him. "I'll feel better if you say you love me, too."

"Christ, you know it's true." He captured her mouth with his and gave in to the wash of relief. He held her close and ran his hand along the skin of her neck.

"Then say it. Please," she whispered, blood shimmering like wildfire under her skin. Her heart skipped and danced with a joy she thought she would never feel again.

"I love you." His eyes found hers, and he cupped her face in his hands. "You won't convince me to leave you again, Grace. It's not happening. I'll follow you to Chicago if I have to."

"You don't." She let out a shaky laugh, biting her lower lip. "I'm not going back there. I want to come with you. And when we're not on the road, I want us to stay here."

"You have this all figured out, don't you?"

She reached for his hand, pulling him with her toward the house. "Plans change, people change. I realized the new me couldn't live without you."

"Lucky for me, then." He followed her, leaving the dock

behind.

"Besides, ghost hunting is a lot more fun than I realized. Maybe I can be the medical expert for your new show and give insight into how the people may have died."

"You're brilliant."

"I know." She beamed up at him. "I told you that you would need me."

"You have no idea."

As they walked up to the house, they missed the violent war being waged beneath the surface of the harbor. Where the rotted legs of the dock met the rocky sand beneath and clumps of seaweed and scuttling crabs thrived, a woman fought against the bonds that held her.

Mercy twisted and writhed with fury and pain, her efforts wasted. She was trapped, unable to move on.

With black hatred in her soul, she tossed her head back and screamed.

EPILOGUE

"Here's a good one. Name the infamous home planet of Luke and Anakin Skywalker."

Grace sighed. "I don't know, Pluto?"

Alex smacked his forehead and groaned. "Oh, Grace. Your lack of nerd knowledge is killing me. It's Tatooine."

"Hey, I only watched that movie for Harrison Ford, okay?" she shot back, snatching the bag of Doritos from his hands. She crunched into a chip and eyed him from the front seat. "How about I ask you some medical questions? Like, what day of the week are you most likely to have a heart attack?"

Alex grabbed the bag back from her with a devious grin. "Monday."

"Lucky guess." Grace rolled her eyes and turned to Ian, who was busy driving. The road ahead of them was dry and dusty, nothing visible for miles around but lonely desert. She couldn't even remember the last time they'd seen another car. "At least you're not a nerd."

Ian bit back a laugh as Alex erupted in the back seat. "Wait till you hear about his collection of *Dungeons and Dragons* cards."

"Oh, my God."

"Shut the hell up, Alex," Ian replied, a warning tone in his voice.

"What? It's true."

"So is your unhealthy obsession with *Spiderman* comics, but you don't see me bringing that up."

"You just did, thanks." Alex sat back in his seat, pouting.

Jackie curved into him, tweaking his nose playfully with her finger. "I always loved Spiderman."

"Yeah?" He wrapped his arm over her, then looked triumphantly at Ian. "See? You can't bring me down, man. This nerd's got game."

"Somehow," Ian mumbled, shaking his head even as a slow smile spread over his lips. He felt Grace's hand trail over his thigh.

"You know, when I was a kid, I had a set of those cards, too."

"Seriously?" He tore his eyes off the road and gaped at her.

She shushed him, then smiled wickedly. "You tell a soul and you're dead."

He recovered with a grin. "Your secret's safe with me, Doc."

"So, what's the story with this ghost town we're headed to?" Jackie asked as Gatsby hopped into her lap. She scratched his ears lovingly.

Ian met her eyes in the rearview mirror. "Just a little place called Goldfield, Nevada."

Her eyes widened.

"I take it you've heard of it?" Alex asked.

She nodded. "It's notorious."

"Why?" Grace turned in her seat, confused. When the three of them exchanged knowing looks, she sighed. "Okay, seriously. Tell me."

"The buildings there are some of the most haunted locations in the country. Every crew that goes there captures incredible evidence," Ian told her, adrenaline bringing a fierce smile to his face. "I want my shot at it."

"Let's just say the likelihood of us bringing a pissed off spirit home with us is pretty high." Alex put in cheerfully.

Grace fought back the uneasiness his words gave her. "You'd like that, wouldn't you?"

"Damn right I would."

Ian's hand found Grace's and squeezed, urging her to look at him. "Still sure you're up for this?"

"Absolutely." A determined fire chased away the anxiety in her eyes. "Bring it on, ghost hunter. I'm ready."

* * *

"Love is merely a madness; and, I tell you, deserves as well a dark house and whip as madmen do; and the reason why they are not so punished and cured is that the lunacy is so ordinary that the whippers are in love too."
–William Shakespeare

ABOUT KATIE JENNINGS

Katie Jennings is the author of the popular fantasy series *The Dryad Quartet* as well as the award-winning romantic family drama series *The Vasser Legacy*. Her paranormal romance, *So Fell The Sparrow*, won an Honorable Mention in the 2014 Readers' Favorite International Book Awards. Her bestselling contemporary romance, *Things Lost In The Fire*, is a semi-finalist in romance in the Kindle Book Awards. A Los Angeles native, she now lives in beautiful North Idaho with her husband, who thinks she's the biggest nerd ever. She's a firm believer in happy endings and loves nothing more than a great romance novel.

PREVIEW OF

UP IN THE PINES

FROM THE BESTSELLING AUTHOR OF
THINGS LOST IN THE FIRE

UP IN THE PINES

KATIE JENNINGS

CHAPTER ONE

"THE BODY'S THIS way."

Deputy Sheriff Lark Galloway stepped nimbly over a fallen tree trunk carpeted with moss, her weathered hiking boots sinking into the rich soil beyond. Faded pine needles and the skeletal remains of pine cones littered the forest floor and crunched beneath her feet.

"You sure you remember the way?" she asked, her breathing practiced and consistent as she navigated the terrain. Her length of dark brown hair was swept back in a neat tail, clear of a long face made masculine by smooth angles and a notable cleft in her chin.

The young man adorned in flashy new L.L. Bean outerwear that she followed wasn't nearly as capable. He huffed and puffed and shivered with what she imagined were more nerves than a chill, though the October air did have a distinct bite to it. Pieces of black hair poked out from beneath his bright red beanie, a sharp contrast to the pasty white of his face.

He gave a curt nod. "Yep. It was right up here." He paused, his eyes scanning the expanse of trees. "Somewhere…"

Lark stopped beside him, her hand lowering instinctually to her holstered pistol as she followed his gaze. "You said you found it near a damaged tree?"

"Yeah. The tree looked like it'd been struck by lightning or something." He glanced up as a light mist began to fall, scrunching his face against the wetness. "Oh, great."

"Let's keep moving." Lark urged him onward, wondering if he was leading her on a wild goose chase. She never knew what to expect with tourists, but generally they were as green as the pines were tall. "Keep an eye out for bears. It's nearing dusk."

He faltered. "You really think we'll run into one?"

She regarded him through heavy-lidded jade eyes, unamused by his lack of preparedness. "This is their home you're intruding upon, Mr. Lowry. You'd do well to remember that."

He gulped, but nodded before continuing.

As they walked, she felt the sick feeling in her gut grow stronger. When Kevin Lowry had shown up at the sheriff's department in a panic declaring he had discovered a body in the woods, she hadn't really believed him. It was common for tourists' imaginations to run wild while on a hike through the desolate forests of Montana, leading them to believe they had seen all manner of odd things. She thought she had heard it all. Of course, no one had ever claimed to have found a body before.

In her eight years as a deputy sheriff, the worst she had dealt with were drunk locals starting bar fights and the occasional domestic dispute. She had been trained to handle more, but in the tidy mountain communities of Missoula County life was often quiet and predictable. It suited her, as she valued the constant and the familiar. But every once in a while, she found herself craving a little more excitement.

She was seriously regretting that desire now.

There was a distinct change in the air, like she had walked through an invisible wall. The atmosphere was heavier, charged with an electricity that prickled the hairs on the back of her neck. Whatever caused it had her instincts on high alert. They screamed at her to run, to flee to safety. It was exactly the sort of feeling she imagined animals got when they scented the death of one of their own.

Only this wasn't a smell. It was a sensation. A sudden, tremulous shiver that told her this was the site of something terrible. Something tragic and wrong.

At that moment, she saw the tree several yards in the distance. The lightning bolt had severed the trunk neatly down the center, carving a vertical line of exposed bark. The light amber wood stood out like a flame among the sea of charcoal gray trunks.

Kevin pointed. "There it is!"

He took off at a run, leaving her no choice but to race after him. Adrenaline pumped in her veins, joined by a horrible sense of dread. Her finely tuned body seemed to pull her back, advising her to stay away from her destination. Her equally focused mind wouldn't let her.

"Stand back, Mr. Lowry," she ordered just before he reached the tree. He doubled over, panting as he pointed once again, this time at the forest floor.

"It's there. See it? Sticking up out of the ground."

She did see it. Tucked into the bed of needles and cones was the perfectly rounded skull of a human being. Beside it, what she imagined to be rib bones and perhaps a leg or arm jutted up out of the earth. One look at the jagged slope of the ground had her determining that rainwater must have exposed the grave some time ago.

Kevin inched closer, his hands shoved deep inside the pockets of his jacket. "See? Told you I wasn't crazy."

Lark ignored him and knelt beside the bones, careful not to disturb them as she took a closer look. She was no expert, but she'd wager they had been buried for a very, very long time.

"Who do you think they were?" Kevin wondered aloud.

Lark reached for her radio and motioned for him to stand back. Just as she was about to call her partner to give him her location, she spotted the hole on the front of the skull. Her eyes narrowed as she lowered her radio and shifted closer, needing to confirm what she saw. Though her fingers itched to examine the neat, half-inch diameter circle cut through the yellowed bone, years of training had her resisting. Instead, she rested back on her heels and released a long, unsteady breath.

Kevin's shaky voice broke the silence. "Wait, is that a bullet hole?"

Not willing to confirm or deny it, Lark raised the radio to her lips.

"Russ, come in."

"*Hear ya loud and clear, Sparky. Go ahead.*"

Lark rolled her eyes at her partner's nickname for her. "I've got possible human remains up here on Heller Ridge. Request back up."

"*Hot damn. So the tourist wasn't kidding, huh?*"

"Just get your ass out here."

"*Ten-four. On my way.*"

Clipping her radio back onto her belt, Lark refocused on the pile of neglected and weathered bones. She felt the first stab of remorse hit her like an ice pick to the stomach.

There was no doubt in her mind that this person, whoever they were, had been shot point blank in the head. Murdered in cold blood, right in the heart of her forest. At that moment, the how and the why of it were unimportant. She simply took the time to ponder the heavy weight of death and how it would inevitably shake up the remote mountain town she'd been sworn to protect.

Murder, it seemed, had come to leave its mark on Eden Falls, Montana.

THE FORENSICS TEAM combed the area surrounding the body. When dusk set in, the use of high-powered flashlights became necessary. Clad in blue windbreakers and khakis, the team of four broke off on assignments; two to meticulously photograph and exhume the remains, two more to search for shell casings, weapons, or any other sort of evidence that might relate to the case.

Lark stood by with her partner, Russ, at her side, her arms folded and a thoughtful frown on her face. She watched the team with scrutinizing eyes, feeling protective over the dead person not just because she had been the first on the scene, but because this was her hometown. Even if he or she had not been a resident, they still died in Eden Falls. That made the case all the more personal for her.

She could sense Russ vibrating with energy, like a restrained horse impatient for a race. As a young rookie just shy of twenty four years old, he thirsted for action like he had seen in the movies. Soon enough, he would see that this kind of thing wasn't anything like Hollywood made it out to be. For one, in reality, someone actually had to die. While he may not feel the weight of death hanging in the air, she certainly did. And what mattered most to her was not that there was a body in the forest, but that someone, somewhere, was missing a loved one and it was up to her to bring the family closure.

A hand fell over her shoulder, and she turned to face the lead detective of the Missoula County Sheriff's Department, Matt Fisher. He was a tall, mild-tempered man in his mid-thirties with a crop of dusty blond hair and quietly discerning brown eyes. At one time, she had considered him attractive, supposed she still did. But when he had married his high school sweetheart and had a couple of kids that infatuation faded into nothing more than a solid friendship.

"No sign of the bullet just yet," he informed her. His gaze swept over the area, his lips pressed into a tight line. "Hell of a thing, isn't it?"

Russ grinned, his thumbs tucked through the belt loops of his beige slacks. "You kidding? This is exciting."

"Maybe for you," Lark said drily. She turned back to Matt, all business. "So, what *can* you tell me?"

"Honestly? Not much." He paused as one of the crew swept by with a clear plastic evidence bag holding the skull, another crew member following with a bag full of rib bones. They loaded both into a plastic container to be hauled back to the road where the cars waited. "For now, all we can tell is that the remains have probably been buried for twenty years or more. It's pretty obvious that's an entry wound in the skull, but until we examine it closer, we won't know for sure. In the meantime, we'll keep looking for the bullet. It might be buried here somewhere."

Lark cocked her head. "Unless the victim was killed elsewhere."

Matt nodded. "That's a possibility. Unfortunately, given the amount of time that's passed, there won't be much evidence to go on. We'll pick up what we can but the key now is to identify the body."

"I'll look up missing persons' reports for the area from around twenty years ago and get you some names to start with," Lark offered.

"Good." Matt squinted up at the darkening sky, then whistled to the forensics team members, waving them over. "Time to go for tonight, guys. It's getting too dark to do much good."

A brisk wind blew past them, shivering through the trees above. Lark zipped up her jacket and nudged Russ with her elbow. "Ready to hike back?"

"Sure." He held out a hand to shake Matt's. "Always a pleasure, Detective. See ya around."

"I'll have Bev fax over the reports to you as soon as possible," Lark told Matt, giving him a curt nod before following Russ through the trees.

Russ, for all his childish humor and laid back attitude, was a trained outdoorsman. Much like her, he had been going out in the woods his entire life, learning everything it took to survive. It was because of this that she valued his addition to her team, even if his immaturity got under her skin from time to time.

People often mistook them for siblings, if only because they had the same sable-brown hair and similar eyes, though his were more hazel than green. Lark felt the resemblance ended there, as Russ was all long limbs and height while she was lean and athletic in a compact, five-foot-seven frame. One time he had nearly outrun her during a training exercise, and she had learned not to underestimate his physical abilities. Despite his habit of inhaling an entire pepperoni pizza on his own, Russ was no slouch.

He was a good partner and the closest thing she had to a best friend. The five-year age gap between them made her feel slightly his superior, even if he was just as much of a deputy as she was.

The drive back to town took only minutes. They curved around a tight bend with a wall of trees on both sides, then crested over a ridge that took them within eyesight of Eden Falls.

No matter how many times she saw it, the town tucked among the rocky-faced mountains and towering pines took her breath away. Even now, with the sun long gone and the sky murky and dark, the view of log homes with warm yellow light shining through windows and smoke rising from their chimneys calmed her. This was home. Always had been, always would be.

The road straightened out into a mile-long strip that made up the heart of Eden Falls, lined with wood-paneled buildings with sloped roofs in varying sizes and colors. There was the Eden Falls General Store, the tiny shack-of-a-Post Office, the hardware and snow equipment store, the steakhouse slash cocktail bar where most of the locals spent their evenings, the sheriff's department, ranger station, and several small boutique shops carrying Native American trinkets and wildlife souvenirs for the touristy crowd. Tiny roads twisted off the main strip into the hills around the town, branching off every which way so that the old-fashioned, log style homes had both privacy and stunning views of the Lolo National Forest and the jagged, white-tipped mountains.

Eden Falls was, in Lark's opinion, the best kept secret in Montana. Over the years more and more people had discovered its abundance of hiking trails, scenic falls, and majestic mountain views, allowing the town to grow and flourish. Lark had watched it all happen, but as much as she valued progress, part of her wished for nothing to change at all. She wanted her little portion of heaven on earth to remain just as it was—charming, rugged, and a little bit wild.

With just shy of seven hundred residents year-round, there was very little that went on in town that everybody didn't know about within one twenty-four-hour gossip cycle. The body would be the latest victim of a slew of rumors and bullshit, making it all the more important to get a jump start on identifying the remains and the exact cause of death.

Until then, her goal was to keep Russ from losing all control and spilling the beans prematurely.

She parked the cruiser in her usual spot in front of the sheriff's department, latching onto Russ's forearm before he could hop out. She fixed him with a no-nonsense stare.

"As much as it kills you, I need you to refrain from telling everybody in town about this, okay? I mean it."

Russ patted her hand. "Gotcha. I won't tell *every*body. Just some people." He grinned and exited the car before she could stop him again.

She sighed and followed him up the wooden steps to the station, envisioning strapping duct tape over his mouth. Her lips twitched at the thought seconds before she was bombarded by a wave of questioning from her team.

"Well? What did it look like?" Dispatcher Bev Campbell fluttered over from her desk at the front of the station. She was a pleasantly heavy-set woman in her early fifties with jet black curls that framed an excitable, surprisingly youthful face. She always applied a bit too much blush to the apples of her cheeks and enough mascara to make spider legs out of her eyelashes, but Lark thought her joyful, albeit gossipy, personality made her lovable all the same. "I want details. *All* the details."

When Lark said nothing, Russ jumped in. "Bones, Bev. Nothing but bones left out there. With a bullet hole to the forehead."

"Oh, my." Bev fanned herself, beyond horrified and excited all at once. "That poor soul."

Lloyd Miller, an older deputy with a balding head of scruffy brown hair and guileless, laughter-lined eyes, placed a calming hand on Bev's shoulder. "Now, Bev, don't look too thrilled. A man—or woman—is dead, after all." He winked at Lark, who appreciated his move to inject seriousness back into the conversation.

Russ was bouncing on the balls of his feet, unable to stand still. "Hey, I get it. Dude's dead. But what's done is done. I just want to know who did it. And why." He faced Bev with wide eyes, his mouth falling open. "What if it's a serial killer and we're gonna find more bodies in the woods? What if he's still out there, biding his time to kill again?"

Bev cried out in alarm and looked ready to faint. Lloyd helped her back to her desk where she plopped into the squeaky desk chair, her hand clutching at the gold cross she wore around her neck. While Russ continued to bounce theories off Bev and Lloyd and fill them in on all the details, Lark shook her head and started for her office. She paused when her father stepped out of it.

"Hey, what are you doing here?" she asked, straightening her stance out of habit. He may have been her father, but he was also a fellow deputy. Though these days, he was enjoying a well-deserved retirement.

Roy Galloway fixed his gaze upon his only daughter and offered her a grave smile. "Bev called me. Said a hiker found a body up on Heller Ridge."

Lark gave a brisk nod and rested her hands on her hips. "The forensics team came up from Missoula to cordon off the area and exhume the remains, but we won't know more until they have a chance to really look at them." She hesitated, feeling that heavy weight fall over her again as she recalled the details. "There was a noticeable entry wound in the forehead. A bullet hole."

Her father blew out a long breath. "Hell of a thing."

"Yeah." Concern came over her as she noticed the strain in his eyes. "Everything all right? You look tired."

He brushed off her question. "Just a bit upset, is all. Nobody ever likes hearing about things like this."

Lark snorted. "Unless you're Russ or Bev. I swear, if I hear this around town tomorrow morning, I'll—"

"You know how this town works as well as I do. Nothing stays secret for long." Roy gave her shoulder a friendly pat. "Get some sleep, honey. There's nothing more that can be done tonight."

Although she disagreed with him— in her mind there was always more work to be done—she gave him a placating smile. She took in his thick, graying hair and the familiar features of his cragged face, his green eyes edged with stress lines and laughter lines and everything in between. He had a reputation for being a fair, balanced man with a firm but charismatic disposition, never quick to anger but always prepared to serve justice.

He had been with the Missoula County Sheriff's Department for all her life and for most of his. Ever since she had been a teenager, he had groomed her to become a deputy herself and take over for him at their little station in Eden Falls. He had never once asked her if she wanted the job—he simply expected her to take it. As with many things in her life, whether she wanted it or not didn't matter to him.

She followed him as he headed out of the station, coming to a stop before Bev's desk. Russ was busy on his cell phone ordering a pizza and Lloyd had taken a bathroom break, so Lark seized the opportunity to actually get some work done.

"Can you pull up all the missing persons' reports for the county from say 1990 to 1994? I need to send them over to Matt so he can pin down the identity of our victim."

Bev motioned to Lark's father just as he was about to leave. "Roy, you'll remember this. Wasn't George Murray the only missing person's report we filed in the early nineties?"

Lark's brows rose. "There was only one?"

Bev donned one of her bless-your-heart looks. "I think I'd remember filing any others. This is a safe place, honey." She caught herself, her amusement fading. "At least, it *was*. Goodness, do you think that might be George up there on that mountain, Roy?"

He chuckled, still halfway out the door. "I always figured George just ran off. But if it is him, we'll know soon enough. Goodnight, ladies."

After he was gone, Lark pointed to Bev's computer. "Search for any other reports just in case, and get everything over to the Missoula Office as soon as you can. Oh, and see if Dr. Grogan has dental records on file for Mr. Murray and send those over to Matt, too."

"Will do, sweetheart." Bev tapped at the keyboard, though her eyes raised to Lark before she could walk away. "You remember George, don't you? Big tall man, balding. He walked with a limp but nobody knew why since he was barely forty years old. He lived in that old cabin on Elkhorn Drive."

Lark stared at her blankly for a moment as the memories came back. "Oh, right. Everyone called him the hermit because he never talked to anyone and rarely left his house."

Bev hit a few keys and the printer jolted to life, spitting out a report. She handed it to Lark and lowered her voice conspiratorially, a subtle grin lifting the corner of her painted mouth. "Way I remember it, one day he was just gone without a trace. Left behind all his things, little that he had. Now what makes a man do such a thing?"

Lark stared at the report, running over Bev's words in her head. She said nothing as she took it with her into her office and shut the door, recalling the eerie, bone-chilling feeling she'd gotten up on Heller Ridge.

AVAILABLE NOW ON AMAZON

IN EBOOK AND PAPERBACK

Visit *www.katieajennings.com* to learn more!

www.ingramcontent.com/pod-product-compliance
Lightning Source LLC
Chambersburg PA
CBHW030404180626
46812CB00005B/1922